PROLOGUE

Dim light filled the underground cavern. A drop of water splashed from the ceiling into one of the dark, quiet pools that filled the cavern floor.

A hooded figure stepped out of the darkness. He faced seven others. They all wore dark clothing, and each face was hidden beneath a mask.

"Our enemies have been tested. Our allies are in place," said the man. His eyes glowed red from underneath his hood. "The hour is upon us. It's time to cover the world in shadow. Which of you will lead us to battle?"

One of the figures stepped forward. The tall, young man with brown hair wore a long, brown coat over his brown shirt. A sinister-looking mask in the shape of a bird's beak covered the top half of his face. A red jewel glittered on the mask, on the man's forehead. A broken gold medallion hung around his neck.

"I'll be the first to go, master," he said.

...may be reproduced in whole or...
...itted in any form or by any mean...
...cording, or otherwise, without w...
...ormation regarding permission,...
...ons Department, 557 Broadw...

ISBN 0-439-88831-X

© 1996 Kazuki Takahas...
© 2004 NAS TV Toky...

Published by Scholastic I...
associated logos are traden...
trademarks of Scholastic

4 3 2

Designed by Phil Falc...
Printed in the U.S.A...
First printing, November

Me...

SHO

Yu-G
6

HADO

Adapte

SCHOLASTIC and

12 11 10 9 8 7 6 5

New Yor

Their hooded leader nodded approvingly. "Nightshroud. So be it."

Nightshroud's eyes shone behind the mask. "I will not fail," he said. He held out his left arm, which had a Duel Disk attached. He activated the disk. "Academy Island's prize will be ours!"

• CHAPTER ONE •

THE STORM

Storm clouds rolled across the night sky, forming a gray blanket over Academy Island. Thunder roared like an angry dragon. Moments later, jagged lightning lit up the gloom.

In the buildings below, most of the students at the world's most elite Duel Monsters school slept peacefully.

The students in the Obelisk Blue dorm slept in their soft, comfortable beds, dreaming the happy dreams of students considered to be the best of the best.

The students in the Ra Yellow dorm slept in their slightly smaller, comfortable beds, dreaming the peaceful dreams of students who don't have to worry about failing their classes.

In the Slifer Red dorm, rain dripped through holes in the leaky roof. The claps of thunder seemed to shake the rickety wooden building that the Slifers shared. No one slept. Well, almost no one.

Syrus Truesdale and Chumley Huffington cowered under the covers of Chumley's bunk bed. Below them, Jaden Yuki snored loudly.

"I really don't get it, Chum," Syrus said. His own frightened face was as white as his spiky hair, and his blue eyes were wide behind his glasses. "There's thunder and lightning. How can Jaden sleep?"

"Forget the guy who *can* sleep," replied Chumley. He was twice as big as Syrus — but just as afraid. "Think about the guy who *can't*! Hold me!"

The two boys grimaced as another blast of thunder rocked the dorm. Jaden just smiled and rolled over.

Across the island, Chancellor Sheppard, the director of Duel Academy, paced across his office. Something about the storm made him uneasy. It wasn't the thunder and lightning. It was . . . the darkness. It seemed unnatural, somehow.

Sheppard looked out of his large window. A shadow flew across the sky. At first, it looked like a bird. But as the shadow came closer,

Sheppard realized it was too large to be a normal bird. This was human: a man in a glider.

An intruder.

"So it begins," Sheppard said softly. "The fight. The war."

Sheppard hung his head. A heaviness filled his heart. He knew what he had to do.

On the ground below, Nightshroud glided to the ground. He tossed off the glider that had carried him to Academy Island. It burst into flames behind him.

Nightshroud turned and faced the buildings of Duel Academy. He grinned.

Soon . . . soon, it would begin.

• CHAPTER TWO •

THE SHADOW RIDERS

The next morning was bright and sunny on Academy Island. Students from all three dorms sat in Professor Banner's class. They sat in stadium-style seats that rose from the floor to the ceiling. The long-haired professor sat in a desk in the center, stroking a large cat on his lap.

Jaden Yuki was sleeping — again. He had made a cardboard mask of his wide-awake face so he could close his eyes and sleep. His wavy brown hair stuck up from behind the mask. Eventually, he yawned, opened his brown eyes, and took off the mask.

"Time to get up," Jaden told Syrus.

"For the next class?" Syrus asked.

"Of course not," Jaden replied. "For lunch!"

Jaden took a lunch box out of his backpack and began to dig in.

"Oh yeah!" Jaden said. "This is one subject I can't get enough of!"

Professor Banner smiled at Jaden, his eyes kind behind his glasses.

"Just a moment there, Jaden," he said. "I'm afraid your lunch will have to wait. It seems Chancellor Sheppard wants a word with you."

"Huh?" Jaden grunted.

Chumley leaned down. "Jaden, I'll watch your lunch for you," he offered. "Especially if you have grilled cheese in there!"

"You wish!" Jaden replied.

Syrus shook his head nervously. "Chancellor Sheppard? What did you do?"

Jaden shrugged. "Maybe it's good! Like an award."

A few rows up, a student in an Obelisk Blue uniform stood up. He had dark eyes and wavy black hair.

"No way," Chazz said. He looked happy — happy that Jaden might be in trouble. "It's never good news with Sheppard. You are *so* busted!"

"Actually, Chazz, he wants to see you, too," Professor Banner said.

Chazz looked shocked.

"And two others," Banner continued. "You, Bastion."

A tall boy with short, brown hair wearing a Ra Yellow uniform stood up.

"And you, Alexis."

A pretty girl with long, light-brown hair stood up as well. She wore an Obelisk Blue shirt and skirt.

Jaden frowned. What did Sheppard want with all of them?

"This doesn't sound good," he muttered.

The four chosen students walked to Sheppard's office. Jaden noticed that Banner was following them, holding his cat.

"We're not gonna make a run for it, Professor," Jaden assured him. "You don't have to escort us."

"Yes, I do," Banner replied. "He wants to see me as well."

As they reached the hallway near Sheppard's door, another professor walked toward them. Professor Crowler wore a blue uniform with a frilly collar, lace cuffs, and shiny buttons. His yellow-blond hair was tied in a ponytail. Crowler had a pale face, a long nose, and a smile like a crocodile. He was smiling now.

"Well, well," he said. "Look at this convocation of students! Some of the best duelists in the school, I see."

Then he looked at Jaden and sneered. "Uh-oh! Which one of these is not like the others? Clearly someone here is a little bit lost."

Crowler spent most of his time trying to

find someone who could beat Jaden in a duel. Jaden didn't mind. He loved a good challenge.

"He is not," Jaden replied innocently. "Chazz was invited!"

"He means you!" Chazz scowled.

Jaden was surprised to see one more student arrive. It was Zane Truesdale, Syrus's older brother, who stayed in the Obelisk Blue dorm. Jaden quickly counted — there were seven people altogether. What did Sheppard want with them?

He couldn't believe it when Sheppard told them.

"Three Sacred *what* Cards?" Jaden asked.

"Beast," Sheppard said. He stood behind his desk, looking strong but worried. "And due to their immense power, their colossal might, they were hidden here."

"Sweet!" Jaden cried. "Like under someone's mattress? Or in a cookie jar?"

"Hey! Let him finish!" Chazz complained.

"They're not in a cookie jar," Sheppard said. "They're actually much closer than you'd ever think. They're right below you!"

Everyone gasped. Three Sacred Beast Cards? On Academy Island?

"You see, this academy was built, in part, to protect the Sacred Beast Cards," Sheppard explained. "They were buried deep underground, their powers sealed safely away. Legend says that if these cards ever see the light of day, terrible things will happen. Buildings will crumble. Lights will fade. Souls will fall. Our world will be no more!"

"So where are these cards?" Jaden asked. "I say we take them out for a spin!"

"Haven't you been listening?" Professor Crowler snapped.

"So that's why the seven of you are here," Sheppard continued. "To protect these cards from the wicked ones: seven duelists known as the Shadow Riders who covet the cards. And I'm afraid one of them is already here. He arrived in the thick of last night's storm."

Bastion Misawa frowned. "Naturally."

"Okay. So how do we protect these cards?" Alexis Rhodes asked.

Professor Sheppard's dark eyes clouded. He opened a drawer in his desk and took out a black box. He placed it on the desk.

"By protecting the Seven Spirit Gates," he said. "To get to the cards, one must unlock them. And one must gain the seven keys for each gate. That is how we will protect the cards. By protecting the keys. There is one for each of you to guard."

Everyone stared at the black box, quiet for a moment. Seven keys. Seven duelists. It was a big responsibility.

Bastion spoke first. "If we hold the keys, won't that make us targets?"

Sheppard nodded. "It's true. With these keys, the Shadow Riders will seek you out."

"Uh, *seek* us out? You mean take us out," Chazz said.

"Only in a duel," Sheppard said. "Fortunately for our side, the keys can't simply be stolen. An ancient edict commands the keys must be won in a duel. So I've called on our school's seven best, to take up the challenge and fight the good fight!"

He looked sheepishly at the two professors. "Well, five best, really, but I needed seven, so you know . . ."

Professor Banner frowned. Crowler looked around. "He certainly doesn't mean *me*!" he protested, pointing at Jaden.

"Of course, if any of you feel like backing

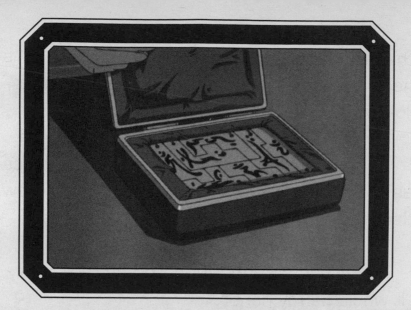

out, I won't blame you. These Shadow Riders play for keeps," Sheppard said. He put his hand on the lid of the black box. "So, who feels like saving the world?"

Chancellor Sheppard opened the box. The flat, metal keys looked like angular puzzle pieces that fit together to form a rectangle. Each key was gold-colored and etched with strange black symbols. A cord looped through the top of each key.

The seven chosen duelists stared at the keys for a moment. Then Jaden reached into the box and grabbed one. He put it around his neck. It dangled against the broken gold medallion he wore as a trophy from a victory.

"How about that! It's my size," he joked.

There was a moment of awkward silence as the other duelists decided whether to follow Jaden's lead. Then Zane reached for a key.

"I, too, accept," he said.

Bastion stepped forward and took a key. "It would be my honor."

Alexis was next. "I don't want you boys having *all* the fun!" she said.

Chazz grabbed the next key without a word. Then Professor Crowler stepped up.

"How could I refuse? I mean, our very world is at stake," he said. He hung the key around his neck. "And if I said no, I wouldn't get this very posh piece of jewelry!"

"Good to know you're doing it for the right reasons . . . kind of," Sheppard muttered.

"Well then! I am the last one!" Professor Banner said, smiling his usual smile. He picked up the key, and the cat hit it with his paw.

"Well, let's get started!" Jaden said, excited about the new challenge. "I think the best duelist should go first, and that would mean . . . well, me!"

Crowler's face turned red with anger. "You? You couldn't beat a drum!"

Jaden glared at him.

"Obviously, I should duel first," Crowler said. "If not, I say Zane. After all, he *did* beat Jaden."

Jaden groaned. That match had been unofficial. How did Crowler know?

"Forget them both!" Chazz said boldly. "I'm clearly the best choice."

"There is no choice," Sheppard said, his voice solemn. "This isn't some tournament where we choose who goes first. This is a war. You can be attacked by your enemy at any time, at any place!"

Jaden looked into the chancellor's dark eyes. They were filled with fear and concern.

"So, my students," Chancellor Sheppard warned. "Be on guard!"

CHAPTER THREE

NIGHTSHROUD

Jaden couldn't concentrate at all for the rest of the day. He kept touching the key around his neck. It was real. The Shadow Riders, the Sacred Beast Cards, everything. That meant he was in store for some amazing duels.

That night, he told Syrus and Chumley everything that had happened in Sheppard's office. They sat on chairs in the dorm room they shared.

"So that's pretty much the story, guys!"

Jaden finished. "Pretty sweet, huh? So now, I just wait!"

"Aren't you scared?" Syrus asked, shivering. The Shadow Riders sounded pretty terrifying to him.

"No joke," Chumley added. "Creepy shadow guys looking to beat you so they can destroy the entire world? I mean, that's pretty intense!"

"Not to mention exhausting," Jaden said, yawning. "Which is why I'm gonna hit the hay."

"What?" Syrus cried, panicked. "You can't just go to sleep right now! I mean, what if a Shadow Rider shows, Jaden?"

Jaden casually put his hands behind his head.

"I'm sure they'll wake me up," he said. "I only hope it's not before ten. Actually, make that eleven, so I have time to shower and stuff."

Syrus shook his head. No matter how

much pressure Jaden was under, he always seemed so cool about it.

"Wow, Jay," Syrus remarked. "You sure seem chill."

"Hey, maybe twelve," Jaden continued. "So I can have breakfast, too."

"The fate of the world's in your hands. Maybe you can skip breakfast?" Syrus suggested.

"Sy's right," Chumley said quickly. "I'd be happy to look after it for you."

"Yeah, sure, Chum," Jaden said sleepily. "Now that that's settled, I'm gonna settle myself between the sheets."

Jaden climbed into the bunk and pulled the sheets over his body. "I'll see you guys tomorrow. When I save the world . . ."

Chumley shrugged and looked at Syrus. "At least he'll be well rested!"

As Jaden slept, Alexis walked quickly across the dark campus toward the Slifer Red dorm. She knew that if the Shadow Riders decided who they would duel, they would go after the weakest duelist first. They'd probably avoid the Obelisk Blue and Ra Yellow students and go after a Slifer Red student first.

I've got to warn Jaden, she thought, as she hurried to the dorm.

Back in Jaden's room, a strange white light appeared outside the window. A small, round creature with wings floated out of Jaden's Duel Disk. It was Winged Kuriboh, a card given to Jaden on the day he tried out for Duel Academy. Winged Kuriboh had helped Jaden win many battles since.

Now it was trying to warn him. The little monster squeaked and flapped its wings in Jaden's face.

Jaden woke up, groggy. "Whoa, Kuriboh. Can you keep it down?"

Kuriboh flew to the window. Jaden saw the bright light. It slowly filled the room with an eerie glow.

Jaden jumped out of bed. "Guys, wake up!" he cried. He shook Syrus, then climbed to

the third bunk and shook Chumley. "You gotta check this out!"

Alexis burst in the door just as the white light engulfed them all. The light grew brighter and brighter. And then . . .

The light transformed into a large, flat circle, like a battlefield, right under their feet. The air was suddenly hot and smelled of ash and sulfur. Jaden felt off-balance. He looked around. The battlefield hovered over a pit of bubbling, steaming lava. They were inside a volcano!

"Jaden!" Alexis cried.

Jaden turned around. Alexis was here, but what about Syrus and Chumley?

Suddenly, the lava began to bubble and churn. A huge creature made of lava and flames rose up — a dragon of some kind. It swirled around them, hissing as it moved, and then it sunk back into the lava pit.

"What's happening?" Alexis asked.

A voice echoed through the volcano.

"The first duel is happening!"

Alexis looked around. "Where are we?"

"In one very weird dream," Jaden replied.

"Or nightmare," Alexis added.

On the opposite end of the battlefield, Nightshroud stepped out into view from the shadows.

"It's neither!" he cried.

"What's going on?" Jaden asked him.

"You mean you don't know?" Nightshroud asked.

Jaden didn't like this guy's attitude. "Call me a slow learner."

"And call *me* Nightshroud," the masked man replied. "I'll be the one taking that key around your neck."

"Wow, you guys don't waste much time, do ya?" Jaden joked. He looked down at his key. Then he noticed something else — the medallion he wore was glowing.

He looked at Nightshroud, and noticed for the first time that he wore an identical medallion. Nightshroud's medallion glowed, too.

"Nice medallion. The Gravekeeper must be getting sloppy," Nightshroud said. "But if you think you'll be able to beat me as easily as you beat him, you have another thing coming."

Jaden's eyes narrowed. His Shadow Game against the Gatekeeper hadn't been easy at all. It had been one of his most difficult battles yet. If Nightshroud wore the medallion, it meant that he had beaten the Gatekeeper, too.

Jaden's heart began to beat quickly. This was going to be some duel.

"I'll get that key," Nightshroud continued. "And just to make sure of that, I brought friends."

Nightshroud pointed down into the lava. Jaden and Alexis looked at the bottom of the lava pit. A flat rock sat right in the middle of the lava. A glowing orb of light rested on the rock. And inside the orb were Syrus and Chumley!

"Jaden! Help us!" they screamed.

"No!" Jaden cried. He nearly jumped off the battlefield to get to them, but Alexis held him back.

"Looks like they're in hot water," Nightshroud said, grinning. "Or maybe I should say hot molten lava. But then, such is the nature of a Shadow Game, Key Keeper!"

"Shadow Game?" Jaden's voice faltered. "Listen, just duel me. But let them go!"

"I don't think so," Nightshroud replied. "I need them to insure a speedy match. After all, that protection orb they're in . . . well let's just say it wasn't built to last."

Jaden looked at his friends. A wave of lava splashed up and hit the orb. He could see the pale blue light flicker as the lava hit it.

Without the orb, Syrus and Chumley would be deep-fried, fast.

"I'm afraid there's more, too," Nightshroud said. He held up a blank Duel Monsters card. A black cloud swirled around it. "For you see, also at stake is your soul. Which will be sealed in this card when you lose!"

⬢ CHAPTER FOUR ⬢

GAME ON!

"Of course, if *I* lose, then *my* soul will be sealed in the card," Nightshroud continued. "But hey, let's be honest with ourselves. Me lose? No way."

Jaden felt his fists clench. He had faced arrogant duelists before. No big deal. But none of them had put his friends in danger.

"So, shall we begin?" Nightshroud asked.

Alexis gripped Jaden's arm. "You can't agree to this!"

"Tell that to Syrus and Chumley," Jaden said. "They're about to become meatballs in a lava stew. They're my friends, and I'm not gonna let that happen to them — or us."

Alexis released her grip. She knew Jaden was right. There was no other way.

"Besides," Jaden said. "It's not like this is my first Shadow Game. I'm just hoping it doesn't hurt as bad as the others!"

Jaden's memories of his match against the Gravekeeper flooded back as though it had happened yesterday. In a regular Duel Monsters game, the only thing that happened when a player was attacked directly was that his Life points dropped. In a Shadow Game, a player felt every direct attack as though it were really happening. At one point, Jaden had felt like his whole body was on fire. He shuddered at the memory.

But he couldn't think about that now. He gritted his teeth.

"Okay, pal," he told Nightshroud. "You want to duel? You got it!"

"Good luck, Jay!" Syrus called from the orb.

"Just let us know if we can help," Chumley added.

"Uh, thanks, Chum," Jaden called back. "But I think I've got all the help I need right here in my deck!"

Jaden pressed a button on the Duel Disk strapped to his left arm. It swung open, ready to deal out the cards Jaden would play during the duel. Across the field, Nightshroud activated his Duel Disk. Both players started with 4000 Life points.

"All right! Let's throw down!" Jaden cried. The Duel Disk shot five cards into his hand. "Get your game on!"

"You wanna see game?" Nightshroud taunted. "How's this?"

Nightshroud held up a card, faceup. A green dragon wearing armor and carrying a sword appeared on the field in front of him.

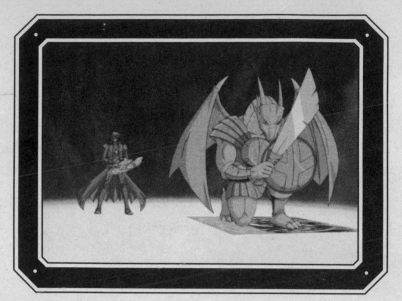

"He's called Troop Dragon and I'll have him defend me," Nightshroud said. "Plus I'll place a facedown while I'm at it."

The tough-looking dragon growled. Its Defense stats appeared: 800 points.

"Not bad," Jaden admitted. "But how is he gonna stack up against my dragon slayer, Elemental Hero Wildheart?"

Jaden put a card on his Duel Disk faceup, and a muscled warrior appeared on the field in front of him. Wildheart wore a loincloth. He had black tattoos all over his body, carried a large sword, and had 1500 Attack points.

"Show him that sword isn't just for show!" Jaden cried. "Attaaaaack!"

Wildheart leaped up and slashed at the Troop Dragon with his sword. 800 Defense points weren't enough to protect the dragon, and it vanished from the battlefield. Wildheart let out a victory roar.

Nightshroud didn't seem bothered by the loss of his monster. "You know, there was something I forgot to mention," he said. "The Troop Dragon's special ability lets me summon *another* Troop Dragon whenever he's sent to the graveyard."

As Nightshroud spoke, another Troop Dragon appeared on the field.

"Hence the word 'troop'" Jaden realized.

"That's right! And I'm not done yet," Nightshroud said. "Now I'll play my facedown, Call of the Haunted."

Nightshroud turned up his facedown card, which had a picture of a graveyard on it. Jaden knew what was coming next.

"This lets me dig from my graveyard a monster that was previously destroyed," Nightshroud continued. "Such as Troop Dragon!"

The first dragon reappeared, and now two Troop Dragons stared at Jaden across the field. And Nightshroud wasn't done yet.

"There's much more where that came from," Nightshroud promised. "Now I'll trade my Troop Dragons to summon . . ."

"Summon what?" Alexis asked.

The lava beneath the field began to bubble again.

"Aw boy," Jaden said.

"Red Eyes Black Dragon!" Nightshroud yelled.

The lava once again formed a long, snake-like dragon. It flew around the volcano. Jaden could feel its searing heat as it sped past his face.

The lava dragon brushed against the orb, which wobbled uncertainly. Chumley pushed his hand against the wall.

"It's cool, Sy," Chumley said, punching the blue light of the force field. "The wall's still in one piece — *whoa!*"

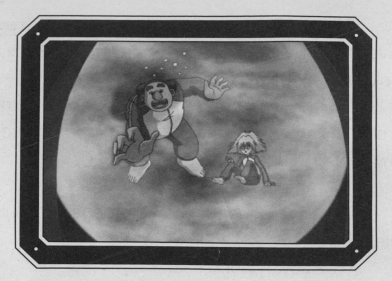

Chumley's hand went right through the wall. The orb was weakening before their eyes.

"It's disappearing!" Syrus wailed.

The dragon landed behind Nightshroud. Then it transformed from a dragon made of lava into a huge, black dragon with wide wings. Its eyes glowed as red as flames. Jaden and Alexis gasped — this monster had 2400 Attack points.

"Now, Red Eyes, attack Wildheart!" Nightshroud commanded. "Inferno Fire Blast!"

The towering dragon blew a huge ball of flames at Elemental Hero Wildheart. The raging fires claimed Wildheart, who disappeared from the field. And because Wildheart wasn't in defense mode, Jaden took whatever his hero couldn't absorb. He screamed as the flames licked at his body. Then he fell to his knees.

"Jaden!" Alexis cried. She watched as his Life points dropped from 4000 to 3100.

Jaden winced and tried to catch his breath. "Hey, that hurt!" he said.

"That's right. And it's about to hurt a lot more, Key Keeper," Nightshroud warned. "Because the true pain is about to begin!"

• CHAPTER FIVE •

ATTACK OF THE DRAGONS

"Hurry up and make your move!" Nightshroud taunted Jaden. "I've got a Doomsday to start!"

"Doomsday?" Chumley repeated. "I'm too young!"

Alexis gripped Jaden's shoulders. "Come on," she coaxed him.

Jaden took a deep breath.

"Sorry, Nightshroud," he said, his dark

eyes glittering. "But the only doom that's com-ing around here is to *your* monster!"

Jaden rose to his feet and took a new card from his Duel Disk. "It's my draw! And I play the spell card Polymerization!"

Jaden put down two more cards. A big clay monster and a female monster in a red costume with wings and black hair appeared on the field.

"With Clayman and Burstinatrix in my hand, I'll fuse them to create the Elemental Hero Rampart Blaster!"

The two monsters flew up from the field. They joined together to become a new monster,

a giant robot with a red helmet. Her left arm ended in a red shield, and a cone-shaped weapon pointed from the end of her right arm. The new hero had 2000 Attack points and 2500 Defense points.

"Even in defense mode, she can still blast you with half of her attack points," Jaden said. "So go ahead and let him have it, Blaster! And don't pull any firepower. Rampart Barrage!"

Three missiles shot out of the cone at the end of Rampart Blaster's hand. The missiles exploded in front of Nightshroud and the Red Eyes Black Dragon. When the smoke cleared, Nightshroud's Life points dropped from 4000 to 3000.

"Yes!" Alexis cried.

Nightshroud glared at Jaden.

"Don't forget, she's still in defense," Jaden reminded him. "So if you want to get to me, you'll have to get through her. Pretty sweet there, don't you think?"

Nightshroud shuddered, trying to shake off the missile attack.

"Hmm, okay. Maybe not so sweet for you, but you know what I mean!" Jaden said cheerfully.

"Enough!" Nightshroud shouted angrily. "You fool! The Blaster doesn't change a thing. But you can bet this next card will. I'm going to change your Life points, Jaden. And not in a good way."

"All right, I'll bite," Jaden said. "Why not?"

"Because this time his attack is an actual card!" Nightshroud held up a card for them to see. "Inferno Fire Blast!"

Jaden gasped. The card had 2400 Attack

points. He had never heard of an attack being a card. That couldn't be good.

A red ball of fire shot from the card and slammed into Rampart Blaster. She reeled from the impact. The flames fanned over Jaden, burning his skin with searing pain. He screamed.

"Nice card, huh?" Nightshroud asked. "It's just as strong as my Red Eyes's attack. The only difference is, it hits your Life points directly."

Through a haze of pain, Jaden watched his Life points drop from 3100 to a dangerously low 700.

"I'm not through with you yet, Key Keeper," Nightshroud said. "Next I summon Attachment Dragon!"

Another dragon appeared on the field. This one had the wiry body of a serpent, with blue-green skin and purple wings.

"Don't worry," Nightshroud said. "He's not the attacking type, see. Like his name suggests, he's a lot more the *attaching* type. Show him, Dragon!"

The Attachment Dragon let out a piercing scream. It flew across the field and picked up Rampart Blaster in its claws, lifting her high above the field.

Nightshroud grinned. "Blaster's made a new friend. A friend that *forces* her into attack mode. And because she is . . . no more direct attacks!"

"Oh, no," Alexis said. Jaden was in trouble. Big trouble.

Down in the lava pit, the glowing orb rocked. Syrus and Chumley screamed as they almost fell forward through the

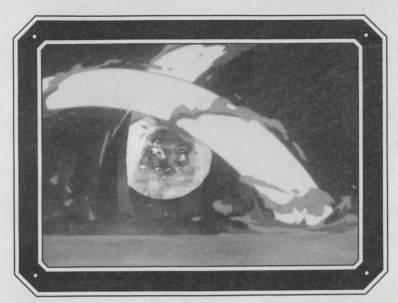

thinning wall — the only thing protecting them from the lava.

"It's so hot!" Chumley wailed. "Now I know what grilled cheese feels like!"

Jaden panted, trying to get his strength back after that last attack. He raised his head and looked directly at Nightshroud.

"All right," he said. "My turn!"

And at the rate that orb's disappearing, maybe my last chance to save my friends, Jaden thought. *And the world!*

• CHAPTER SIX •

THUNDER GIANT VS.
RED EYES BLACK DRAGON

"Do your friends a favor and make your move now!" Nightshroud challenged him.

Jaden managed to smile. "If you knew what I was packing, Nightshroud, I don't think you'd be so eager!"

Jaden put a card faceup on his Duel Disk.

"I play the spell card Pot of Greed!" Jaden cried. "It lets me draw two cards. And if that's not enough for you, I play De-Fusion, too!"

Jaden held up the card, and a bright light

flashed on Rampart Blaster. The hero split up into its two parts, Elemental Hero Clayman and Elemental Hero Burstinatrix.

The Attachment Dragon hissed in surprise. Jaden looked up at it.

"Attachment Dragon, attach yourself to the graveyard!"

Attachment Dragon disappeared from the field. Nightshroud frowned.

"Next from my hand, I'll activate Fusion Sage!" Jaden announced. "It lets me add a Polymerization from my deck to my hand."

Jaden looked through his deck and found Polymerization. He placed it on his Duel Disk.

"That means I can now fuse the Clayman on the field with the Sparkman in my hand to create the Elemental Hero Thunder Giant!" Jaden cried.

Sparkman appeared on the field, a hero with sleek, blue-and-gold body armor. Then Sparkman and Clayman fused together in a blast of bright light. When the light faded, Thunder Giant towered over the field. The hero

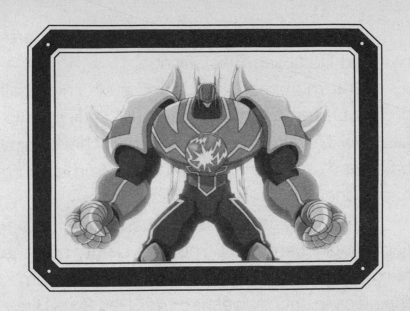

had a shining body of gold and purple metal. A blue energy orb glowed in its chest. 2400 Attack points appeared next to him.

"It's an even match up," Alexis said.

"All right, time to see who blinks first!" Jaden said. "Elemental Hero Thunder Giant attacks Red Eyes Black Dragon with Voltic Thunder!"

A lightning bolt formed in the orb on Thunder Giant's chest. The hero formed the electric energy into a glowing ball. It hurled the ball at the dragon.

"Go Inferno Fire Blast!" Nightshroud commanded Red Eyes Black Dragon.

The monster roared, and a churning ball of fire blazed from its mouth. The fiery missile flew through the air, meeting the energy ball head-on. The two forces slammed into each other.

Wham! The explosion rocked the battlefield. Angry flames hit Thunder Giant, and the hero collapsed on the field. At the same time, the electric energy washed over Red Eyes Black Dragon. The creature screeched and dove back into the lava pit.

Nightshroud was stunned. "Both destroyed?"

"What was the point, Jaden?" Alexis asked.

"The point is, now that Red Eyes is gone, Nightshroud is directly in Bursinatrix's line of fire — and I do mean fire!" Jaden answered. "Attack, Flare Storm!"

Burstinatrix jumped up, a fiery vision in her red uniform. She held out her hands and a ball of swirling flame appeared. She hurled the ball at Nightshroud. He held up his arms to protect himself as the hot fire engulfed him. His Life points dropped from 3000 to 1800.

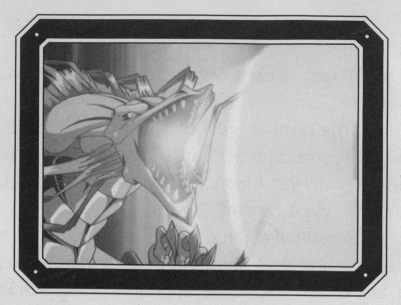

"Aw, come on, aren't you going to flinch or anything?" Jaden asked. "How about a wince? Can I get a cringe?"

The flames died. Nightshroud's clothes were charred, but he wore the same calm expression on his face.

"Sorry. I leave that to my opponents," he replied.

"Oh yeah? Well we'll just see what we can do about that, Nightshroud!" Jaden cried. "I play Mirage of Nightmare!"

He threw a card onto his Duel Disk.

"With this spell card, during your standby phase, I get to draw cards until I have four in my hand," Jaden explained. "But then, during my standby phase, I have to randomly discard the same number of cards I drew to the grave."

"Do whatever makes you happy," Nightshroud said.

"In that case, I'll throw a facedown, too!" Jaden said, putting the card on his disk. "And that's it."

"Good. My draw!" Nightshroud said. He reached for new cards.

"Yeah, and mine, too, thanks to my Mirage of Nightmare!" Jaden said happily. "Here I go."

Jaden drew cards from his Duel Disk until he had four in his hand.

"Whatever," Nightshroud said, scowling. "Just don't forget to discard the same amount of cards you draw next turn, okay?"

Jaden grinned. "Actually, Nightshroud, I was kinda thinking I wouldn't," he said. He held up one of the cards in his hand. "I play Emergency Provisions! Now, by destroying one spell card on my field, I gain 1000 Life points."

Jaden's Life points jumped from 700 to 1700 in a flash.

"And the card I think I'll destroy is Mirage of Nightmare!" Jaden cried. The card shattered.

"Now Mirage's discard rule is no longer in effect!" Alexis realized. Jaden could keep all of the cards in his hand.

Jaden faced Nightshroud, proud of his last move. He felt confident that he could take whatever Nightshroud had to dish out next.

"So you were able to avoid Mirage's unpleasantness," Nightshroud said. "But you won't be avoiding *this* one's — Mirage Dragon!"

Nightshroud put a card on his disk. A dragon with a long, reptilian body appeared on the field. It had gleaming gold scales, sharp blue teeth, and 1600 Attack points.

"Despite his name, his attack is no illusion!" Nightshroud said. "Go, Spectrum Blast!"

Mirage Dragon let loose with a stream of rainbow-colored fire. The hot blast shattered Burstinatrix and then reached Jaden, who fell to his knees. His hero had absorbed most of the damage, but he still lost 400 Life points. Now he was down to 1300.

"I can't let it end here," Jaden said.

"You don't have to," Nightshroud said. "Mirage Dragon will end it for you!"

• CHAPTER SEVEN •

RED EYES DARKNESS DRAGON

Syrus and Chumley watched the duel from their orb. Waves of lava splashed against the glowing ball, sizzling as they made contact.

Syrus looked at Chumley. "If we don't make it through this, I just want you to know that you've been a great friend!"

Chumley pounded on the wall of the orb. "Hurry, Jay! Sy's getting mushy!"

Alexis watched them. "Jaden, that orb's disappearing fast!"

Jaden nodded. "Yeah? Well not as fast as that Mirage Dragon's about to. I summon Elemental Hero Bubbleman!"

A blue hero appeared on the field. Big muscles bulged under his blue uniform, and a blue cape waved behind his back. Two weapons were strapped to his arms.

"*And* I activate his ability!" Jaden cried. "See, when he's summoned out all by himself, I can draw two more cards."

Jaden took the two new cards from his Duel Disk. He looked at them and grinned.

"One of which I'm gonna use right now,"

he said. "Silent Doom! It lets me summon one monster from my graveyard to the field in defense mode."

Elemental Hero Sparkman reappeared on the field, with 1400 Defense points.

"Next I'll play the field spell card known as Fusion Gate," Jaden announced.

He held up the card. A gray storm cloud appeared above the field, swirling menacingly.

"What?" Nightshroud was shocked.

Jaden grinned. "Oh yeah. A storm's coming. And it's coming for you, Nightshroud! 'Cause now that Fusion Gate is out, I can fuse Bubbleman and Sparkman, who are on my field, with Avian to create the mighty Elemental Hero Tempest!"

Avian — a hero in a green feathered uniform — appeared, but only for a second. A bright light flashed over Avian, Bubbleman, and Sparkman. When the light faded, a newer, bigger hero stood in their place.

A combination of all three heroes, Tempest wore blue armor and had white wings

edged with green. He wore a blue mask and a shining gold helmet. The hero had a massive 2800 Attack points.

"Yeah! That's more than Mirage Dragon!" Chumley cheered.

"Now go, Tempest!" Jaden yelled. "Attack Mirage Dragon with Glider Strike!"

Tempest spun around and aimed the heavy weapon on his right arm at the Mirage Dragon. Waves of sizzling blue energy raced across the room and slammed into Mirage Dragon. The monster shattered.

Then the energy waves slammed into Nightshroud, knocking his Life points from 1800 to 600 in a split second. Nightshroud stumbled backward, moaning.

"There's the flinch I was looking for," Jaden said.

"No, it wasn't. That was a twitch. It's not the same!" Nightshroud protested. "I had something in my eye, that's all. You got that? It was a twitch!"

"Hey, call it what you want," Jaden said. "But there's one thing you can't argue with. I'm winning this Shadow Duel now, Nightshroud! And I think I'll end my turn leaving you with that thought, *plus* a facedown!"

Jaden put his last card on his Duel Disk, feeling more confident than ever. With only 600 Life points left, Nightshroud was in real trouble.

"Ha! You chump. Life points don't decide who's winning the duel." Nightshroud took a card from his hand and held it up, keeping the face of the card toward him. "It's the cards you hold! And if you don't believe me, I'm quite certain this one here will prove it to you."

"Yeah, right," Jaden said. "I bet you're just bluffing."

Suddenly, the waves of lava below the field began to rise and fall, churning faster and faster. Six lava dragons rose from the bubbling pit and began to fly around the volcano. Jaden felt a wave of heat as one passed near his face.

"Did you honestly think, Key Keeper, that you could get rid of all my dragons so easily?" Nightshroud asked. "That you could simply banish them to the graveyard and be done with them?"

"That's kinda what I was hoping," Jaden admitted.

"Well you can just keep on hoping, because I summon the Red Eyes Black Chick!" Nightshroud cried.

A huge purple egg rose up from the lava. The egg hovered in the air for a moment, and then began to crack. Two red eyes glowed from within.

Jaden had been expecting something much worse. "That's your big card?"

"That's right," Nightshroud said. "Until I use Chick's special ability, that is!"

Nightshroud moved the card into his graveyard, and the egg exploded.

"You see, by sending Chick to the grave, I'm allowed to summon from my hand . . . his daddy! The full-grown Red Eyes Black Dragon!"

Jaden watched in disbelief as the huge monster appeared behind Nightshroud again, flapping its large black wings.

"And as big as this Red Eyes is, they can

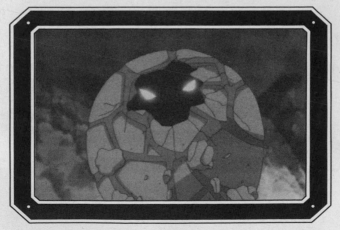

still get bigger!" Nightshroud said. Jaden froze. What could be bigger than this monstrous dragon?

Nightshroud continued his move. "Red Eyes, I now sacrifice you to bring out... Red Eyes Darkness Dragon!"

Red Eyes Black Dragon dove into the pit. The waves in the lava pit grew higher and higher. Syrus and Chumley screamed as the hot goo disintegrated the flimsy orb protecting them.

Red Eyes Black Dragon flew back out of the pit, a flaming lava dragon now. It flew up and joined the burning dragons flying about the battlefield.

"Now, the molten ashes of my fallen dragons boil up from their fiery graves, ablaze with new life, each granting my Red Eyes Darkness Dragon 300 additional Attack points!"

That gave the fiery dragons 4500 Attack points!

Alexis gasped. "4500? Jaden can't withstand that!" One attack from the Darkness Dragon would end the duel immediately.

The dragons fused together, changing shape, forming a black dragon twice the size of any of them. He had red jewels on his legs and wings.

"It's over!" Nightshroud crowed. "The spirit key, your friends, your soul. With Darkness Dragon's attack, they're all mine!"

Nightshroud looked up at his massive monster. "So go. Inferno Darkfire! End this!"

• CHAPTER EIGHT •

MYSTICAL SPACE TYPHOON!

While Jaden and Nightshroud's duel raged on, energy from the duel rippled across Academy Island. The other Key Keepers felt it.

Zane noticed when the key around his neck began to glow. "There's something amiss . . . a Shadow Rider. This key's telling me one's close."

Bastion sat in his dorm, studying, when the key around his neck began to shake.

An invisible force pulled them toward the volcano. . . .

In his office, Chancellor Sheppard felt it, too. A duel was underway. He slowly sank into his chair.

"What were you thinking, Sheppard? Getting your students involved in a battle with such stakes," he said, nervously rubbing his hands over his bald head. "But then, what other choice did you have? After all, if those Shadow Riders get ahold of those three Sacred Beast Cards, they'll be destroyed no matter what."

Sheppard put his head in his hands. "We all will!"

Back in the volcano, Jaden readied himself for the attack of the Red Eyes Darkness Dragon. The huge beast reared its head and let loose with a huge wave of flame the color of blood. It raced across the field toward Tempest.

Syrus and Chumley closed their eyes. This attack would be the end of Jaden. The end of them all. . . .

"Don't think so!" Jaden cried. "I've got a trap!"

Jaden held up a card. "Go Negate Attack!"

"What!" Nightshroud cried.

A green protective bubble appeared around Tempest. The flames blasted against the bubble, but couldn't penetrate it. They slowly died out.

"That's right, your attack's been cancelled!" Jaden said. "And Negate Attack ends your battle phase so you can't attack me anymore this turn!"

"Oh well," Nightshroud said, trying to stay calm. "Till next time."

"My draw!" Jaden cried. "First off, I summon Wroughtweiler in defense mode."

A tough-looking dog made of metal appeared on the field with 1200 Defense points.

"And I'll switch Elemental Hero Tempest to defense, as well," Jaden added. 2800 Defense points appeared next to Tempest. "Then I'll call it a turn."

Nightshroud sneered. "That's funny. You know what I'd call it? A waste of time. And time, in case you forgot, is very much of the essence right now. Well, at least for your friends who are about to be deep-fried, it is!"

"Don't you listen to him, Jaden!" Syrus called out. "Just concentrate on winning the duel!"

"Aw, deep-fried!" Chumley moaned. "I'll never be able to look at a french fry again. Though I'll probably be able to eat them."

"Jaden, hurry up!" Alexis warned.

Jaden nodded. "Yeah, I know. That lava is beginning to look really restless."

Jaden looked up at Nightshroud. He didn't seem to be in any hurry.

"How about you make your move?" he asked angrily.

"Oh right, it's my turn," Nightshroud said. "Sorry! I summon Spear Dragon in attack mode!"

A compact, dinosaur-like dragon appeared on the field. It had leathery, tan-and-blue skin and a long, curved snout.

"Now, Spear Dragon, give that Wroughtweiler something to chew on. Attack, Cyclone Blast!" Nightshroud yelled.

Green light poured from the dragon's snout. It blasted Wroughtweiler, destroying Jaden's monster.

"Wroughtweiler doesn't roll over that easily!" Jaden said. "See, by sending him to the graveyard, his special ability now activates. One that lets me fetch an Elemental Hero and Polymerization from the grave and put them into my hand!"

Jaden reached for the cards, but

tumbled backward as a stray energy blast hit him.

"Don't get ahead of yourself," Nightshroud warned. "When Spear Dragon attacks a monster in defense mode, if its Attack points are greater than your defending monster's Defense points, the difference is dealt to *you* as damage."

Jaden cringed as his Life points dropped to 600.

"However, as you can see, Spear Dragon must then switch to defense mode," Nightshroud explained. The monster had no Defense points at all.

"And now for the matter of your Tempest and his special ability?" Nightshroud continued. "Since you can save him from being destroyed by sending one card on your field to the graveyard, I'll get rid of the card on your field by playing Mystical Space Typhoon!"

Jaden groaned. He was counting on Tempest's special ability to win him the duel. Nightshroud was good — maybe too good.

A strong wind swirled from the card. It blew across the field and hit Jaden's Duel Disk, wiping out the card on the field. Jaden gasped.

"Now, Key Keeper, just try saving your Tempest!" Nightshroud taunted him. "Red Eyes Darkness Dragon, attack! Inferno Darkfire!"

Darkness Dragon roared again, letting loose with another fiery blast. This time, the flames hit Tempest full force. Alexis screamed as the monster vanished from the field.

Jaden fell to the ground as the flames swept past him.

"It's your move, if you have any strength to make it," Nightshroud said.

Jaden tried to get up, but he was too weak. He groaned and sank back to the ground.

Alexis ran in front of Jaden.

"Enough!" she called to Nightshroud. "This duel is over!"

• CHAPTER NINE •

JADEN GETS WILD!

"Says who?" Nightshroud shot back.

"Says me, and this!" Alexis said. She held out her key. "I have a Spirit Gate key, too. Let my friends go, and I'll let you duel me for it and have my soul either way."

Nightshroud paused. He frowned. "I know you . . ." he said softly.

"You can't lose, so just let them go and deal with me!" Alexis pleaded.

"No," Jaden grunted. He slowly got to his

feet. "I won't let you, Alexis. I mean after all, I'm about to win this!"

"He's delirious," Alexis said.

"I am not," Jaden said, straightening up to stare at Nightshroud. "What I am is about to get my game on!"

Below, Syrus and Chumley watched the orb slowly disappear.

"Well, you better hurry!" Syrus called out.

"I don't want to be a french fry!" Chumley screamed.

Jaden drew a card from his Duel Disk.

"It's now or never," Jaden said. "I summon Elemental Hero Wildheart in attack mode!"

Back from the graveyard, Wildheart appeared on the field with all his 1500 Attack points. The muscular hero thumped his chest.

"Next, I'll activate the spell card Wild Half from my hand," Jaden said. He held up a card with a picture of a wild dog on it. "Wild Half is gonna cut your monster in half!"

Darkness Dragon's Attack points dropped to 3300. Then a duplicate dragon appeared next to it. It had 3300 Attack points, too.

"See, what it does is take the original Attack points of your Red Eyes Darkness Dragon and split it by summoning a monster token with the same Attack points to the field," Jaden explained.

Alexis frowned. Normally, Darkness Dragon had 2400 Attack points. Divided in half, that would leave each monster with 1200. Jaden could deal with that. But there was a problem.

"But, because of all the dragons in Nightshroud's graveyard, they still have 3300 Attack points each," she pointed out.

"I'm getting to that," Jaden said. "Next up is Polymerization, which I'll use to fuse Wildheart and Elemental Hero Bladedge!"

Jaden called up Bladedge, a hero wearing sharp gold metal armor from head to toe. He fused with Wildheart to create a bigger, tougher hero. Elemental Hero Wildedge had Wildheart's muscles and weapons, Bladedge's armor, and an impressive 2600 Attack points.

"One of the things that puts him on the

edge of being wild is that he can attack all of the monsters you have out at the very same time!" Jaden said.

"You just go ahead and do that then," Nightshroud replied. "He *still* has less Attack points than my dragons."

"Again with the Attack points," Jaden shot back. "I guess it's time I finally address this issue for you guys. Or better yet, let Skyscraper do it for me!"

Nightshroud frowned. "What?"

"That's right," Jaden said. "I play the field spell card Skyscraper!"

Tall skyscrapers rose out of the lava, surrounding the floating battlefield.

"And once Wildedge is done with your dragons you're going to be scraping them off the pavement," Jaden promised. "Because here, heroes gain 1000 Attack points!"

As Jaden spoke, Wildedge's Attack points shot up to 3600.

"Impossible!" Nightshroud cried.

"Now go, Wildedge!" Jaden yelled. "Attack the Red Eyes Dragons and Spear Dragon with Scimitar Slash!"

Wildedge pulled out two curved blades. He sprang across the field with a mighty leap. Then he threw the blades at the Darkness Dragons. They shrieked and vanished in flashes of orange light.

Then Wildedge turned to the Spear Dragon, who stood in front of Nightshroud in the defense position — with zero defense points. Wildedge raised a sword and slashed the Spear Dragon.

The Spear Dragon vanished, and Nightshroud screamed as his Life points

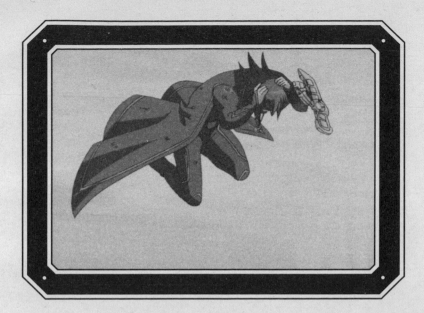

drained from 600 to zero. He fell to his knees.

"That's game!" Jaden cried.

With Nightshroud weak, the battle-field weakened, too. Geysers of flame shot up through the field, breaking holes in its foundation.

"Syrus! Chumley!" Jaden cried. He ran toward the edge of the field, but the heat over-whelmed him.

Then his whole world went black.

• CHAPTER TEN •

THE END. . .
AND THE BEGINNING

Syrus and Chumley screamed as a wave of hot lava engulfed the orb.

Then, in the next instant, they found themselves outside the volcano.

"We're alive! We're alive!" Syrus cheered.

Then they heard a groan. They turned to see Alexis facedown on the rocky ground. The two boys ran to her side.

"He did it! Jaden did it!" Alexis said, as they helped her to her feet.

"Yeah!" Chumley cried.

Then Alexis frowned. "But where *is* Jaden?"

They looked around. The morning sun was just beginning to light up the sky. Brown rocks jutted out from the hard ground. Then Chumley pointed.

"Jaden!" Syrus screamed.

They ran to Jaden. He lay on the ground, flat on his back, his eyes closed.

Alexis knelt by him. "Wake up!" she pleaded. She grabbed his wrist.

"He's not moving!" Syrus wailed.

But Alexis had felt a pulse. "Sy, he's fine," she said, relieved. "Tired, maybe, but who could blame him?"

"Not me," Chumley said. "I'm tired and I didn't do a thing."

But Syrus didn't believe it. He shook Jaden's body. "Jay! Don't do this!"

"He's fine," Alexis assured him. Then she

noticed something on the ground next to
Jaden. A card. "Which is more than I can say
for Nightshroud."

Alexis picked up the card. Nightshroud's
mask was there, held back by thick chains.

"At least we'll be safe from him for now,"
she said softly.

A soft groaning distracted Alexis. She
looked to the right to see another figure
sprawled on the ground. It looked like
Nightshroud. Curious, she walked to him and
knelt down.

Nightshroud's mask was off. He opened
a large brown eye and looked right at her.

"Alexis," he whispered.

Alexis suddenly felt faint. She knew that eye . . . that voice . . .

"It can't be . . ." she said.

Then a familiar voice rang through the morning air.

"Jaden! Hold on! We're coming!"

Alexis turned. It was Bastion Misawa, climbing up to them with Zane and Chazz. They ran up and surrounded Jaden.

"What happened?" Chazz asked.

"One of the Shadow Riders challenged Jaden to a duel," Syrus told him.

Chazz sighed impatiently. "So? Did he win?"

"He sure did," Chumley replied. "And it was a lishus battle. There was lava, dragons, and some talk of french fries!"

Zane looked toward Alexis and Nightshroud.

"Is that him? The Shadow Rider?"

Then Zane heard Alexis sobbing. He ran up to her.

"Alexis?" he asked.

"It's him, Zane," she said, tears running down her face. "I don't understand how, but it's him. I thought I'd lost him, but he's back. He's finally back."

"What are you talking about?" Zane asked. "Who's back?"

Alexis moved aside to reveal Nightshroud's face.

"Look at his face," she said. "It's my brother."

Zane was stunned. "Atticus?" He had

known Alexis's brother. How had he become a Shadow Rider?

"It wasn't him before, but that card took away whatever darkness was holding him," Alexis said. "He's back now."

Chumley picked up Jaden and carried him on his back. Syrus, Chazz, and Bastion followed him to Zane's side. Alexis stood up. The duelists looked out into the horizon and watched the rising sun.

"If this is how it is after you *win* a duel, just think what it's like when you lose," Zane

said, his voice somber. "The sun may be coming up now, but night will fall again soon. And
when it does, we must be ready."

The duelists looked at one another. Zane
was right.

But there was nothing to do but wait.

CHAPTER I

"WELL DONE, June!" said Mrs. Cresswell as her daughter cantered out of the ring with yet another rosette.

"Tie it on, Mummy," said June.

"Golden Wonder does look smart with two red ones," said Mrs. Cresswell.

"I hope both the prizes are cups," said June, "then I'll have thirty; though, actually, two of them are challenge cups."

"Well, you'll only have to win them twice more and then they'll be yours," said Mrs. Cresswell. "And I don't suppose that'll be very difficult, since all the children round here are such appalling riders. I've just been having a look at the Barington-Brown child's pony," she went on, "and a very good one it is too. You'll have to be careful next time there's a showing class, for I don't think there's much to choose between her and Wonder."

"Riding makes a lot of difference," said June, "and if Susan rides like she did to-day it'll be another walk-over for me. What a bore these gymkhana events are. I suppose we've got to sit and watch them until the prize-giving."

"Why don't you enter?" asked her mother. "You might win another prize."

"Oh, Wonder's no good at that sort of thing," replied June, "and I don't want to be made to look a fool."

"Perhaps you're right," said Mrs. Cresswell. "Though I think you would probably win—riding must count, even in gymkhana events."

"I dare say it's all right for those cart-horsy old ponies with mouths of iron," said June, "but I don't want to spoil Wonder's mouth, and she'd be sure to hot up. I do wish they'd hurry up and have the prize-giving."

The competitors for class three, children's bending race,

were waiting in the collecting ring. Among them sat John Manners, a stocky, dark-haired boy of about thirteen, on a roan cob. John was in a very bad temper, and Dick Turpin, the cob, was rather excited. He danced about and barged his quarters into the other ponies. John jagged him in the mouth and said, "Stand still, can't you?" at intervals. It was the jumping that had put John in a bad temper. It was all very well for mum to say that Turpin was getting on and couldn't be expected to jump as well as he used to. *She* didn't know how maddening it was to be beaten, time after time, by June Cresswell. It wasn't as if he could beat her in the races either, for she never went in for them— she probably realised that she wouldn't stand a chance against him and the Radcliffes. He did wish dad would buy him a pony that could jump. As for the best-rider class this morning, that simply hadn't been fair. June Cresswell had only won because Golden Wonder was a properly trained show pony, which could change legs, while Turpin had never been taught to do that sort of thing. He was more of a hunter.

Next to John, on a small bay pony with a very large head, sat Noel Kettering. Her jodhs, which were too big for her, had slipped up and her shirt, which was too small for her, had come untucked from her jodhs. But Noel was past caring; she felt icy cold and slightly sick. She thought, this awful "needle", and I'm sure to let Topsy down again. Miss Lamb says she's marvellous at bending, so it must be my fault, but I don't see how I can get her to turn quicker at the end when she won't stop. I do hope she doesn't charge out of the ring again . . . it was awful in the jumping . . . I'm sure Miss Lamb was furious, but I don't see how I was to get Topsy over; she's so nappy. How I wish I were a better rider, could jump four foot and win the novice jumping.

"Mummy, Mummy," shrieked Jill Morrisson, "I can't get Wendy's girths to meet, and I ought to be in the collecting ring!"

"All right, darling," said Mrs. Morrisson in the affected voice in which she always talked to children, "don't panic, there's plenty of time."

"Oh, Jill, you are stupid. Can't you even saddle a pony yet?" asked her brother Richard in patronising tones.

"Of course I can," said Jill. "But Wendy keeps blowing herself out, and I bet you couldn't do it."

"I bet I could," said Richard. "I can always saddle Peter, and he's nearly two hands bigger. But, then, you're only a girl, and girls can't do anything."

"Girls can," said Jill. "I can do lots of things you can't."

"Now, children," said Mrs. Morrisson, "stop quarrelling. You must be overtired. I think you'd better go home directly after the potato race."

As he waited in the collecting ring, Richard thought how tiresome his mother was, and wondered what the boys at his school would say if they could see him now. Peter was a pretty good-looking pony—he sometimes won in showing classes—but, of course, he didn't touch Golden Wonder. Richard wished Peter was better at gymkhana events. He would like to show that conceited John Manners that he wasn't the only person who could ride; but, best of all, he would like to win the jumping. Peter wasn't bad; they generally got round. . . .

Jill Morrisson thought that none of the other ponies was nearly as pretty as Wendy, with her long mane and tail. Richard might say she looked like a Shetland pony and jolly silly, but he was awfully tiresome since he had been at a boarding-school. Once he had liked Wendy's mane and tail *and* her name—she'd been given to them just after they had seen *Peter Pan*—now he said *Peter Pan* was only fit for girls, and he had been livid when mummy had made him call his new pony Peter Pan so that he would go with Wendy. . . .

Susan Barington-Brown, dressed in expensive riding clothes, rode her dark brown pony Beauty into the collect-

ing ring. It was Susan's first show, and she almost wished that she had stayed at home, in spite of the third prize, which she had won in the best-rider class. She loved riding, but she didn't think she liked gymkhanas. Daddy hadn't been able to come—he had had to go to London on business; and mummy was afraid of horses; and neither she nor Valerie, Susan's sister, would take any interest in riding. In the end, Bob, the gardener, who looked after Beauty, had been sent, and he was awfully tiresome. When she had won the third prize he had told her how marvellous she was, though Susan had explained that it was entirely due to Beauty, which had gone on the right leg every time when she, Susan, had forgotten the aids again. He had said "shoo," and waved his arms as they went over the practice jump—a thing Mrs. Maxton had told her you must never do. Then, when she had three refusals at the first jump in the children's jumping, he had said that Beauty needed someone behind her with a whip. Susan knew very well that it was because she hadn't used her legs enough. But far worse than Bob's tiresomeness were the things she had overheard the Radcliffes saying. They always did shout. One of them—she thought it was Evelyn—but they all had red hair and freckles—was telling the others what a frightful rider Susan was, and how she would never have won third in the riding class but for the fact that her father was very rich and could afford to buy her a perfectly schooled pony and pay a groom to look after it. Susan knew this was true, but Evelyn had gone on to say that she was frightfully feeble and was ruining Beauty's mouth and manners. . . .

The five red-headed Radcliffes were, as usual, making more noise than all the rest of the competitors put together. The three eldest—Roger, and the twins Hilary and Evelyn—were entering for the bending, but James and Margaret were considered too young to ride in gymkhanas. However, they were discussing, in very loud and perfectly audible voices, whom they would like to be bucked off so that

10

their family could be first, second and third.

Major Holbrooke, M.F.H., sat on his shooting-stick in the middle of the ring with his fellow-judges, Sir William Blount, M.F.H., and Captain Julian Barton, a well-known equitation expert. Their tempers, already frayed by the best-rider class, were becoming shorter and shorter every moment as they watched the jumps removed from the ring and the bending-poles put up. They agreed that the stewards were incompetent, the committee impossible, and the standard of riding shocking. Captain Barton said that he didn't mind bending competitions if they were used as a means to an end; but at gymkhanas, most of the competitors were far too keen on winning, and nearly pulled their wretched ponies' heads off in the process. Sir William said he agreed, and that he knew from experience that the children in these parts were exceptionally bad about that sort of thing. But now that Holbrooke had taken over the Pony Club he expected things would change. Major Holbrooke didn't say anything, for he was wondering whether Blake, his stud-groom, and Gay Crusader had arrived safely, and whether Crusader was much upset by the crowd, for it was his first show.

Then, at last, the bending race started. There were a great many heats, but a very low standard of riding. Noel Kettering and Susan Barington-Brown both fell off, while Jill Morrisson was removed from the ring, on the word go, by her rather stubborn Dartmoor pony. John Manners, Dick Hayward, Richard Morrisson and the three Radcliffes all won their heats, and in the end the event was won by John Manners, with Roger and Hilary Radcliffe second and third. Evelyn Radcliffe won the potato-race, with John Manners second and Hilary third.

Then, as all the children's events were over, most of the parents began to make their families collect their possessions. John Manners had lost his riding-stick, and he was afraid his father would be cross, as he had given it to him for Christmas. But in the end he found it under

11

the Morrissons' car. The Radcliffes had lost two crash caps, a satchel and a dandy-brush; but after a frantic search they found everything except the dandy-brush, and, as they wanted to see Major Holbrooke jump, they had to stop looking.

Major Holbrooke was the only competitor to do a clear round. There wasn't a very high standard of jumping, for Brampton was only a small local show. Mrs. Maxton, who owned the riding-school at Basset, was second with three faults. Susan Barington-Brown was pleased at this, as she had riding lessons from Mrs. Maxton and liked her very much. Joan Brent, a local farmer's daughter, was third. She had ridden a cob with a Roman nose, which jumped very well. Then, after the prize-giving and several very dull speeches, everyone went home.

Susan Barington-Brown rode with Bob bicycling beside her. He was an annoying companion, as he would tell her what a marvellous rider June Cresswell was, and although Susan had been wishing all day that she were half as good, she found this very irritating. Also, he wanted her to trot, and Mrs. Maxton had often told her that you shouldn't trot much on the roads, as it is bad for your pony's legs. But the rosette on Beauty's bridle made up for a great deal, even though it was only a third, and Susan knew that she didn't deserve it. . . .

June Cresswell sulked most of the way home because her mother hadn't let her have the trailer. She had said that it wasn't worth while, when they only lived three miles from the show ground, and that the hack would do Wonder good.

The Radcliffes took a long time to ride the four miles back to Little Hogshill, where they lived, for, like all large families, they had to work out the complicated turns. James and Margaret had to ride home, as they hadn't entered for anything, so they had Pixie and Darkie; while Roger, Hilary and Evelyn took it in turns to ride Northwind and the two bicycles, whose names were Satan and Spitfire.

12

Noel Kettering gave Topsy to Miss Lamb, who was going to lead her home off her flea-bitten grey horse Warrior; because it was too late for Noel to ride all the way to the Hatch-gate, where Miss Lamb lived, and then walk home. So, after thanking her for the loan of Topsy, Noel started for Russet Cottage, which was only a mile from the show ground if you went across the fields. At first she pretended to be a nervous thoroughbred, and cantered along, bucking and shying, but after a bit she became more serious, and walked sedately, trying to think of ways to make money to buy a pony of her own. . . .

Richard and Jill Morrisson actually managed to get home without quarrelling. They discussed everyone's riding, and finally agreed that, if Richard had had Golden Wonder and Jill had had Beauty, they would certainly have won something; but that all the same they would rather have Wendy and Peter any day. . . .

John Manners was one of the last of the competitors to get home; for Basset is five miles from the little market town of Brampton and Lower Basset Farm, where John lived, is some two miles farther on. Colonel and Mrs. Manners, who hadn't gone to the horse show because the Colonel was helping with the harvest, were both waiting at the gate when John arrived, and they were delighted to see the first and second rosettes on Turpin's bridle.

"Well done, my boy! Well done!" shouted the Colonel as soon as John was within hearing distance. "In the money again, I see."

"Yes, Dad," said John. "First in the bending and second in the potato-race. Not bad, was it? But old Turpin simply *wouldn't* jump—that conceited June Cresswell won both the jumping and the riding class."

"That Cresswell girl won the riding class?" roared the Colonel. "Those judges ought to be shot. Look how she jumps—half-way up her pony's neck! . . ."

Major Holbrooke called the dogs and went out into the velvet darkness of the fast-gathering dusk. He walked

down to the stable yard to give the three horses, which were stabled, a last pat. Nothing Venture, the big chestnut showjumper, whinnied softly, Gay Crusader's bay head and the grey one of Harmony, the Anglo-Arabian show hack, appeared over their loose-box doors—Major Holbrooke produced three apples from his pockets . . .

CHAPTER II

MAJOR HOLBROOKE finished his bacon and eggs, threw *The Times* on the floor, and started to open his post. After opening letters from people who wanted to sell him horses, hounds' food, and saddlery, he found one from a "horsy" cousin who lived in Hampshire. While he was reading it, Mrs. Holbrooke came to breakfast.

"Really, George," she said, "must you throw the paper on the floor? I haven't read it yet."

"Sorry, dear," said Major Holbrooke meekly, as he picked up *The Times* and threw it on the nearest chair. "But I have a very interesting letter from Cousin Harry. You know those pony foals he bought several years ago, when they were so cheap they were being killed and sold as veal?"

"Yes, I remember," said Mrs. Holbrooke. "I thought it was the best thing that that bore Harry ever did."

"Well, anyway, these ponies are now four-year-olds, and, though they are quiet to handle, they have never been ridden, and Harry is at his wits' end to know what to do with them. Apparently there is no one small enough who is capable of breaking a pony in his part of the world."

"I expect Harry thinks breaking is a Wild West operation," said Mrs. Holbrooke. "But what does he expect you to do?"

"Perhaps he thinks the Pony Club is full of efficient young horse-breakers," suggested the Major.

"It's an idea," said Mrs. Holbrooke. "But I doubt whether you'd find six children good enough whose parents would allow it. Let's see. There'd be June Cresswell——"

"It's not only the riding which counts," interrupted the Major; "it's horse-sense and tact—so they'll keep out of trouble. That's more important than being able to stick on when you've started it."

"Well, there's the Radcliffes," said Mrs. Holbrooke dubiously. "But they're rather wild and noisy."

"I should be near to help anyone who got into difficulties," said the Major thoughtfully. "Yes, I think it might be done. Anyway, I'll write to Harry to-night, and, if he thinks it a good plan, I'll suggest it at the Pony Club rally. . . ."

Friday was a perfect day: the sun shone out of a clear blue sky and there was a slight breeze.

The Radcliffes hadn't far to go—it was only a matter of three miles from Little Hogshill; and as, for once, they started in good time, they didn't have to hurry their ponies, which arrived looking very smart. John Manners, on the other hand, had lain in bed much later than he meant to, and when he *had* got up he had been hindered at every turn. First of all Turpin had been tiresome to catch—partly because John had forgotten his usual apple. And when at last he did catch him, it was only to find he had a loose shoe. John knew this was his own fault; his mother had reminded him to look at them the day before, and he, thinking she was interfering, had rudely replied that of course they were all right. Knowing he was in the wrong did nothing to improve John's temper, and, as he rode the four miles to the forge at Little Hogshill, he vented his anger on Dick Turpin, whacking him whenever he shied and making him trot nearly the whole way. When he got to the forge, John said he *must* have his pony shod by half-past ten. This didn't make Mr. Hodges, the blacksmith—

who was a very obstinate man—at all inclined to hurry, and it was five minutes to eleven by the time Turpin was done. As John mounted and rode away, without even saying, "Thank you," Mr. Hodges vowed that it would take longer still next time.

John rode the three miles back to Folly Court in twenty minutes, and arrived, hot and cross, with Turpin dripping with sweat, to see June Cresswell riding up the drive without a hair out of place.

However, John wasn't the last member to arrive. In spite of living only half a mile away, Susan Barington-Brown was late. At the last moment she discovered that Bob had put Beauty's bridle together wrong. She had spent ages taking it to pieces and putting it together again, only to find that it was still wrong, whereupon she had put it on in despair. Last of all were the Morrissons. They both arrived in very bad tempers—Richard because his mother had made him ride over with Jill, and Wendy, besides being a much slower walker than Peter, had stopped to graze at intervals, and Jill, because Wendy had been so naughty, and Richard had ridden on, stopping occasionally to shout remarks about her feebleness or Wendy's manners. They joined the other members in the big field behind the house, and they were just in time to hear the Major finish a short explanation of the programme. Then he asked them all to walk in single file round the four white posts which marked out a "school" in the middle of the field. At first Major Holbrooke merely told them not to bunch and that there should be a horse's length between each of them; then he began to look at the riders individually. The standard of horsemanship really was rather low, but it wasn't the children's fault, for there had been no one who really knew about riding to teach them. Mrs. Maxton, who ran the riding-school at Basset, had old-fashioned ideas, and though she taught her pupils to stay on and to control their ponies, they were bad at jumping, and knew nothing of advanced equitation. Miss Lamb, who lent

16

Noel Topsy, and Miss Mitchell, the secretary of the Pony Club, were both indifferent riders, and neither of them had studied horsemanship enough to be able to explain it to anyone else.

The first thing which caught Major Holbrooke's eye was Susan's bridle. He showed her how it should be, and put it right. Then he called a brother and sister, whose names were Anthony and Felicity Rate, into the centre, and explained to them that if they wanted their ponies to walk they must give them a loose rein and allow them to extend their necks. Anthony, who thought he was too old to be taught anything—he was seventeen—tried to argue. He said that Tinker and Topper always jogged, and that if you didn't hold them on a tight rein they bolted. He was told, quite sharply, that no pony would walk with him hanging on to its head, and that, if they did gallop off, they were only trying to escape from their aching neck muscles.

Then Major Holbrooke made Anthony and Felicity walk round him, and when their ponies jogged—through force of habit—he said, "Pull them up to a walk," and when they walked, "Now, quickly, give them a loose rein as a reward." After a few minutes Tinker and Topper seemed to understand, and when they were sent back to their places they only jogged occasionally. This caused a general loosening of reins, for a good many members had thought it necessary to have a firm "feel" on their ponies' mouths. Then the order to trot was given, and straight away Noel was called in and told not to lean so far forward and not to rest her hands on Topsy's withers. Several of the smaller children—Jill Morrisson, Simon Wentwood and the Minton boys—were corrected, and then the order was given to canter. Major Holbrooke let those who *had* got their ponies to canter, canter half-way round the school, and then he called everyone into the middle and asked if *any-one* besides June knew the correct aids to canter on the off leg. Most of the members looked rather blank, and for a bit no one answered. Then a girl of about eighteen, called

17

Joan Melton, said that you pulled with the right rein and kicked with the right leg.

"That's one way of doing it," said the Major, "but I prefer the diagonal aids—that is, to make your pony lead on the off leg you would 'feel' your right rein and press with your left leg. To lead on the near leg you would, of course, reverse your aids—'feel' the left rein and press with the right leg. Now you," he said, pointing at Susan, "make your pony canter round on the off leg."

"Oh, dear," thought Susan, "I know I shall make a mess of it," she gave Beauty a kick and forgot to "feel" either rein.

"You're on the right leg," said Major Holbrooke. "But that was your pony—you didn't give any aid at all." And he patiently showed her all over again. This time Susan understood, and she made Beauty lead off correctly to either hand. Several more people tried with varying success, and then Noel, who, after making a complete muddle of it, was forced to admit that she didn't know her right hand from her left, the near side from the off, and hadn't the faintest idea how you told which leg you were on. Major Holbrooke explained, to the relief of several of the people who instantly pretended they had known all along. Noel wasn't very successful, for Topsy much preferred the near leg, and she obstinately went on it, in spite of the most violent aids to lead on the off one. When she had had about a dozen tries, the Major said it was hopeless, and called the next person. Noel did feel disheartened; she thought drearily that she was doomed to go through life a third-rate horsewoman, when she had so wished to be good.

Scarcely anyone managed to get their pony on the right leg the first time; in fact, June Cresswell and Mary Compton were the only ones, and they sat and watched the other members getting hot and bothered with what John Manners told Richard Morrisson were conceited smiles on their faces. John felt particularly cross, because

18

he had always despised this sort of thing and termed it show riding. As he told Richard, his father had never bothered about which leg he was on, and he'd been pretty good at polo. Richard said that this fancy stuff was safe and suitable for girls, but for those who weren't nervous, races were much more fun.

When everyone, except Noel, Jill Morrisson and the Minton boys, who were all dismissed as hopeless, had mastered the diagonal aids, the Major taught them to ride circles, and then they tried some jumping.

The jump was only a small one—in fact, several people were heard to remark that it was "potty"—but Major Holbrooke found fault with everyone's seat. Even June was corrected. To the great delight of most of the other members, she was told to shorten her reins and put more weight in her stirrups.

"Of course Major Holbrooke believes in the forward seat," said Mrs. Cresswell to Mrs. Radcliffe, who was beside her, "but it's impractical for showing purposes, and I'd so much rather that June rode with her reins on the long side than too short, like that Kettering child."

Mrs. Radcliffe, who disliked Mrs. Cresswell and was only polite to her because she was one of Dr. Radcliffe's patients, said that *she* thought Noel looked rather nice. Mrs. Cresswell gave an affected laugh, and said that of course it was a matter of taste, but she would die of shame if her daughter was mounted on such a scruffy pony.

But it was John who did the worst jump of all; he decided that his father knew just as much about riding as Major Holbrooke, who, after all, was only a major, and would have to do as dad told him if they were still in the Army. So when his turn came he jumped with the backward seat as usual. The Major gave a loud roar, which meant, apparently, that the jag John had given Dick Turpin's mouth was enough to put a pony off jumping for the rest of its life, and that he *must* lean forward, keep his legs back and his hands down.

"But that's the forward seat," said John, deciding that he wasn't going to be shouted at for nothing, "and my father says it's hopeless for hunting—if your pony pecks you can't help going over his head."

"Oh, heavens," said Major Holbrooke rather wearily, "I thought that tiresome old theory had died out long ago!" He went on to explain that a lot of people thought that anyone who leant forward was jumping with the forward seat, and unfortunately the number of people who really jumped with the forward seat was small compared with those who tried to imitate it without knowing the principles. These people generally jumped in "advance" of their horses, with their legs too far back and very little balance or knee grip. They were therefore liable to come off it if anything unexpected happened; but with the correct seat you were perfectly secure. From the horse's point of view he likened the rider who jumped with the forward seat to a well-balanced, firmly-fixed knapsack, while riders like John were satchels, bumping their horses' loins as they jumped. As for jagging a pony's mouth, the Major couldn't believe that the most old-fashioned of fathers thought that a good thing.

John was furious. For a moment he thought he would ride away and never come to a beastly Pony Club rally again; but then the Major asked him whether he would like another try, and John, resolving to show he could jump with the forward seat if he wanted to, rode at the jump, hurled himself forward, and banged his nose on Dick Turpin's hogged mane, which was very prickly, and made his eyes water. However, Major Holbrooke, who was already haunted by remorse for having been so squashing, said that that was jolly good, and John would soon pick it up.

When everyone had done at least one jump fairly well, the Major said it was time to stop. He showed them where the water-trough was, and told them they might tie their ponies to the park rails while they ate their lunches.

20

Noel had forgotten her halter, so she had to tie Topsy up with her stirrup leathers; and Jill Morrisson forgot to loosen Wendy's girths. But this was soon pointed out to her by June, much to Richard's annoyance; for once he took Jill's part, telling June that she hadn't forgotten, but was just about to loosen them. However, June squashed him by saying that you should see to your pony before you even *unpacked* your lunch.

The Radcliffes rescued their mother from Mrs. Cresswell, and then they ate their lunch lying on the grass in the park, except for James and Margaret, who climbed one of the giant oaks, which they said was a lighthouse, and made the rest of the family hand their food up to them.

The Morrissons were made to go right away from the ponies and sit on a rug by the car to eat their lunch, which consisted mainly of Rivita and lettuce; while Noel and Susan, neither of whose parents had come, ate theirs together, and found they had many dislikes in common, the chief being June Cresswell and geometry.

Noel was in the middle of telling Susan what sort of a pony she would buy if she was rich, when their attention was attracted by a view-holler from the Radcliffes, and Noel saw, to her horror, that Topsy had slipped out of her stirrup leathers and was grazing at the far end of the field.

"Oh, dear," she said, "I'm sure I shall never catch her."

"Well, there are plenty of people to help, that's one good thing," said Susan, "and I've got an apple."

Together they advanced on Topsy, Noel holding the apple out invitingly, with the stirrup leather concealed behind her back; but Topsy was enjoying the grass far too much to care about apples, and she merely rolled her small, mean eyes, swished her tail, and walked away. Noel and Susan followed her. This went on for some time, and then Topsy got fed up. With a squeal, she swung round her heels and lashed out at them. They both retreated hastily.

21

"Oh, she is beastly," said Noel. "I know we shall never catch her."

"I'm glad Beauty isn't like that," said Susan, and they stood looking despondently at Topsy, who tore huge mouthfuls of grass in a triumphant manner. The Radcliffes —who prided themselves on being able to catch anything— soon decided that Noel and Susan were being "jolly feeble," so they all came across the field to suggest driving Topsy into a corner. Noel, glad of any ideas, agreed, and Roger and Evelyn arranged everyone in a large half-moon; then they all advanced on her. Eyeing them warily, she walked a few steps towards the corner of the field; suddenly she whirled round. She was intimidated by the waving arms and hair-raising yells of the Radcliffes, but she dodged between Noel and Susan.

"Oh, you are feeble!" shrieked Evelyn. "Why on earth didn't you head her off?"

"Sorry," shouted Noel, as Topsy, headed by John Manners, came galloping back.

"Look out, Roger; she's coming your way!" shrieked Evelyn. But Topsy dodged Roger and doubled back up the field, to be turned by three of Mrs. Maxton's pupils— Cynthia Burke and Pat and Charles French. They chased her down the field again, and then several more people joined in, among them Anthony Rate on Topper. They all chased Topsy in different directions, waving their arms and giving view-hollers. She grew more and more excited, and finally she dodged everyone, galloped through the gate —which no one had thought of shutting—and up the drive towards the house. The Radcliffes raced after her, taking a shortcut across the corner of the park. Noel tore after them, arriving in the garden several lengths behind, but in time to see Topsy career across the smooth green lawn, smash through the herbaceous border, and disappear round the corner of the house.

Major Holbrooke was in the stable yard seeing if Harmony was ready for her demonstration. Hearing the

22

sound of galloping hoofs and the shrieks of the Radcliffes, he hurried into the garden, to see Topsy pursued by a pack of shrieking children. The Major took one look and then, in his best hunting-field voice he bellowed, "Stop chasing that pony!" The result was instantaneous. Everyone stopped in their stride, except Topsy, who disappeared down the path which led to the kitchen garden. The Major took a glance at the rose garden and asked angrily, "What *do* you think you're doing?"

"Trying to catch Topsy," said Evelyn in a voice which meant, surely any fool can see.

"Well, that's not the way to catch a pony," said Major Holbrooke. "Don't you know yet that you must never chase them? I can't see much point in my trying to teach you which leg to canter on if you can't even catch your ponies." Everyone looked very sheepish except Evelyn, who could never believe she was in the wrong. She said, "Topsy's not my pony—we can always catch ours; and anyway, we tried to corner her first."

"Well, it doesn't make the slightest difference whose pony she is," said Major Holbrooke sternly. "There is no excuse for chasing her about whatsoever. Who does she belong to, anyway?"

"Me," said Noel miserably, stepping out from behind the ranks of Radcliffes.

"Why can't you tie your pony up properly?" asked the Major.

"I'm awfully sorry," said Noel, wishing the earth would open and swallow her, "but I forgot to bring a halter, so I had to tie her up with stirrup leathers."

"If you'd asked me I could have lent you one," he said. "Well, you'd better come and help me catch her, but everyone else can go back to the paddock." While the Major collected a scoop of oats and a halter, Noel gazed about her. There were twelve lovely loose-boxes, built of mellow red brick on three sides of a square, and over the green doors looked the wise head of Nothing Venture, the

23

alert one of Gay Crusader, Harmony's exquisite little grey one, and the inquisitive ones of the two youngsters which Major Holbrooke was breaking. The rest of the horses were still out at grass, for it was only the beginning of September. They were exactly the stables Noel had always dreamed of, and she stood spellbound until the Major said, "Come on, let's go and catch your wretched pony before she does any more damage."

"I'm awfully sorry about the garden," said Noel.

"Oh, that's all right," said the Major, "but I shall expect you to come and tidy up if the gardener gives notice—ah, there she is!" as they turned a corner and saw two men, chasing Topsy off a cabbage bed. "Don't chase her," he shouted. "I want to catch her," and he approached Topsy quietly, holding out the oats and talking to her all the time. She stood like a statue, a cabbage leaf hanging out of one side of her mouth, and let the Major go right up to her. The oats did the rest—she greedily buried her muzzle in the scoop while he slipped the halter round her neck.

"Hurray!" said Noel, though at heart she felt rather annoyed that the Major should catch Topsy so easily when she hadn't been able to get near her. "Thanks awfully."

"That's all right," said Major Holbrooke.

Noel led Topsy up the path, past the wrecked rose garden and the trampled herbaceous border, to the paddock, where she was met by Susan, who inquired anxiously:

"Was he very cross?"

"No, he was quite agreeable after you'd gone," said Noel, "but, of course, he hasn't seen the herbaceous border or the lawn yet."

"You managed to catch her, then," said Hilary.

"Yes," said Noel. "Major Holbrooke caught her quite easily with some oats."

"I bet you got a blowing up," said John.

"No, not at all," said Noel. "He was quite agreeable."

"Whew!" said John. "He wasn't very agreeable when I was there."

"I should have thought that anyone who really loved horses would like hoof-marks on their lawn," said Evelyn.

"Not if they liked gardens too," said Susan.

"Well, she didn't do much damage," said Evelyn. "She only squashed a few dull old flowers."

"Shut up!" said Hilary. "Here he comes."

Everyone turned as Major Holbrooke rode into the paddock on Harmony, and almost everyone said, "Isn't she lovely?" She was beautiful: her perfect proportions, her generous eye, noble head, and grey satin coat. The proud carriage of her Arab sire, allied with the lithe gracefulness of the thoroughbred, combined to make her almost unreal.

"I'm just going to ride round a few times to loosen her up," said the Major, "and then we'll try to show you a few things," and he trotted off round the field.

"Golden Wonder isn't a patch on her, is she?" said John to Richard.

Mrs. Cresswell turned to Mrs. Morrisson, whom she had captured, and said, "That's just the sort of thing I want for June when she grows out of Wonder."

"Oh, yes," said Mrs. Morrisson; "but I suppose your little girl is going to take up riding as a career—it's all she thinks about, isn't it?

Mrs. Cresswell was saved the trouble of thinking of a rude reply, for at that moment Major Holbrooke, having trotted and cantered round the field, called all the members together and started to give them a short lecture. Then he and Harmony demonstrated the difference between the extended and collected paces, and he showed them how all the things they had learnt that morning—circles, reining back and leading off at the canter—should be done, and he finished up with the flying change of leg, which Harmony could do at every stride. It was a perfect display. As Noel said to Susan, it made one want to get on one's pony and

start improving oneself straight away. She was soon given the opportunity, for, when Major Holbrooke had finished, he said they had time for a short equitation test before tea, and while he took Harmony back to the stable, everyone bridled their ponies and mounted.

The equitation test was quite simple. You were supposed to walk, trot, and canter slowly and extendedly, rein back, and, if you were good enough, jump two jumps of two feet six. Only three ponies had any idea of collection. They were Golden Wonder, Beauty, and Mary Compton's Blackbird. But as June was the only rider in a position to use her legs, she won easily. The Major pointed out to Mary and Susan how difficult they made it for their legs to do any work—Mary, by sticking hers too far forward; and Susan, by being precariously perched on the pommel, instead of sitting down in the saddle. It was impossible to distinguish between the rest of the members' collected and extended paces, and a few—Jill Morrisson, Simon Wentwood, and Martin, the youngest Minton—were unable to make their ponies leave the others, while Anthony Rate got another lecture for holding Topper on a tight rein. Roger Radcliffe on Northwind was second, with a nice quiet performance, and Diana Melton, Joan's younger sister, was third on her grey cob Pewit.

The ponies were tied up and each given a small feed to eat, while the Pony Club members had tea on the lawn. Mrs. Holbrooke had provided for large appetites, and there were platefuls of egg sandwiches, fruit-cakes, and chocolate biscuits. But for Noel, the whole meal was ruined by the sight of the trampled herbaceous border and the hoof-marks on the lawn.

When everyone had eaten as much as they possibly could, and those parents who were present were telling their families that it was time to go home, Major Holbrooke announced that he had something to say. Everyone crowded round, and, when they had stopped talking, the Major told them about his cousin's New Forest ponies,

and said that anyone who weighed under eight and a half stone and was a fairly competent rider, and whose parents would allow it, could have a pony to break. He explained that the ponies were halter-broken and quite quiet, so that there would be no "rodeo business," and that he was going to hold special instructional rallies for those who had the ponies and anyone else who was interested in breaking and schooling. He also said that two people could share one pony if they liked, as they would want fairly regular exercise. Anyone who wanted a pony was to ring him up before Tuesday.

"Oh, I should love one," said Susan, as the Major finished speaking. "Wouldn't you, Noel?"

"I'm not nearly a good enough rider," said Noel gloomily. "I shouldn't even dare to ask, for I'd probably be told to learn how to tie a pony up properly before I tried to break one in."

"Well, I don't suppose mummy will let me have one, even if Major Holbrooke thinks I'm good enough," said Susan, "and I expect it's awfully difficult. I wonder who will have them," she went on. "I expect June will."

"She's sure to," said Noel, "and the Radcliffes and Clarissa, if she's not too fat."

"I'm sure she weighs at least nine stone," said Susan, but there's Dick Hayward, he's small; and John and Richard, besides Cynthia Burke and the Frenches, who are sure to want them, for they haven't ponies of their own."

"Do you think you'll be allowed one, John?" asked Richard.

"Goodness knows," said John. "Dad won't mind if I catch him in the right mood, but mum might think it was dangerous—she's like that."

"I don't think my father would mind," said Richard. "He doesn't really care what I do as long as I get a good report; but mummy may think an unbroken pony will kick Jill."

27

"It would be pretty good if we could have them, though," said John. "I bet June thinks she's the only person who can break in ponies."

"I bet she does," agreed Richard. "I think it would be a good plan if I asked my mother whether I can have a pony now," he went on, "for she's talking to Mrs. Cresswell, and she won't like to say no if June's having one." And he hurried off across the lawn.

"Mummy, mummy!" shrieked all the Radcliffes, "we *must* have at least one pony."

"For goodness' sake be quiet," said Mrs. Radcliffe. "I can't hear a thing when you all talk at once, and of course you can have a pony—only James and Margaret aren't to ride it until it's quiet."

"Thanks awfully," said Hilary.

"Hurrah," said Evelyn.

"Oh, Mummy, why not?" asked Margaret.

"I'm much too heavy," said Roger gloomily. "I was nine stone two *last* holidays."

"Can't we have two?" asked Hilary, "then we would each have a pony to ride?"

"Yes, we must," said Evelyn. "It would save all the arranging of turns."

"No," said Mrs. Radcliffe, "one will be plenty. Major Holbrooke said they needed a good deal of exercise, and when Roger's at school you won't want more than four ponies."

Major Holbrooke was unpopular in a good many homes that night. Tired fathers just back from the office were greeted with: "Can we have one of Major Holbrooke's ponies, Daddy? Mummy said we were to ask you." "You'll drive me into a lunatic asylum if you mention those ponies again," threatened exasperated mothers.

The Frenches' father said he would stop their riding lessons for the rest of the holidays if they uttered another word about the Major's ponies; Mrs. Minton almost sent her family to bed; Clarissa Penn nearly drove her parents

28

mad because she spent the whole evening grumbling about her fatness, and saying she was going to slim; while Dick Hayward sulked because his parents said that, since he was away at school all the term and had to be coached all the holidays, he couldn't possibly find time to exercise two ponies; Susan Barington-Brown, having persuaded her father that there was no safer or more fashionable amusement than breaking ponies, hastily retired to bed, and left him to tackle her mother; Margaret Radcliffe grumbled because she wasn't allowed to ride Hilary's and Evelyn's pony; and Hilary and Evelyn grumbled because they weren't allowed two ponies, and apparently it would be no fun at all if they had to share one. At first Mrs. Radcliffe stood firm, and said one unbroken pony would be plenty. But as the evening wore on she became exasperated by their grumbling, and finally she said she didn't care what they did as long as they went away and left her in peace. So Evelyn said, "Hurrah!" and Hilary said, "Thanks awfully!" and they both rushed off to ring up Major Holbrooke before she could change her mind.

Mrs. Kettering was nearly driven crazy by Noel wishing she were a good enough rider to have one of the ponies, and cursing fate, which, she said, had condemned her to be a rotten one. To her mother's suggestion that they should save up for a few lessons at Mrs. Maxton's, Noel asked what was the good when she didn't teach you the diagonal aids, and what was the good of knowing the diagonal aids when Topsy wouldn't go on the off leg whatever you did? Mrs. Kettering said that perhaps when daddy came home and wrote his book they would be richer, and then they would be able to buy Noel a pony. But Noel, who was in a bad temper, said that no one would want to read a book about boring remains in Egypt, so they would never be any richer, and she would have to go riding ponies like Topsy all her life, and she stamped off to bed in a rage, leaving Mrs. Kettering very upset. Noel was generally very good about being poor, and never grumbled when she had

to wear her clothes when they were too small or her cousins' out-grown ones, which were always too big, and Mrs. Kettering wondered whether she had been silly to let her ride when other children were so much better mounted.

CHAPTER III

DURING the week-end Major Holbrooke had several telephone calls, and on Monday he was able to tell his cousin that he had found people to break all six of his ponies, so would he send them off as soon as possible? Cousin Harry, who was a retired colonel with a walrus moustache, usually took weeks to arrange anything, but to the Major's surprise he announced that the ponies would arrive next day on the ten-twenty train.

Next morning he almost wished that he hadn't started the idea, when he and Blake had to make three journeys to Brampton station to fetch all the ponies, none of which liked the thought of going into the trailer at all, and he cursed Cousin Harry heartily in the evening, when he had to ring up the Radcliffes, June Cresswell, John Manners, Susan Barington-Brown, and Richard Morrisson, and tell them all to come to Folly Court on Thursday at ten-thirty.

Of course, all the people who were having ponies became very excited when the Major rang them up; they began to wonder what the ponies would be like, and how he would decide who was to have which. In fact, they talked of nothing else. Mr. Morrisson forbade the mention of ponies, or anything connected with them, at meals; Colonel Manners told John that children should be seen and not heard, when he had tried to tell a dull golfing story for the whole of one lunch-time, and had been unable to get a word in edgeways; Dr. Radcliffe complained bitterly that he had raised a family of horsy bores. But Mrs. Cresswell

30

and June had a new subject of conversation. They never ceased discussing how the other members would spoil their ponies and how riding would count and give June another victory. Susan Barington-Brown's mother disapproved of the whole idea, and, if Susan mentioned the pony, she got a lecture on how it would be her own fault if she broke her neck or spoilt her appearance, for she should be playing nicely with some other little girl instead of galloping about the countryside. In vain did Susan point out that she didn't gallop much—it would be bad for Beauty's legs and manners—her mother, spurred on by Valerie, who was twenty-two and had been brought up in the days before Mr. Barington-Brown had made his money, was prepared to find fault with everything Susan did. Unfortunately, Mr. Barington-Brown, who generally kept the peace, was away in Manchester on business, so Susan had no one to support her. On Wednesday morning, after a particularly unpleasant breakfast time, when Valerie said Susan was spoilt, bad-mannered, stupid, ought to be sent to a boarding-school, Susan felt she could bear it no longer; she saddled Beauty, without looking for Bob, and rode over to Russet Cottage to see Noel.

Noel was also feeling fed-up, for Miss Lamb had gone to Ireland for a holiday, and she had turned Topsy out for one too. As Noel had particularly wanted to practise the diagonal aids, she felt very cross and grumbled that there was nothing to do. When her mother suggested occupations, she replied that she didn't feel like doing that, or it was no fun by yourself. She had just taken Simple Simon, the golden cocker spaniel, for a walk, and was sitting on the five-barred gate into Farmer Trent's forty-acre meadow, which was opposite Russet Cottage, trying to think of something else to do, when she heard the sound of hoofs and saw Susan riding up the lane.

"Hallo!" shouted Susan, "The ponies came yesterday, and we're going to Folly Court to share them out tomorrow. Are you coming?"

31

"I don't think I'd better," said Noel, getting off the gate and patting Beauty. "I mean, I'm not having one, and anyway the Major will probably say he doesn't want an idiotic person, who can't even tie her pony up properly, listening to lectures on breaking ponies."

"Of course he won't," said Susan. "He's probably forgotten all about it by now."

"Not if the gardener gave notice," said Noel. "He might give me some weeding to do."

"That would be rather fun," said Susan. "I'd help you, and when he wasn't looking we could explore the stables."

"I hate weeding," said Noel.

"Oh, do come," said Susan.

"But I haven't got Topsy, because Miss Lamb has gone away for a holiday; so how am I to get there?" asked Noel.

"Well, if you could walk to my place," said Susan, "we could take it in turns to ride Beauty to Folly Court, and then perhaps you could come to lunch with me afterwards. I'll ask mummy. And then we could take it in turns to ride back here."

"I should love to," said Noel, unable to resist the thought of so many turns on Beauty, "but I don't see why I should ride your pony while you walk."

"Oh, don't be so silly," said Susan. "Anyway, you'll come?"

"O.K.," said Noel. "What time?"

"We've got to be there by half-past ten," said Susan, "so you'd better come early—ten o'clock at the latest. Would you like a ride on Beauty now?"

"I should love one," said Noel, "but I don't want to spoil her."

"I've done that already," said Susan, "and I don't suppose you'll make her any worse. Is there a field you could ride her in?"

"Farmer Trent lets me ride in here," said Noel, opening the gate. Susan gave her Beauty, and she mounted and

rode round the field several times. Then, coming back to Susan, she said, "She's *lovely*—quite different from Topsy; she's got such a soft mouth and she cantered on the right leg straight away."

"She is nice, isn't she?" said Susan. "For, though she's fresh, you can always pull her up and she's never nappy."

"You are lucky," said Noel, patting Beauty. "I wish I had a pony like her; but I expect she was awfully expensive."

"Daddy wouldn't tell me how much she cost," said Susan, "but I think it was quite a lot, because mummy said it was a waste of money, and Valerie said daddy had never bought *her* such an expensive present."

"Is Valerie your sister?" asked Noel.

"Yes, worse luck," said Susan.

"Don't you like having a sister?" asked Noel in shocked surprise. "I always wish I had one—it's so boring doing things by oneself."

"Yes, but Valerie's twenty-two," said Susan, "and she certainly wouldn't do anything with me. She says I'm spoilt."

"I suppose it's because she's so much older than you," said Noel thoughtfully. "I mean, she counts as a grown-up. . . ."

Thursday was a wet, windy day, and to John Manners, walking up the winding road which led to Folly Court, it seemed that the first breath of autumn was in the air. He thought, regretfully, that the holidays were almost over, and soon he would be back at school. It wasn't that he minded school, but it was more fun to ride about on Turpin, drive the tractor or help on the farm. The real trouble about going back to school was that he would only have a fortnight in which to break his pony, and by the Christmas holidays it would have forgotten everything he had taught it. That, thought John, is where the girls are going to have an advantage, for none of them are at

33

boarding-schools, and, though it will be dark in the evenings, they will have the week-ends.

By this time John had reached the gates of Folly Court, and he was hailed by shrieks from Noel and Susan, who were approaching from the opposite direction. John waved and waited—he was very glad to see them, for he hated to arrive by himself.

"Hallo," said Susan, "I see you walked over too."

"Yes," said John. "I thought it would be hopeless to try to lead an unbroken pony off Turpin."

"That's what I thought," said Susan. "So Noel is going to ride Beauty home, and I hope my pony will follow her."

They were walking up the drive during this conversation, and suddenly Noel, who was riding Beauty and could see over the hedges, said, "There they are!"

"Where?" asked John and Susan both at once.

Noel pointed. There, in a little paddock close to Folly Farm, grazed the six ponies—a grey, a skewbald, two bays, a chestnut, and a black.

"Don't they look lovely?" said Susan, separated from them by several acres but determined to be pleased.

Meanwhile the long, grey rambling Priory, where the Radcliffes lived, had been the scene of a good deal of argument and excitement. The Radcliffes had decided to go to Folly Court in full force, for, in spite of Major Holbrooke's assurance that the ponies were quiet, they all felt sure that they would have a difficult journey home. They had each prepared themselves for any eventuality, and as they hurried along the quiet country road, Margaret and James in front, riding Pixie and Darkie, and the elder three, who were going to lead the youngsters, walking behind, their pockets bulged with things that *might* be useful. James had a compass, a long piece of cord to rescue people from chalk quarries, and a box of matches so that they could light a fire as a beacon if they were lost, or to warm them if they had to spend the night out. Margaret had a very large handkerchief to bind up any one

34

—horse or human—who cut his arteries, and some acid drops in case they all fell into a quarry and shouted themselves hoarse. Hilary had oats for the ponies and bars of chocolate for the humans; while Evelyn had enough apples for everyone; and Roger carried the halters and some money.

The walk to Folly Court seemed very short. They spent it imitating the other Pony Club members and inventing the things they would say when their ponies were naughty. Evelyn was June Cresswell when she had been bucked off into a puddle; she complained bitterly that she had been made to look a fool, and told Hilary to send for Dr. Radcliffe, as she had swallowed a mouthful of muddy water. Hilary replied that she would never be able to bear the shame of Evelyn looking so scruffy. Margaret was alternately Noel, when she said in a squeaky voice, "Oh, dear! Whatever shall I do? I'm *sure* I shall *never* be able to catch her." And Susan when she whined, "Daddy, Daddy, the horrid pony's bucked me off. I *must* have another groom to exercise her." Roger imitated Richard Morrisson. He told his sisters that they were *only* girls and couldn't do anything. James' thoughts were far away. He stood at the helm of his good ship *Dauntless* and steered her through the coral reefs with unerring judgment.

Jill was very pleased when Richard asked if she would ride over to Folly Court with him and then lead Wendy home off Peter while he walked with the youngster. Generally he wouldn't let her ride Peter, saying she would spoil his mouth or let him have his own way, and it was very flattering to be thought capable of leading one pony off another when you were "only a girl."

They rode to Folly Court in the best of spirits, imagining all sorts of triumphs for his youngster. They arrived to find John, Noel and Susan gazing across the fields at the ponies. They all admired and discussed them for a few minutes, and then John said he thought they ought to go up to the house in case everyone else had arrived.

They found the Radcliffes talking to the Major, who, after everyone had said "Hallo," asked if they would like to see round while they were waiting for June. They were in one of the big shady paddocks looking at the brood-mares and their foals when they heard the sound of a car, and on going back to the stable yard they found that Mrs. Cresswell and June had arrived, complete with trailer. Mrs. Cresswell apologised for being late, and the Major led the way across the fields towards the Home Farm. Mrs. Cresswell kept up an unending stream of conversation about June, to whom, she said, the breaking would be a wonderful experience, for, though she hadn't much more to learn about riding, she had never done anything with young horses.

The sight of the ponies stopped Mrs. Cresswell's flow of words. Hearing the Major's call, they all hurried across the field and began to look in people's pockets in the most friendly manner. They were all about the same size—between twelve-two and thirteen-two—and four of them were mares, and two, the chestnut and one of the bays, were geldings.

"Oh, aren't they lovely?" said Susan.

"I want the black one," said John.

"We *must* have the skewbald," said Margaret Radcliffe.

"No, no, the grey," said Evelyn.

Mrs. Cresswell turned to June and said, in an undertone, "I do hope you don't get the skewbald—she's too 'circusy' for words."

"I'm going to give you five minutes to make up your minds," said the Major; "and then, if more than one person wants any pony, they'll have to draw lots." And he sat on the gate while they decided.

"Oh, we *must* have the skewbald," said Margaret.

"For goodness' sake shut up," said Evelyn. "It's not you who's having a pony, and anyway, I want the grey."

"A good horse is never a bad colour!" quoted Hilary, "but personally I rather like the chestnut."

36

"Yes, he's awfully nice," agreed Roger, "such a glorious golden chestnut, and I like his star."

"I like the black," said James. "You could be a highwayman on her."

"Ugh," said Evelyn. "I hate blacks! Anyway, you can be a highwayman on a grey. What about Katerfelto?"

"A black's better, though," said James, "because you can't be seen at night."

"Well, I don't want to be a highwayman," said Evelyn. "I'm going to have the grey."

"If no one else wants her," said Roger.

"Mummy," said June, "don't you think the grey has the best hocks?"

"Don't talk so loud," whispered Mrs. Cresswell, "or all the others will want her too."

"I don't know which I want," said Susan. "They're all so lovely. Which do you think, Noel?"

"I've no eye for a horse," said Noel drearily. She was feeling very envious. "But I don't think colour matters much, and you can't tell what their characters are like until you've known them some time. I should just let fate take its course."

"Have you decided which you want, Richard?" asked John.

"The grey, I think," said Richard. "But I don't really mind. Have you settled on the black?"

"Yes, I like her the best," said John.

Then the Major got off the gate and said time was up, and who wanted which?

"The grey," shouted June, Richard and Evelyn all at once; while John said, "The black"; and Hilary, "The chestnut."

"One at a time, *please*," said Major Holbrooke. "You nearly deafened me. Now who wants the grey—and please don't shout."

"Me," said June, Evelyn and Richard more quietly.

"Well, you'll have to draw lots, then," said the Major.

37

"But first of all, what about you other people?"

"Can I have the black?" asked John. As no one else wanted her, he was settled. Hilary asked for and was given the chestnut, and then, as Susan still hadn't decided which pony she wanted, the Major made three lots, and June drew the longest, so, to Evelyn's intense disgust, she chose the grey. Then Susan, Richard and Evelyn drew for the three remaining ponies. Richard, who got the longest lot, had the bay gelding, which was the tallest pony; Susan, who got the middling lot, had the bay mare; while Evelyn, who had the shortest lot, had the smallest pony, which was the skewbald. She was very cross, but Margaret was delighted, and whispered to James that they would be able to have a circus.

"Thank goodness, that's settled," said the Major. "I only hope everyone knows which pony they've got, for I certainly don't. And now," he went on, "if you will all come back to the stables, I want to show you a few things about lungeing on one of my youngsters."

As they walked back across the fields, Major Holbrooke explained about lungeing. He said he expected they had all seen it done, but, for the benefit of anyone who hadn't, it was simply making a horse walk, trot and canter on a long webbing rein fixed to his head-collar and held by the trainer who, by standing more or less in the same place, causes the horse to go round in a continuous circle. Lungeing was, he said, an excellent thing for the young horse, as it balanced and suppled him, besides teaching him the words of command, which were so important when you first started to ride him.

When they reached the stables they found The Merry Widow ready in a head-collar and lunge-rein. The Major led her out to a small paddock on the west side of the house and started to lunge her, first of all at the walk. He pointed out the way in which he held the rein and whip, and said that of course they mustn't expect their ponies to go as well at first, as The Widow had been broken in six

38

weeks and knew all about it. When he had lunged her at the walk, trot and canter to either hand, Major Holbrooke asked if anyone would like a try. "Me," said everyone but Noel.

The Major handed the lunge-rein and whip to Evelyn, who had spoken most loudly. While she had been watching, Evelyn had thought lungeing looked easy, and as she knew she was a very capable person, she had expected to be able to do it straight away, but, to her chagrin, The Merry Widow, who had behaved perfectly with the Major, refused to walk round at all. After she had tried for a few minutes, with very little success, Major Holbrooke pointed out that she was standing absolutely still in the centre and expecting the horse to walk round her, while she should move round with the horse, though on a very much smaller circle and slightly behind her, with the whip out, ready to send her on if she should try to stop or turn, in exactly the same way as one used one's legs when riding.

When Evelyn got the idea of this she managed the Widow much better, and when she had made her walk and trot round to either hand several times, the Major said it was someone else's turn, and Richard took the rein. He was quite good, but he would show off and try to crack the whip. Susan, who had the next turn, tangled the lunge-rein round her legs and was nearly pulled over; but apart from this she controlled The Merry Widow well, as did Hilary. When Hilary had had her turn, the Major said The Widow had done enough, and he sent John for Black Magic. She was more difficult to lunge, for not only had she a more excitable temperament, but she had barely been broken in a month. In spite of this, both John and June managed her well. Then, Major Holbrooke asked Noel if she wanted a turn.

"Oh, I should love one," said Noel, "but I'm not having a pony."

"That doesn't matter," said the Major, "come on."

So Noel gave Beauty to Susan and took the lunge-rein

She managed Black Magic quite easily.

and whip. Black Magic looked huge and formidable but Noel found that she could manage her quite easily and she had no critical audience for the others had lost interest in lungeing and were questioning the Major about saddling and bridling for the first time. She was sorry when her turn was up.

"You had better have a go now, Roger," said the Major. And then, when Roger had finished, he told James and Margaret Radcliffe, to their annoyance, that they were too small, and, taking the rein, he showed the way to teach a horse to jump, beginning with a pole on the ground and working up to two feet six—the highest Black Magic had learned to jump so far.

At the end of the jumping, Mrs. Holbrooke, who had been good naturedly keeping Mrs. Cresswell out of the way by showing her round the aviary in which she kept her collection of exotic birds, came into the paddock to point out that it was already half-past twelve, and that most families lunched at one.

"Oh, heavens," said Major Holbrooke guiltily, "why didn't someone tell me before? Come on, all of you; we'd better catch those ponies. Have you got your halters?"

"Oh, dear!" said Susan. "We've come without one."

The Major said he would lend her a halter, and he sent Noel to fetch one, for she knew where they were kept, and he asked Roger to put Black Magic away. Noel helped Roger to settle Black Magic, and then they ran across the fields, to find that the others had already caught the ponies. When everyone had thanked the Major, who said that anyone who got into difficulties was to ring him up and that he would arrange another rally before the end of the holidays, Noel, Margaret and James mounted and, followed by the six led ponies, they set off for home. When they came to the drive, the Radcliffes took the back way, which led to the Hogshill road, while everyone else, except June, went down the main drive to the Basset-Brampton road. There John had a little difficulty in persuading his black

41

mare to go alone to Lower Basset while all her friends were led off in the opposite direction, but he got her along in the end, though she neighed hopefully long after the others were out of sight.

Mrs. Cresswell and June had great difficulty in getting the grey into the trailer. The Major, who was feeling hungry, and therefore rather cross, became very annoyed with Mrs. Cresswell, who would wave her arms and say, "Shoo!" to the pony, which, of course, only upset her the more. At last Major Holbrooke could bear it no longer. He gave Mrs. Cresswell a lecture, and, taking the halter-rope from June, who was trying to pull her pony in, he picked up each of the grey's fore-feet in turn and put them on the ramp; then, holding out a cow-cake, he walked up in front of her. Finding that the ramp was quite firm and didn't collapse as she had expected, the grey followed him into the trailer. Mrs. Cresswell thanked the Major effusively, and then he, muttering, "Not at all," and "Don't mention it," hurried into lunch, to find Mrs. Holbrooke also in a bad temper, partly because she was hungry, partly because the lunch was overdone, but mainly because she had had to spend the whole morning making conversation to Mrs. Cresswell.

Meanwhile, as Mrs. Cresswell and June drove home to their lunch, which was to be sausages and mash followed by bread and butter pudding, they discussed the events of the morning.

"Wasn't it a good thing I got the grey," said June, "and not the cart-horsy old skewbald or the dull bays and black? I wouldn't have been seen dead on the skewbald."

"The grey is certainly the pick of the bunch," replied Mrs. Cresswell, "and I'm glad you got her, June, for I hardly think those other children would have done her justice. Of course, the chestnut was a showy little animal."

"Well, he soon won't be," said June. "Hilary Radcliffe is sure to spoil him. Why, she doesn't even know how to

change legs, so what's the good of her trying to break in a pony?"

"That's quite true," said Mrs. Cresswell; "and really," she went on, "after the exhibition those children made of themselves at the rally, I don't know how the Major can bring himself to entrust them with his cousin's ponies. I suppose he thinks he can chase round after them all showing them what to do, but in spite of the nasty way he spoke when we were boxing her, he can rest assured that one pony—and probably only one—will be properly trained."

"Susan," said Noel as they parted from the Morrissons and turned up the drive to Basset Towers, "I know I shall upset something."

"That's all right," said Susan calmly. "I often do. Mummy makes rather a fuss, and Valerie says my table manners are disgusting, but they won't be able to say anything to you—you're a guest."

"But it's so awfully embarrassing," said Noel.

"I don't see why," said Susan. "Everybody upsets things."

"Not as often as I do," said Noel. "I hardly ever go out without upsetting something."

By this time they had reached the stables, and the bay pony, which had led perfectly all the way, suddenly refused to go any farther. In vain did Susan try to tempt her with apples or pull her along. In vain did Noel take Beauty on ahead. They pushed and pulled and tempted her for about ten minutes, and then, just as they were despairing, Mr. Barington-Brown came rolling up the drive in his Daimler, driven by Cookson, the chauffeur. The pony didn't take any notice of the car; she just stood, her fore-legs braced out in front of her, and refused to move. Cookson brought the black, shiny Daimler smoothly to a standstill, and Mr. Barington-Brown jumped out and said in jovial tones:

" 'Ullo, Susan. Won't the bucking broncho go?"

"Oh, Daddy, you're just in time. *Do* come and help us."

So Mr. Barington-Brown, who in the days of his youth, long before he became a rich shoe manufacturer, had looked after a pony called Snowball, belonging to his father, a greengrocer, pushed, while Susan tempted the pony and Noel rode ahead on Beauty. Suddenly the bay gave in and walked quietly into the stable. They put her in the box next to Beauty, in which she looked very small and forlorn, for it was the old-fashioned type, with iron bars all round, so that she couldn't look out or speak to Beauty next door. To Noel she seemed like an unjustly sentenced prisoner.

Susan made sure that there was water and hay in the youngster's box and a feed for Beauty, and then, when he had finished mopping his brow, Mr. Barington-Brown said that it was half-past one, and that if they didn't hurry into lunch they'd have mother after them.

Basset Towers was a very ugly house. It had been built by an eccentric shipowner, who had a great deal of money but no taste. Besides being built in a hideous red brick, it was too high for its length, and at each corner there was a pepper-pot turret, which made it look quite absurd.

The Barington-Browns had only lived at Basset for about a year; before that they had had a house in Manchester near Mr. Barington-Brown's factory. When Susan's mother, who was rather a snob, decided to live in the country, she had chosen Basset Towers, partly because it was the right size and she thought that the rooms were convenient, and partly because she thought that Basset Towers would be a smart postal address.

Noel took an instant dislike to Mrs. Barington-Brown, who was tall, gaunt and acid looking, and whose hand, when Noel shook it, was cold and fish-like. Noel thought she looked awfully old—more like Susan's grandmother than her mother. Then Valerie came in. She, too, was tall and thin; her blonde hair was piled on top of her head, and she had sticking-out teeth and a discontented ex-

pression. Noel shook hands with her, and then Mrs. Barington-Brown told Susan to take "her little friend" to wash, so Susan took Noel upstairs to a very pink bathroom. They washed with pink soap, and afterwards Susan did her hair, which was in two neat, fair plaits, and Noel made a feeble attempt to flatten her unruly black shock. When Susan was ready they cantered down to lunch, which was saddle of mutton, followed by chocolate soufflé. Noel was given enormous helpings, far more than she could eat, and, except for offering her more, no one made much conversation. Mr. Barington-Brown told one story—a very dull one—about Snowball, while Mrs. Barington-Brown argued with Valerie as to whether the lounge needed redecorating.

After an even longer pause than usual, when everyone looked at their plates and Noel felt terribly embarrassed, Mrs. Barington-Brown asked:

"When is your father coming home from Egypt, Noel?"

"Not until next summer," replied Noel, rather surprised that she knew he was there.

"He's one of those people who dig up china and mummies, isn't he?" asked Mr. Barington-Brown.

"Really, Albert!" said Mrs. Barington-Brown before Noel could reply. "How can you be so ignorant! Professor Kettering is an eminent archæologist, and he's written several very deep books on the subject."

"He's written some books," said Noel, "but they look rather boring to me."

"Oh, well," said Mr. Barington-Brown with a laugh, "I'm sure no one expects you to bother your little head with such things. . . ."

CHAPTER IV

IT WAS ON the following Wednesday that Major Holbrooke, having once again summoned all the horse-breakers to Folly Court, gave another lecture and demonstration—this time on the second stage in breaking, that of backing the young horse, and teaching him the elementary aids.

Beforehand, Noel hardly knew whether to be glad or sorry that she was unable to go—she was in bed with a very bad cold—but afterwards, when Susan had told her all she could remember, which was not a lot, Noel thought it sounded so interesting that she was very disappointed not to have been there.

The Major had asked everyone a great many questions about the behaviour of his or her pony and what it had been named. June's, which, as you know, was called Grey Dawn, had apparently learned a great deal. She could walk, trot and canter on the lunge-rein; she could be groomed, have her feet picked out and wear a saddle and snaffle bridle. He said he hoped June hadn't hurried Grey Dawn in her lungeing, but June and Mrs. Cresswell both assured him that she hadn't; they said that Dawn lunged perfectly, and was not at all hotted-up or excitable. Some of the other children were rather downcast by this long list of Grey Dawn's accomplishments. John wondered whether June would beat them all again; it looked like it.

Then the Radcliffes had told how their ponies, which they named, after a good deal of argument, Rocket and Romany, were both behaving quite well. Evelyn's, which was Romany, could canter on the lunge-rein, but would not let her hind-feet be picked up, and though Evelyn didn't mention this, she cow-kicked when she was groomed or girthed up, while Rocket, though not so far on with his

46

lungeing, would let you do anything with him in the stable, and Hilary had already lain across his back on her tummy without any objection on his part. Major Holbrooke seemed to think Rocket a promising pupil when he heard this, which surprised Evelyn, for though she hadn't said anything to Hilary, she privately thought him much too quiet and lazy, and while Romany had learned to canter after her second lesson, Rocket still couldn't after his sixth.

Richard, in a fit of rashness brought about by a foolish desire not to sound "small" in front of June Cresswell, gave Red Rufus an untruthfully good report. He said that he could walk, trot and canter on the lunge-rein, but he did not mention that he usually escaped at least twice in a lesson. He said that Rufus could wear a saddle and bridle, but he did not add that it sometimes took half an hour to put the bridle on.

Then John explained that he hadn't settled on a name for his pony. He had thought of Black Bess, Jackdaw, Nightmare, and Midnight, but he didn't think that any of them suited her. For the moment, he called her Blackie.

Susan was the last person to give her account. She said that Sunset was very quiet to lead, but would not lunge to the right without a struggle, and, though quiet to groom, was very naughty to saddle.

Major Holbrooke explained that probably Sunset was stiff to one side—horses often were—and, naturally, she preferred going round the way that was easier. The cure was to twice the work on the difficult rein, but to do this tactfully, a bit more each day and breaking it up with rests and spells on the easy rein. It was no good giving in, but one had to remember that one was asking the pony to do something that was difficult for her.

As for the saddling, either Susan had put the saddle on with a bang or else she had pinched Sunset with the girth; unless, of course, the saddle didn't fit or the pony had girth-galls. Susan said she was sure that Sunset hadn't any

47

girth-galls; and, as the saddle, which her father had bought specially, fitted perfectly, she thought it must be her bad saddling. Major Holbrooke told Susan to be very careful in future, and then, when Sunset found she wasn't going to be hurt, she would give up making a fuss. He went on to give them all a great deal of good advice, and, among other things, he suggested that those at boarding schools should ask a parent, brother or sister to pay their ponies an occasional visit, and perhaps even put a halter on and lead them about during the term. Then, when he had reminded them that anyone who got into difficulties was to ring him up, they all went into the house for lemonade and cake.

When everyone had gone and the Holbrookes were drinking a before-lunch glass of sherry, Mrs. Holbrooke asked the Major how the children were getting on.

"The Barington-Brown child was the only one which seemed to have had any trouble," replied Major Holbrooke. "Her pony is evidently a bit one-sided, and it looks as though she's pinched her with the girth, but, apart from her, they all seem to be doing well."

"Mrs. Cresswell seemed pleased with the grey's progress," said Mrs. Holbrooke.

"Well, actually," said the Major, "I'm afraid they may be taking her a bit too fast, but they insist she's going well."

"I shouldn't worry," said Mrs. Holbrooke. "I expect Mrs. Cresswell was laying it on a bit thick. You know what she is: June must always be one better than the others."

"It's a most tiresome complex," said Major Holbrooke, "and so bad for the child, but I suppose it's an excess of maternal instinct. What that woman needs is *six* children."

"Mummy," said June on the way home from Folly Court, "I'm going to back Grey Dawn this afternoon."

"Are you sure she's ready?" asked Mrs. Cresswell.

"Major Holbrooke seemed to think we were taking her too fast."

"That's only because he doesn't want me to get ahead of the others," said June. "I expect he's afraid that he'll have to give me special instructions on how to teach ponies the flying change while he's still trying to drum the turn on the forehead into them—if they ever get as far."

"Yes, perhaps that's it," said Mrs. Cresswell, "though it hardly seems fair to hold you back because the rest are dolts. Of course, he's made a mistake. How can that Barington-Brown child or those two hopeless boys turn out a properly broken pony? Now, if I had been the Major, I should have asked you to help me with the lot, and then I should have known that the job would be done properly. But there it is—there's such a lot of jealousy and spite about."

The backing of Grey Dawn was very successful. Following the Major's instructions, June began by putting her foot in the stirrup as if to mount, and increasing her weight on it each time. Then she lay on her tummy on Grey Dawn's back, and finally as, like all properly brought up ponies, she made no fuss, June mounted. Except for a slight stiffening of her back, under the unaccustomed weight, Grey Dawn did nothing, and after she had been given several handfuls of oats by Mrs. Cresswell, who was holding her, she relaxed, and allowed herself to be led a few steps round the box. This, Major Holbrooke had told them, was the most they should do at the first lesson; so June dismounted, and when they had given Dawn some more oats they hurried jubilantly into tea.

At Hogshill Priory all was not going so smoothly. Roger and James had gone for a ride, but Margaret had said she would stay at home and help Hilary and Evelyn back their ponies. They began by lungeing, and Hilary asked Rocket to canter for the first time. He cantered very calmly

and on a loose lunge-rein, which caused Evelyn to remark to Margaret that she did wish Hilary would wake him up, for he looked like a worn-out hireling. Romany certainly didn't need waking up; in fact, it was impossible to make her walk on the lunge-rein until she had cantered round for some time, and was so out of breath that she couldn't do anything else. When Hilary pointed this out, Evelyn said happily that Romany had a hotter temperament than lazy old Rocket, and since she could ride stubborn old Pixie if she wanted to use her legs, it was a jolly good thing. Hilary was furious. She said that Evelyn was being perfectly beastly about Pixie, and that if she had paid the slightest attention to Major Holbrooke she would have heard him say that you should use your legs for turning, pulling up, and reining-back.

"That's only for training show horses," said Evelyn. "I don't want Romany to be one of those silly ponies that have to be told what to do with their legs and are always falling flat in the hunting-field."

"I can't say I've seen many of Major Holbrooke's horses fall flat out hunting," said Hilary shortly.

"Old Georgie Holbrooke is different," said Evelyn. "He's gifted. You're not so conceited as to think you'll ever be able to ride like him, are you? Good hands are born, not made, and you're just as mutton-fisted as the rest of us."

"If you think I intend to go on riding as badly as I do now all my life, you're mistaken," said Hilary with dignity. And she marched out of the field leading Rocket.

"Gosh," said Evelyn to Margaret, "she *is* getting touchy. She seems to fly off at the least little thing nowadays."

"I expect it was because you said Rocket was lazy," said Margaret.

"Well, so he is," said Evelyn, "and if Hilary thinks I'm going to say he's wonderful, when I don't think so, she's mistaken."

For a while she lunged Romany in silence. Then she

said, "Marga, do you think you could hold Romany while I back her? It's no good asking Hilary if she's got the sulks."

Margaret was delighted. She said of course she could hold her; *she* was jolly nearly as strong as Hilary. So they led Romany into one of the loose-boxes, and Margaret took her head while Evelyn put her weight in the stirrup several times and then mounted.

"Hurrah," shouted Margaret, frightening Romany, who threw her head up and hit Evelyn a blow on the nose.

"For goodness' sake shut up," said Evelyn. "Can't you see you're frightening her?"

"Whatever does she want to be so jolly nervous for?" asked Margaret impatiently.

"Perhaps Georgie Holbrooke's cousin was beastly and chased her with whips," suggested Evelyn. "Poor old lady," she went on. "Give her some more oats, Marga." And when Margaret had given her another handful, "Now lead her round the box."

At first Romany was very nervous, and, as Margaret found her hard to control, they went round in rushes and jerks, but she soon became quiet to all outward appearances, though an experienced horseman would have known her rigid back and tense muscles for a "go-slow" signal. Unfortunately, Evelyn was not an experienced horseman, nor did she remember the advice of one who was. "Marga," she asked, "do you think you could hold her if we went outside?"

"Yes, easily," said Margaret. "She's awfully quiet now, and I'm sure no one has got on half as fast as this."

Encouraged, Evelyn said, "Come on, then; open the door, but for goodness' sake don't let her go."

Margaret led Romany out across the yard at the back of the house. All went well until they passed the corner by the back door for the second time; then some tea towels, hung out to dry, flapped idly in the breeze. Romany, already keyed up to breaking point, was terrified. She

51

leaped forward with a snort, and Margaret and Evelyn, who had been chattering gaily about the surprise they would give Hilary, were taken by surprise themselves. The head-collar rope was jerked out of Margaret's hand, and Evelyn shot forward in the saddle and clutched at Romany's mane, frightening her still more. She bucked, and Evelyn flew through the air to land on the ground with a smack. "Oh, you are feeble," she said to Margaret as she scrambled to her feet. "Why on earth did you let her go?"

"I couldn't help it," said Margaret. "It all happened so suddenly. Anyway, it wasn't a very big buck, so I don't know why you came off."

"Well, if I hadn't she would have gone on until I did," said Evelyn disagreeably.

Romany allowed herself to be caught, but, when Evelyn tried to remount, she twirled round and round, and in spite of all Evelyn's instructions Margaret was unable to hold her still. They had to take her back to the loose-box, and even there it was some time before Evelyn managed to scramble on. When she was in the saddle Margaret gave Romany some more oats, and then, as they heard the sound of Northwind and Darkie returning from their ride, they decided it was time to stop.

While they unsaddled Romany, Evelyn said. "Mind you don't say anything about me falling off to anyone, Marga, or there's sure to be a fuss."

"Not even to the others?" asked Margaret.

"No, not to anyone," said Evelyn, "or I shan't let you help again."

Later, at tea, when Hilary, who had quite recovered from her outburst, asked how Romany had behaved, Evelyn replied, "Fine, thank you," and asked Roger to pass the cake.

After tea Hilary, with Roger's help, backed Rocket. He was very quiet, and they were able to lead him a few steps round the box without mishap.

Two days after the second rally, John Manners was sitting on his garden gate in the depths of despair. He had to go back to school the following week, and, for lack of an assistant, he still hadn't ridden his pony. Once more he wracked his brain for someone to help him. He didn't want his father to, for Colonel Manners was inclined to take charge of anything and always made you do it his way. He knew the farm hands would say they were too busy, and he was far too independent to consider asking any of the other Pony Club members.

There's no one, thought John, no one at all. That beastly June Cresswell will beat me again, and he fell to kicking the gate savagely with his heels.

Mrs. Manners was weeding the rockery. She knew John was in a bad temper, and at intervals she cast anxious glances at him and wondered whether she dare ask him what was the matter. At last she could bear his scowling face and the drumming heels no longer. She stood upright with a grunt—her back ached from stooping—took off her gardening gloves, and pushed back a few wisps of her greying brown hair. What a pity it is, she thought, that in youth one is always bothering about small things— what one wears, what people think of one, and when, as middle age draws near and one develops a sense of proportion, one is too old to enjoy life to the full.

"John," she asked, "how is little Blackie getting on?"

"Not at all," said John in a cross voice.

"Why, what's the matter with her?" asked Mrs. Manners.

"Nothing's the matter with her," said John. "But how's a person to break a pony with no one to help them?"

"Couldn't dad help you?" suggested Mrs. Manners.

"No, thanks. I don't want to be organised," said John.

"Oh, John, you mustn't speak of your father like that," said Mrs. Manners reproachfully. She bent down and absently pulled a sow thistle from the gravel path. Then

53

she asked, "What has the assistant to do? Would I be any help?"

"Would you really help me, Mum?" John asked as he jumped down from the gate.

"Of course," said Mrs. Manners, "if I don't have to do anything too complicated."

"No, it's quite easy," said John. "You just hold her and give her handfuls of oats. I'd better go and catch her," he added, and ran to the stable feeling as if a load had been taken off his mind.

He caught the ponies, which were turned out in a large meadow, and, mounting Turpin off the gate, he rode up the cart-track to the farm-yard leading Blackie. He put her in Dick Turpin's box and tied him in one of the cart-horse stalls; then, whistling merrily, John fetched the tack, which he hadn't cleaned since the first Pony Club rally.

When he was ready, John fetched his mother and, while she held Blackie, he went all through the business of putting his weight in the stirrup, lying on his tummy on her back, and finally slipping his leg across and sitting in the saddle. Then, as the pony seemed quiet, John asked his mother to lead her round the box.

"Thanks awfully, Mum," said John as he dismounted. "Will you help me again to-morrow?"

Mrs. Manners said she would, and then she asked whether he had thought of a permanent name for Blackie yet.

"No," said John despondently. "Nothing I think of seems to suit her. Now Jackdaw is an awfully nice name, but it's no good for a mare, and it's the same with everyone I think of. If only she were a gelding, I'd have had the choice of dozens of super ones."

"Have you thought of Sweep or Jet?" asked Mrs. Manners.

"No," said John. "Sweep isn't bad, but it's rather common, and, of course, it's really more suitable for a gelding—you don't have women sweeps. But Jet," he went

54

He hit her savagely several times with the whip.

on reflectively, "I like that better. It's nice and short. It's all right for a mare, and Blackie is certainly jet black enough. You know, Mum, I think that's what I'll call her." And, fetching the lunge-rein, he added, "Thank goodness that's settled at last."

"If you're going to lunge her before lunch, you'll have to hurry, dear," said Mrs. Manners, "for you know how dad hates you to be late."

"All right," said John. "I shan't be long." And, pulling Jet round roughly, he led her into the dairy-cows' field, which was the nearest, and started to lunge her. For some unknown reason Jet, who usually behaved perfectly, decided that she was not going round to the left, and when John told her to, she just swung round and trotted off to the right. The first few times John did his best to obey Major Holbrooke's instructions for dealing with this sort of trouble: he shortened the lunge-rein and placed himself even more behind Jet, so that he was in a better position to drive her forward, but, unfortunately, he wasn't quick enough in anticipating her, and his aid to go forward generally arrived after she had turned, and only served to make her go round in the wrong direction faster than ever. It was about the sixth time Jet did this that John, who had become hotter and crosser with every moment, lost his temper completely. He hit her savagely several times with his whip. Terrified, she leaped forward, and, pulling the lunge-rein out of John's hand, she galloped to the far end of the field. Red in the face with rage, John ran after her. She had pulled up in the shelter of a group of chestnut trees, but when she saw John coming she walked nervously away, though not before he had grabbed the end of the trailing lunge-rein. Pulling her up short, he struck her across the nose with his clenched fist. Jet was terrified; she trembled and shook all over, but John was too angry to care. Picking up the whip, he made her canter round and round on the lunge-rein, hitting her if she showed the slightest sign of slowing up. At last, when his rage had

56

burned itself out, John turned the exhausted, giddy and frightened pony out in her field and wandered morosely in to lunch.

Susan had to wait until Saturday to back Sunset, for Noel, who had promised to help her, was still in bed, and Susan was determined not to ask Bob, because she felt the other members might think it unfair if her groom helped her and because she knew that Bob's ideas on breaking were, almost entirely, culled from "cowboy films." So she resigned herself to await her father's return on Saturday. Mr. Barington-Brown wasn't really interested in horses, but he was a good-natured man, and, since Susan was the only member of his family whom it was possible to satisfy, he liked doing things for her.

They had very little trouble, for Sunset was not at all nervous, and since Susan, who had taken Major Holbrooke's advice very much to heart, had been careful not to pinch her with the girth, she had almost given up being difficult to saddle. Mr. Barington-Brown was very impressed by the way in which "his little girl", as he always thought of Susan, handled her pony, and he thought what a good thing it was that he had braved Mrs. Barington-Brown's displeasure and bought Beauty.

Richard did not back Red Rufus until the last day but one of the holidays. Each day he put it off to the next. First he had promised to go for a bicycle ride with Michael Thorpington, a friend of his, who lived at Friar's Fenchurch; next it was too wet; then he had no one to help him; and when Jill offered to, he felt too tired. But at last he realised that the holidays were almost over, and, deciding that it was a matter of now or never, he borrowed Wendy's felt saddle and jointed-snaffle bridle and began the tedious task of putting them on Rufus, who from the first had learned to dread being bridled, for Richard carelessly banged his teeth, poked his eyes, tweaked his ears, and was generally too lazy to alter the bridle to fit him. It

was not surprising that, as soon as he saw Richard carrying the tack, he began to dash round the tree to which he was tied—the Morrissons had no stables. Richard dumped the saddle on and made a grab for the girth, but Rufus, with the memory of many painful pinches, cow-kicked at him.

"Stop it, you little brute," said Richard, jumping out of reach and hitting him sharply on the shoulder. Rufus whirled as far round the tree as his halter would allow him. The saddle fell off and he trod on it. Richard said several words which would have shocked his parents, but not his school-fellows, and tied Rufus up much tighter. Then, picking up the now muddy saddle, he tried again, this time with more success.

He fetched Jill to help him with the bridle, and it took the pair of them at least ten minutes to put it on. Both of them were hot and cross and Rufus upset and excited when they led him into the hen-run—the only enclosed place they could think of—and Richard tried to mount. But Rufus did not even give him time to put his foot in the stirrup; he just whirled round and round, and Jill was quite unable to hold him still. Richard hopped after him, becoming hotter and hotter and grumbling at Jill, who said it was his fault for being so slow at mounting.

When he was exhausted from hopping, Richard suggested that Jill should have a try while he held Rufus. Jill didn't like the idea at all, and she was just about to refuse when Richard said, "Oh, well, never mind if you're afraid."

"I'm not afraid," said Jill, stamping her foot at him, "and I didn't say I wouldn't try." Flinging the halter-rope at Richard, she rammed her foot into the stirrup and, digging her toe in Rufus' side, she landed with a crash in the saddle. Rufus braced himself for a buck, but Richard just managed to pull his head up in time.

"Jolly good," he said. "Now hold tight and I'll lead you round a bit."

Now that Jill's rage had evaporated, she felt very nervous, and this made Rufus more frightened than ever. Neither of the children spoke a reassuring word to him. The pinching girth, the tight bridle and the unaccustomed weight on his back were almost unbearable. He tried to buck, but Richard held him in an iron grasp. Rufus wondered how he could get rid of all these horrible contraptions. He wished he were back in the big field in Hampshire. Suddenly he felt so miserable and lonely that he stopped to neigh. He neighed to the five other ponies to ask if they were being treated like this, but his neigh wasn't loud enough. . . .

"Come on, can't you," said Richard crossly as he dragged Rufus forward, "and stop making that beastly row."

CHAPTER V

JUNE was the only horse-breaker whose pony was far advanced enough to be ridden loose by the end of the summer holidays. Evelyn Radcliffe tried to ride Romany one day when none of her family was about, but she was bucked off twice, and then gave up. The rest of the Pony Club members remembered Major Holbrooke's advice about making *quite* sure that their pony understood the leg-and rein-aids before trying to ride without an assistant to help if he became excited or started to play up. The Major had pointed out that there was nothing brave or clever in riding a pony off the lead-rein before he was ready. It was asking for trouble, and, when trouble came, the only way to control a pony which didn't know the aids was by strength. That, he had said, was the old-fashioned rough-rider's method, and quite out of place in modern horsemanship.

Certainly neither Jet nor Rufus understood the aids, and

John and Richard went back to their boarding schools grumbling bitterly about the unfair advantage the girls would have because all of them were at day schools except for Hilary and Evelyn, who were weekly boarders at St. Crispin's, in Gunston.

It was in the second week of the term that Margaret told James they must begin to teach Rocket and Romany their circus tricks.

"But won't Hilary and Evelyn be cross?" asked James. "You know they said we weren't to touch them."

"Of course not," said Margaret. "You wait till they see the ponies doing their tricks—they'll be simply amazed. They only meant we weren't to ride or lunge them. Besides, you know Major Holbrooke said the ponies needed handling in the term-time; and if we don't handle Romany and Rocket, June's pony will beat them easily 'cause she's a day-girl."

James, all his doubts allayed by Margaret's arguments, entered into the idea at once. They planned wildly as they collected halters and a bucket of oats, and by the time they reached the field they had visions of Rocket and Romany standing on tubs and leaping through flaming hoops.

"Now," said Margaret. "I've bagged Romany, so you'll have to have Rocket. Here's his halter."

They caught the ponies easily enough, and then, as Margaret thought it would be the simplest trick to start with, they began to teach them to shake hands—picking up their hoofs, shaking them, and then rewarding the ponies with oats. For a little while they were each intent on their pupil, then suddenly James shouted excitedly, "Look, Marga! Look!" Turning, Margaret saw Rocket waving his forefoot wildly in the air. "Jolly good," she said. "That's fine." But at heart she was not so pleased; she felt that James had beaten her, which was annoying, for, being the elder, she should naturally be the best at everything.

60

"You are stupid," she told Romany. "You're not half as intelligent as Rocket. Now for goodness' sake attend."

A few minutes later there was another shriek from James. "Look," he said, "I've taught him another trick; he'll follow me anywhere." And he ran a short way to demonstrate. Rocket trotted after him, his ears flat back, and a threatening expression which said, "Give me those oats, or I'll kick and bite you to bits," on his face. Unfortunately, as each time James stopped he rewarded him with a handful of oats, Rocket believed that his blackmailing faces were having the desired effect. Margaret was even more annoyed when she saw this trick. "Will you come on, you obstinate old thing," she said, giving Romany's halter an impatient jerk. "Rocket's learnt two tricks, and you can't even do one yet. Jim," she went on, "come and help me with this brainless animal; you can tie Rocket to the gate."

James tied Rocket up and went to Margaret, who said:

"You slap her leg at the top while I push her weight back." And to Romany, "Now come on, shake hands?"

So far Romany, who did not in the least understand what she was supposed to do, had stood meekly while Margaret thumped and pushed her, but the combination of James slapping her leg and Margaret jerking the halter-rope was too much; she reared. For a moment both children were speechless with amazement. Then Margaret said:

"Oh, isn't she wonderful! Just like a real circus pony. You are a clever little pony; that's a much better trick than either of Rocket's." And she gave Romany several handfuls of oats.

"I bet Rocket could do that," said James, defending his pupil. "I bet *he* could learn to lie down; but you shouldn't teach them too many tricks the same day. Anyway, I don't expect Romany will do it again."

"Yes, she will," said Margaret. "Come on, old lady, you show him. Up, up," she went on, jerking the halter-rope.

After a few moments Romany realised what she wanted and once again she reared up.

"There you are," said Margaret triumphantly. "I knew she would." And she gave Romany another handful of oats.

"Won't it be lovely," said James, "when they're all trained? Roly, Poly, and Cinders, if Doc. will lend her to us, must all come in, and we must think of some tricks for the other ponies. Even the cats might come in, if only they'll attend instead of *always* thinking about food. It'll be an awfully big circus; we might even have a lion later."

"Yes," said Margaret, "it'll be an *enormous* circus. Everyone will come miles to see it, and we shall make our fortunes."

On the following afternoon Margaret and James gave the ponies another lesson. Romany knew her trick perfectly: she would rear at the slightest jerk of the halter, but Margaret still could not persuade her to shake hands. Rocket began to paw the air wildly as soon as he smelt the oats, and, when rewarded with a handful, he bit James' hand, which made him cry. After that they swopped ponies, and while James tried to teach Romany to shake hands, Margaret did her utmost to make Rocket rear. She didn't succeed, but she had one of her coat buttons ripped off and a hole torn in her pocket from his attempts to get the oats. James managed to persuade Romany to pick up her hoof when asked to shake hands, but she would not wave it out like Rocket. Still, they were very pleased with their pupils' progress, and they constantly thought what a lovely surprise they were going to give Hilary and Evelyn. On Friday they had a dress rehearsal. They decorated the ponies with ribbons and coloured feathers from a Red Indian head-dress belonging to James, and they plastered their own faces with flour and their mother's lipstick in an attempt to look like clowns. Unfortunately Rocket was even more excitable. He bit James' pockets every few seconds. He shook hands so wildly that he hit him on the

arm with his hoof and reduced him to tears, and later, when he was supposed to be following James, he barged his quarters into him, knocking him over and upsetting the bucket of oats which he was carrying. James began to cry again; he said that Rocket had trodden on his toe and hurt his arm.

"You *are* feeble," said Margaret crossly. "Do stop crying."

James said Margaret was beastly, and that he hated her, and she said he was a cry-baby, and that she hated him. James said all right then, he wouldn't help with the circus any more, and stamped off across the field in a rage. She shouted after him that he needn't think he was going to help next day. So when at lunch on Saturday Margaret told Hilary and Evelyn that she had a surprise for them, James stared moodily at his plate. Afterwards, when Margaret had gone, telling them to follow in ten minutes, he collected his six favourite small boats and wandered off to sail them in the water-butt.

Hilary and Evelyn were both very curious about Margaret's surprise. As they changed their school clothes for jodhpurs they discussed what it could be.

"I expect it's something dull like a hut," said Hilary.

"She's not going to drag us all the way up there just to see a beastly hut, is she?" said Evelyn.

"Well, we can catch the ponies on the way back," said Hilary. "I hope she hasn't been messing about with them."

"I shouldn't think so," said Evelyn. "Doc. forbade her to ride them until they were quiet; though Romany is pretty quiet now. I think I'll ride her by myself to-day."

"I don't think we'd better ride them together," said Hilary, collecting her crash cap and riding-stick. "I'll stand in the middle while you ride Romany, and grab her if she starts to fool around, if you'll do the same when I ride Rocket."

"I don't suppose Romany'll do anything," said Evelyn. "But I don't mind hanging around if you think Rocket's

63

likely to play up. Are you ready? Come on, then; let's go and see this tiresome surprise."

When they reached the hill field, Hilary and Evelyn were not at all pleased to see Romany and Rocket, adorned with ribbons and feathers.

"She has been mucking about with them," said Evelyn.

"I hope she hasn't done anything silly," said Hilary.

"Look here, Marga," said Evelyn, when they were within speaking distance, "we told you to leave those ponies alone."

"All right, keep calm," said Margaret. "I haven't hurt them, and when we've all made our fortunes you'll be grateful."

"Grateful for what?" asked Hilary.

"Wait a minute and you'll see," said Margaret as she untied Romany from the gate. "Shake hands," she ordered. And, as Romany obeyed, Hilary breathed a sigh of relief. "If that's all," she said to Evelyn, "she hasn't done any harm." But scarcely were the words out of her mouth when Margaret said, "Up, Romany, up!" and jerked the halter-rope. Romany reared high. Both Hilary and Evelyn gasped with what Margaret wrongly took to be joy.

"Isn't she good?" she asked, her voice full of pride. "Doesn't she do it beautifully?"

"Good!" echoed Hilary. "Good! Don't you realise what you've done? Don't you know that rearing is incurable?"

"Well, of all the interfering, idiotic, silly, half-witted fools you're about the worst," said Evelyn furiously.

"You are beastly," said Margaret, bursting into a loud roar. "After all the trouble I'd taken to train them so as to give you a lovely surprise."

"A *lovely* surprise!" said Hilary. "What have you taught Rocket?"

"Only to shake hands and trot after me," replied Margaret through her tears. "But I shan't show you now."

Hilary, who had untied Rocket and was taking the ribbons and feathers out of his mane, found, to her dismay,

that the friendly expression which she had grown so fond of was replaced by a threatening mask, and the once gentle pony nipped her about a dozen times in the space of a few minutes.

"Oh, Marga," she said in a despairing voice, "what have you done to him? He's quite different." Just at that moment Rocket, who had grown tired of waiting for his oats, struck out impatiently with his hoof, narrowly missing Hilary, who dodged to one side. He thought he had frightened her, but as she still did not give him any oats, he made a blackmailing face and seized her pocket in his teeth. Hilary smacked his nose, and in a fury he swung round his heels and barged his quarters into her. Hilary could bear it no longer. She pulled Rocket's halter off, and, ignoring both her sisters, ran in the direction of the house.

Mrs. Radcliffe hadn't heard much of the conversation at lunch, for she had suddenly thought of a design for an evening dress, and afterwards she had gone to the Prior's room—which she used as a sort of studio—and started to draw it. She had just fetched her paints, and was wondering whether black and crimson or turquoise and silver would be the more striking, when Hilary burst in. Her face was as red as a beetroot, and she was obviously on the verge of tears.

"Mummy," she said, "whatever shall we do? The little half-wit has absolutely ruined them." Flopping into a chair, she produced a large red handkerchief.

"Who's ruined what?" asked Mrs. Radcliffe.

"That little idiot Marga," said Hilary. "She's been trying to teach them circus tricks, and they're completely spoilt. Heaven knows what Major Holbrooke will say."

"Margaret is the limit," said Mrs. Radcliffe crossly. "Your father and I both told her to leave those ponies alone. What has she actually done?"

"She didn't mean to do any harm," said Hilary. "She meant to give us a surprise, but she must have simply

65

C

stuffed Rocket with oats, for he nips all the time, makes horrid faces, and barges into you if you won't give him anything. He used to be such a nice friendly pony."

"What about Romany?" asked Mrs. Radcliffe.

"She's taught her to rear," said Hilary between sniffs, "and it's supposed to be incurable. We haven't tried riding her yet, but it's ten to one she'll do it if she doesn't want to go somewhere—they always do—and, if she's vicious, Major Holbrooke's cousin won't be able to sell her as a child's pony; he'll have to send them both to some beastly market and they're sure to get bad homes." Mrs. Radcliffe did her best to be consoling. She said:

"Surely, if we keep Marga away from them and you and Evelyn scold them every time they do their wretched tricks, they'll forget them in the end."

"I suppose they might," said Hilary without much conviction. "It does seem such a shame. They were getting on so well, and Rocket was so gentle, he would have made a lovely pony for children."

"I dare say he will yet," said Mrs. Radcliffe in the most cheerful tones she could muster. "After all, it's not as though they've been doing them long. I think you'll find that when Rocket discovers that his faces and nips don't intimidate you into giving him titbits, he'll realise they're pointless and give them up."

"I hope you're right," said Hilary, cheering up a little. "But I shall have a job to get him right by the Christmas holidays. I think I'd better start retraining him at once." And stuffing the red handkerchief into her pocket, she leapt to her feet and hurried out of the room.

Hilary spent that week-end and most of the succeeding ones in re-educating Rocket. It was a thankless task, not made any easier by Margaret's and Evelyn's constant quarrels; for Evelyn now attributed every fault of Romany's to Margaret's circus tricks.

"Darn that kid," she would say when Romany cow-

kicked as she was girthed up. "She's ruined this pony's temper." Or when she was bucked off, "Another of Marga's circus tricks, I suppose." Naturally, Margaret hotly denied all blame for these innumerable and varied wickednesses. Apart from his bullying habits, Rocket was behaving well, and the week-end before half-term Hilary took him out for a ride, accompanied by James on Darkie, to give him confidence. Evelyn found hacking Romany rather dull, for the pony was too unfit to go fast or far. She preferred riding in the field, sometimes with Margaret and sometimes alone, where she practised competitions: potato and bending races, musical chairs and jumping, for the gymkhanas. Secretly she hoped to win an untold number of events on Romany—a perfectly schooled gymkhana pony. Let June, she thought, who is sure to be best anyway, excel at niggling show-riding.

To Noel the term seemed endless. Each dreary day dragged by even more slowly and monotonously than its predecessor, while, in comparison, the week-ends passed like a flash of lightning. Every Saturday morning she would walk over to the Spinneys to fetch Rusty, Simon Wentwood's dark-brown pony, which she had been told she could borrow during the term. Rusty, who was about thirteen hands high, was slightly fresher and a much nicer ride than Topsy. But he had one or two faults: he pulled with his head down when he was excited. He was nappy, and he was sometimes difficult to catch. It was his jumping that pleased Noel most; she had never been able to persuade Topsy to jump higher than two feet, but on Rusty, who hardly ever refused, she had cleared three feet three inches.

Some days Noel rode and jumped in Farmer Trent's meadow, and occasionally she went for a solitary hack, but more often she rode to Basset Towers, put him in a box, and then rode Beauty out with Susan on Sunset. It was on one of these rides, when they had been across the Hogshill

fields and were going home by the Basset-Fenchurch road, that they had to pass Dormers, the Elizabethan cottage where the Cresswells lived. Seeing June riding Grey Dawn in the field, they pulled up and, standing in their stirrups to see over the hedge, they watched her. June had some white posts to mark out a school round which she was trotting Grey Dawn, turning and zig-zagging across it at intervals. Occasionally she would pull up and turn on the forehand.

"Oh, goodness!" said Susan. "I hope I haven't got to teach Sunset all that."

"You'll have to," Noel said, "unless you want her to be the worst trained of all the ponies." Susan was saying that she would be anyway when a voice asked, "Would you like to come in and watch? I'm sure June won't mind." Looking round, they saw Mrs. Cresswell standing at the gate.

"Good afternoon," said Noel, thankful that they hadn't been criticising June. "We should love to. We were just wishing we could do turns on the forehand and all that sort of thing."

"Well, I'm sure June will give you a few tips," said Mrs. Cresswell. "She's always willing to help anyone; and you can take it from me she knows what she's talking about. June, June!" she called. "Here are Noel and Susan; they want you to show them how you do it."

June turned Grey Dawn and cantered up.

"Hallo," she said, seeming to give all four of them, riders and ponies, a critical stare.

"Hallo," answered Noel and Susan.

"Look, dear," said Mrs. Cresswell to June, "they were watching you over the hedge, so I brought them in, and Noel wants to know how to do the turns."

"Dawn knows both," said June. "This is on the forehand." As she turned her, Mrs. Cresswell said, "For that you use lateral aids, and the fore-legs should stay still, while the hind ones move round."

68

"This is the turn on the haunches," said June. "It's more difficult; beginners shouldn't try to do it."

"You see, you pull one rein, neck-rein with the other, use one leg, rather far forward to push the shoulder round, and the other to keep the quarters still," explained Mrs. Cresswell. "Now, June," she went on, "give them a little show; let them see what you've taught her."

"All right," said June. "I'll begin by doing the diagonal change of hand at the extended walk."

"Whatever's that?" asked Susan.

"Don't you know the school figures?" asked June, thinly veiled scorn in her voice.

"No, I've never heard of them," said Susan, not in the least squashed.

"But how do you manage to school your little pony, then?" asked Mrs. Cresswell.

"I haven't given her any proper schooling yet," replied Susan. "I just ride and lunge her."

"I see," said Mrs. Cresswell. "Then I don't suppose she can do anything like Grey Dawn, who is really becoming quite accomplished, but perhaps you're wise not to attempt this advanced stuff if you don't really understand it."

Meanwhile June, having ridden the diagonal change of hand, which, to Noel, looked exactly the same as a figure of eight, only with straight sides as it was ridden round the school, broke into a trot and then a canter.

"She's got her on the right leg," said Mrs. Cresswell with pride. Noel peered wildly to see how you distinguished the leading leg, which, in spite of all Major Holbrooke's instruction, she still could not do.

"To-morrow," said Mrs. Cresswell, "June is going to teach her the change of leg. That just shows how she's getting on, doesn't it?"

"Yes, rather," said Noel. "I should think she's miles ahead of all the others."

"I'm sure she is," said Mrs. Cresswell complacently. "But that is to be expected. After all, June has ridden,

and won, at some of the biggest shows in the country."

When June said she had finished, Mrs. Cresswell suggested, without consulting Susan, that she might ride Sunset. Saying rather ungraciously that she might as well try her, June mounted and rode round the field several times. When she came back she said, "Of course, she's completely unschooled, her mouth is like iron, she doesn't understand any of the aids, and she's awfully nappy—you can feel her edging towards the gate the whole time."

"You mustn't be too critical, dear," said Mrs. Cresswell. "You have to remember that you'd never ridden anything but good ones until you had Dawn, and now that you've trained her you've forgotten what she was like to start with. I expect Susan thoroughly enjoys playing around with little Sunset, and she'll make a nice mount for a small kiddy on the leading-rein."

"Oh, yes, she'll do for a beginner," said June contemptuously.

Then Mrs. Cresswell told June that they must take Dawn in or she would catch a chill. They all walked up to the stables, three portable wooden loose-boxes, and, while June put Dawn away, Mrs. Cresswell showed Noel and Susan Golden Wonder, who looked very smart—clipped and rugged up—and all the rosettes June had won, which were displayed in a glass case in the saddle-room. She offered to take them indoors and show them June's cups and the nineteen riding-sticks she had won, but they said that they really must go, and after thanking both Mrs. Cresswell and June, they rode hastily away.

"Have you noticed how accomplished Beauty is becoming, Susan?" asked Noel as soon as they were out of earshot.

"I knew she'd swank," said Susan. "We've wasted hours of our ride and not learned a thing."

"Yes, I have," said Noel. "You wait, I'll give you a few tips next Saturday. *I've* ridden at some of the biggest shows in the country."

"Oh, do shut up," said Susan. "If you learned anything I didn't, and I don't see why they should be so beastly about Sunset. Why should she cart horrid, whining children about on the leading-rein?"

"It's no good going on like this," said Noel, becoming serious. "You've simply got to school her properly."

"I can't," said Susan. "You know I'm hopeless at that sort of thing."

"Well, I can't tell my right hand from my left," said Noel, "and that makes it difficult to work out complicated aids, but if we don't learn somehow we shall never be famous horsewomen."

"I'm sure I shall never be famous," said Susan, "however hard I try."

"Don't be such a defeatist," said Noel.

"How are we to learn?" asked Susan. "We can't ask Major Holbrooke before the holidays."

"There are other experts," said Noel, "and they all write books. Surely we could learn from them?"

"I'm sure I couldn't," said Susan. "I've got a book on riding. Uncle Vic. gave it to me last Christmas, but I only got to page six—it's terribly dull."

"Can I borrow it?" asked Noel, willing to catch at any straw. "You never know, it might be just what we need. Wouldn't it be lovely if we schooled Rusty and Sunset and *we* were able to give *June* a little show?"

"You can borrow it," said Susan. "But it's no good expecting me to teach Sunset anything. How can I, when I still don't understand the diagonal aids?"

CHAPTER VI

ONE MORNING, at the beginning of the Christmas holidays, Roger Radcliffe was seated in the middle of Brampton market-place on the stone water-trough, wondering what he could buy Margaret for a Christmas present, when he saw John Manners coming out of the ironmonger's shop, several awkwardly shaped parcels clasped in his arms.

"Hallo," shouted Roger. John waved and came across.

"Hallo," he said. "I'm doing my Christmas shopping."

"Same here," said Roger. "At least I've done most of it. I'm waiting for Hilary and Evelyn. You haven't seen them?"

"No," said John. "But I've only been in Stanlakes' and Flapton's. Would you like to see what I've bought my father?" he asked after a short pause. "I hope he'll like it; but he's an awfully difficult person to think of presents for." And without waiting for an answer he unwrapped a large rake-like implement for scratching moss out of lawns.

"I should think he'd love that," said Roger, "especially if he's keen on gardening."

"He's fairly keen," said John. "And this is what I bought mum." He unwrapped a smaller parcel and produced three pink coat-hangers. Each had a lavender-bag attached.

"I shouldn't want them myself," he said, "but I thought she would like them."

"Oh, definitely," said Roger. "Especially as she's rather a feminine sort of woman, isn't she?"

"That's right," said John.

"At last!" said Roger as Hilary and Evelyn came up. Ignoring him, they said hallo to John, and Hilary asked:

"How is your Holbrooke pony getting on? Have you named her?"

"Yes!" said John. "I named her Jet last holidays, but I haven't had time to do much with her; I only got back yesterday."

"Isn't it a bore about old Georgie's son?" said Evelyn. "It doesn't look as though we'll have any rallies these holidays."

"Whose son?" asked John.

"Major Holbrooke's," explained Hilary. "It's the middle one—the scientific one—he's fallen off a mountain and Major and Mrs. Holbrooke have had to rush off to Switzerland, where he's hovering between life and death."

"What a sell!" said John. "That means we shan't get on at all these holidays."

"And no decent children's meet," said Evelyn. "Old Sir Charles Dent is Acting-Master, and you know what he's like."

"Yes," said John. "I'll say I do. It looks to me as though we're going to have some dreary holidays."

"We'll have to get something up ourselves," said Roger. "It's no good sitting back and grumbling. Surely we could organise a paper chase or something?"

"That's a super idea," said John enthusiastically, while Evelyn asked:

"Where could we have it?"

"Obviously the hares, or whatever you call them, would have to decide where to go," said Roger. "But there are masses of places, and one could ask the farmers' permission, though, actually, they never mind at this time of year as long as one shuts the gates."

"I bags be a hare," said Evelyn.

"Bagging isn't allowed," said Hilary.

"I thought of it," said Roger, "so I ought to be one."

"But who will be the hounds?" asked John. "We need more than two."

"We can invite some of the Pony Club members," said Hilary.

"Not June Cresswell," said Evelyn firmly.

"No, we don't want her," agreed John. "She'd soon start bossing us all around."

"We'd have Mrs. C. organising everything," said Hilary.

"What about Richard?" asked John rather diffidently.

"Oh," said Roger, "must we have him?"

"Well, what about Susan and Noel?" suggested Hilary.

"Oh, Hilary," said Evelyn, "they're *awfully* feeble. They're sure to fall off."

"Who is there, then?" asked Hilary. "It's no good asking people like the Meltons—they live too far away—and that only leaves Mary Compton and the Rates."

"There's Michael Thorpington and the Mintons," said John.

"Michael Thorpington is even worse than Richard," said Roger, "and the Mintons can't jump."

"If you and Evelyn are going to object to everyone we can't have any hounds," said Hilary in exasperation. "You're both so intolerant."

"I know what we can do," said Roger, "we can each invite one person, and I'll have Dick Hayward."

"Oh, yes," said John. "Why didn't we think of him before? I wish I had. But still, I can have Richard."

"I'll have Noel," said Hilary. "After all, it's not her fault she's only got that dreadful Topsy."

"I don't see why I should be left with that beastly Susan," said Evelyn.

"We had each better tell the person we've decided to invite," said Roger. "And, personally, I think our place would be a good spot for the meet—it's fairly central."

"Yes," agreed John. "But who is going to be the hare?"

"I should think we'd better have two," said Hilary, "and that would leave eight hounds, counting Marga and Jim."

"Shall we four toss up?" suggested Roger. "After all, we thought of it, so I don't see why two of us shouldn't be the hares." As the others agreed, they tossed, and Roger and Hilary won. Then, after some more discussion, they

decided to hold the paper-chase two days after Boxing-Day, and meet at the Priory at ten o'clock.

Dick Hayward was delighted, Richard faintly condescending, and Susan surprised and pleased, when they were invited to the paper-chase. Hilary was slightly annoyed when she discovered that Noel wasn't on the telephone, but on Christmas Eve she decided to ride Rocket over to Russet Cottage. As Dr. Radcliffe had insisted that neither of the youngsters was to be ridden out alone until they were absolutely reliable, James said he would go with her for he much preferred Hilary's company to that of his other sisters.

Noel was schooling Rusty in Farmer Trent's field when Hilary and James rode up the lane. They stood at the gate and watched her for some time before she noticed them. When she did see them, she felt very self-conscious. I bet they've been criticising my riding, she thought, pulling our turns on the forehand to pieces, but I suppose I shall have to see what they want. And, turning Rusty, she cantered across the field.

"Hallo," said Hilary. "Isn't that Simon Wentwood's pony?"

"That's right," said Noel. "I was allowed to ride him all through the term, and now the Wentwoods have gone away for Christmas, which is marvellous, as I shall be able to hunt him on Boxing Day.'

"How lovely," said Hilary. "But when do they come back? Not before the twenty-ninth, I hope."

"No, the first of January," said Noel. "Why?"

"Well, you see, John Manners and all of us are getting up a paper-chase, because we thought it would be so dull these holidays with no rallies, and we wondered whether you would like to come."

"I should love to," said Noel, "but what do I have to do? I mean, I'm awfully bad at jumping. Shan't I be a nuisance?"

"Oh, no," said Hilary kindly, but not very tactfully.

"Marga and Jim are coming, you can't be worse than them."

"I should love to, then," said Noel. "But why aren't there going to be any Pony Club rallies?"

"Haven't you heard about Major Holbrooke's son?" asked Hilary, and she went on to explain about the accident and how tiresome it would be having Sir Charles as Acting-Master. Then, after reminding Noel to be at the Priory by ten o'clock on the twenty-ninth, she said they must go, for she hadn't wrapped up any of her presents.

When they were out of sight Noel put up her course of jumps, which she had to keep stacked in the corner of the field, as they were very untidy; two hen-coops made the first jump, a heap of hedge trimmings posed as a brush-fence, the wall was an old door, the in-and-out was built of bales of straw, and the triple bars were supported by petrol cans and kitchen chairs, borrowed from the cottage.

Rusty jumped a clear round with everything, except the in-and-out, at three feet. This was an enormous improvement, due, Noel felt, to Susan's book, which had proved a mine of information, and, luckily, agreed with Major Holbrooke's views on all important matters. She felt very elated as she gave Rusty some carrots and turned him loose, and, as she put her jumps away, she imagined the run of the season on Boxing Day. She was still flying over enormous fences, with only the Master in front of her, when she went indoors to tell her mother about Hilary Radcliffe's unexpected invitation.

The next few days passed in rather a whirl. First there was Christmas, which was celebrated in the traditional manner, though Richard refused to hang out his stocking. On the whole, everyone was delighted with his or her presents, though Noel was indignant at being given *The School Girl's Annual* by her godfather, and Dr. Radcliffe complained bitterly as he opened the thirty-nine calendars he had been sent by grateful patients.

On Boxing Day everyone was feeling morning-after-the-

Rusty jumped a clear round with everything.

night-before-ish, especially Sir Charles Dent and the weather. It poured with rain from six o'clock in the morning until the late afternoon, and the wet, combined with his liver, made Sir Charles even more irritable than usual. He quarrelled with the Huntsman, shouted at the field, lectured the children, and took the hounds home at half-past three after a completely blank day. In spite of this, all the Pony Club members enjoyed themselves.

Then, two days later, there was the paper-chase. It was wet and misty at half-past seven when Noel opened her bedroom's tiny window and looked out. Rivulets of water were coursing down the sodden thatch, the gaunt elms in the field across the lane dripped miserably, and the air was damp and raw. She wondered whether the Radcliffes would postpone the paper-chase, but she decided that they were much too tough to be deterred by a little rain.

By nine o'clock it had stopped raining, and by half-past a faint but persevering gleam had appeared in the sky. Roger and Hilary, stuffing haversacks with sawdust, made encouraging noises to it, but Richard cursed it heartily. Besides losing everything in his effort to hurry, he had a furious row with his mother, who suddenly said he was to take Jill with him. In vain he argued that she hadn't been invited, couldn't jump high enough, and as he wasn't going to hang about while Wendy grazed and refused, would certainly get lost. Mrs. Morrisson insisted. At the Priory, there was also an atmosphere of thinly veiled unpleasantness; for Susan, seeing Evelyn mount Romany, had asked, in slightly shocked tones, if she was going to ride her in the chase.

"Yes, why not?" replied Evelyn.

"I don't know," said Susan. "I only thought it wasn't supposed to be a good thing for young horses to be galloped and raced, but I suppose otherwise you wouldn't have enough ponies for all of you."

"Romany isn't as young as all that," said Evelyn, "and I haven't the least intention of letting her become one of

those pampered show ponies; she's going to be a hunter and gymkhana pony, and she may as well begin now. I could have ridden one of Mrs. Maxton's ponies if I had wanted to," she went on, "but she would only let me have Woodcock, and he's so jolly dull and lazy I decided that it would do Romany good to have a gallop."

"I like Woodcock," said Susan, "and he's quite a good jumper, you know."

"Personally, I like a hot pony," said Evelyn, "not a worn-out riding-school hireling."

"Woodcock isn't worn out," said Susan furiously. "He's nice, and Mrs. Maxton doesn't let her horses out for hire."

"Here's Richard," said Roger, glad to see him for once, and wishing Evelyn would keep her mouth shut. "Come on, Hilary, hadn't we better get going?" Richard rode up, looking very disagreeable, and said to Roger in an angry undertone:

"I'm sorry I've brought Jill, but mummy made me, and now she'll ruin everything, I suppose."

"That's all right," said Roger, though at heart he didn't think so. "She's no worse than Marga and Jim, so she can keep with them." Margaret gave him a furious look and said loudly: "I can jump three feet one and a half inches."

"You'll start in a quarter of an hour, then," said Roger, mounting Sky Pilot, the black gelding, which Mrs. Radcliffe had given her three eldest children as a Christmas present.

"O.K.," said John, looking at his watch, "it's ten past ten now."

"Cheerio!" said Hilary, mounting Northwind, and the hares rode off down the drive.

The hounds watched them in silence. Noel, who had the "needle," though she repeatedly told herself that it was ridiculous to have it for a game, racked her brain for something to say. Then she and John both started to speak.

"Sorry," said Noel. "Go on, you started first."

"I was only going to say that they'd been five minutes," said John. "What were you going to say?"

"I was only going to ask whether we are hunting in a pack, in pairs, or separately," said Noel.

"Separately, of course," said Evelyn firmly. "It's a race, so if you can get ahead, you do." There was another silence, then Richard said:

"I presume that if anyone gets lost they make their way back here?"

"Either that or ring up," said Evelyn, "otherwise we shan't know whether to send out search parties or not."

"Ten minutes," said John.

"I'm simply frozen," said Richard. "My feet are like blocks of ice."

After another pause, John said:

"Awfully bad luck for Dick getting 'flu, wasn't it?"

"Yes, his mother said he was fearfully fed up," said Evelyn.

"Fourteen minutes," said John. "Are you ready? Go!"

Everyone swept down the drive at a brisk trot, with Margaret in the lead. They passed under the grey stone arch into the road, and there, on their right, was a thin trickle of sawdust. Evelyn let Romany, who was pulling, trot faster, and took the lead from Margaret. John rammed his crash cap down and shortened his reins. Susan, mindful of Mrs. Maxton's warnings, took Beauty on the grass verge; Noel and James followed her.

Evelyn flung open the five-barred gate leading into a large stubble field.

"Last through, shut the gate," she shouted and, giving Romany her head, she galloped flat out beside the now wide line of sawdust. James was last through, but Susan and Noel, who had waited, shut the gate. As they galloped on Noel found, to her delight, that Rusty was fast for a pony of his size. He held his own with Beauty, who was a couple of inches taller, and together they passed Wendy, Darkie and Pixie, and drew near to Turpin and Peter, who

were racing neck and neck. Suddenly John and Richard turned sharply to the left. The trail had turned, but Evelyn, in the lead, had been going too fast to notice. When she saw that the others were no longer following her and realised what had happened, she tugged Romany round and tore after them. Everyone was exhilarated by the gallop. John and Richard urged their ponies even faster in an effort to pass each other. Noel and Susan, galloping side by side, gave themselves entirely to the enjoyment of speed, and the feeling of the wind and the sting of the rain in their faces. James' pleasure was slightly marred by the strain of looking out for rabbit-holes. Margaret was enjoying herself thoroughly. Occasionally she gave vent to a hunting cry, partly as an outlet for her excitement, but mainly as an encouragement to Pixie to go faster still. In spite of Jill's frenzied kicking Wendy was dropping farther and farther behind the other ponies, and in a panic Jill saw herself deserted, lost, wandering aimlessly about the fields. Evelyn's annoyance at losing her lead soon evaporated as she felt Romany's lengthening strides beneath her and saw the way in which she put every ounce into covering the distance between her and the rest of the ponies. She passed Wendy, flashed by James and Margaret, and inch by inch drew close to Rusty and Beauty. Just as she was level with them, the trail turned. It led along the hedgerow for a little way, and then over a bank and down into the road. They clattered across, and then pulled up to a walk as, with John, Richard and Evelyn in the lead, they followed the wet, yellow trail down the Nut-walk, a steep and narrow lane with a close hedge of nut trees on either side, which overhung so low that you had to lie on your pony's neck to pass beneath.

"I bet Roger had a job to get down here on Sky Pilot," said James.

"Can't see why he had to go down such a beastly place," grumbled Richard. "I've scratched my face all over." Behind, Noel was hoping that Rusty wouldn't slip, and

Over a bank and down into the road.

telling herself not to be such a coward; and Susan was giving small shrieks as the branches whipped her face and clutched at her clothes. Suddenly there was a wail from Jill. "My saddle's slipping. Whoa! Whoa!" she cried. "It's right up her neck."

"Get off and put it back," said Evelyn.

"I told you to tighten your girths," said Richard. Susan, who was just in front of Jill, stopped. "Jump off," she said, seeing the saddle perched precariously on Wendy's neck.

"I can't, I can't," whined Jill. "It's wobbling. I'm going to fall." Susan dismounted and Noel, who was just ahead of her, took Beauty's reins. With Susan at Wendy's head, Jill managed to scramble off.

"You'd better lead her the rest of the way down," said Susan, "and we'll put it right at the bottom."

"Come on," said Noel, "the others have gone." She gave Beauty to Susan, who led her until the Nut-walk came out into a huge downland field. There they put Wendy's saddle back and Jill mounted. They could see Richard, Margaret and Evelyn, dim specks, fast disappearing in the distance, while John stood half-way across the field, an indecisive figure, torn between the thrill of the chase and the obvious unfairness of deserting Susan and Noel.

"Is your saddle O.K., James?" asked Noel.

"Yes, thank you," replied James.

"Come on, then," said Susan, "we must catch them up."

"The others have gone towards Stark Dyke," John shouted as they drew near, and, turning Turpin, he took the lead. Soon the ponies began to blow, and the children let them canter more slowly until they reached the brow of the hill, where they pulled up, and looked down on the dyke and the faint line of the Roman road in the valley below.

"That's odd," said John, scanning the view. "Where can they have got to?"

"They must be in that wood, I should think," said Noel.

"There's lots of sawdust down here," said James excitedly. He was the only one who had remembered they were supposed to be following a trail and not the other people.

"Yes," said John, riding over to him, "lashings of it. Come on." And he started off down the side of the hill, where a track led round the edge of a chalk quarry. At the bottom the trail led over a small post and rails into the next field. Turpin jumped it beautifully, Beauty and Rusty followed, and then Wendy refused.

Jill turned and rode at it again. Still Wendy refused.

"What about James giving you a lead?" suggested Susan.

"Look out, then," said James. He rode at the jump, and Darkie cleared it easily, but Wendy refused again.

"Try a short run," said Susan, but still she refused.

"Do you think one of us could get her over?" asked Noel.

"That's not a bad idea," said John. "You'd better try first; you look much the lightest."

Noel scrambled on and giving Wendy two hits, turned her at the jump. She was so surprised at being ridden in a determined manner that she jumped it straight away.

"Hurrah!" said James.

"Well done!" said Susan. Jill felt rather annoyed, but still anything was better than being left refusing. They both remounted and cantered on, following the trail across a couple of fields and into a wood. They were trotting down a broad ride, when Susan pointed and said, "Look, there's another trail leading off here."

"A false scent, I expect," said John. "By the hoof-marks, the others have gone this way."

"Let's go the other way, then," said Noel, "because if they took the right one they'll probably have caught the hares; but if they've taken the wrong trail, we might get there first."

"Oh, yes," said James. "Besides, this trail is an awfully thin one; the others may not have noticed it."

"Come on, then," said John, "let's get cracking." And, leaving the path, they began to follow the smaller trail, which led through the undergrowth and twisted in and out of the rhododendron bushes. They walked the ponies for some time, and then they trotted until they came to a pair of hurdles, which led into a ploughed field. James fell off over them, but he didn't hurt himself, and while John caught Darkie, Noel mounted Wendy, who had had six refusals with Jill, and jumped her over second try. The trail led round the headland of the ploughed field and through a gap into the next one—a barren, untilled field, treacherous with rabbit-holes and mole-hills, through which the children picked their way, to find themselves on the deserted grass-grown track that had once been a busy Roman road.

Suddenly Jill said, "Look! There's a fog coming up."

"Gosh, yes," said John as he looked round and realised with dismay that, while they had been so intent on the trail, the fog had been creeping up, minute by minute, until the surrounding hills were completely blotted out.

"We shall be lost," said Jill. "I know we shall."

"I've got my compass," said James, "though it doesn't work very well."

"I think the best thing we can do," said John, "is to keep going, because if we manage to catch up with Roger and Hilary they'll know the way home." They cantered on and on. All five felt anxious as they watched the fog become thicker and thicker, but no one, except Jill, said anything. She sniffed continuously, and whined that she didn't want to be lost, and have to sleep out in the dark and the fog at intervals. Soon they couldn't see the trail, but no one remarked on it. They followed John along the Roman road at a trot in grim silence. Then Susan said, "Beauty seems awfully tired. Shall we get off and lead them for a bit?" They all dismounted, and Noel suggested,

"Oughtn't we to shout? Some of the others may be lost too." So they shouted and made hunting cries as they walked along, which cheered them for a little, but when they had to stop, through hoarseness, the silence which fell seemed deeper, heavier, and more eerie than before. John spoke, more to break the stillness than for any other reason. "Has anyone the faintest idea where this road comes out?" he asked. No one had.

"We're heading due north-west," said James. . . .

When John had seen Noel and Susan stop to put Jill's saddle back at the bottom of the Nut-walk, he had shouted to Evelyn and Richard, who were a few yards ahead of him, "Oughtn't we to wait for them?"

"No, they'll be all right," Evelyn had answered. But at the top of the hill John's conscience forced him to wait. Margaret pointed this out to Richard, who said, "Well, that's his look-out. I'm blowed if I'm going to nursemaid Jill," and had kicked Peter on faster than ever in an attempt to catch up with Evelyn. When they reached the wood, all three of them had been galloping too fast to notice the smaller trail leading off through the undergrowth; they had gone straight on, through a field and down a lane, until they had seen hats, which looked like Hilary's and Roger's, bobbing in the distance.

"There they are," said Evelyn, who saw them first. "Now we can take a short cut." She turned and rode Romany at a solid, three-feet-six post and rails into the next field. Romany refused. Evelyn hit her and rode at it again. This time Romany jumped, but she hit the top bar, which was firmly nailed, and nearly fell. Evelyn let her stand for a moment while she watched Richard and Margaret ride their ponies at the fence. They both refused.

"Oh, come on," said Evelyn impatiently, "Well, I'm not going to wait; you'd better follow the trail," and she galloped off in the direction of the bobbing hats. The sight of Evelyn disappearing into the distance lent strength to

Richard's legs, and Peter, ridden really determinedly, cleared the timber easily. They galloped on, and Margaret was left. She tried everything she could think of to get Pixie over: short runs and long runs, showing her the fence, hitting, kicking and patting her, but Pixie simply said that it was much too high, and she wasn't going to consider jumping it. And when she had had thirty-nine refusals, Margaret reluctantly decided to follow the trail. They cantered down the lane and into another wood, but somewhere they went wrong, and instead of finding the trail they came out on a heath, covered with gorse and bracken and intersected by a mass of small winding paths. Then she noticed the fog creeping up, and at the same time Margaret realised that she was completely lost. "Oh, Pixie," she said, "what on earth shall we do?" And she almost started to cry before she remembered that only feeble people—people like Jill Morrisson—cried when they were lost. She rode on until she came to a clearing. Five tiny paths led off in different directions. She stood in a quandary, unable to decide which path to take; they all looked exactly alike. Suddenly she thought, perhaps Pixie knows the way home—perhaps she will be like a pony in a book. And, dropping the reins, she said, "Come on, take me home. Home, Pixie, home." Pixie put down her head and grazed. "Oh, you are a horrid, greedy pony," said Margaret tearfully as she wrenched it up. "The fog's thicker than ever and I don't want to stay out all night." And in spite of it only being feeble people who cry, she burst into tears. Pixie grazed for a few moments, then she turned and set off at a purposeful trot down the smallest and steepest of the little winding paths.

Evelyn had galloped away from the timber jump with the lightest of hearts. She was well in the lead, and, as she had sighted the hares, it could not be long before she caught up with them.

"You're much the best of them, old lady," said Evelyn

impulsively as she lent forward and patted Romany's sweat-soaked neck, marvelling that the pony was still pulling, though lathered from head to foot. When they reached the clump of trees near which Evelyn had seen the bobbing hats, she pulled up and looked about her. To her disappointment there was no one in sight.

She turned at the sound of hoofs behind her, to see Richard galloping up. She said, "You got over, then?"

"Yes," said Richard. "Where are they? Can you see them?"

"Do you think I'd be standing here if I could?" asked Evelyn disagreeably.

"All right, keep your hair on," said Richard. "But I suppose that means we've lost them; that's what comes of leaving the trail and trying to take short cuts."

"Why didn't you stick to the trail, then?" said Evelyn. She rode on at a trot. There was no sign of the hares and fog was blotting out the landmarks, swallowing the trees. Richard came alongside her.

"This fog's getting worse every minute. We shan't be able to see in front of our noses soon. Have you any idea where we are?"

"None at all," answered Evelyn, enjoying his discomfort. "I expect we're going round and round in circles."

"It's getting thicker than ever," said Roger, pulling Sky Pilot up and gazing into the fog. "I think we shall have to call it off; they won't be able to see the trail in another ten minutes if it goes on coming up as fast as this."

"Oh, darn it!" said Hilary. "Why does the weather always have to spoil everything?"

They turned their ponies and retraced their steps. They rode through the thickening fog, and with each moment their forebodings grew. Hilary said, "Do you think anything's happened to them? They ought to be here by now."

"Heaven knows," said Roger gloomily. "They'll be

hopelessly lost if they've missed the trail; but there's just a chance they turned back earlier and have gone home. Sssh, did you hear a shout?"

"No," said Hilary, listening intently. "Yes, wait a minute. What was that?"

"Them, I think," said Roger excitedly, and he gave a blood-curdling scream, which was meant to be a view-holloa. As it died away they both listened, and, to their delight, they heard an answering yell.

"It's them all right," said Hilary. "Come on."

"Wait a sec.," said Roger. "It sounded more on our right to me; they may still be on the Roman road."

"Probably they missed the trail where it turned off into Downley Wood," said Hilary, "but we can't go back there. Shall we take a short cut across and risk getting lost?"

"It's the only thing to do," said Roger, "and I think there's a gate on the right in a minute; I noticed it on the way down." They soon came upon the gate, and they were delighted to find a footpath, which led across the fields in the direction of the Roman road. They followed, shouting as they went. Gradually the answering calls became louder, until they were separated from Noel, Susan, John, James and Jill only by a broken-down hedge. Both parties were overjoyed to see each other, but this turned to dismay when they realised that Evelyn, Margaret and Richard were still missing.

"Oh," said Roger dispiritedly, "you got parted, then?"

"Yes," said John, "but they were so far ahead, we felt sure they would catch you before the fog got thick."

"Which was the right trail in the wood?" asked James.

"They both led to the Roman road," said Roger; "but the one that went straight on was a longer way round."

"I think the best thing we can do," said Roger, "is to try to find our way across the footpath and down Lindon's Lane, where I laid the false trail. I should think they must be over that way somewhere, but if they're not—well, we shall be on our way home."

"We've got to find a way into your field, first," said Susan.

"Yes," said John, "and we can't jump, because there's a strand of barbed wire in the hedge."

"There's a post here that looks pretty rotten," said Noel, who'd been investigating. It *was* rotten, and, when she and John both pushed, it broke off close to the ground. Then Roger and Hilary stood on the wire while the others led their ponies across. The ponies all seemed tired except for Sky Pilot; he was nervous and shied at gates, bushes and cows as they suddenly appeared out of the fog. The riders, who were cold, hungry and anxious, tried hard not to show it. Every few minutes they all shouted together, and at last, when they were riding down Lindon's Lane, Roger in the lead, they heard an answering call.

"There, that must be them," said Hilary, as relief surged through everyone. They all felt inclined to hurry in the direction of the shout, but they were prevented by the fog, which seemed thicker than ever concentrated between the tall overgrown hedges of the lane.

"What about singing?" suggested John. "That might guide them to us."

They were in the middle of the second verse of "John Peel" when there was a shout quite close, and in a few moments Evelyn and Richard were among them.

"But haven't you got Marga?" asked Hilary in a horror-struck voice. "The others said she was with you."

"She was," said Evelyn, "but she got left behind. We took a short cut, because we saw you, and, as she couldn't get Pixie over the jump, she was going to follow the trail."

"This is the last straw," said Roger. "Never again will I organise anything."

"She's awfully scatterbrained," said Hilary. We must find her. What will mummy say?"

"I'm sure she's fallen into a chalk quarry," said James.

"Nonsense, Jim," said Roger, trying to sound cheerful. "If it was you I'd be much more worried, because, in spite

of your compass, you always get lost; but though Marga's rash, she's awfully good at finding the way."

"We must do something," said Evelyn. "We can't just stand here."

"Personally," said Richard suddenly, "I think we had better go back to your place, and, if she hasn't got there first, we can call the police and have a proper search party."

"Oh, yes," said Jill. "Do let's go home, I'm so cold."

"I'm not going home," said Hilary. "We've got to find Marga."

"Nor am I," said James, giving Richard a challenging look.

"Wait a minute, though," said Roger. "I'm not sure that Richard isn't right. By now the parents will have realised we must be lost; but they can't search for us, because they don't know where we were going. The best thing would be to ring up, but I should think the nearest telephone is the Cresswells' and that's at least three miles away. If we search in parties, we're bound to lose each other. Neither party will know if she's been found, and meanwhile she'll probably get home and turn everyone out to look for us."

"Perhaps you're right," said Hilary slowly.

"Come on, then," said Richard impatiently, "let's get going." They rode on, speaking very little, but occasionally giving a view-holloa, in case Margaret was about. At last they came out on the Basset-Fenchurch road, and they parted from the Morrissons at the lane which came out opposite Orchard Cottage. Roger apologised for the unpleasant time they had had, Richard replied that it wasn't his fault, and Jill didn't bother to answer.

Roger said, "We must be nearly at the Cresswells' now. I think I'd better brave her and ring up mummy. Don't you?"

"Yes," said Hilary. "But I'll go. I'm better at escaping than you."

"Well, if you're sure you don't mind," said Roger.

"We'd better keep our eyes open," said Hilary, "or we shall ride past. I'm sure the fog's thicker here." When they reached Dormers, Roger held Northwind while Hilary went in. She was quite a long time, it seemed ages to the others waiting in suspense, and when she came back every hope was dashed: Margaret hadn't got home, she told them, and Mrs. Radcliffe was waiting for them to get back before she started to look for her in the car. They rode gloomily on. Roger dropped back beside Hilary and asked in a low voice, "What did mummy say? Was she very upset?"

"She was—rather," said Hilary. "She was cross with Evelyn, she told her to keep an eye on Marga and Jim."

When they reached the cross-roads where the Basset and Hogshill roads parted, Noel and Susan said good-bye, and that they hoped the Radcliffes would find Margaret waiting for them. Then they rode off together, for Noel had to drop Rusty at the Spinneys. But John insisted on going back to the Priory. He said he would help search, or, if Margaret had turned up, use Major Holbrooke's drive as a short cut home. They clattered up the Priory drive, a depleted party, with very different feelings to those they had started with that morning. Mrs. Radcliffe appeared; there was still no sign of Margaret.

Drearily they settled the ponies: Turpin in Pixie's place, and then they hurried into the house, to find Mrs. Radcliffe answering the telephone. "That's very kind of you," she was saying. "I'll start right away, but I expect it'll take me some time, the fog is so terribly thick." At last she put down the receiver and said, "It's all right, she's turned up at Flinton-under-Fenchurch. That was Colonel Cagemore. He says he'll keep Pixie for the night, as she seems dead beat, and we're to fetch Margaret in the car."

"Hurray!" said everyone.

"Thank goodness for that," said Roger. "I'll come with you, mummy."

"Well, I suppose I'd better go now," said John in

disappointed tones, "unless I can be of some use."

"You can't possibly ride all the way home now, John," said Mrs. Radcliffe. "Turpin must be exhausted. Look! If Pixie is staying with Colonel Cagemore, Turpin can keep her box."

On the day after the paper-chase, the hounds and hares all gave their ponies a well-earned rest and lay late in bed themselves. Colonel Cagemore telephoned the Radcliffes to tell them that Pixie was slightly lame, and would have to stay with him for another day or two. The Radcliffes thanked him several times, and then they rang up John and told him he need not fetch Turpin until next day.

On the next day, which was Friday, Mrs. Radcliffe went to London, and the children, who felt very bored now that the excitement of Christmas, hunting and the paper-chase was over, spent most of the morning quarrelling. In the afternoon John came for Turpin, and Hilary and Roger decided to ride back with him and see how Jet's education compared with Rocket's. Evelyn said she was going to give Romany a jumping lesson.

Evelyn waited impatiently until the sounds of Sky Pilot's, Turpin's and Rocket's hoof-beats had died away in the distance, and then, taking Romany to the paddock, she put all the jumps up to three feet six and mounted, filled with high hopes. Unfortunately, Romany, who had been made hotter than ever by the paper-chase, became half-crazy with fear and excitement at the sight of the jump. Snatching the reins out of Evelyn's hands, she tore at it, much too fast, and then, her heart failing her at the last minute, refused dead. Evelyn almost shot over her head; but she quickly recovered her seat and, bitterly disappointed, she beat Romany, who galloped off round the field. It took some time and a good deal of wrenching before Evelyn was able to pull Romany up; then, though she was blowing hard, Evelyn rode her at the jump again. This time she whipped round before she was within the wings, and, expecting another beating, shot off across the

field. Evelyn tried again and again, and every time she got hotter and angrier, especially when she noticed that James and Margaret were watching from the gate. It took her nearly half an hour before she was able to force the pony through the jump. Then, feeling very pleased with herself at having conquered this display of obstinacy, and hoping to put Margaret in her place, she called out, "Want a ride?" To her dismay Margaret answered, "Yes, *please*," and, leaping down, ran towards her. For a moment Evelyn contemplated telling Margaret that she hadn't meant it, but that, she decided, would make her more conceited than ever, for she would guess that Evelyn had expected her to be afraid. She shrugged her shoulders and thought, it's the little fool's own look-out; she shouldn't be always bothering me.

Evelyn held Romany, who wouldn't stand still, while Margaret mounted and altered her stirrups. Then Evelyn said, "Just ride her down to the end of the field and back." Margaret turned Romany, who shot straight off into a canter, increased her pace as she went down the field, swerved round the corner—luckily Margaret had a firm hold of her mane—and galloped back to the gate, flat out, stopping dead with a bounce at the last moment.

"She's lovely," said Margaret. "Awfully fast. Do you want a try, Jim?"

"No, thank you," said James.

"You're afraid," said Margaret accusingly.

"I'm not," said James, going red in the face.

"Why won't you have a ride, then?" asked Margaret.

" 'Cause I don't," replied James.

"Coward!" said Margaret.

"You shut up," said James, clenching his fists and taking up a threatening attitude.

"Baby!" said Margaret, not in the least intimidated.

"Leave him alone," said Evelyn. "You know he's nervous."

"I'm not nervous," shouted James furiously.

94

"You are," said Margaret. "You're a nervous baby."

"All right, then," said James. "I'll ride her, just to show you."

Seizing the reins from Evelyn, James scrambled on Romany and gave her an angry kick, which made her tear off even faster than usual, shooting him up her neck. She galloped down the field and swerved round the corner, which unseated him still more. "Pull her up, you idiot," shouted Evelyn, while Margaret, already repenting her rash dare, shouted, "Whoa, Romany, whoa!" But Romany, frightened by the shouting and James clinging round her neck, started to buck. Minus both stirrups and losing his head as he began to slip sideways, James, too, shouted. "Whoa!" in far from soothing accents. Terrified, Romany galloped round the field at full speed, and then, in a last desperate attempt to rid herself of her horrid, clinging burden, she leaped the hedge, which was about four feet high. James fell off, and Romany galloped on, across the little paddock, through the open gate, into the stable yard.

Dr. Radcliffe, who had returned home early, was walking towards the house, after putting the car away, when he heard shrieks of "Whoa!" and the sound of galloping hoofs. He ran to the paddock gate, and was just in time to see Romany jump the hedge and James fall off. Muttering words he would not allow his children to use, Dr. Radcliffe ran across the field. Evelyn and Margaret, too, ran towards James. Evelyn reached him first.

"Are you all right?" she asked.

"I don't know," said James. "I think so, but my arm hurts."

"Well, get up, then," said Evelyn, and, seeing her father, she added, "Quick, Doc's coming. Gosh, there'll be a row." James staggered to his feet and stood holding his arm as his father arrived on the scene.

"Are you all right, James?" he asked.

"Yes, thank you," said James, looking distinctly green.

"What's the matter with your arm?" asked Dr. Radcliffe.

"It's all right," said James firmly. But his father was not a doctor for nothing. "Let me have a look," he said, and after a brief examination, "Um! We'd better go straight into Gunston and get it X-rayed."

"No, no," wailed James. "It's all right, I tell you. I don't want a beastly X-ray."

"Now, don't be silly," said Dr. Radcliffe patiently. Don't you want to see what your bones look like?"

"No, I don't," said James, starting to cry. The doctor picked him up, carefully avoiding the broken arm, and walked briskly towards the house.

Romany, who was in the paddock, still wearing her saddle and bridle, reminded everyone of the cause of the accident.

"Evelyn," said Dr. Radcliffe, looking very stern, "I thought I told you that on no account were Margaret and James to ride that pony."

"You said not until she was quiet," said Evelyn.

"Which, as you know very well, she is not," said Dr. Radcliffe.

"Well, Marga managed her all right," said Evelyn. "I should think she's as quiet as she's ever likely to be. It was Jim's own fault for shrieking."

"I didn't shriek," protested James weakly. "I only said 'whoa' when she wouldn't stop."

"You didn't," said Evelyn, "you *screamed*."

"All right," said Dr. Radcliffe, "we'll discuss that later. Margaret, you catch that pony before she breaks her reins; and Evelyn, run indoors and fetch a couple of cushions and a large silk handkerchief from the top right-hand drawer of my tallboy." Evelyn and Margaret hurried off. Then, with his arm in a sling and Evelyn beside him in case he felt queer or fainted, James was propped up with cushions and the Doctor drove briskly to Gunston.

When Hilary and Roger arrived home, just before tea-

time, they were surprised not to find either their sisters or brother about, but, after they had made a few hunting noises, Margaret appeared from the hayloft, where she had obviously been crying, and said that Jim had fractured his arm and Doc. had taken him to hospital. Of course, Roger and Hilary wanted to know how it had happened, and, when Margaret told them, they both said Evelyn must be absolutely half-witted and that there would be a fearful row.

As the Radcliffes had anticipated, there was a row that evening. When James, his arm encased in plaster, had been put to bed, and Mrs. Radcliffe, back from London, had had the whole business explained to her, the Doctor announced that, as Evelyn was obviously unfit to be entrusted with a young pony, Romany was to be returned to Major Holbrooke next day. Evelyn, white to the lips, said that her father couldn't send Romany back; she wasn't his pony; he had said that she could have her, and it wasn't her fault that Jim was such a baby. Dr. Radcliffe said that he had definitely forbidden both Margaret and James to ride Rocket and Romany, and Evelyn had agreed to this condition before she had the pony. Yet she had been there, and allowed, if not even encouraged it; though why was entirely beyond his comprehension. James, the Doctor had gone on, was punished, for he would not be able to ride for several weeks, and Romany going back would put an end to all further temptation. He had already arranged with Coles of Folly Farm for Romany to be turned out there until the Major, to whom he would write that night, came home. Evelyn stormed, argued, and in the end cried, but all in vain. The Doctor stood firm, and when Roger and Hilary, who thought the punishment much too hard, joined in the argument, they were told to mind their own business. Then Margaret pointed out that it was her fault; *she* had called James a coward and dared him to ride Romany, not Evelyn. But the Doctor, though agreeing that Margaret had caused the broken arm and

behaved in an extremely thoughtless, and even dangerous way, since James might easily have had a worse accident, said that this was no excuse for Evelyn. Romany was to be taken to Folly Farm next morning, and as he saw no reason why Margaret should go unscathed she was not to ride again for the rest of the Christmas holidays.

CHAPTER VII

IT WAS the first day of the Easter holidays. But Noel, riding Rusty back to the Spinneys, was heavy at heart, for Simon Wentwood was coming home, and after to-day she would have no pony to ride. Susan was very kind, and would, Noel knew, let her ride Beauty, but that was far from being the same thing as having a pony lent one for the whole term and being allowed to keep him at home.

When she had turned Rusty out in his field and thanked Mrs. Wentwood for the loan of him, Noel crossed the road to speak to Romany, who was turned out in one of the Folly Farm fields opposite the Spinneys. Everyone had heard about James Radcliffe's arm, but no one seemed to know exactly how it had happened, or why she had been sent back to the Major. When Romany saw Noel, she whinnied and trotted across the field, for she found it very dull turned out alone.

"I wish I could have you," Noel told her. "But I wouldn't even dare ask the Major. Besides, it would sound awfully conceited to suggest that I could manage you when Evelyn, who is miles a better rider, has had to send you back."

None of the horse-breakers was very pleased when, on the first Saturday of the holidays, they received a post-card from Major Holbrooke asking them to bring their

98

ponies to Folly Court at ten o'clock on the following Saturday.

Susan had Beauty saddled at once, and rode over to Russet Cottage to tell Noel.

Noel was very pessimistic. She said that Sunset didn't know half as much now as Grey Dawn had at the beginning of the Christmas holidays, and she thought all the ponies would look completely unschooled beside her, except, perhaps, Rocket Radcliffe, who, John Manners had told her, was "pretty good." Susan begged Noel to go to the Towers on Monday afternoon and help her school, and also offered to lend her Beauty to ride at the rally. Noel accepted the invitation for Monday, but she said she was sure that Major Holbrooke wouldn't want her to go to the rally when she wasn't one of the horse-breakers. But in the end Susan persuaded her by saying that it would take hours to ride Sunset to Folly Court alone, as she would dawdle and shy the whole way.

Richard was thrown into a frenzy by his postcard. He suddenly realised that Rufus was still unshod, and had never been ridden without someone leading him. Mrs. Morrisson looked up from her own letter to ask whom his was from.

"Major Holbrooke, the old bore," Richard replied. "What does he want to start stirring things up for? I thought he was going to be away for ages."

"But you know you like rallies, darling," said Mrs. Morrisson. "You ought to be pleased he's back. What does he say?"

"Just: 'I should be very glad if you could bring Rufus here on Saturday the ninth at ten o'clock for an instructional rally.' That means a lot of fuss and criticism for everyone, except his dear little June, who, of course, will do everything perfectly," said Richard.

"Well, you must train the pony a bit more," said Mrs. Morrisson. "You really ought to be able to put up a better show against that Cresswell girl. I'm sick and tired

99

of her mother crowing over me at every gymkhana."

"It's easy to say that," said Richard, "but how can I beat her? To start with, she's got the best pony; we all wanted the grey, but I suppose the Major wangled it somehow."

"Oh, Richard," said Jill, "you know he wouldn't do that, even if she is his favourite."

"I don't know so much," said Richard. "It was a queer coincidence, anyway. To go on with, she doesn't have to go to a boarding school, so she can train her wretched pony every day, and I bet her mother helps her. It's not fair," he went on, becoming more indignant as he thought about it. "Rufus can't do anything yet, and I don't see why I should make a fool of myself. I'm blowed if I'm going, and I don't care what old Holbrooke says."

"No, you'd better not, if you're going to make a fool of yourself," said Mrs. Morrisson. "But are you sure you can't train the pony in time?"

"How can I," said Richard, raising his voice, "with no one but Jill to help me? I tell you the wretched animal knows nothing—literally nothing."

"Don't shout at me like that, Richard," said Mrs. Morrisson sharply. "It's entirely your own fault for not riding more last holidays. I wish we'd never said you could have it. You'd better write a note to Major Holbrooke and say you are very sorry, but you have an appointment at the dentist's on that day, and meanwhile, if you don't settle down and train the animal seriously, I'll speak to your father and he'll send it back." Richard would have liked to be rude, but after all, he thought, his mother had suggested a way out; so he confined himself to scraping back his chair which he knew annoyed her, and saying, "All right, I'll write and then I'll try to knock some sense into that wretched pony. . . ."

"Look at this, Mummy," said June, handing her mother Major Holbrooke's postcard, "I don't want to go. He'll be

teaching the others how to make their ponies walk and trot and I shall have to stand about doing nothing. I think it's mean," she went on, "the way he always does everything to suit the worst people."

"It does seem a shame," said Mrs. Cresswell. "You'd think he'd take more trouble with the best ones—the ones that would do him most credit—instead of wasting time on the duds. I see your point of view, my pet, but what do you want to do? Wait a bit and hope the others get on?"

"I can't see much good in doing that," said June. "I should think Grey Dawn knows more now than the Major will have taught the others by the summer holidays. Supposing I just go to the gymkhana or test he said he was going to have to decide which is the best schooled pony before they go back to his cousin?"

"It would be nice to show that you could do it all without help," said Mrs. Cresswell. "But I'm afraid he has the right to insist on you taking Dawn to the rallies, for he would be failing his cousin if he didn't keep an eye on all of them."

"Well, I suppose I might go to some of the later rallies when there may be jumping," said June. "But this one is sure to be dull. Do think of an excuse, Mummy."

"Well, dear," said Mrs. Cresswell, "we could say you had an appointment at the dentist's. . . ."

Hilary Radcliffe found her postcard on the breakfast table. She picked it up with a feeling of curiosity, but one glance told her what it was, and she quickly stuffed it into her pocket, though not before Margaret's sharp eyes had seen it.

"Who is your postcard from, Hilary?" she asked.

"Really, Margaret," said Mrs. Radcliffe, "you mustn't be so inquisitive. It's Hilary's letter, and she'd tell you if she wanted you to know."

After breakfast Hilary went to the Prior's room to look for her mother; instead, she found Roger.

"Look," said Hilary, handing him her postcard, "I suppose you guessed whom it was from."

"Yes,' said Roger, "it was pretty obvious."

"I don't want to go," said Hilary as he finished reading it. "I know it won't be any fun, but I can't think what to say; I must give a reason."

"I think you ought to go," said Roger, balancing himself precariously on the fender. "After all, there is Rocket to consider."

"Yes, but it'll be beastly," said Hilary. "I mean, one can't mention Rocket, much less Major Holbrooke, now."

"But you can't let that put you off," said Roger. "Anyway, it ought to have blown over by now. I was most surprised when I came home these holidays and found Evelyn was still sulking."

"She's not sulking," said Hilary. "But no one likes to have their pony sent back, and, if I do go to the rally, what am I to tell everyone?"

"If they are tactless enough to mention the subject, they deserve to be told to mind their own business," said Roger; "but I don't think they will, except perhaps June Cresswell."

"What has that poor despised creature done now?" asked Mrs. Radcliffe as she came into the room.

"It's not what she's done, but what she might do," said Roger.

"Look," said Hilary, handing her mother the postcard.

"Don't you think she ought to go, Mummy?" asked Roger.

"Of course she must," said Mrs. Radcliffe. "But don't you want to, Hilary?"

"No," said Hilary. "It won't be any fun without Evelyn, but I can't think of an excuse."

"Now you mustn't be silly about it," said Mrs. Radcliffe, "you can't give up schooling Rocket now; it wouldn't be fair to him or Major Holbrooke. Besides, it's not as bad for Evelyn as you seem to think. She's not so

interested in breaking and schooling as you are, and it's obvious that while she is much the best of you at jumping impossible heights, she's too impatient to be good with young or nervous ponies. Except for the blow to her pride," Mrs. Radcliffe went on, "I don't think she feels the loss of Romany as much as you think."

"Besides, Hil," said Roger, "I'm positive that you're the only person who can beat June Cresswell."

"Letter for you, John," said Colonel Manners when John came into the sunny, oak-panelled dining-room on Saturday morning. "Can't you *ever* be in time for breakfast?" the Colonel added angrily, rustling the paper, which was full of the iniquities of the Government.

"Sorry," muttered John sulkily, as he helped himself to porridge, and then, sitting down, he read his postcard between the mouthfuls. Only a week, he thought. This morning he would take Jet to the forge and then lunge her; tomorrow, he would go out for a ride and that would leave five days for schooling. He sighed despairingly. He knew Jet would seem untrained beside Rocket and Grey Dawn. Looking up, he found his parents eyeing him.

"It's from Major Holbrooke," he explained. "About a Pony Club 'do' next Saturday. I wish it wasn't so soon. I shan't have much time to get Jet in practice again."

"Huh," said Colonel Manners, "Holbrooke's back, is he? I shall have to go up and see him. There's that new type of tractor I wanted to ask him about, and I must find out if he still wants a load of mixture hay."

When Susan told her parents that her postcard was from Major Holbrooke, Mr. Barington-Brown said that now she'd catch it. She'd have the Major after her, when Sunset turned out to be the worst-trained pony of the lot. Susan had to have somewhere to lay the blame, so she said that no one could possibly school a pony in the park; it was too full of trees and bracken, not to mention rabbit-holes and molehills. To her surprise, her father said he

would make a bargain with her: If she would agree to school Sunset regularly, at least five days a week in the holidays, he would fix it with Hodges, the farmer who rented all his land but the park, that she should have the big flat field by the stables, and he'd tell Bob to mark out a school and put up some jumps. Susan, who was delighted, readily agreed to her side of the bargain, and when Noel arrived at the Towers on Monday she was surprised to find a school neatly marked out, while Bob was giving the finishing touches to four little jumps. Susan, who had groomed and saddled both the ponies so that the jumps might be finished, was delighted to see Noel's surprise. She said that now they would be able to give June Cresswell a show.

Sunset had forgotten everything: she dawdled at the walk, trotted much too fast, with her head low, and couldn't halt, back-rein or turn on the forehand. Even Susan, who generally thought she went rather well, was disheartened, and at the end of five minutes' schooling she said, "What about having some races—at the trot, of course?"

"Don't you think we ought to school seriously?" asked Noel. "Sunset must be able to pull up and make turns by Saturday."

"Yes, I suppose we ought," said Susan with a sigh. "But it's awfully dull, and surely we can invent some races with a lot of turning in them to make her more handy."

"The experts seem to think schooling is better," said Noel. "I mean, one never hears of people training horses by trotting races. Anyway, Sunset trots too fast now, so I should think it would be definitely bad for her."

"Oh, dear," said Susan, "I suppose we'll have to school, but I've forgotten the aids for the turn on the forehand."

Noel felt impatient with Susan. She thought, you simply don't try to remember; you know I'll tell you; but I'm not going to. Aloud she said, "Your book is on the gate, and the turns are at the beginning of chapter three."

"Oh, I can't be bothered to get off and look it up," said Susan. "Do tell me, Noel; I'm sure you haven't forgotten."

"Lateral aids," said Noel, relenting. "The rein and leg on the same side."

"Oh, yes," said Susan. "Now I remember. You know Grey Dawn is sure to be first," she went on, "but I wonder which'll be second."

"Not Sunset, at this rate," said Noel tartly. "Probably Hilary Radcliffe's Rocket, I should think."

"Why?" asked Susan.

"I don't know," said Noel reflectively. "Hilary's always struck me as being a good rider, that's all."

"Yes, but we thought Evelyn was a good rider," said Susan, "and she's had to give up."

"We don't know why," said Noel.

"Well, I think John will be second," said Susan, "and I hope Richard is last."

"He never talks about Rufus," said Noel. "So perhaps he's marvellous, and Richard is keeping it a secret so that he can give everyone a terrific surprise."

"I hope not," said Susan, "because, then, Sunset will be the worst of all."

"You are a defeatist," said Noel. "But for goodness' sake let's get on with the schooling."

Richard enlisted the help of Clayton, the jobbing gardener, on the three days a week when he worked at Orchard Cottage, and, while he held Rufus down, Richard rode him round and round the hen-run. Clayton, who was very dark, and locally supposed to be descended from gipsies, had one theory on the treatment of animals, and that was, to show them " 'oo was master." After three days of Clayton's help Richard rode Rufus, with only Jill near-by, in case he started to buck. But he was too cowed to play up; he just walked sorrowfully round the hen-run, his head low and his eyes dull and sad. On Friday Richard took him to be shod.

By Friday, Susan, with Noel's help, had retaught Sunset

all the things she had learned before, but forgotten: to walk fast, trot slowly, canter round the field on the appropriate leg, to rein back, turn on the forehand, and jump one foot six quietly. They didn't ask her to canter round the school, because the author of Susan's book wrote that you should never make your young horse canter slowly, or in a confined space, until he was really well balanced at the trot, for there was a distinct danger of forcing him behind the bit and shortening his stride.

John, too, found that his pony had forgotten most of what she had learned. The first day that he had schooled Jet he had lost his temper because she wouldn't rein back. He had beaten her furiously, which had upset and muddled her more, and it wasn't until John cooled down and thought of making her face a hedge, as Major Holbrooke had told them to do when they taught the ponies, that she remembered what the aids meant, then she backed perfectly. On the whole John was most pleased with Jet's jumping. He began with a pole on the ground and raised it daily, until by Friday she was jumping two feet perfectly, and it was only by great strength of mind that he prevented himself from raising the jump another six inches.

At first, Hilary had slunk guiltily away by herself to school Rocket, but when Roger discovered this, he decided that he wasn't going to have another holiday spoilt by Romany lurking, an unmentionable skeleton, in the cupboard, and he said at lunch that, if Hilary intended to school Rocket that afternoon, he would join her on Sky Pilot.

To Hilary's surprise everyone agreed, including Evelyn, who said that Northwind was getting disgustingly fat and lazy, and must improve his jumping before the gymkhanas.

They spent a very pleasant afternoon riding in the flat field. To start with, they had a competition for the best mannered pony, which Rocket won; then a jumping contest, in which Sky Pilot had the jumps at three feet six, Northwind at three feet, and the three smaller ponies at

two feet six. Sky Pilot and Pixie both jumped clear rounds, and Rocket was third. Then, while the others rode races, Hilary practised turns on the forehand and reining back, as well as teaching Rocket to open gates and lead in hand.

On Saturday, the day of the rally, Major Holbrooke's temper was stretched to its limit long before ten o'clock. To begin with, it was raining—pouring steadily and relentlessly out of one of those steel grey skies in which even the most confirmed optimist can find no hope of change. Then the bath water was cold—and finally, the Major found one of his grooms hitting Southwind's foal with a pitchfork and had to give him the sack.

Altogether it was in an extremely disagreeable mood that Major Holbrooke strode out of the house at the sound of Beauty's and Sunset's hoofs coming up the drive.

"What did you come without a mackintosh for?" he asked angrily as he noticed Noel clad only in a school blazer.

"Sorry," said Noel.

"I offered to lend her my other mack," said Susan. "But it's a tartan cape, and she thought it would be an insult to Beauty."

"I suppose I'd better lend you one," said the Major, ignoring Susan. "Not that it'll be much good now; you're simply soaked." You'd better take those ponies into the barn until the other children come." He turned on his heel and marched into the house, banging the elegant white front door behind him.

"Goodness," said Susan, "he was in a temper, and it's not your fault if you haven't got a mack."

"Oh, do shut up about mackintoshes," said Noel.

"Well, it's nice and dry in here anyway," said Susan in soothing tones as she rode into the huge tithe barn, which stood by itself a little way from the stables. They both dismounted and waited in silence, Susan wondering what it must feel like to be poor. She knew that her parents

107

hadn't always been rich, but in all Valerie's sombre stories of her impoverished childhood—when, apparently, she hadn't had one half of the pleasures and advantages which Susan enjoyed—there had been no mention of the inconvenience of not having a mackintosh.

Soon John joined them. "Hallo," he said, riding into the barn. "Isn't it a beastly day?" And then, catching sight of Noel, "You didn't come without a mackintosh, did you?"

"Yes," said Noel firmly. And she began to wonder why people despised one for not having clothes when ponies, pictures, books, and even music, were so much more important. She wondered, too, why she always thought she was going to enjoy rallies beforehand when she had been disillusioned so many times. John felt awkward waiting in silence. Why couldn't one of the girls say something, he wondered, instead of standing there.

"Stand still, can't you?" he said crossly to Jet as she changed her weight to rest the other hind leg.

At last Hilary arrived. She rode to the barn door, closely followed by the Major, and said to the other horse-breakers, "Hallo, isn't it a foul day?" They said Hallo, and the Major, after silently handing Noel a mackintosh, said, "Come on, then, it isn't going to stop, so we may as well resign ourselves to getting wet," and he led the way down the drive to the field where the rallies were always held.

"But aren't Richard and June coming?" asked Susan, trotting to catch up with him.

"No," said the Major. "They both had appointments at the dentist's."

By the time they reached the field Noel had managed to struggle into the mackintosh. It wasn't much too big, except for the sleeves, and she guessed that it must belong to Mrs. Holbrooke. The Major opened the gate and asked the children to walk round the school a length behind each other. At first Hilary took the lead, but Rocket, who didn't like the look of the strange field, would stop and

108

Sunset lashed out.

shy every few yards, upsetting all the other ponies. Major Holbrooke shouted instructions to Hilary. He told her to pat and speak to Rocket, then to use her legs, and when it seemed that he was just being naughty, to hit him. But Rocket went on shying, and when the Major gave the order to trot, he caused havoc. Every time he stopped, the other ponies ran into him and each other. Hilary was becoming more and more flustered, and Rocket was beginning to believe in his up to now imaginary bogies when the Major, in exasperation, shouted to Noel, "You're riding a schooled pony; for goodness' sake take the lead."

"What?" asked Noel before his words had had time to sink in, and then, realising what he had said, she gave Beauty a kick which made her leap forward and bump into Rocket. Apologising to Hilary, Noel disentangled herself and took the lead. For a few moments all went well. They walked and trotted round the school, and Noel was just thinking that perhaps leading wasn't so bad when Major Holbrooke shouted, "Change the rein."

"What?" asked Noel, though she had heard perfectly.

"Change the rein," he repeated. Noel panicked. She knew that the Major meant her to go round the school the opposite way, for they had often done this at rallies before, but then she had blindly followed the person in front of her and never noticed how it was done. She wavered indecisively at the corner of the school. "Turn right," shouted the Major, but Noel couldn't remember which way was which; she took a chance and turned left out into the field. Susan, who was behind Noel and knew her right from left, turned right, and John and Hilary followed. Suddenly Sunset noticed that she was leading. She stopped dead, and Rocket and Jet ran into her. Giving an angry squeal, Sunset lashed out, catching Rocket on his forearm.

"Can't you people keep off each others' tails?" asked the Major angrily. "What is the good of me trying to teach you to school ponies when you can't even ride a length apart?"

110

"Sorry," said John and Hilary hastily.

"Is Rocket hurt?" asked Susan anxiously.

"He's bleeding from this leg," said Noel, pointing. Hilary dismounted, and she and the Major examined the wound.

"I don't think it's much," said Major Holbrooke. "Just a cut. It was lucky she caught him on the forearm and not on the knee; I don't think it'll make him lame. You'd better take him up to the stables and ask Blake to bathe it, then bring him back and we'll see if he's sound." Hilary led Rocket away and Major Holbrooke turned to the others. "Now, for goodness' sake keep away from each other," he said. "The next one may not be so lucky. Now, where had we got to? Oh, yes, I remember," he went on. "Noel had just tied everyone up in knots. Don't you know how to change the rein?"

"No," said Noel miserably.

"But we've done it at every rally," said the Major. "You must be half-asleep if you've never noticed." Noel didn't say anything; she stared hard at Beauty's wet mane and felt herself grow redder and redder.

"Well, lead on round," said Major Holbrooke. "I'd better try to teach you."

Noel rode round the school, wishing she had never joined the Pony Club. Suddenly she realised that the Major was speaking. "Turn right," he shouted. "Right, at the corner." Noel felt near tears; she had forgotten which way was right again. Then John rode up beside her. "That way," he said, pointing across the school.

"Where?" asked Noel.

"Look," said Major Holbrooke, walking up and trying to speak calmly, "Imagine you are riding in a covered school, keeping as close to the wall as you can. There will only be one way you can turn, won't there? Inwards. When I tell you to change the rein," he went on, "turn inwards, and ride diagonally across the school. Trot on."

Everyone was glad when Hilary returned with Rocket,

111

and they were able to stop schooling while she trotted him up and down for the Major to see if he was lame. Happily he wasn't, but Major Holbrooke gave Hilary another lecture about keeping off people's tails, during which John would wink at Noel and Susan. Noel was too downcast to pay much attention, but Susan giggled until the Major heard. He thought she was laughing at him, so he was crosser than ever, and gave her a long lecture on how it wasn't funny to kick another person's pony, and how, if she had used her legs, Sunset wouldn't have jibbed.

John, the only unscathed member of the party, did not remain so for long. The Major, having asked them all to ride circles, soon discovered that John wasn't giving with his outside hand, and was, therefore, preventing Jet from following the order—to turn her head and neck inwards, that his inside rein was giving. When he remembered to do this, John forgot to use his outside leg, so that Jet's quarters, which should have been turned inwards, were straight with the rest of her and she wasn't making a circle at all. When John had learned to circle properly the Major asked if there were any questions. Then, seeing glassy expressions spread over the members' faces, he said that they would do some jumping.

"Oh, goody!" said Susan.

"That'll be super," said John, who had practised the forward seat a lot since the last Pony Club rally.

"Nothing very exciting to start with," said Major Holbrooke. "Just a pole on the ground. Noel, lead over at a walk, please." When everyone had walked over the pole twice, the Major told them to trot, and no one was corrected, except John, who, in excess of zeal, pulled Jet up too sharply when she cantered.

"They all do that very nicely," said the Major when each pony had had several turns. "Now we'll try a jump," and he led the way across the field to where there was a course of jumps of various types and sizes. He lowered a white bar to about one foot six and told Noel to lead on at

112

a trot. All the ponies jumped it perfectly, but Susan's legs were too far back and Hilary's hands rested on Rocket's withers instead of sliding up on either side of his neck.

"How high have you been jumping these ponies?" asked Major Holbrooke. "They're all going very well, but I don't want to overface them."

"Rocket's jumped two feet six," said Hilary.

"Jet's never jumped higher than two feet," said John.

"One foot six is the highest I've ever put Sunset at," said Susan, "but I'm sure she can jump much higher."

Then Major Holbrooke told Noel to stand aside while the young ponies jumped and he would give her something more difficult at the end. So Noel watched and tried to decide which was the best schooled of the three ponies. Rocket's head-carriage was the highest and his jumping was excellent—he never tried to run out or refuse, but Noel thought he seemed lazy, and certainly Hilary had to kick hard to make him canter. Jet, on the other hand, though not so well balanced and apparently difficult to keep straight at her fences, was much more willing, and obeyed a more elegant leg aid. Sunset wasn't as lazy as Rocket, but her head-carriage was lower, and she had an uncomfortable habit of cat-jumping, which unseated Susan over almost every jump. Noel was wondering what sort of a test the Major would give the horse-breakers in the summer and which of them would win, when she heard him say, "Come on, Noel, stop day-dreaming; here's a nice little course for you," and, looking up, she saw that he had raised all the jumps to a little over three feet.

"But they're enormous. *I* couldn't *possibly* jump them," said Noel, speaking without thinking.

"Don't be absurd," said Major Holbrooke. "In the first place, they're not at all large, and, secondly, you're riding a jolly good pony. Why can't you jump them? Do you mean you don't want to?"

"No," said Noel, wishing she could cut her tongue off. "No, of course not."

"Well, stop dithering, and come on, then," said the Major. "The brush fence is first."

Noel turned and rode Beauty at the brush fence. They cleared it, and went on over the five other jumps.

"Jolly good," said Susan as they cleared the last one.

"A perfect round," said Hilary.

"Beauty *can* jump," said John.

"They weren't quite so enormous as you thought, were they?" asked Major Holbrooke as Noel rode back, patting Beauty. "It wasn't a bad round," he went on, when she didn't reply, "but you took the parallel bars too slowly and only just cleared them. And now, I am afraid, we must stop," and, turning from Noel to the official horse-breakers, he said, "I want you to remember that the main object of schooling is to teach your pony the aids, and to balance and supple him so that he can obey the lightest possible aid in the shortest possible time. There are no short cuts to this. As for jumping," the Major went on, "at the moment they are all going well, but don't forget that lungeing over fences is invaluable, especially if you are heavy for your pony, and remember that breadth, rather than height, should be your aim. By the way," he finished, "Mrs. Maxton is kindly organising a picnic ride on Friday, and there will be an instructional rally here to-day fortnight; you can bring either your own ponies or the youngsters. Now it's very late, so good-bye and thank you for coming."

"Thank you for having us," said the horse-breakers in one voice, and, following him out of the field, they said good-bye, and took their different directions down the drive; Noel, John, and Susan together, Hilary alone.

"He wasn't in a very good mood to-day," said John to Noel and Susan as soon as they were out of earshot.

"Poor Noel caught it," said Susan. "And so did the rest of us when we rode on each other's tails."

"What about the blowing up I got when I didn't circle properly?" said John.

114

"Didn't Beauty jump well?" said Susan. "You were awfully good on her, Noel; much better than I am. I know I should have fallen off over those jumps. I think they were enormous, and I don't care what the Major says."

"They didn't seem so big when you got close to them," said Noel. "And Beauty was marvellous. I only had to sit there while she did everything, but I'm sorry I held her back too much at the parallel bars."

"Well, she cleared them," said Susan, "and that's all that matters."

"But if she wasn't such a good jumper she mightn't have cleared them," said Noel.

"You're as bad as the Major," said Susan, "always bothering about small details. I can't see much fun in riding if you're going to be so particular."

As Hilary rode homewards through the faint drizzle, she thought over the rally. Roger had been right in saying that no one would ask tactless questions about Romany. Even the Major hadn't mentioned the subject, and, on the whole, the rally had been much more fun than she had expected. Rocket, apart from being nappy at the beginning, had gone well, but she wished that June had been there, for she would have liked to compare him with Grey Dawn. Hilary felt glad that her mother and Roger had persuaded her to go. It would have been awful if three of the horse-breakers had had appointments with their dentists, especially as there were only two in Brampton.

It had stopped raining by the time Noel reached home, and a thin, watery gleam of sunshine was filtering through the clouds. Mrs. Kettering, who was planting out sweet-williams, looked up at the sound of the gate shutting and said, "Hallo, did you have a good time?"

"Yes, thank you," said Noel. "But why did it have to rain?"

"Are you very wet?" asked Mrs. Kettering.

"No," said Noel. "The Major was a bit fussy and would lend me a mack, so I'm fairly dry. Beauty jumped mar-

115

vellously," she went on. "She did a clear round, and it was quite a high course—at least three feet."

"Good heavens," said Mrs. Kettering. "You are getting on; I must come and see you at the next rally."

"I don't suppose I'll be able to borrow Beauty for the next one," said Noel. "I expect Susan will ride her, because it's for everyone, not just horse-breakers. I do wish," she went on, "that I could have Romany. It does seem such a waste for her to be turned out at Folly Farm and never ridden."

"Why don't you ask the Major?" said Mrs. Kettering.

"I'm not a good enough rider," said Noel. "I wouldn't dare."

"But he can't say more than no," said Mrs. Kettering. "And that won't kill you."

"I'm sure he'd think I was awfully conceited," said Noel.

"My good girl," said Mrs. Kettering violently, "what does that matter? If no one ever thinks anything worse about you than that, you'll be jolly lucky. You can't go through life weighing up what people will say or think to every action before you make it. Think of all the great books that would never have been written, the great pictures that would never have been painted, and the lands that would never have been discovered, if the writers, the artists, and the explorers had stopped to wonder what people might say or think. If you want Romany, for goodness' sake ask the Major and stop dithering."

As Noel ate her belated lunch, it occurred to her that this was the second time she had been told to stop dithering that day.

Remembering his mood of the morning, Mrs. Holbrooke tactfully let the Major eat his lunch and start drinking his coffee before she asked, "Well, and how did the rally go?"

"Not too badly," replied Major Holbrooke. "The ponies all seem quiet enough and I don't think Harry will be able to grumble by the time we've finished with them. The

116

Barington-Brown child's pony kicked Hilary Radcliffe's Rocket, but luckily it was only a slight cut, and perhaps it will teach them not to ride on each other's heels."

"I doubt it," said Mrs. Holbrooke. "I've never known anything, but advancing old age, teach children that."

"It is extraordinary how long it takes to get anything into their heads," said Major Holbrooke. "I spent about twenty minutes trying to teach Noel Kettering to change the rein and I'm sure she doesn't know now."

"Well, of course, she is rather a vague child," said Mrs. Holbrooke.

"Yes," said the Major. "But it's really amazing the way she's got on with her riding."

CHAPTER VIII

ALL THROUGH the next week Mrs. Kettering's words rang in Noel's ears. Each night she resolved to ask Major Holbrooke if she could have Romany. But each morning she wakened wondering how she could have been mad enough to dream that he might say yes, or even, when it came to the point, that she would have the courage to ask him. It was Richard Morrisson who decided her. They met in Bond's, the Brampton bookseller. She was looking for a book to buy with a birthday book-token. Richard was rummaging among a pile of maps.

"Hallo," said Noel.

"Hallo," answered Richard. "Isn't this an inefficient shop? One can't get anything in these wretched cock-eyed provincial towns. London is the only place to shop."

"Ssh," said Noel, looking anxiously at Mr. Bond. "He'll hear."

"I hope he does," said Richard. "I want a map of

Buttonshire, and all he says is that if he *has* got one it'll be among this pile; and I've been searching for *hours*."

"Are you going for a riding tour?" asked Noel.

"No," said Richard. "A cycling one, with Michael."

Noel said, "You are energetic. But what about Rufus?"

"I'm not going to be away all that long," replied Richard peevishly. "And anyway, I don't see why I should devote my life to him. I'm not June Cresswell, you know. I have a few interests besides horses. Anyway, if we do teach the wretched animals all this stuff the Major's so keen on, they'll only be mucked up by some feeble beginner."

"If beginners are properly taught they don't muck ponies up," protested Noel. "Anyhow, the idea was that the Pony Club members should learn to break and school."

"I believe it was, *partly*," said Richard. "But there was an ulterior motive, don't you worry. I bet the old Colonel wanted his ponies broken in cheap. But apart from that, if you can ride decently, you don't need to be taught—I mean it's obvious, there's nothing in it."

"I don't agree with you," said Noel. "I think there's a great deal in it."

"Oh, well," said Richard in a patronising voice, "I wasn't really including you. I mean, to put it frankly, you're not much of a rider, are you? Not that it's your fault. I dare say that if you could get hold of a decent pony, and if you were to ride for as many years as I have, you'd be quite reasonable." Noel felt herself go red with rage. She was filled with an almost overwhelming desire to smack Richard's pink, self-satisfied face, but she controlled it, and said instead, "The Major seems to think that Susan is good enough and she hasn't been riding more than two years." Richard looked up in surprise when he heard the angry note in her voice.

"Don't get in a bait just because I said you weren't all that good," he advised. "You weren't thinking of asking the Major if you could take over Romany?" He gave an

118

incredulous laugh, as though the mere thought was out of the question. Noel didn't reply. She couldn't trust her voice, and Richard said, "I shall ask my father to get the map in London. I'm not going to waste my time messing about here," and walked out of the shop.

Noel stood gazing with sightless eyes at *Sunshine Sayings, a book of moral verse by Pansy Paisley*. Her brain whirled furiously. I'd like to push him in a really stagnant pond, thought some outraged part of her; and she saw the pink face peering through a curtain of slime and the straw-coloured hair festooned with duckweed.

Ah, but why get in such a fury when he agrees with you? asked some cooler part of her annoyingly. You know you said you couldn't ask the Major about Romany because you weren't a good enough rider.

Yes, but there's no need for him to rub it in, replied the hot-headed part of her sulkily.

It was a little tactless, certainly, allowed the level-headed part, but nothing to get in a temper about. If you ask me, you had a sneaking feeling that you *were* good enough.

"Can I help you?" asked Mr. Bond in his high crackling voice.

"Oh," said Noel, jumping; "er—no, I mean—yes. Have you got *From Shetland to Show Hack*, by Colonel Archibald Snake, or *The Lane to Success*, by 'Clear Round'?" Mr. Bond peered round his shop, looking like a very elderly tortoise, and then said he was afraid he hadn't either work in stock, but that he would be pleased to order them. After some thought Noel decided to order *From Shetland to Show Hack*. When Mr. Bond had written down the particulars she walked into the street and continued her argument, gazing at the fascinating confusion of knives and tools in the ironmongers window.

It's no good losing your temper, the cool half of her told the other; you've got to face facts. Either you believe you ride well enough to break a pony, or else you're the sort of person who flies into petty tempers about nothing.

119

I can't go on like this, thought Noel. I shall go raving mad. I'll have to ask Major Holbrooke, and that'll settle it one way or the other. Filled with determination, she glanced at the Town Hall clock, and decided that she just had time to get to Folly Court and back before lunch.

At first Noel walked fast, whistling. But the nearer she drew to Folly Court the slower she walked; and when she reached the Towers she gave up whistling and began to feel cold and sick, as though she was going in for a horse show or some vital exam. As she walked through the gates she imagined the Major's scornful laugh and heard him say, Whatever put that fantastic idea into your head? I'm sorry, but I couldn't dream of it; I've my cousin and the pony to consider, and where Evelyn Radcliffe failed how can *you* hope to succeed?

Oh, thought Noel, stopping dead in her tracks, I'd better go back. But then she thought of Shelley, Van Gogh, Charles Goodyear, and Winston Churchill—they had all had horrid moments and they had all taken the plunge. She walked on, feeling herself grow smaller and smaller under the critical gaze of the eyes, which she was, quite wrongly, sure were looking from the tall Georgian windows of Folly Court. She knocked with the shining brass door-knocker. She waited. Nothing happened. She knocked again.

With her knees feeling weaker than ever, she crossed the rose garden and walked under the red brick archway into the stable yard.

Major Holbrooke was talking to a tall man in corduroy trousers, whom Noel recognised as Mr. Thomas, the vet.

"Well, thank you very much for coming."

"That's quite all right," said Mr. Thomas. "I don't think you'll have any more trouble with her, but I should certainly keep her on a light diet for a day or two."

"Good morning, Noel," said Major Holbrooke as he turned and caught sight of her hovering in the background.

"Good morning," replied Noel.

"Well, cheerio," said Mr. Thomas, and he got into his car and drove down the drive.

"A lovely day, isn't it?" said Major Holbrooke.

"Yes, it is a lovely day," she mumbled as she racked her brain for a way to get on the subject of Romany.

"Southwind has had a bad attack of colic," said Major Holbrooke, wondering why Noel had come to see him.

"I hope she's better," said Noel, wishing for an earthquake.

"Yes, she is, thank you," said Major Holbrooke. "But the routine of the stable has been upset; Blake had to spend most of the night with her, so he has gone to bed and left me in charge. I was in the middle of feeding when Thomas came. Have you seen our forage-room? It's really rather nice," and, picking up a bucket, he led the way to the long low building where the forage was kept.

"I came to ask you if I could have Romany," said Noel, taking the plunge. "I mean to school; but I suppose I'm much too bad a rider." Her voice trailed away, and she stood looking at her feet.

"Well, it's like this," said Major Holbrooke slowly as he seated himself on a corn-bin, "officially Romany was sent back because Evelyn let her younger brother and sister ride her, which, quite rightly, she had been forbidden to do, and, as I expect you know, James came off and broke his arm. But, besides this, Dr. Radcliffe told me that he didn't think Romany was going very well; he said she seemed far too excitable and that it was all Evelyn could do to control her. Now there's nothing vicious about her; she's a very nice-tempered little thing, and, personally, I think you should be able to manage her. You've improved a lot lately and you've a good deal of horse-sense. You must realise, though, that you'll have to put a good deal of work into her. It's not all fun reschooling a spoilt pony. But if your parents agree, and if you're quite sure you want to, you can try your hand with Romany."

"Oh, thanks awfully," said Noel. "Mummy has already
121

said I can have her if you think that I'm good enough."

Major Holbrooke got up from the corn-bin. "Have you a saddle and bridle?"

"No," said Noel, "not at the moment, but I can acquire them."

"There's no need to do that," said the Major. "I've got the tack which belonged to my youngest son's first pony. I'm keeping it for my grandchildren, it'll do it good to be used." When he had fed Gay Crusader and Harmony, Major Holbrooke led the way to the saddle-room, and produced a saddle and a bridle with a snaffle-bit. Then they walked down to the field where Romany was turned out. She looked lovelier than ever, thought Noel, in spite of being much too fat and covered with mud and grass stains. Her candid brown eyes shone, her absurd mane, half-chestnut and half-white, stood on end, and the neat white star on her otherwise chestnut forehead gave her a very intelligent expression.

As usual, Romany was delighted to see humans. She trotted up, whinnying. Noel slipped the halter on, and held her while Major Holbrooke saddled and bridled. Then he said, "Hop on and let's see how she goes." Noel felt that this was torture—to ride alone in front of the Major, the only object on which his critical eye could rest. She mounted, from the wrong side, and, marking out a school in her mind's eye, rode round it. Romany jogged and threw her head about, snatching the reins from Noel's hands. Noel forgot the Major while she tried to persuade her to walk, pulling her up when she jogged, and then, the moment she stopped, giving her a loose rein. After a little, Romany began to walk, and Noel circled and rode round the school the other way at a trot. Now Romany wanted to canter. She pulled and cantered sideways, throwing her head about worse than ever. Noel tried to calm her, but in vain, and after a few minutes the Major said, "I should canter her round for a bit—she hopelessly overfresh." Noel gave Romany her head; she shot forward into a

122

gallop and gave three bucks. Noel flew off.

Oh, I am feeble, she thought as she scrambled up. Now he'll say I'm not good enough to have her.

"Are you all right?" asked Major Holbrooke.

"Yes," said Noel firmly, and she mounted quickly so that he wouldn't have time to say she wasn't a good enough rider. This time she kept a feel on Romany's mouth, and when she started to buck, Noel pulled her head up and drove her on with her legs.

"Well done," said Major Holbrooke quietly. Noel cantered Romany round until suddenly the Major said, "Good heavens. It's a quarter-past one! We shall be unpopular. For goodness' sake go home, Noel, but ring up or come over if you get into difficulties. You know the way out through the farmyard, don't you?"

"Yes," said Noel. "Thanks awfully for letting me have Romany."

"The pleasure is entirely mine," said Major Holbrooke.

. . . . .

John slammed the green door of the square white farmhouse and ran down the flagged path to the farm buildings, muttering angrily beneath his breath. Three times he had been called back by his parents, and since he was already behindhand through breaking his resolution to get up early, he couldn't imagine how he was going to find time to ride both Jet and Turpin before lunch, and he had arranged to go bicycling with Michael Thorpington and Richard in the afternoon. John saddled Jet quickly and rode down to the Basset Bottom field, where he had put his jumps. At first all went well. Jet knew everything, and behaved perfectly until John rode her at the in-and-out, which he had made for Turpin the day before. She approached it warily. Snorting loudly and paying no attention to John's kicks, she stopped and peered nervously at the second fence. John looked at his watch, and knew he ought to fetch Turpin if he was to ride him before lunch. "Come on, can't you?" he said to Jet, "and stop fooling around." Hitting her

123

sharply, he turned and rode at the jump again. Once more she slowed up and refused. Then John lost his temper completely; he hit her with all his strength. Jet was terrified; she leaped about and tried to gallop off, but John jagged her in the mouth and went on hitting her. Unable to think of anything else to do, Jet reared. John hit her, and she reared again, this time higher, and John, who had taken his feet out of the stirrups, slid gently over her tail. He was furious. Seizing the reins, he began to belabour her from the ground. Jet whirled round and round, but John held her firmly and hit her harder than ever. Suddenly a voice shouted, "Hi! Stop that," and, looking up, John was horrified to see Major Holbrooke on Black Magic opening the gate to the field.

John's rage evaporated in a flash.

The Major came across the field at an extended canter. He looked furiously angry.

"What the devil do you mean by knocking a pony about like that?" he demanded as he pulled Black Magic up. "What do you think you're doing? You're not fit to be trusted with an animal if that's how you treat them."

"I'm awfully sorry," said John, and, trying to keep his voice steady, he said, "I'm awfully sorry, sir, but I lost my temper."

"You've no business to lose your temper," said Major Holbrooke sternly. "You're quite old enough to control it, and, if you can't, you oughtn't to have a pony. Anyway, why did you lose it?"

"Because she wouldn't jump the in-and-out," said John, looking at his feet.

"How many times have you jumped her over it before?" asked the Major.

"None," admitted John.

"And how many times did she refuse?" asked the Major.

"Twice," muttered John almost inaudibly.

"Twice!" said Major Holbrooke. "And you consider

that a reason to knock her about as you were doing when I came along? If your maths master, having taught you addition and subtraction, suddenly gave you a long division sum and told you to do it, and you said, 'What's this? How on earth does one do it?' and he, losing his temper, began to knock you about, I suppose you'd think that quite fair and just?"

"No," said John, "I wouldn't."

"And yet," said Major Holbrooke quietly, "that is exactly what you were doing to Jet." There was a silence, broken only by occasional sniffs from John—he didn't seem to have a handkerchief—until the Major said, "Do you think I ought to leave Jet with you? Dare I let her run the risk of it happening again?"

"Oh, please don't take her away," said John. "I won't do it again; honestly I won't."

"Have you ever done it before?" asked the Major.

How John would have liked to lie! He felt sure now that the Major would take Jet away, and he had never realised, until that moment, how fond of her he had grown. "Yes," he replied in a strangled voice. Major Holbrooke lit a cigarette and smoked thoughtfully for a few moments. Then he said, "It's not easy to learn to control your temper, and it's no good thinking you're going to do it in five minutes, but if you don't learn now it'll be more dangerous when you grow up, because you'll have more people and animals in your power. Look," he went on after a pause, "if I let you keep Jet, will you do your utmost? If she seems stupid when you're teaching her anything new, put yourself in her place—try to imagine how she is puzzling it out. But if you do feel yourself getting hot and bothered, dismount, tie her to the fence or something, and go away and look at the view until you cool down."

"Now get up and we'll see if we can get her over this in-and-out."

John mounted, and, following the Major's instructions, jumped Jet over the second of the two bars. She did this

125

without any fuss. Then he jumped the first bar, and the second one lying on the ground, and, finally, both at their original heights.

"You see," said Major Holbrooke, "she was worrying about the second bar, but when we showed her how to take it she jumped it perfectly. Now don't do it again, and I may as well tell you that I shall come round to have a look at you occasionally, so you'd better behave yourself."

Noel was rather embarrassed by Susan's delight when she rode into the stable yard at the Towers on Romany; especially as Susan seemed to take it for granted that the Major must think Noel a better rider than Evelyn. They argued about this for some time, and then Noel said, "Well, anyway, I'm positive I'm going to be bottom when it comes to the test, for Romany's terribly bad mannered."

"No one will blame you for that," said Susan. "That's Evelyn's fault."

It was true that Romany was bad mannered, and Noel, who found her hard enough to control by herself, soon found she was far worse with other ponies. She seemed to think that schooling with Sunset should be one long race. She pulled Noel's arms out, jogging when she should be walking, cantering sideways when she was meant to be trotting, and galloping wildly about the field when she was asked to canter. If Susan expected to have plenty of races and jumping contests now that Noel had a pony of her own, she soon found she was mistaken. Noel spent half the morning persuading Romany to walk on a loose rein and the other half trying to make her trot. By the end Noel had decided that until Romany was better mannered she would school her alone, but since Susan found riding by herself dull, Noel agreed to school Romany in the mornings, and go over to the Towers, as often as possible, to ride Beauty in the afternoons.

When the rally drew near, and Romany, though quieter, still couldn't walk over a pole on the ground, and simply

126

wouldn't dream of walking beside another pony out for a hack, Noel began to despair.

"What on earth shall I do?" she asked her mother. She's silly enough if I school her with Sunset, I just can't imagine how she's going to behave with twenty other ponies."

"Why don't you ring up Major Holbrooke and explain the trouble to him?" suggested Mrs. Kettering. "After all, he's the expert."

"Oh, I couldn't," said Noel. "He'd think I was awfully feeble—he'd probably think I was afraid."

"Nonsense," said Mrs. Kettering. "You're imagining things again, but if that's how you feel you may as well go to the rally; he'll tell you how to cure her."

"Well, my pet," said Mrs. Cresswell when she had read June's second postcard from Major Holbrooke asking her to bring Grey Dawn to a rally, "you'll have to give her some practice. I know that she's the best trained of the ponies, but you haven't ridden her for three weeks, you know, and you don't want to risk being made a fool of."

"I haven't had time to ride her," said June. "I can't waste hours schooling her while there's Wonder to keep up to the mark. It isn't as though I can enter her for any shows—I mean, she's not good looking enough for the showing classes and she can't jump well enough for even the under-thirteen-two jumping."

"Why don't you teach her to bend and potato race?" asked Mrs. Cresswell. "She's not of such an excitable temperament as Wonder, so she might do well."

"That's not a bad idea," said June. "I'll try her and see if she seems promising."

While June schooled Grey Dawn, she grumbled that the pony was too fat and out of condition, and when Mrs. Cresswell told her, in exasperation, that it was her own fault for not riding Dawn regularly, she sulked. She became crosser still when Dawn wouldn't change legs

127

behind, and said that she was wasting her time trying to school an ugly, common pony without a drop of blood, and that if Major Holbrooke's cousin had known the first thing about ponies he would have let Grey Dawn be sold for veal, which was all she was fit for.

Hilary lay on the nursery sofa. She had had to stop reading because her eyes felt queer, and, bored by solitude, she wondered impatiently how much longer she would have to wait for the return of her brothers and sisters. It was a shame, she thought, that Rocket's schooling should be completely upset through her catching 'flu. He had missed seven lessons, three hacks, and now the rally. Then, hearing the sound of hoofs she tottered across the room on her weak legs and sat down on the window seat. Soon Sky Pilot's head appeared through the archway, and then, some way behind as usual, for he walked too fast for them, came Darkie, Pixie, and Northwind. No one could have four nicer ponies, thought Hilary.

Margaret was the first person to get her pony settled for the night. She rushed into the nursery and said, "Something awful has happened, but I'm not allowed to tell you till the others come, but it really is the limit and we're all furious. Oh, I do wish they'd come. They are slow. I'll go and hurry them up." And she shot out of the room, leaving Hilary to imagine all the horrible things which could have happened. The ponies had looked all right, but perhaps the Major had said something about Rocket or Romany. At last she heard the sound of voices on the stairs.

Roger was evidently squashing Margaret. "It's a good thing we're not all slapdash speed-merchants like you," he was saying. "At least we have time to see that our ponies have plenty of water."

"What shall we do?" asked Evelyn, bursting into the room. "Noel Kettering's got Romany."

"What?" said Hilary, flabbergasted.

128

"Yes," said Roger. "Noel Kettering of all people."

Hilary said, "Do you mean that he's given Romany to Noel to school?"

"Apparently," said Evelyn. "But he must have been drunk or something."

"I bet she can't jump as high as I can," said Margaret.

"She'll ruin Romany," said Evelyn. "She couldn't control her at all."

"She was galloping all over the place," said James. "She nearly knocked Darkie over. I gave her a look."

"I should imagine that the Major's regretting it already," said Roger. "He kept taking Noel aside and explaining things to her."

"Yes, but it didn't seem to make much difference," said Evelyn, "and I'm sure that she's afraid of Romany. She didn't jump her over anything but a pole on the ground, and considering that she can clear three feet six, I thought it pretty feeble."

"I should think that Noel wishes she hadn't got her," said Margaret. "She was scarlet in the face the whole rally."

"But how do you suppose she got Romany?" asked Hilary. "Do you think she asked the Major?"

"I wouldn't put it past her," said Evelyn.

"It's an absolute insult," said Roger, "to take a pony from us and give it to a complete beginner like Noel."

"You should have seen June Cresswell's face," said Margaret.

"And June actually had the cheek to ask me if I'd been unable to manage Romany," said Evelyn indignantly. "I was furious. I gave her a frightfully disdainful look and said, very coldly, 'I never had the least difficulty in controlling her, I assure you, or I would certainly have asked for your valuable advice and assistance."

"You squashed her all right," said Margaret.

"Grey Dawn didn't behave too well," said Roger. "The Major gave June a long lecture. What was it about? Did

129

anyone listen? It sounded much too complicated for me."

"Oh, it was a lot of twaddle about collection," said Evelyn impatiently. "I could have told him that it was pointless to try to teach the ponies that from the start. It's such a waste of time when they'll never be show ponies. Anyway, June's gone and overdone it, which'll mean another good pony spoilt through too much theory."

Richard's mind was in a turmoil as he rode home, reliving the disasters of the day. They began on the way to Folly Court when Rufus cast a shoe, a fact which June had pointed out to everyone on his arrival. The sight of so many other ponies had upset Rufus completely, and he had done nothing but plunge and buck. That feeble Noel Kettering had made him ten times worse by continually getting in his way. One consolation was, thought Richard, that, in spite of falling off, he hadn't looked quite such a prize fool as Noel. He frowned angrily as he remembered the laughter which greeted him as he crawled out of the rhododendron bush into which Rufus had bucked him. Even Major Holbrooke had been grinning like an ape. He blushed as he thought of the time the other horse-breakers and Pony Club members would have discussing and tittering over Rufus' manners. It was all very well for them, thought Richard; *they* had everything in their favour and then they hadn't done so well as they had expected. June had had a nasty shock, for, though Grey Dawn knew a tremendous lot and could do passes, the Major had said that she overbent, and given June a long, boring lecture, to which no one, except Noel, had bothered to listen. Altogether it had been a beastly rally, and Richard wished that he had never had Rufus. He had spoilt the Christmas holidays, he was spoiling these holidays, and there was every sign that he would spoil the summer ones too. He rubbed his shoulder where he had fallen on it, and wondered how he could tactfully get rid of him. If he was going to ride he much preferred Peter, and he hadn't time

130

to ride both of them when Michael Thorpington was always inviting him to bicycling and bathing parties, which were much more fun than walking round and round the hen-run on a pony which might buck you off at any minute.

Noel spent the evening after the rally wallowing in the depths of despair. Romany had behaved worse than she had thought possible, and she had become so flustered that she had muddled the school work even more hopelessly than usual. Though Major Holbrooke hadn't said much more than "Keep calm," or "Don't lose your head," Noel felt sure that he had decided that she was unteachable, and that any day she would get a letter asking her to return Romany.

Mrs. Cresswell and June wrangled ceaselessly as they drove home, with Grey Dawn behind in the trailer.

"It's all very well for you to say that I should do this and that," said June when her mother complained that she hadn't used her legs enough. "You haven't tried Dawn. She's perfectly horrid: she's got a short stride, nothing in front, and a badly-joined-on head, and you expect me to make her go like a show pony. I bet that no one, not even Major Holbrooke, could make her go any better."

"Now, my pet," said Mrs. Cresswell, "don't be silly. I admit that Dawn's not much to look at, but it's no good laying all the blame on her. You know you haven't been schooling regularly—that's the trouble. You've been resting on your laurels, and you can't afford to do that, with all these children around chock-full of spite and jealousy. They're all out to beat you, and you really mustn't give them the satisfaction. It would be too humiliating, especially when it's just through slackness."

"It's not, Mummy," said June. "If I schooled that wooden-necked, cow-hocked, stupid animal every day for a year, she still wouldn't know as much as Wonder. She's common, and that's all there is to it."

John rode home from the rally feeling happier than he had for a long time. The Major had been agreeable, and had said that Jet had improved immensely, and that he could see that John was keeping his side of the bargain. John had felt terribly embarrassed. But still the Major was quite right; he hadn't lost his temper since that horrid day. It was also true that Jet had improved: she could jump grids and in-and-outs perfectly, she was much easier to keep straight than she used to be, and not nearly so nappy, besides being a faster walker and good at turns on the forehand. Susan had been much more friendly than usual, he thought, as he unsaddled Jet. She had invited him to tea at the Towers, and also to school Jet with Sunset and Romany, which John thought would be a nice change from riding alone.

CHAPTER IX

THE SUMMER TERM passed quickly. The horse-breakers who were at day schools devoted most of their spare time schooling their ponies in preparation for the Pony Club gymkhana.

Only the thought of boring Romany prevented Noel from schooling her every evening as well as at the weekends. She was determined to do better at the gymkhana than she had at the rally, and though she was often disheartened, she was, on the whole, pleased with her improvement. At first she had rather a dull time, riding round and round the school at the walk and trot. Then half-way through the term she began to canter and jump her. Jumping took a lot of patience, for Romany would get wildly excited and gallop about the field. But walking over a pole on the ground had a quietening effect, and gradually Noel was able to raise the jumps.

Richard came home from school with a new craze—architecture—everything had to be given up for it. Rufus was a bore, Major Holbrooke a pest, and the Pony Club a waste of time. When his mother lectured him on his lack of perseverance, he said that she wanted him to be a horsy nitwit like June Cresswell. Each morning he mounted his bicycle and pedalled off in search of Roman remains, Norman churches, or Gothic arches, and in the evenings he read guide-books to find more buildings of architectural interest. Every day he put off schooling Rufus until the next.

John, helping on the farm all day, generally schooled Jet in the evenings and it wasn't until the second week of the holidays that he found time to ride over to the Towers to practise with Noel and Susan.

They were schooling. Susan stopped at once. "We *must* have a jumping competition now that John's here," she told Noel.

"I want to compare Jet with your ponies," said John. "I'm sure she's miles behind and there's only ten days to catch up."

"Oh, don't talk about it," pleaded Noel, "I've got the most terrible needle already."

"You can't have it yet," said Susan.

"But I have," argued Noel. "And it comes on every night in bed. It's all very well for you, Sunset's reliable, but Romany's quite likely to turn into a maniac at the gymkhana."

"Come on," said John. "If we're going to jump, we'd better start."

Jet won the jumping contest with one refusal, Susan was second with four faults, while Romany had a knock-down and a circle. Then Susan and John decided to have some races, and Noel was persuaded to join in, against her better judgment. Romany became thoroughly over-excited: she kicked the bucket over in the potato race and refused to stop at the poles to allow Noel to grab the potatoes. In

the saddling-up race she galloped off, bucking with Noel half-on, and, of course Noel fell off. But, worst of all, she broke three of Susan's poles in the bending race.

John's and Susan's obviously tactful attempts to find excuses for Romany's bad behaviour made Noel feel more crestfallen than ever, and as she rode homewards she wondered what Major Holbrooke would say when Romany behaved like this at the gymkhana. His cousin would be there, she supposed, and all the people who usually judged, besides hundreds of spectators and competitors, and everyone would say pityingly that Noel Kettering would never make a horsewoman and that the Major must have been mad to let her have Romany. Probably the cousin would be so furious when he saw his best-looking pony completely ruined that he would have a terrific row with the Major there and then, and it would be all her fault.

There had been unpleasantness among the Radcliffes about their entries right up to the eve of the gymkhana. As they cleaned their tack they still argued.

"All you people think about is yourselves," complained Evelyn. "You don't care about the honour of the stable. I tell you Darkie won't be anywhere if Jim rides her; if he must enter why can't he have Rocket, Hilary? You know that he hasn't a chance either."

"I know," said Hilary, "but I still want to ride him and, even if Doc. would let him, Jim doesn't want to. Anyway it's a well-known fact that you shouldn't put an inexperienced pony and rider together and you couldn't have a less experienced pair than Jim and Rocket."

"Well, you jump both ponies," said Evelyn. "Jim's sure to fall off."

"I wouldn't dream of it," said Hilary. "Besides, what does it matter if he does come off? He's got to begin riding in shows some time, you know."

"Oh, all right then, have it your own way," said Evelyn

134

disagreeably. "But it'll mean another walkover for June."

"We shall survive that," said Roger.

"Do you think Pixie's got a chance?" asked Margaret.

"About as much as the rest of the family, which is none at all," said Evelyn.

"How can I clean my tack when there's no saddle soap?" asked Richard in a melodramatic voice as he flung himself despairingly on the drawing-room sofa.

"Well, who's fault is that?" asked his mother tartly.

"I suppose Jill finished it while I was away at school," said Richard. "How like a girl not to get any more!"

"I didn't finish it," said Jill. "I never cleaned Wendy's tack in the term. You threw the soap away in the middle of last holidays because you wanted the tin to boil glue in."

"Well, you ought to have cleaned Wendy's tack in the term, then we should have known that there wasn't any saddle soap," said Richard.

"I've cleaned Wendy's tack later than you've cleaned Peter's," said Jill. "You haven't cleaned his since the very beginning of the Easter holidays, and I did clean Wendy's half-way through."

"It's easier for you," said Richard. "You're a girl and girls like cleaning things. Anyway, you have much more time, and Wendy's tack is much easier."

"Girls don't like cleaning things," said Jill.

Mrs. Cresswell and June rose early on the morning of the gymkhana. Wilson, the groom-gardener, hadn't arrived when they went out to the stables, but they fed both the ponies and started to groom them. At least Mrs. Cresswell did. June's part in the proceedings was limited mainly to criticism of her mother's work. By eight o'clock, when Wilson came, Wonder had had her socks washed and Grey Dawn had been bathed, and they were left in his charge while Mrs. Cresswell and June had breakfast. Afterwards

Mrs. Cresswell plaited Grey Dawn, while Wilson body-brushed Golden Wonder and June watched.

"Oh, Mummy," she said when the first plait was finished, "it's all bristly. Look at those bits of hair sticking up."

"All right, my pet," said Mrs. Cresswell, "I'll undo it and try again presently."

"Mummy," wailed June when the second plait was finished, "they're so fat that they look like the Radcliffes' —simply awful."

"I know, darling," said Mrs. Cresswell patiently. "But her mane is so terribly thick; it's not like Wonder's."

"Beastly common animal," said June. "I'm glad it's not a big show. I shouldn't like to be seen dead on her by Priscilla Exemouth or the Fredericks."

"Nonsense, my pet," said Mrs. Cresswell. "There's nothing to be ashamed of. She's not your pony, and everyone knows that you only broke her in for fun."

"Well, after to-day I needn't ride her any more, thank goodness," said June. "I'll just get that red rosette on her bridle and then I'll say 'good riddance to bad rubbish' and send her back to the Major. He'll sell her to a complete beginner, which'll ruin her, but I shan't care; I'm never going to mount anything but a blood pony again."

"You're getting over-excited, my pet," said Mrs. Cresswell. "Would you like to go and lie down for a while?"

"Oh, Mummy," said June, "you are stupid. Of course I'm not over-excited; I'm not even excited over a potty little show like this one. I know that it'll be a walk-over for me, so what is there to get excited about?"

"Pride comes before a fall, they say," said Wilson.

The gymkhana, which was held in the park at Folly Court, started punctually. It was uncomfortably hot even at eleven o'clock, when the competitors for the first class, which was to decide which was the best trained of the New Forest ponies, walked into the ring. June, as usual, led the way. Thanks to Mrs. Cresswell's washing, Grey Dawn's

136

coat was dazzling. Her plaits, in spite of June's criticisms, were the best in the class, and her tack had been cleaned up by Wilson. But something was lacking. Grey Dawn did not step out proudly to show off her smartness, nor were her ears pricked, or her eyes alive with interest. She dawdled, and each time June kicked her, with the heel on the side that the judges couldn't see, she swished her tail; she had been schooled five or six days a week since the rally, when June had made her mother "feel a fool." Close behind Grey Dawn walked Jet. John's arms still ached from the grooming, and his fingers were sore from the pricks they had got as he plaited her, but it was worth it; and he felt justly proud.

Richard followed John. Beside the other ponies Rufus looked very untidy. His mane was unplaited, and there were several burrs in his tail. Sweating from the gallop Richard had given him to get his back down, with his head low and his eyes dull and sulky, he was a forlorn sight, and looked more like an old pony than a young one. Rocket was a striking contrast: his golden coat shone like a ripe cornfield, and his plaits were only second in neatness to Grey Dawn's. He walked briskly, looking about him with pricked ears and an air of complete confidence. After Rocket came Sunset. Her coat shone, but not with such brilliance. Her plaits were lumpy, and one was already coming unsewn, but her tack was clean and shining. Her broad blaize gave her a look of placid contentment which was not belied by her manner. Last of all, and quite a long way behind the others, came Romany. She was excited; she wouldn't walk, but jogged and went sideways. Noel was becoming more hot and bothered with every moment. "Walk, Romany, walk," she muttered, wishing that such things as gymkhanas did not exist. But Romany felt too excited to walk. Her rich chestnut parts shone, her white parts sparkled as she bounced round the ring.

Major Holbrooke, Colonel Shelbourne, and the three judges, Lady Wrench, Captain Barton, and Sir William

Blount, stood in the middle of the ring. The spectators hurried to the ringside to see the fruits of the horse-breakers' labours, and the gymkhana had really begun.

Good gracious, thought Mrs. Cresswell, some of them *have* come on. June *must* be careful, and she felt quite ill as she saw how unwillingly Grey Dawn was going.

"Doesn't Rocket look lovely?" said James Radcliffe.

"Much the nicest pony there," agreed Margaret.

"There's Romany," said Evelyn. "She looks quite different. But why *is* Noel hanging back? She ought to be in the lead. Wait for the others to come round again," she shouted to Noel as she passed. "You *must* take the lead."

"O.K.," said Noel, pulling Romany up and waiting. June was annoyed when she saw what Noel was doing, though it was to her advantage, for Dawn was nappy and followed better than she led. Once Romany was in the lead she settled down and walked out with her longest stride, peeping coyly at the judges to see if they were admiring her. The order to trot was given.

Jet was going well, thought John. Of course he hadn't a chance, but he felt sure that Major would be pleased with her, and that, after all, was the main thing.

"Canter on," said one of the judges. All the competitors remembered the aids, and all the ponies, except Rufus, who had never been taught, remembered what they meant. Suddenly the people at the back of the line found themselves overtaking the ones in front. Romany and Grey Dawn cantered too slowly for the rest of them. Rufus put his head down and started to pull—he galloped, passed everyone, and took the lead. John, Hilary, and Susan passed Noel and June. Soon they were told to walk, and then they were all called into the centre. They lined up in no particular order, though June was careful to put herself at the top. Noel was between Susan and Hilary.

"I got Sunset on the right leg," Susan told her joyfully. "She was going awfully well. How did you get on?"

"Not too badly," said Noel. "Romany was rather
138

excited at first, but she's calmed down now."

Captain Barton came up to ask June to give a show. Now I'll surprise them, thought June. She hadn't paid much attention to the other competitors, but she felt sure that they had made fools of themselves as usual, and, full of confidence, she gave Grey Dawn a kick and rode out from the line. Grey Dawn wanted to be nappy. She edged towards the other ponies, but June kicked her into a canter and rode a figure of eight. Though Dawn dropped her nose and flexed her lower jaw, she did it without energy or impulsion. Her hocks trailed out behind her, and when June gave her the aid to change legs she only changed in front.

"Disunited!" said Noel in surprise.

June pulled up and backed.

"Her head's too low," said Susan.

"Yes," said Hilary. "I believe it is. In fact she looks over-bent to me." John, who was next in the line, wracked his brain for an original show. Richard hit Rufus, who was trying to graze.

"What is she trying to do now?" asked Hilary as Grey Dawn ran backwards across the ring.

"A turn on the haunches, I think," said Noel.

"Well, it doesn't look much like one," said Susan. "Not that I shall do any better." June finished her show by riding passes at the trot, but Grey Dawn was behind the bit, which spoiled them completely.

"Next, please," shouted Captain Barton as June cantered back to her place.

"It's me," said John, riding forward.

"Good luck," said Susan. John gave a watery grin as he trotted off. He cantered a circle to either hand, pulling up to change legs in the middle. He reined back, turned on the forehand, dismounted and mounted. Jet stood perfectly, and finally jumped the brush fence very neatly.

"That was good," said Hilary in a surprised voice, and she tried to think of some more things for Rocket to do.

Richard was supposed to follow John, but Rufus didn't want to leave the other ponies, and each time Richard got him away he charged back with his mouth open and his head down. Richard's face became red with rage and exertion as he tugged at the reins and kicked furiously. But he was unable to get Rufus under control, and after a few minutes Sir William waved to him to stop, and called for the next person.

Susan, who followed Richard, started badly. Flustered, because she was called sooner than she had expected, she gave a terrific kick. Sunset leaped forward into a canter. Susan looked for the leading leg and cantered a circle on it, then she pulled up to canter on the other leg. Unfortunately, Sunset didn't change, but cantered gaily round until Noel shouted to Susan as she passed, she pulled up and started again. Afterwards she turned on the forehand and backed. Now it was Noel's turn. As she had watched the other horse-breakers' shows, she gradually became sure that hers was too difficult. "You've bitten off more than you can chew," she told herself. But it was too late to make any alterations.

She rode forward and suddenly her needle disappeared. Conscious of her audience, Romany broke into her most elegant trot. She circled neatly, led smoothly into the canter and, looking as though she'd spent a lifetime in the show-ring, made a shapely figure of eight with two well-balanced changes of leg. She reined back, she circled and jumped the triple fence. She walked back on a loose rein with a smug expression on her face. Noel felt like hugging her, but had to make do with a dignified pat. Hilary had felt fairly confident until she had seen Noel's performance. Now she trotted out from the end of the line, feeling sure that, however well Rocket went, she could only be second. She walked a circle, cantered a figure of eight, she turned on the forehand, reined back, and started straight off into a canter. To finish, she jumped the stile.

"Well done," said Susan as Hilary came back.

"Thank goodness it's over," said Hilary.

"I do wish they'd hurry up," said Susan.

"I can't imagine what Noel's done to her," said Evelyn, of Romany, to her family. "She looks quite different— like a show pony. Honestly, I can hardly believe my eyes."

"She goes just like one of Major Holbrooke's horses," said Margaret. "But I'm sure Noel can't have schooled her."

Mrs. Cresswell stood by her car at the ringside, twisting her fingers together in suspense. In her heart she knew that June had lost, but it was too late now to do anything. The things that might have made a difference flitted through her mind in a mournful procession. But the horrid fact remained: the only thing now that could make the judges award June the first prize would be force of habit. As she watched Noel, Hilary, and John lined up, Mrs. Cresswell felt furious. It was only spite, she thought, that had urged them to improve their riding.

No one was more surprised than Noel herself when Lady Wrench handed her the red rosette and as Hilary was given the blue rosette and John the yellow, it gradually dawned on Noel that she had won the best trained of the New Forest ponies' class.

"Well done, you three," said Major Holbrooke when Lady Wrench had finished presenting the rosettes. "I'm very pleased with you. This is my cousin, Colonel Shelbourne," he added, and, pushing him forward, "Go on, Harry, say something." Cousin Harry, who was a kindly looking man, in spite of his soldierly figure and walrus moustache, seemed rather nervous. "By jove," he began, and the Pony Club members hastily riveted their attention on their ponies' ears and tried not to giggle. "You've done wonders, all of you. If every child's pony was as well trained as these, we'd have a great many better riders. I don't know all the ins and outs of schooling myself, but I do know a well-schooled pony when I see one, and I've seen three to-day. I hope that you will never forget the

lessons which you have learned from these ponies and my cousin, and that you will all break and school many more ponies and horses just as successfully." The Colonel mopped his brow as he finished speaking, and, turning to Major Holbrooke, said, " 'Fraid I'm not much of an orator, George, but I hope that will do."

"Yes," said Major Holbrooke, "an excellent speech; you covered everything, and now I am sure that the children would like me to thank you for entrusting us with your ponies."

"Yes, rather," said Hilary and Susan.

"Gosh, yes," said John.

"Thanks awfully," said Noel. Richard and June didn't say anything. Neither of them ever wanted to see a New Forest pony again.

"Well, I think that's everything," said Major Holbrooke, "so perhaps we could go on to the next event."

Noel led the canter round the ring and Romany went beautifully. Her gay carriage and shining skewbald coat earned her extra applause from the spectators. Once out of the ring, all the horse-breakers, except Noel, hastily mounted their own ponies, for the next event was the showing class for ponies under 14.2.

"I'm determined not to go on the wrong leg this time," Susan told Noel as they waited in the collecting ring. "I let Sunset down, but I mustn't do the same to Beauty."

"It might have happened to anyone," said Noel. "And, if you ask me," she went on, "winning is mostly luck."

"Oh yeah," said John. "Do you know what Mrs. Cresswell's telling everyone?" he asked. "That she understood that the ponies were to be made suitable for tiny tots and she 'can't think' how Romany won.' "

"And didn't June look furious?" said Susan. "I'm sure she expected to win."

"Oh, dear," said Noel. "Do you think it was really unfair?"

"Of course not," said John.

142

"Will class two come into the ring at once, please, instead of gossiping?" shouted the collecting steward.

Said Noel, "Where's June? She always leads."

"Go on, Noel, you idiot," shouted Evelyn from behind —she was showing Northwind. Collecting her scattered wits, Noel rode into the ring, but before she had gone far Captain Barton began to shout and wave his arms.

"What did you say?" Noel shouted back.

"Go round to the right," he shouted again.

"The opposite way, you idiot," said Evelyn. Behind, half the competitors had turned round and were going the other way. Pixie and Martin Minton's pony, Sir Galahad, were having a kicking match.

Noel felt very depressed. Oh, dear, she thought. Of course one always goes round this way in a showing class. Why did Evelyn make me lead? She might have known that I would only do something silly.

"Wake up, Noel," said Evelyn's voice. "He said trot on."

The judges soon collected a long back row, and when there were only seven competitors left cantering round, they called them in and told them to line up.

"Is this the back row?" Noel asked Richard, who was beside her.

"Of course not," he said. "Use your eyes. Can't you see that June's here?"

June and Golden Wonder gave an excellent show, and Susan, who followed them, changed legs perfectly. Charles French riding Mrs. Maxton's Billy Boy, and Felicity Rate on Tinker, were both hopeless. No one could understand what they were trying to do. Mary Compton's weak seat spoiled Blackbird's chance as usual; then it was Noel's turn. Once more she rode a figure of eight, passes, and reined back; once more Romany behaved beautifully.

Richard was the last person to give a show. Surprisingly, he rode Peter—who was rather lazy—well, and put up a far better performance than Charles French.

It seemed to the competitors that the judges talked endlessly before they made up their minds. Then, to everyone's amazement, Susan and Beauty were placed above June, and Noel crept up to third, while Richard was reserve. Susan's delight knew no bounds. She patted Beauty profusely and thanked Lady Wrench for her rosette three times. Noel didn't dare look at June. She felt sorry for her. It must be awful, she thought, to lose one's assured position so abruptly. Meanwhile Lady Wrench had asked her twice whether Romany had ever been to a gymkhana before.

"No, I don't think so," said Noel, suddenly realising that she was being spoken to. "At least—I mean—I know she hasn't."

"I think she does you great credit, then," said Lady Wrench as she handed Noel the yellow rosette. "You ought to be proud of her."

"Thanks awfully," said Noel, going scarlet in the face.

During the lunch interval the mistakes and surprises of the morning were discussed.

"I told you that it would happen," said Mrs. Cresswell to June. "They've made you look a fool—to be beaten at a little show like this when you've won at *Wembley.*"

"Well, you can ride Wonder at the next show if you think that you can make her beat Beauty," said June. "It's not *my* fault that Mr. Barington-Brown is richer than you are and can buy Susan a better pony than Wonder."

"But riding must count, my pet," said Mrs. Cresswell.

"I expect the judges favoured Susan, then," said June. "Probably Mr. Barington-Brown bribed them."

"You mustn't say things like that, however likely they seem," said Mrs. Cresswell. "And, though I admit that the result of the showing class left room for doubt, the class for the New Forest ponies didn't. That dreadful Kettering child—who *still* hasn't got a riding coat—had the skewbald going like a show hack, and though John Manners didn't do anything spectacular, his pony knew

what it did know thoroughly. But you, my pet, I really was disappointed. Running backwards, cantering disunited, and Grey Dawn's head carriage was just appalling—there's no other word for it. We shall be the laughing-stock of the whole county."

"Nonsense, Mummy," said June rudely. "Why should anyone laugh? I can't help it if Grey Dawn is so stupid. After all, you were there and helped choose her."

"That sort of talk won't get us anywhere," said Mrs. Cresswell. "The only thing you can do is to take care to win the jumping this afternoon and do better at the next show."

Dr. Radcliffe was greeted by shouts from Margaret when he arrived on the show ground with the lunch. "Romany was first and Rocket second," she yelled. "But I bet Major Holbrooke helped Noel."

"I thought that he helped everyone," said Dr. Radcliffe, and turned to congratulate Hilary. Just as they were about to begin their lunch, the Radcliffes discovered that Evelyn was missing and Roger noticed her riding Romany on the other side of the ring.

"Oh," said Margaret, "do you think she asked Noel for a ride? She is a nuisance. We wanted to have a blood feud, didn't we, Jim?"

"Yes," said James. "We had thought of nine different ways to murder her."

Passing Evelyn on the way out of the ring Noel had stopped to thank her for her instructions, without which she might easily have made a mess of things.

"Oh nonsense," said Evelyn. "But you always will creep about at the back and Romany goes miles better in the lead. But what I want to know is how you improved her so much between the last rally and to-day?"

"Well, I can ride in the evenings as well as at the week-ends," explained Noel.

"But just riding wouldn't have made that difference," said Evelyn. "I mean what schooling?"

145

"Round and round the school mostly, trying to get to go quietly," answered Noel. "Millions of circles. And then, just when I thought she was never going to improve, she did."

"It sounds easy," said Evelyn. "But of course it isn't. It's queer, you suddenly coming out like this—it seems such a short time ago that you were falling off Topsy every other minute. You've certainly surprised everyone. They say that Mrs. Cresswell is furious."

"Oh, dear," said Noel, and then, a happy thought striking her, "Look, would you like a ride on Romany?"

"I should love one," said Evelyn. Noel handed her the reins and she mounted. It was with some trepidation that Noel watched her; she knew that it was conceited to think that other people couldn't control Romany as well as she could, but she did hope that Evelyn wouldn't excite or upset her, for she still had three events—jumping, bending, and musical poles—to enter for. However, Evelyn didn't do anything that could have upset the most highly-strung of show ponies; she had never ridden a well schooled pony before, and she was interested to discover what it felt like. After she had walked, trotted, and cantered Romany round, she rode up to Noel and said, "You've certainly improved her."

"She looks lovely with you. I wish she went as well for me," said Noel wistfully.

"Don't be a goose," said Evelyn. "Of course she does, or you wouldn't have won." But secretly she hoped that Noel was right. It took some of the sting out of being no good at breaking and schooling to think that one could show a pony to greater perfection than the poor wretch who had spent months of toil doing the schooling. Aloud she said, "I'd better go now or my family will be wondering where I've got to, or, worse still, eating my share of the lunch. Thanks for the ride."

"Not at all," said Noel. Mrs. Kettering wasn't coming to watch until later in the afternoon, so Noel ate her lunch

146

sitting beside Romany, and wishing that she had four brothers and sisters and could ride like Evelyn.

"Oh, Daddy, wasn't Beauty good?" said Susan. "Didn't she go marvellously?"

"It was nice to see my little girl in the front row," said Mr. Barington-Brown. "But I always knew you'd get there. I've told mother time and time again that you'd do it one day. Haven't I, Mother?"

"Now then, Albert, you'll make Susan too big for her boots," said Mrs. Barington-Brown. "If she was as good at her lessons I'd be better pleased."

"You can't talk about lessons in the holidays, Mummy," said Susan. "And anyway, I shan't get a swelled head. I know that it's Beauty who does it."

"Come on, now, don't talk so much, but eat some lunch," said Mrs. Barington-Brown, handing out paper napkins and cold chicken.

"I'm sure," said Susan between the mouthfuls, "that I'm going to fall off in the jumping."

Colonel Manners was quite delighted over John's success in the best-trained pony class. "I always knew the boy had it in him," he had told Mrs. Manners at least three times while John was being given his rosette. "Perhaps he has learned something from Holbrooke after all."

"John has certainly changed a good deal lately," said Mrs. Manners. "He's much quieter with the animals, and not nearly so thoughtless of other people's feelings."

"He's growing up, my dear," said the Colonel. "St. Philips is knocking the rough edges off him. It's always the same with boys. I ought to know, I was a boy once."

At lunch, John would only say that Jet had behaved wonderfully, and that he had only done what "old Holbrooke" had told him. But he found it very pleasant, though a little embarrassing, to sit between his proud parents and be thoroughly approved of for a change.

The Morrissons' lunch-time conversation was even more disagreeable than the Cresswells'. The only consolation for Richard's complete failure was, in Mrs. Morrisson's eyes, that June hadn't won anything either in the best-trained pony class. But she said it was obvious that Rufus was the worst-trained of the ponies, if, indeed, he was trained at all. Richard said that Rufus was a brute, and had simply been playing him up. And Jill said that Richard always blamed his ponies, when all the time it was his own fault for not schooling them.

The judges had an excellent lunch at Folly Court, and they were all in the best of tempers when they returned to the ring at two o'clock. Class three was the senior jumping competition, in which there was no height limit for horses, but their riders had to be between fourteen and twenty-one years. There was a good entry, for the Pony Club possessed quite a number of older members, and though few of them came to rallies, they hunted and rode in the annual gymkhana. David Gore-Simmonds, the first competitor, was one of these, and there were loud comments from the regular attendants at rallies about his backward seat. He rode a lovely chestnut mare from Ireland, which jumped well, despite his riding, but made four faults—at the wall. Robert Penn, Clarrissa's elder brother, who jumped next on a huge grey hunter, scattered everything, and, when the course had been repaired, Anthony Rate refused the first jump three times. Some of Mrs. Maxton's pupils followed him, but none of their rounds was spectacular. Dick Hayward had one refused on his fourteen hand, sixteen-year-old pony, Crispin, but Roger, who was the next competitor, jumped a clear round. The Radcliffes were beside themselves with delight, but this was damped when, a few minutes later, Diana, the youngest of the Meltons, also made a faultless round. Then there were only two competitors left. One was Valentine Dale, a thin girl with fair plaits and sticking-out teeth. She was galloped out of

the ring by her cob, Bounce, which surprised everyone, as he was professionally turned out in bandages and a hood, and there was a rumour that he had won a high-jump competition. Last of all was Mary Compton. She had two refusals at the first jump, and then, when Blackbird jumped it, she fell off and lay groaning in the ring. The first-aid party, which had been longing for something to happen, rushed to her rescue, but they were annoyed to find that she wasn't hurt. When Mary had been removed from the ring and told not to make a fuss by the doctor in charge, the judges called Roger's and Diana's numbers. They were told to jump the whole course, which had been raised, and the excitement was terrific as Roger rode at the first jump.

"He *must* do another clear round," said Margaret.

"He's over that one," said James. "Now steady."

"And the gate," said Margaret, jumping about in her excitement.

"He'll hit the wall; he's sure to," said James. "It's enormous." But Roger and Sky Pilot didn't hit the wall; they cleared everything until they came to the triple.

"Four faults," said James with a groan as it fell.

"Diana mustn't do a clear round," said Margaret. "Come on, Jim, will her to knock the gate." In spite of James' and Margaret's willing, Diana cleared the gate, but she had two refusals at the wall. The Radcliffes were overjoyed; they clapped their brother as he, Diana, Dick and David Gore-Simmonds, rode in for their rosettes.

"I'm awfully glad that Dick's won something," said Hilary.

"Class four in the collecting ring, please," shouted the collecting steward. "Jumping for ponies under fourteen-two, riders under fourteen years."

"Noel's teeth were chattering as she obeyed. This was much worse than anything that she had done before —worse than showing classes, or exams.

"It's sporting of you to enter Romany for the jumping," Evelyn told her. "You haven't a chance, have you?"

"No," said Noel, "not the slightest chance."

"Hilary's entered Rocket," said Evelyn. "She hasn't a hope either."

"It's nice to think I've someone to keep me company," said Christopher, the eldest of the Mintons. "I've been schooling Mousie for ages, but I'm sure that we're going to refuse the first jump three times."

"I bet I do a better round than you, Charles," said Pat French to his brother.

"I bet my lucky coin to your South African stamp that you don't," said Charles.

"Why don't they start?" asked Susan. "I've got the most awful needle."

"So have I," said Noel. "And I know that I'm going to let Romany down."

"Hallo, Clarrissa," said Hilary. "We're all expecting you to do a clear round."

"I'm afraid Sweet William isn't jumping very well," said Clarrissa. "I think I'm getting too heavy for him—if only I wasn't so fat. I weighed nine stone thirteen at the end of term. Isn't it ghastly?"

James Radcliffe sat on Darkie without saying a word. His face became greener with each moment. He felt that the honour of the stable was at stake. He must get round.

"For goodness' sake tighten your girths, Jim," said Roger. "They're frightfully loose."

"Mummy," said June, "tighten my curb chain and take off my tail bandage."

"All right, my pet," said Mrs. Cresswell. "Now mind you take the double slowly. Nearly all the riders in the last class took the corner too fast."

"Yes, I saw," said June. "But they've no idea how to ride over a course, in spite of all the hunting they do."

"I do hope that none of the other children do a clear round," said Mrs. Cresswell. "They've improved so much that you really must take care, my pet."

"Mummy," said June, who wasn't listening, "do ask the

collecting steward if I can go first. I don't want the take-off spoiled by everyone refusing. You know what it's like at Pony Club Gymkhanas."

"Yes, darling, I will," said Mrs. Cresswell. "Just a moment." Collecting stewards invariably gave in to Mrs. Cresswell, so June was the first competitor. As she cantered down to the start people pointed her out to each other. "She'll win. She always does," they said. Or, "There's the Cresswell girl; she's sure to do a clear round." Mrs. Cresswell was tense with suspense as June rode at the first jump —the usual brush fence. She cleared it easily, and also the gate. Mrs. Cresswell sighed with relief as June increased her pace for the parallel bars, and again as she steadied Wonder for the double. The stile, wall, and triple were all straightforward, and in a few moments June had done a clear round. The spectators clapped, Mrs. Cresswell relaxed, and there was an unsporting silence from the collecting ring.

"Next competitor, Hilary Radcliffe on Rocket," said the collecting steward."

"Good luck, Hilary," shouted the other competitors.

Rocket shied at the jumps as he cantered down to the start, and when Hilary rode him at the brush fence he slowed up and refused. Evelyn groaned.

Hilary patted him and said, "That's all right, old man, have a look—it's only a jump." Rocket sniffed the brush fence, and then, to the amusement of the crowd, he began to eat the gorse. Hilary turned him and rode at it again. This time Rocket knew what she wanted. He approached the fence slowly and cat-jumped, unseating Hilary slightly; but in spite of being ridden most determinedly, he refused again at the gate. Once more Hilary made him inspect the jump, and once more he cleared it easily the second time.

"She's out of it now," said Evelyn. Rocket cleared the parallels, but knocked the second part of the double. He jumped the rest of the course without mishap. Evelyn was the next competitor and Northwind, careless as usual, just

tipped the stile. Christopher Minton followed Evelyn. He fell off three times, but everyone clapped because he finished the course. As he rode out of the ring, grinning broadly and patting Mousie, he shouted, "I never expected to get round," to the people who were still waiting in the collecting ring. Felicity Rate, like Anthony, had three refusals at the first jump, and, as the relieved Tinker cantered briskly out, Clarrissa Penn came in to jump a clear round on Sweet William. Everyone applauded wildly except Mrs. Cresswell.

The Frenches jumped next, and Pat lost his South African stamp. Simon Wentwood and Rusty jumped a good round until they came to the triple, where they refused three times; and then James Radcliffe's number was called. He rode into the ring with a set expression, ignoring the cries of "Good luck" from sympathetic people who knew that it was his first show. Darkie jumped the brush fence and the gate in fine style, but James didn't ride her fast enough at the parallel bars, and they fell behind her. She cleared all the straight fences, but, again, James let her take the triple too slowly. "Eight faults," said Hilary. "Well that's not too bad for his first show."

"Go on, Marga," said Evelyn. "Good luck!" Margaret had expected to have fewer faults than James, but, where he rode too slowly she rode too fast, and taking off haphazardly, she brought down the parallels and stile.

At last, thought Susan, when her number was called. "Come on, Beauty," she said and they cantered up the ring. They cleared the brush fence and the gate, but crashed the parallel bars. Susan remembered to steady Beauty for the double, and they made a lovely jump over both them and the stile. But Beauty didn't like the look of the wall. Oh, golly, thought Susan, I mustn't refuse. She rode at it using every ounce of energy that she possessed. Beauty flew over. Susan patted her and turned for the triple. They cleared that too, and galloped out of the ring. Richard followed Susan, but his round was not a

good one. He had two refusals—at the gate and at the wall—as well as crashing the parallel bars, which were becoming rather battered in appearance. Michael Thorpington, who jumped next, had even more faults than Richard. John had to wait while the stewards mended the wall, and then he rode into the ring, trying to feel calm and confident. "We must do a good round," he told Turpin as he turned him for the brush fence, and evidently Dick Turpin decided to oblige, for, to Mrs. Cresswell's horror, he cleared everything.

"I've never seen Turpin jump so well," said Hilary as he rode out.

"It's the forward seat," said John.

"Is number forty-six here?" asked the collecting steward.

"Will number forty-six come at once," bellowed the collecting steward, wishing that he had not let Major Holbrooke persuade him to take this tiresome job.

"Noel, you're forty-six," said Evelyn. "Half-asleep as usual," she said to Hilary. Noel rode hastily into the ring.

"Why can't you attend?" asked the collecting steward crossly. "I've been calling you for about half an hour."

"I'm awfully sorry," said Noel.

"That *is* a nice pony," said Sir William.

Noel wished that she hadn't entered for the jumping as, with her heart in her mouth, she rode at the brush fence. Never had a jump looked so formidable, and the nearer she drew, the taller it seemed to become. Romany, who was nervous too, jumped high into the air, clearing the brush by nearly a foot, and unseating Noel, who was unable to get back into the saddle in time to ride her at the gate, which she refused. But, second try, Romany flew over, and cantered on to clear the parallel bars, the double and the stile. Now Noel was really enjoying herself. The jumps had shrunk to a reasonable height, and she felt she could go on flying over them for ever. They jumped the triple perfectly, and galloped out of the ring amid applause from everyone who knew that Romany was

153

one of the New Forest ponies. In the collecting ring the Pony Club members patted Romany. The judges called for June, Clarrissa and John to jump off. Everyone agreed that the course was now enormous, just as big as in the senior jump-off. June looked cool and collected as she rode to the start. Her mother was making frantic signals from the ring-side, but she ignored them. She took the brush fence and gate slowly and carefully, but she didn't increase her speed enough for the parallels and Wonder just couldn't clear them, spoiling an otherwise faultless round. Sweet William found the whole course too high, he had three fences down. "Bad luck," shouted the Pony Club members regretfully, they knew now that June would win. The jumps loomed and leered at John as he waited at the start, but Turpin seemed fresh and eager to be off which gave him confidence. "Come on, boy," he said as he rode at the first jump. They cleared it and the gate and the parallels; John's spirits soared. They nipped neatly over the double, steadied for the wall, turned for the triple. John strained every nerve to get the take-off right. Turpin was pulling, but he held him back, gradually letting him gain speed. Three strides away he let him go, they soared into the air, and by the clapping John knew that they had cleared it. He jumped off Turpin as soon as they were out of the ring, and gave him all the oats and bread that he had in his pockets.

"He *did* jump well," said Susan.

The collecting steward called John's, June's, Clarrissa's, and Noel's numbers, and the first three who were expecting the summons rode into the ring. "Number forty-six," shouted the collecting steward again. "Noel," shrieked everyone as they recognised her number.

"You're fourth," said Susan. "Quick!"

John was feeling very pleased with himself. He had remembered to take his hat off to Lady Wrench, and she had said that she thought Turpin jumped in such good style. June felt furious; she hadn't a single red rosette, and

154

for her the show was over. Clarrissa thought how good
Sweet William had been. She was sure that he would have
won but for her being so fat and heavy. When Noel had
been given her rosette, they cantered round the ring, and
John was most indignant because June galloped past him
and took the lead though she was only second.

There was a short interval for tea while the bending
poles were being put up and the judges for the gymkhana
events took over. The bending, for which, as usual, there
was a very large entry, took a long time. But the collecting
steward put Noel into the first heat before, he said, she
had a chance to disappear or go to sleep. She was against
Christopher Minton and Charles French. Romany went
fearfully fast, too fast, and she knocked down the last
pole but one. Christopher was slow and Charles won easily.

"Bad luck, Noel," said Susan. "But you don't need any
more rosettes."

"She's been marvellous," said Noel. "But the show's
nearly over," and she rode sadly away to find her mother.

She found her talking to the Major and his cousin.

"Ah, here she is," said Major Holbrooke, looking
round. We were just discussing your prize," he told Noel.
"My cousin's had a brainwave."

"I don't know that I'd call it that," said Cousin Harry,
"but I'm delighted with this little skewbald—really
delighted. But to keep to the point, the Major wouldn't
let me decide on the prize; he said I was to wait and see
who won it. Well, now, it seems that you haven't a pony
of your own, and I have an unbroken four-year-old—
fourteen hands—which I found in dreadful condition just
recovering from strangles. I had to buy her, but ever since
I've been at my wits' end to know what to do with her,
now your mother's agreed that I can give her to you."

"Give her to me?" asked Noel, quite incredulous. "Oh,
I should love her."

"Well, that's settled then," said Cousin Harry. "And
you needn't worry about Romany; Sir William's made me

a very good offer for her. He's determined to have her for his little daughter. She sounds a sporting kid, eh, George?"

"Definitely," said Major Holbrooke. "Romany couldn't have a better home."

"This new pony of yours," said Cousin Harry. "She's dapple grey, and she may be quite nice looking when she fattens up, but at the moment she looks ghastly—quite frankly, ghastly; but nothing to what she did when I bought her. However, if you give her plenty to eat and don't ride her too hard at first she'll soon pick up."

"There's one condition about having her," said Major Holbrooke.

"What's that?" asked Noel quickly, hoping that it was nothing to shatter the wonderful plans which she was already making.

"That you help me re-school Rufus and Grey Dawn," said Major Holbrooke.

"Grey Dawn?" said Noel. "But I couldn't possibly improve her. I mean, June's taught her an awful lot. She could change legs in the Easter holidays."

"Small wonder she's behind the bit now," said Major Holbrooke. "But do you agree to the condition?"

"If you really want me to," said Noel.

Some time later, when Evelyn, Hilary, and Margaret came out of the ring with their rosettes for the musical poles, they were greeted by shrieks from James. "Oh, Hilary," he shouted, "isn't it wonderful? Doc.'s bought Rocket."

"Bought Rocket?" asked Hilary. "Are you sure, Jim?"

"Yes, I was there," said James. "Look, there he is, still talking to Colonel Shelbourne. He said that Rocket would do for Andrew when the rest of us got too big."

"Oh, how marvellous," said Hilary.

"But who's Andrew?" asked Susan.

"Well, we're not sure he is Andrew until he arrives," explained Hilary. "But we're hoping for another boy to even things up. If it's a girl it may be Frances."

156

John looked at her with an expression of horror, "You don't mean there's going to be *another* Radcliffe in the Pony Club?"

"Not for years," said Hilary, "you'll be an instructor by then."

Mrs. Cresswell and June sat in arm-chairs in the lounge. They were silent, exhausted by their post-mortems on the show. They had argued throughout supper, but it had got them nowhere, and now Mrs. Cresswell toyed with the thought of moving to a less horsy part of the country, where June could once more reign supreme. June's own conscience was clear. It wasn't her fault, she thought, that Romany had turned out a better-looking pony than Dawn, and, because of her conformation, had been easier to school. It wasn't her fault that Mr. Barington-Brown could buy Susan a more expensive pony than her mother could afford. As for Dick Turpin in the jumping, he had never jumped like that before, and the only thing she could think of was that John had practised him over the jumps—he lived near enough to Folly Court. Still, thought June, Wonder had knocked the parallel bars the second time round. She must be getting past her prime after all; she was nearly twelve. June decided that she would need a new pony next summer, something that would win in novice classes. "Mummy," she said, "how much do you think we'd get for Wonder?"

John nailed Turpin's first and second and Jet's third rosettes close to the others beside the saddles and bridles, and stood back to admire them. He had never thought this morning that he would do so well, and he didn't suppose that anyone else had either. Turpin had been wonderful. Jet had behaved awfully well too. He was going to miss Jet but he would probably be too heavy to ride her next holidays, and he knew that the Major would see that she had a good home. Perhaps someone who lived near would buy her, and then he would see her occasionally.

As she ate her dinner, Susan's eyes turned at intervals to

157

the cup she had won in the showing, which had been put in the middle of the dining-room mantelpiece. Beauty had been good. She had gone better than ever before, and quite made up for Susan's disappointment over Sunset. On the whole, she was glad that Noel had won it. She had taken more trouble than any of them and now that she was going to have a pony they would be able to ride together, and perhaps their parents would allow them to hunt.

"Wake up, Susan, and help yourself to vegetables," said Mrs. Barington-Brown.

"She's going to be worse than ever now that she's won a cup," said Valerie. "I wish you'd spent as much on my education as you have on her riding, Dad. It's easy to do these things if you've got money behind you."

"And if you're any good you'll do just as well without money," said Mr. Barington-Brown.

"At least I won a rosette, so I did better than you," said Richard to Jill. "And I wasn't so feeble as to let Peter cart me out of the ring."

"Rufus nearly did," said Jill. "Everyone asked what was the matter with him, and said he looked so unschooled beside the other ponies."

"Well, it's none of their business," said Richard, "and if they minded their own they'd get on much better."

"What about the Major?" asked Jill. "Didn't he say anything to you?" Richard didn't reply. He wasn't going to tell Jill that during the tea interval the Major had taken him aside and asked, "Well, Richard, what was the matter with Rufus?"

Mrs. Kettering was really delighted at Noel's success with Romany, and with her luck at being given a pony. She didn't say, as many richer mothers might, that feeding it would be an expense, nor did she point out that Noel had no saddle nor bridle in which to ride it. As they sat on opposite sides of the fire, after a celebration supper of pea-soup, bacon and eggs, apple tart and cider, they tried to think of names. "It's so difficult," said Noel, "when one

hasn't even seen her. I can imagine her perfectly, but I may be imagining her wrong."

"Surely there's no need to settle on a name to-night," said Mrs. Kettering. "I should write down all the possibles and decide when you've seen her."

"I'm terribly pleased," said Noel. "But it's going to be awful parting with Romany." In her mind's eye she saw her: young and inquisitive at the shareout; covered in sweat when Evelyn rode her in the paper-chase; fat, round, and muddy when she was turned out at Folly Farm, but never had she looked so lovely as that evening, grazing peacefully against a background of elms.

"I know it's silly," said Noel. "But, even though I'm too big for her, I'd rather keep Romany than have the grey."

"Quite a successful show, I think," said Major Holbrooke, when the last of his guests had gone to bed.

"Very good indeed," said Mrs. Holbrooke, poking up the dying embers of the drawing-room fire. "Everyone said so, except Mrs. Cresswell."

"She certainly had a nasty shock, poor woman," said Major Holbrooke. "It's rather hard on her, really, considering how she dotes on that child."

"She wasn't the only person who was surprised," said Mrs. Holbrooke. "I was myself. You told me that some of the children had improved, but, honestly, I could hardly believe that they were the same children that competed in the gymkhana last year."

"They only needed teaching," said Major Holbrooke, "and I think that Harry's six ponies were the best schoolmasters of all."

THE END

has a whole shipload of exciting books for you

Armadas are chosen by children all over the world. They're designed to fit your pocket, and your pocket money too. They're colourful, gay, and there are hundreds of titles to choose from. Armada has something for everyone:

Mystery and adventure series to collect, with favourite characters and authors . . . like Alfred Hitchcock and The Three Investigators – the Hardy Boys – young detective Nancy Drew – the intrepid Lone Piners – Biggles – the rascally William – and others.

Hair-raising Spinechillers – Ghost, Monster and Science Fiction stories. Fascinating quiz and puzzle books. Exciting hobby books. Lots of hilarious fun books. Many famous stories. Thrilling pony adventures. Popular school stories – and many more.

You can build up your own Armada collection – and new Armadas are published every month, so look out for the latest additions to the Captain's cargo.

Armadas are available in bookshops and newsagents.

Armada

Author's note: "Six Ponies" was first published in 1946. The illustrations included in the Armada edition were drawn for the original edition at a time when there were no regulations about the wearing of crash caps. Since then it has been made a ruling by The Pony Club that children wear crash caps at all Pony Club functions. The author is in full agreement with this ruling.

First published in Great Britain in 1946 by
William Collins Sons & Co. Ltd., London and Glasgow.
First published in Armada in 1971 by
Armada Paperbacks, 14 St. James's Place, London SW1A 1PS

This edition 1979.

© Josephine Pullein-Thompson 1946.

Printed in Great Britain by
Love & Malcomson Ltd., Brighton Road,
Redhill, Surrey.

SIX PONIES

JOSEPHINE PULLEIN-THOMPSON

Armada

SIX PONIES

Contents

About the authors

The authors of *Practical Teaching Skills for Driving Instructors* each have a considerable amount of experience in the driver training industry and in instructor training. They originally wrote the book (in 1992) in response to requests from numerous ADIs and trainee instructors for material that sets out, in straightforward and practical terms, the best teaching practices needed to produce safe and effective drivers. It has been regularly updated by the authors and, since Margaret Stacey's death in 2005, by John Miller.

John Miller has been involved with the driver training industry for more than 35 years. He is an experienced instructor trainer and a qualified LGV instructor. For many years he ran his own driving school for car and lorry drivers in Chichester and is now a training consultant. His qualifications include the City & Guilds Further Education Teacher's Certificate and the ADINJC Tutor's Certificate as well as the ADI and RTITB instructor qualifications. His driving qualifications include the DSA Cardington Special Test and the IAM Advanced Test.

He is the author of *The LGV Learner Driver's Guide* and co-author (with Margaret Stacey) of *The Driving Instructor's Handbook*.

Tony Scriven was involved in the formation of ADITE – The Approved Driving Instructors' Training Establishment directory (now ORDIT) – and served on its committeee for several years.

Margaret Stacey ran a driving instructor training facility in Derbyshire and had been an ADI for more than 30 years. Margaret held the City & Guilds Further Education Teacher's Certificate, the Pitman NVQ Assessor Award, the ADINJC Tutor's Certificate and passed the DSA Cardington Special Test, IAM and RoSPA Advanced Driving Tests. She served on several national committees, including ORDIT (The Official Register of Driving Instructor Training) and the steering group that developed the NVQ in Driving Instruction.

Margaret's other books include *The Driving Instructor's Handbook* (co-author with John Miller), *Learn to Drive in 10 Easy Stages* and *The Advanced Driver's Handbook*.

Practical Teaching Skills for Driving Instructors is listed by the Driving Standards Agency as essential material for the ADI examinations. The book is complementary to *The Driving Instructor's Handbook* – now in its 14th edition – which is also listed by the DSA.

While every effort has been made to ensure that the book is as up-to-date as possible continual changes take place in the training industry and with legislation. This means that some changes may have occurred since going to print. To keep yourself completely up-to-date we recommend that you regularly refer to **Despatch** *(the DSA's own periodic publication for instructors) and the DSA website at* **www.dsa.gov.uk,** *and that you join one of the main ADI associations.*

Introduction

Driving instructors use a wide variety of *practical teaching skills* (PTS) in their everyday work. These skills will have been acquired and developed in many other areas of experience, for example:

- at school;
- in college;
- working in other jobs;
- as a parent;
- in life generally.

Practical skills and techniques that have been transferred from previous situations are known as 'transferable personal skills'. This term is used to define the skills that are personal to us as individuals and are capable of being used in different situations. For example, a pedestrian who is about to cross a busy main road uses skills in judging the speed and distance of oncoming traffic.

When recognized and 'transferred' to the new environment of driving, these skills become very useful in traffic situations, for example when:

- waiting to emerge from a junction;
- crossing the path of approaching traffic.

The skills are similar, but the environment is different.

Another example might involve the use of bicycle gears – a combination of decision making together with the physical skill of hand and foot coordination. This type of skill can be directly transferred to the car-driving situation.

To be able to teach learner drivers to cope with the fast, complicated and potentially dangerous environment in which cars are driven, it is essential that we develop our individual transferable skills and our *practical teaching skills*. This will ensure that effective learning takes place.

Remember that as driving instructors we are probably the only teachers whose 'classrooms' are travelling at high speeds along busy roads. In this environment your control and effectiveness as an instructor is a vital factor in the safety of your pupil, yourself and other road users.

To survive (in a business sense) in what is becoming an increasingly competitive market, you need to work continually at improving your:

- practical teaching skills;
- instructor characteristics;
- fault identification and analysis skills;
- business skills and expertise.

This book is designed to help:

- candidates preparing for the Approved Driving Instructor (ADI) exams;
- practising ADIs preparing for their Check Test;
- instructors gathering information and evidence for National Vocational Qualifications (NVQs);
- those involved in driver training at all levels who want to become more effective teachers in their everyday work.

As professional driving instructors we need to be able to persuade our pupils to do what we want them to do, and to do it in the way that we would like it done.

Most of the practical teaching skills (PTS) dealt with in this book are dependent on effective communication skills. Instructors who can communicate and coach effectively are more likely to succeed in transferring their own knowledge, understanding, skills and attitudes to their pupils.

Knowledge of the *Highway Code* and the ability to drive with a high degree of expertise are not in themselves sufficient qualities to be able to teach somebody else how to drive. The number of parents and spouses who have been unsuccessful with their teaching bears witness to this fact!

As a 'Driving Standards Agency (DSA) Approved Driving Instructor (ADI)' you should be aiming to teach your pupils 'safe driving for life' and not just training them to pass the test. As part of the qualifying process you are required to demonstrate not only your knowledge and driving ability, but also your communication skills and instructional techniques.

Whether you are a potential or a qualified ADI, this book focuses on showing you how to improve your teaching and communication skills so that you are better equipped to teach 'safe driving for life'. It also covers the preparation required for all three parts of the ADI examination.

PTS can be developed to help you interact with your pupils, building on existing transferable skills. Many of these skills are not only 'transferable' from one environment to another, but are also 'transferable' from instructor to pupil.

Being a successful driving instructor relies not only on the traditional interpersonal skills, but also on being able to:

- use and interpret body language;
- sell ideas and concepts;
- solve problems;
- identify, analyse and correct faults;
- make immediate decisions with safety in mind.

To become qualified as an instructor you need to have, and to use, all these qualities. You also need to acquire learning and study skills and a basic understanding of role play.

ADIs are required to be able to communicate with their pupils in a variety of ways to suit the perceived needs of each individual pupil. You will be involved with selling, whether it is 'selling' yourself or your services to potential pupils or 'selling' ideas and concepts to existing pupils.

These skills are included because you must master them all in order to develop your career. This book will show you how to improve your effectiveness by developing these practical teaching skills.

As already indicated, PTS and other transferable personal skills are not necessarily developed overnight.

If you want to improve and develop your skills, you need to consider regular refresher training courses in all areas of driving, instruction, business skills and customer care. You will also need to monitor your own performance and effectiveness as part of a programme of Continuing Professional Development (CPD).

The need to practise these skills while you are giving lessons is just as vital as driving practice is to your pupils. To be able to learn from each encounter with a new pupil and to structure a self-development programme you must have an understanding of how studying, learning and teaching can be made effective.

Even more important is your ability to continually develop your own transferable personal skills and to assist your pupils in doing the same. As well as driving ability, the skills of decision making, prioritizing and problem solving are just as important to the learner and qualified driver as they are to you, the instructor.

To drive safely on today's congested roads requires knowledge, understanding, skill and an attitude that shows not only courtesy and consideration for other road users, but also the ability to make allowances for the mistakes of others.

The development of sound PTS will assist you in achieving the objective of teaching driving as a lifetime skill. Many of the skills outlined are just as important to the development of the learner as they are to that of the instructor. They are 'transferable' from one to the other.

It is rather like preparing for the ADI Part 2 (own driving) examination.

The first person you have to teach how to drive is yourself.

If you cannot achieve the right standard in your own driving, how can you expect to be able to teach your pupils to drive properly?

The same principle applies to skills other than driving. If you cannot master the skills of risk assessment, problem solving and decision making yourself, how can you expect to be able to teach pupils how to master them?

In an effort to improve the standards of 'L' driver training and driving instruction skills generally, the DSA have introduced various measures, including:

- the recommended syllabus for learner drivers;
- a driver's record;
- 'Pass Plus' for newly qualified drivers;
- a Hazard Perception Test;
- a CPD initiative.

You should take advantage of, and use, all of these initiatives, as they are useful both for your pupils' learning and in your own contining professional development. For example, you can register with the DSA as a trainer for Pass Plus, offering extra training to your newly qualified pupils. The six-module course aims to improve the skills and knowledge of new drivers in the period immediately after passing their driving test.

Unfortunately, with the performance-based driving test system and the limited amount of time and money that the general public are willing to pay for lessons, ADIs are tempted to teach people how to pass the test instead of teaching them how to drive safely for life.

For similar reasons, the same applies to the ADI qualifying examinations: candidates are often trained simply to 'pass the test'. The practical teaching skills outlined in this book will equip you as an instructor or as a trainer to teach driving as a life skill, but the main responsibility for doing so lies solely with you.

The DSA's Check Test system, which has been upgraded over the past few years, has shown many experienced ADIs to be inarticulate, lacking in initiative and often unable to provide an effective learning environment for their pupils. Many have been found to be reluctant to accept criticism; others were unable to recognize and identify their pupils' basic driving faults – some of which were repetitive and serious.

The skills covered in this book are highly transferable and should be of value to all ADIs who are concerned with improving their interpersonal effectiveness and the skills of their learners. They should be adopted by:

- qualified instructors wishing to improve their career prospects;

- qualified ADIs and new entrants to the profession seeking employment – prospective employers will identify those who are best able to apply effective teaching techniques;

- all those who simply wish to improve, to become more self-confident and to influence their peers;

- ADIs preparing for their 'Test of Continued Ability and Fitness' (the Check Test) who will find that improved communication skills and PTS will give them greater confidence and a better chance of achieving a higher grade;

- instructors preparing for the ADI qualifying examinations, particularly Part 1 (theory) and Part 3 (instructional ability) – a better understanding of the skills required when teaching people to drive is an important part of these exams;

- tutors of driving instructors and staff instructors at instructor training establishments.

Developing the skills contained in this book is essential at this level of training; it is also totally compatible with the criteria for approval for the Official Register of Driving Instructor Training (ORDIT). For details, see *The Driving Instructor's Handbook*.

But there is no real substitute for practical, hands-on training and practice. You cannot learn how to drive from a book; neither can you learn how to teach someone from a book: the best way to learn how to teach is to teach!

The development of PTS is a continuous and lifetime process, with each new encounter offering you the opportunity to improve your skills.

Learning occurs in a variety of ways; however, as in most things, a systematic approach is invariably more effective than one that is haphazard. Trial and error in using skills will give some insight into those that are the most effective in different situations and with different types of pupil.

> *Reflecting on your successes and failures will also assist you in developing your practical teaching skills.*

Formal training and structured learning, both in-class and in-car, is invaluable to instructors wishing to develop their own skills. This is even more relevant when developing active learning strategies, such as role-playing exercises and fault assessment skills. Formal training for the ADI test allows you to practise new skills in a safe and controlled setting before trying them out on learners or trainees in the real world.

Experience gained while watching and listening to demonstrations given by your tutor will be invaluable when you have to demonstrate skills to your pupils.

Training should be a continuous circle of learning:

- trainees learn from their tutors;
- pupils learn from their instructors;
- instructors learn from their pupils;
- information feeds back to the tutors;
- and so on...

The challenge for you is to adopt a frame of mind that welcomes each learning strategy, particularly those that require a more active approach.

> *The key element in teaching driving (and for learning how to drive) is controlled practice.*

When teaching your pupils how to drive you should take every opportunity that arises to practise the skills contained in this book. Some skills training, however, can be seen to be slightly threatening to both learners and instructors. If care is not taken, embarrassment and offence can be caused when analysing someone's behaviour. Because of this factor, teaching a practical skill has to be delivered in a sensitive way. You should accept this fact from the outset. If you adopt too strict an approach, then your learners are unlikely to enjoy the experience and may feel reluctant to participate. Sensitivity must be shown to all your learners and this in itself is an important transferable skill.

Always remember that criticism can be very demotivating.

> *Encouragement when needed and praise when deserved will bring about more improvement than any amount of criticism.*

Chapter 1 explains how people learn. As a learner of PTS and transferable skills yourself, you must accept that training will not necessarily be easy and will demand a high degree of self-motivation and discipline. This is all part of your own learning process and will give you a better understanding of how your learners may feel when they are struggling to master new skills.

You will have to learn how to evaluate your own strengths and weaknesses, and will perhaps for the first time in your life, see yourself as others see you. This is also part of the learning process.

> *It is only when you see yourself as other people do that you can start to modify your own teaching skills.*
>
> *This will promote more efficient learning through the establishment of effective relationship skills.*

Remember – there is no such thing as a bad learner. Some pupils merely find it more difficult than others to acquire new skills or to absorb new information. Some people will have natural co-ordination skills, while others need to work to achieve these. Your explanations may need to be given in a slightly different way, or you may need to adapt your teaching methods to suit the pupil.

To bring out the best in pupils the skill of the good instructor is in knowing when to:

- explain;
- demonstrate;
- repeat;
- analyse;
- correct;
- assess;
- question;
- praise;
- encourage.

Being able to use all these skills, and knowing when to use each one, will enhance your coaching and teaching and ensure that more effective learning takes place. As you will be eventually sharing the road with your learners, this should be the main purpose of your job.

Just as your learners need to learn from any mistakes they may make during a driving lesson, you need to learn from your own instructional mistakes or weaknesses that may have led to that error.

At the end of each driving lesson you should ask yourself:

- How much *effective* learning has taken place?
- Could I have done any more to help my pupil achieve the objectives that we set at the start of the lesson?

Only by continually evaluating your own performance will you be able to improve and develop your PTS.

By using this book in a practical manner you can learn how to improve your PTS. This will benefit your pupils, help you to ensure success in the ADI examination, and help you to achieve the best possible grading on your Check Test.

Remember that learning is a continuous process!

1

Learning to drive

Whether you are a trainee instructor or an experienced ADI, your practical teaching skills will be developed or improved by understanding:

- why people learn to drive;
- what motivates them to learn;
- how learning takes place;
- the factors involved in barriers to learning.

People learn to drive for a variety of reasons, but it is doubtful that they fully appreciate the benefits until some time after passing their driving test.

When your pupils begin learning to drive they may be doing so for any of the following reasons:

- social, domestic or leisure pursuits;
- business and employment requirements;
- personal satisfaction;
- the need for independent mobility.

Whatever their reasons, it is only after they have passed the test that your pupils will understand or appreciate how the other benefits gained will improve or enhance their quality of life, including:

- greater freedom and mobility;
- improved confidence and status;
- better employment or promotion potential;
- increased earning power.

When you consider these benefits, and also take into consideration that a driving licence is effectively valid for life, it will be clear that driving lessons can be regarded as extremely good value for money. These benefits can be outlined to the pupil right from the start of their lesson and in the context of the amount of training required for a life skill.

The main requirement for most learners is to pass their test and obtain a full driving licence at the earliest opportunity, with the minimum of effort and at the least possible cost. In recent years, most young people have started their driver training as soon as they are old enough, but there are now some indications that a significant number of 17 year olds are delaying their training and putting off lessons until they are slightly older. Some 10 years ago, about 50 per cent of all 17 to 21 year olds held a full driving licence, but that figure has now dropped to about 26 per cent. It would appear that the cost of learning, combined with that of insurance, might be influencing their decision.

The cost of insurance is one of the inhibiting factors for a young and inexperienced driver. New drivers in the 17–21 age group are six times as likely to be involved in a road traffic accident than any other group of drivers. For this reason, insurance premiums are increased significantly for newly qualified young drivers. However, several insurance companies offer substantial discounts for drivers who have taken the 'Pass Plus' course. The benefits of Pass Plus should be emphasized to your pupils at the start of their training as a motivating factor, rather than simply introducing the topic at driving test stage.

MOTIVATION

The motivation for learning to drive usually involves several different factors, both personal and external to the pupil. One of the strongest motivating influences is the person's own desire to fulfil the personal ambitions on which their mind is set. Quite often, this need for achievement will be linked to some form of prestige or financial gain.

If you understand some of the personal factors governing the motivation of each of your pupils, it should help you to structure their programme of lessons in an effective way.

Most adults are mainly concerned with the immediate benefits to be gained from learning to drive. They will therefore be more concerned with passing the test than with acquiring an understanding that will prepare them for 'safe driving for life'.

However, as an effective instructor, it is your responsibility to equip your pupils for a lifetime of safe driving. You will therefore need to ensure that any training programme includes an element of anticipation, and hazard awareness and perception.

It is very useful for you to know why your individual pupils are learning to drive, as this will enable you to use those reasons for motivational support. For example, if a pupil is having difficulty with a particular manoeuvre, or they comment on the cost of training, you should be able to respond by emphasising the particular benefits to them such as:

- more flexibility in the workplace;

- not having to queue for buses, trains or taxis after a night out;

- the ability to take children to school/clubs/functions.

Because of the costs involved in learning to drive, it is unusual to come across a learner who is not motivated to some extent. However, they do occasionally exist. For example, someone whose partner has been disqualified from driving but who does not particularly want to drive, or the person who is being pressurised by an employer to obtain a driving licence, but who will not benefit from the added responsibility. Emphasizing the other benefits may overcome the lack of initial motivation.

THE LEARNING PROCESS

Learning can be thought of as nature's way of enabling all of us to adapt and survive in a fast-moving and complicated environment. The driving environment is faster and more complicated than most. Unlike most situations, problem solving and decision making often have to be carried out without the same amount of time to think things through. A driver's incorrect assessment or response to a situation and an inappropriate decision can be disastrous, not only for the decision maker, but for any passengers and other road users.

Teaching can be regarded as creating an environment in which learning can take place. In other words, the teacher or instructor is often a manager of the learning process. As a driving instructor, your classroom is the car.

As professional instructors we need to make a few assumptions:

- learning is 'a good thing' because it enriches people's lives;

- while a certain amount of learning is inevitable and takes place all the time, the quality and quantity of learning can be massively increased if it is organized in a structured way, in a controlled environment;

- learning is a continuous and continuing process;
- shared learning is easier to sustain than solo learning.

You could give a novice driver the keys of a car parked in the middle of a field and say: 'Teach yourself how to drive that car. I'll be back in a couple of hours to see how you're getting on.' Surprisingly, if you came back two hours later, you would probably find that the person would have gained, on their own initiative, some basic ability. On the other hand, a properly constructed programme of lessons and practice would make the learning process much quicker and more effective.

Learning is the acquisition, over a period of time, of various aspects of knowledge, understanding and attitudes. This means that the person's behaviour has been changed so that they can do something that they were unable to do previously.

New drivers have a lot to learn. The controls of a car may look easy to use when observing an experienced driver, but are quite complex to a beginner. The new driver has to learn the theory and then combine this with the operation of the controls, while at the same time dealing with observations, awareness, anticipation and judgement. They also have to deal with varying road and traffic conditions, the weather and other road users.

> *In a structured learning programme, such as a course of driving lessons, both the pupil and the instructor should be able to see and measure any change in behaviour. This should allow both parties to decide how successfully learning has taken place.*

Learning takes place in a sequence involving three interrelated stages. This is known as *the learning circle*.

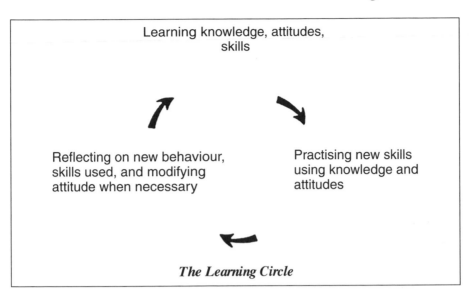

Learning knowledge, attitudes, skills

Reflecting on new behaviour, skills used, and modifying attitude when necessary

Practising new skills using knowledge and attitudes

The Learning Circle

Adults learn mainly through their senses, which provide them with information about the environment around them. These senses are personal to the individual and any two learners receiving the same information from their senses in a given situation, may PERCEIVE things differently. For example, one learner driver meeting oncoming traffic might perceive it as being potentially dangerous and decide to hold back. Another learner approaching a similar situation, might perceive no danger at all and go charging through the closing gap.

From the beginning, you should be aware that no two pupils are likely to react to a given situation in the same way. One of the golden rules of teaching is NEVER ASSUME.

In learning to drive the three main senses used are sight, hearing and touch. However, other senses are sometimes used. For example, the sense of smell could make the driver aware that the engine is overheating or something is burning.

The importance of sight

In the learning process, sight is the most important of the senses. When teaching others to drive you can use this sense in a number of ways to improve the quality of the learning taking place.

Whether giving a demonstration, pointing out actual driving situations or using visual aids, any teaching that involves a pupil's sense of sight will be most effective in fixing new information in their mind.

The following diagram shows the proportions in which our senses gather information. Our use of the diagram in itself shows the effectiveness of sight in the learning process rather than simply explaining the numbers.

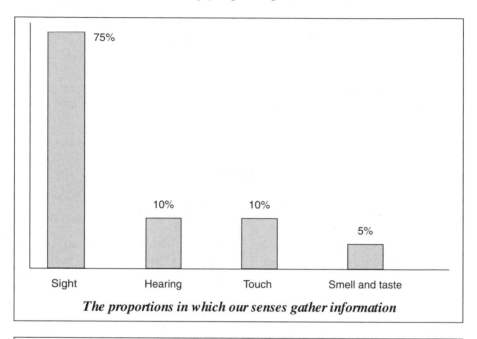

The proportions in which our senses gather information

The ability to persuade pupils to see and perceive things as you do is a vital ingredient when teaching people how to drive.

In driving, hearing and touch have as important a role to play as does sight.

For example, as well as seeing things, when listening and feeling as the noise of the engine changes and the clutch is raised to the 'biting point', pupils should also be developing the awareness and perception that go with these senses.

Awareness

In driving, awareness involves not only the perception and interpretation of one's own vehicle speed, position and direction of travel, but also the recognition of other hazards in time to take the necessary safe action.

Perception and awareness are the first steps towards performing a skill such as driving. Awareness is dependent on the interpretation and meaning the brain attaches to the information it receives from the senses. This involves not only looking with the eyes but also using the mind and calling upon existing knowledge from previous experience to 'see' with the mind. What is actually seen with the eyes is not always the same as what is perceived by the brain.

Optical illusions offer evidence of this. They may be caused by distortion through perspective or by a lack of intermediate visual keys which help the viewer to gauge distance accurately.

THE DISTANCE between A and B appears to be longer than that between B and C. The illusion occurs because the space between A and B is measured out in evenly spaced dots, filling the area for the eye. The distance between B and C can only be guessed at because there are no intermediate points.

This visual distortion, plus a weakness in a driver's ability to judge correctly the width of the vehicle they are driving, or that of approaching vehicles, can have very serious consequences.

What each student actually perceives while learning not only depends on the individuality of their senses but on how that particular person has learnt to see and interpret things. You may need to modify the student's perception to make it compatible with your own.

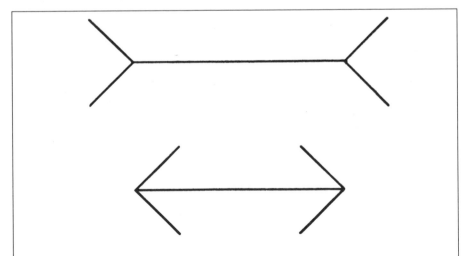

THE LENGTHS of the two horizontal lines appear unequal because of the directional arrows at the ends. Where the arrows branch outward, the line seems to be stretched out beyond its actual length. Where they branch in, the line seems to be strictly enclosed and shortened. Both of the lines are exactly the same length.

Transfer of learning

This happens when a pupil uses skills that have been acquired in previous experiences and in different environments. Examples include:

- problem solving;
- decision making;
- prioritizing.

All of these form a part of everyday life in today's society. You will often be able to relate or transfer your pupil's existing skills to help in driving. However, where the new information is not compatible with established knowledge, it may be totally rejected.

Incoming sensations are instantly compared with existing knowledge stored in the memory from previous experiences. The compatibility of these memories can either help or hinder learning of any new material.

Where the new information is compatible with existing knowledge and thoughts, the established memories will be reinforced. For example, somebody learning to play tennis who is already a good squash player may find the learning less difficult because both sports are very similar. This is called POSITIVE TRANSFER OF LEARNING.

Sometimes previous knowledge can be a hindrance to learning. An example of this could be someone who decides to learn to drive a car and has been used to riding a motorcycle in scrambling trials, an activity where success is dependent on the frequent taking of risks. Put this rider behind the wheel of a car on the road and the difference in the steering, the width and length of the vehicle and the differing speed norms required may all hinder the learning process. This is called NEGATIVE TRANSFER. In this particular case, the learner is likely to be going for gaps which may be narrow, approaching hazards much too fast and struggling to master the steering at the same time.

It will take time for learners to establish the many thousands of memory connections needed to be able to drive safely, along with patience and understanding on your part. What you should try to do is make sure that the pupil 'sees' situations in the same way that you see them.

Other basic requirements which are necessary for learning to take place are:

- PERCEPTION;
- ATTENTION;
- ACTIVITY;
- INVOLVEMENT.

Perception

The senses vary from pupil to pupil and so does their perception. You will need to make your pupil's perception reasonably compatible with your own.

When you are driving along a wet road you will think that you 'see' a three-dimensional scene of slippery tarmac. What you *actually* see (the image in the eye) is neither slippery nor three-dimensional. This can only mean that you create in your mind a 'model' of what is there. You see the road as being 'wet' or 'slippery' because of the previous experience of such things you have 'fixed' in your mind.

A good example of this would be the lights of an oncoming vehicle on a dark country road at night. The amount of sensory information is very limited indeed but with your experience you should not have a problem interpreting it. You cannot see the vehicle but you know that it is there! You will build an image of the type and size of vehicle to which the lights belong and decide whether any defensive action is required.

Drawing on your own experience, you will need to help your pupils to 'fix' such things in their minds. This can be done by using question and answer routines regarding road surface, weather conditions, etc.

The diagram below gives an illustration of how the mind sometimes 'sees' things which may not be there in reality.

The central triangle in each of the figures is an illusion. Although we see the edges as sharp and clear, they are not there. There is no actual brightness difference across the edges; the triangle must therefore be constructed in the mind of the observer.

In the early stages of learning to drive some pupils will have difficulty in judging the width and length of the car they are driving, and the speed, distance and size of oncoming traffic.

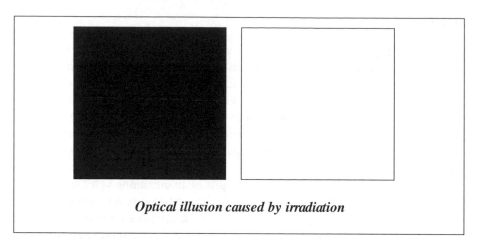

Optical illusion caused by irradiation

At night the problem for the inexperienced driver may be made worse by an optical illusion called IRRADIATION. This is a physiological phenomenon that occurs when the eye focuses on neighbouring bright and dark areas.

Although both squares are identical in size, the image of the white square will to most people appear larger. Light coloured cars can therefore, in some situations, appear to be larger and closer than dark coloured cars of identical size.

Because illusions of this nature could have dangerous repercussions for your pupils, you should encourage them to take some of their lessons at night so that you are there to give guidance and help in resolving any problems that may occur.

> *Perception is not always under the complete control of the learner and occasionally the mind will wander off in an unrelated direction.*

Attention

It is often quite difficult to maintain a pupil's attention for a length of time without either a break or a change of activity. For this reason, lessons in educational establishments are usually about 50 minutes in duration. Instructors who are involved in intensive courses need to take this into account and arrange the programme accordingly.

> *If you do not have the attention of your pupil, learning is unlikely to take place.*

You should watch for non-verbal signals from the pupil which may indicate boredom, impatience or fatigue (see Chapter 2, Body Language).

Activity and involvement

One of the best ways to ensure that your pupils are attentive is to actively involve them in the learning experience. Try to avoid very long briefings or detailed explanations that do not require any active involvement.

Activity, however, should not only be thought of as physical. Learning to drive obviously involves a lot of physical activity but it is often the mental involvement which initiates the physical response to a situation.

The more active and involved novices are in the learning experience, the more they will normally remember. This is why PUPIL-CENTRED LEARNING is so vital when teaching someone how to drive. The good instructor will help learners to think and reason things out for themselves, leading them to the desired conclusion.

Although you can use questions to test pupils' understanding of what they should be doing and why it is important, it is through physically carrying out the task that most learning will take place. This 'doing' VALIDATES the teaching and can be done in various ways. There are several different teaching methods that are commonly used by instructors:

Method 1 allows the passing on of information or facts with little intellectual activity on the part of the learner. Typical examples of this style of instruction are:

● teaching the answers to questions without confirming the pupil's understanding;

● telling the pupil to 'Always look round before moving off' without explaining why or finding out if they know what they are looking for.

Although this teaching method is limited it can be useful, especially in the early stages, provided your learners make use of the knowledge gained during their driving practice.

Method 2 involves asking a series of step-by-step questions that are designed to lead the learner towards the solution of a problem or statement of principle.

Open-ended or pointed questions which encourage active and creative participation, insight and contemplation, will bring about better understanding by the pupil than closed questions which only require a 'Yes' or 'No' response. When teaching a learner how to turn right you might ask:

'What is the first thing you would do before turning right?'

'Well, I would give a signal.'

'Wouldn't you do anything before that?'

'Oh yes, I would check the mirrors.'

'Why is that important?'

'Well, I suppose there could be a motorcyclist overtaking me.'

'That's correct. And what would he be likely to do if you suddenly put on your signal as he was about to overtake you?'

'Well, he might suddenly brake or swerve around me.'

'Yes – so you would have caused him inconvenience or possible danger, wouldn't you?'

'Yes, I suppose so.'

'That's good. So, now you know why the "Mirror-Signal-Manoeuvre" routine is so important don't you?'

Because these open-ended questions are so important they are dealt with in more detail in Chapter 3.

Letting the learner explain correct procedures to you can be a very effective way of bringing about learning.

Method 3 is more 'PUPIL-CENTRED' than 'INSTRUCTOR-CENTRED' because it involves a higher level of participation from your learners, with them having to accept more responsibility for their learning.

Some aspects of driving instruction lend themselves to this 'pupil-centred' approach. For example:

● learning the rules in the *Highway Code*;

● learning about basic car maintenance from a book;

● memorizing basic driving procedures such as M S M, P S L or L A D (see pages 81–82).

Pupil-centred activities are quite useful when teaching in small groups where the instructor should act as a catalyst by:

● providing the necessary resources;

● setting tasks for the learners to involve themselves in.

All knowledge gained through such activities must be transferable to driving practice. You will need to check that your pupils fully understand all the safety implications of practically applying the knowledge they have gained. This will also apply to the setting of homework and in-between lesson tasks which will need to be validated during practical sessions.

PRACTISE WITH FRIENDS AND RELATIVES

Although some people still learn to drive with friends or relatives it has been shown that more than 95 per cent of all learners taking the driving test have had some professional instruction.

It may be that they have their initial instruction with a professional in order to acquire the basic skills required to control the vehicle or, more commonly, they acquire the basic skills with a friend or relative and then come to the professional just before the 'L' test saying, 'I just want to make sure I'm doing everything right!'

Of course, in the latter case it is rather like 'shutting the stable door after the horse has bolted'. It is in this sort of situation that you will have a selling job to do. This may be in the form of selling more lessons, if there is enough time and money available, or selling the idea of postponing the test in order to give the pupil more time to improve and practise the correct procedures.

Unless the friend or relative carrying out the teaching has some form of instructional background, and is a reasonably good driver, it is a distinct disadvantage if the learner has received no lessons at all from a professional instructor.

Most friends or relatives tend to use trial and error methods, and the whole process can end up becoming unpleasant for both learner and teacher. It is also common for the person teaching to be out of date on traffic law, driving techniques and the requirements of the 'L' test. This can result in 'negative' transfer of learning. As in most training, a structured approach is usually much more effective in helping the learners to achieve their objectives.

STRUCTURED TRAINING

The main benefits of learning with a professional instructor should include:

- a better rapport between teacher and pupil;
- a saving in time and trouble;

- a higher level of knowledge, understanding, attitude and skill;
- a better chance of passing the 'L' test and accomplishing safe driving for life.

To achieve these objectives the professional driving instructor needs an understanding of how adults learn. Only through this understanding will the instructor be able to structure a programme of learning to suit the individual needs of each pupil.

One of the most effective methods of instruction is to use educational or instructional BEHAVIOURAL OBJECTIVES. Although there are no hard and fast rules, three main categories of learning have been identified as a basis for deciding the mode of instruction.

1. Behavioural objectives concerned with information and knowledge. This category covers the various mental processes – such as sensation, perception and thinking – by which knowledge is gained. This type of learning will usually involve using conventional issues and formally planned instruction.

2. Objectives that relate to the feelings, attitudes, emotions and values of the trainee. The following sequence shows the usual development of affective characteristics:

    (i)   Learner/trainee becomes aware of feelings about a particular event/activity/topic.

    (ii) Learner/trainee conforms to instructions given by instructor/trainer regarding how they should feel about the particular event/activity/topic.

    (iii) Learner/trainee becomes capable of making value judgements on their own according to codes of conduct and firmly established principles.

    At the lowest level, the role of the learner/trainee is passive and limited to taking in information, with little personal concern. At the highest level, they will be integrating concepts, feelings and values into their own life/world.

    You should help your learners/trainees to develop their feelings and values so that they end up with desirable attitudes. In particular, consideration for all other road users needs to be fostered, especially for the more vulnerable groups such as young children, elderly or infirm pedestrians, and cyclists.

3. This category is concerned with the learning of muscular and motor skills, such as coordination of the foot and hand controls, steering, etc. At the lowest level, behaviour will be clumsy and hesitant with frequent errors.

After following a well-designed training programme, and with practice, complete mastery should be achieved. The pupil should be able to drive to a reasonable standard without assistance. The skilled performance will be efficient and flow smoothly, with only minor errors being made.

During your normal working day you will find that your lessons involve using a combination of all three types of learning.

When taking a structured training course with a professional instructor, learning should be the result of a deliberate and directed effort. The learning plan should include:

- learning to memorize things;
- learning to understand things;
- learning how to do things;
- attitude development;
- developing study skills.

These elements are covered in the following sections.

Memorizing

This is sometimes called ROTE LEARNING or PARROT-FASHION LEARNING and is the method by which most of us learnt our tables at school. Rote learning is rather limited in that it does not necessarily prove an understanding of the subject.

For example, a learner could memorize the overall stopping distances of a vehicle and be able to tell you, 'The stopping distance if you are travelling at 30 miles per hour on a dry road would be 23 metres.' The learner should then be asked to point out something that is 23 metres away!

Even when pupils can do this reasonably accurately, it is still necessary to test their ability to keep a safe distance from the car in front when driving at 30 miles per hour.

Knowledge in itself does not guarantee an UNDERSTANDING, nor the ability to use the knowledge and link it in with the skill of leaving sufficient distance between vehicles. Knowledge is often, therefore, just the starting point.

The good instructor will need to use a skilful question and answer technique to verify understanding and test pupils' ability to put the knowledge into practice.

This is sometimes known as VALIDATION: it involves proving that something has been understood by demonstrating the ability to carry it out.

Memory is vital for those learning to drive as there is no point in learning something if it is forgotten in a short time.

The ability of your pupils to retain information and knowledge, and their capacity for forgetting what they have already learnt, will vary enormously from person to person. This is where the patience of a professional instructor will pay dividends as, with some pupils, there will be a need to explain things several times or in a different way.

Up to the prime of life, the learning rate and the ability to retain information, knowledge and skills increase as the maturity level increases. After maturity both the learning rate and the ability to retain knowledge start to diminish.

Developing long-term memory

The first stage is to put the information in a form which can be more easily remembered by:

- breaking it down into its key components;
- using mnemonics – for example, M S M, P S L, L A D;
- painting pictures – 'What would happen if…?';
- using word associations like 'ease the clutch', 'squeeze the gas' and 'creep and peep';
- using visual keys – for example, 'round signs give orders, triangular signs give warnings', 'think of the thickness of a coin'.

When you have translated the information into a more memorable form, you could write it down and ask your pupils to memorize it by rote. You could then check whether they have remembered it by asking questions at the beginning of the next lesson. If they have not learnt it, do not lose heart. Explain to them that it is difficult to learn and encourage them to do some more studying.

Repetition is a very good way of fixing information in the brain, but care should be taken to ensure that your repetition does not sound like 'nagging'.

You should encourage your pupils to study the *Highway Code*, *The Official Guide to Learning to Drive* and *The Official DSA Guide to Driving: the essential skills*. You will then need to confirm that this has been done by testing their knowledge. You could set simple multiple-choice questions which could be given as homework, thus helping them both to maintain interest in between their driving lessons and to prepare for the theory test.

There are some very good videos, CD ROMs and DVDs that you could loan to your pupils for home use. This should also help to maintain their interest. If you do this, however, you must ensure that you are not infringing any copyright restrictions.

Understanding

An effective way of finding out whether your pupils understand something, is to ask them to explain it to you: '*Why* do we have to look round over our shoulder before moving off?'; '*What* must we do when we get to our turning point *before* we begin to reverse round the corner, and *why*?'

Understanding something means knowing its meaning, whether it be a statement of fact, a concept, or a principle. When a pupil is learning to do something, it is important that, to begin with, the key steps are understood, and then practice takes place until mastery has been achieved. ROTE LEARNING will be of little help to the pupil here and you need to use a technique that involves learning by understanding.

This method involves using mental processes as well as physical ones. It relies on the principle that the whole is greater than the sum of the parts. The easiest way to illustrate this is to use the analogy of a piece of music. Many of us often remember a catchy tune, to such an extent that we cannot get it out of our heads. It would be much more difficult, however, to remember just a few notes, and almost impossible to remember just one note, as this would depend on us having perfect pitch.

When teaching pupils how to approach junctions, you need to outline the complete manoeuvre and then break this down into its component parts. First of all, they need to understand the Mirror-Signal-Manoeuvre routine and then be able to break down the manoeuvre part into the Position-Speed-Look-Assess-Decide routine.

Not only do they need to understand the when, where, how, and why elements involved in these sequences, but they also need to practise carrying them out until a reasonable degree of safety is achieved.

No matter how well pupils understand and can carry out any component parts of the junction routine, unless they can approach and emerge safely, very little will have been achieved.

So the next teaching technique is to go back to whichever component part needs improving in order to get them to carry out the complete manoeuvre effectively. This may involve you in giving more explanation, possibly a demonstration and certainly more practice in order to improve performance.

All of these principles are dependent on the pupils' UNDERSTANDING.

There is little point in getting to the PRACTICE stage if pupils do not UNDERSTAND what is expected of them.

The starting point in teaching understanding is to:

1. ask questions;
2. solve problems.

1.   Asking questions

When giving information to learners, you should ask yourself, '*Why, where, when and how* do we need to do that?' You will then need to ask the pupil the same questions, or give them the reasons. Good instructors will probably use a mixture of asking and telling in order to make lessons more varied. When using a question and answer routine, try not to make it sound like an INTERROGATION as this will only annoy or demoralize, and you may lose the pupil!

Try to relate any new information to what pupils already know (teaching from the known to the unknown). This will allow them to build up a store of understanding. It is of little use for your pupils to know how and when to do something if they do not understand *why* it is important.

We have all had pupils come to us from other instructors, or those who have been taught by friends or relatives, who are making mistakes and do not understand why what they are doing is wrong. For example, you may get pupils who signal every time they move off when there are no other road users in sight. When you ask, 'Why did you signal?' the reply is very often, 'My dad says you must always signal before you move off.'

It is obvious from this response that there is no understanding of what signals should be used for, nor how and when to use them.

Your job is to explain why it is important to assess each situation on its own merits, and then decide whether or not a signal is required. You could confirm this by asking, 'Who were you signalling to?' or, 'What if...?'

---

2.   Solving problems

You need to know how solving problems will help your pupils to UNDERSTAND things.

Solving problems usually relies on learners being able to transfer to new situations any knowledge and understanding already stored in their long-term memory. This should assist learners in working out different possible solutions to a particular problem.They can then evaluate these solutions and decide which is the most appropriate for the problem being dealt with.

> *To solve problems successfully, you will need to use intellectual skills to pose the appropriate questions, which will enable the correct solution to be arrived at.*
>
> *Once the problem has been solved, it is easier to understand why it occurred in the first place and how to prevent it in the future.*

The technique of problem solving is particularly useful when analysing the driving errors made by learners, whether they are in car (errors of control) or outside (errors of road procedure).

An example of this would be a learner driver turning left and swinging wide after the corner. The cause of the error might be obvious to the instructor, but not so obvious to the learner who may perceive several possible reasons for the error. Perhaps the steering was started too late, there was a misjudgement of the amount of lock needed, or the corner was approached at too high a speed, meaning that there was insufficient time to steer accurately enough to maintain the correct position.

> *Having recognized the fault, the good instructor would help the pupil to analyse the fault by using the question and answer technique to arrive at the cause of it.*

The first question could be: 'Why do you think you swung wide after the corner?' After a series of supplementary questions, the pupil should eventually arrive at the correct answer.

Having solved the problem it would be necessary to take the pupil round the block in order to have another attempt at turning the same corner. You might choose to give the pupil a 'talk-through', particularly with regard to when to start braking and how much to brake, in order to ensure that the corner is negotiated more accurately. When success is achieved, the pupil should then be allowed to deal with similar corners unassisted, thus validating their understanding and skill.

This all sounds fairly logical when you put it down on paper. However, it is sometimes surprising how some instructors would, first of all, fail to pinpoint accurately the cause of the error (not just the effect), and then not be able to assist the pupil in working out a solution to the problem, or to put the solution into practice.

Skills training

In learning to drive, it is the practical application of the knowledge, under-standing and attitudes gained that is most important. Whatever the situation, when learning to do something there are three basic steps:

1. determine the purpose – WHAT and WHY;
2. identify the procedures involved – HOW;
3. practise the task – DO.

1.   Determine the purpose – WHAT and WHY

Learners must have a clear understanding of the reason for needing to be able to do whatever it is that you are teaching them. When teaching people how to drive the reasons why things are done in a certain way are invariably to do with:

● *Safety*
● *Convenience*
● *Efficiency*
● *Simplicity*
● *Economy*

One example that covers all of the above would involve the use of brakes to slow the car rather than the gears:

● *Safety:* Both hands are on the steering wheel when the weight of the car is thrown forward; the brake lights come on to warn following drivers.
● *Convenience:* There is less to do if you slow the car with the brakes rather than using only the gears.
● *Efficiency:* The car is being slowed by all four wheels rather than just two.
● *Simplicity:* It is easier to change gear at the lower speed.
● *Economy:* Brake pads and discs are much less expensive than clutches and gearboxes.

2.   Identify the procedures – HOW

The most efficient way for a learner to understand how to do something is to break the skill down into manageable chunks or stages. This can be done by following a few basic guidelines:

- Known to unknown. Start with what the pupil knows, understands and can do, before moving on to new skills and procedures.

- Simple to complex. Setting intermediate targets and moving gradually to more complex tasks will help the pupil through the learning process.

- Basic rules to the variations. Once the basic rules for a particular procedure have been mastered, the pupil will find it easier to deal with the variations.

- Concrete observations to abstract reasoning. Organizing a structured learning process is much less difficult if the learner can start with the more obvious facts before attempting to cope with more complicated or abstract matters.

For more detail on structuring the learning process, see chapter 8 of *The Driving Instructor's Handbook*.

If it is a more complicated task, then you should consider whether or not a DEMONSTRATION would benefit the pupil (see Chapter 3 – Explanation, Demonstration, Practice routine).

3.   Practise the task – DO

What I hear, I forget; What I see, I remember; What I do, I understand.

> *You must never forget that it is the doing that will give pupils the greatest UNDERSTANDING. In each driving lesson you must therefore give your pupil as much time as possible to PRACTISE the skills which have been learnt.*

The more time spent in practising the skill, the more improved the performance should be. As it is much more difficult to correct bad habits once they have become built in to the routines used by learners, good habits must always be encouraged.

Every instructor knows that it is more difficult to correct the mistakes of someone who has received poor instruction than it is to teach correct procedures to someone with no previous driving experience.

Although some car driving routines could be taught initially by ROTE (for example, the M S M, P S L and L A D routines), the application of them requires an *understanding* which then allows the pupil to make connections with any previously established principles.

For example, once your pupil has carried out one of the manoeuvres using the criteria of CONTROL, OBSERVATION and ACCURACY, it will then be relatively easy for them to follow the same pattern in similar but slightly more complicated manoeuvres – ie teaching from the known to the unknown.

As an instructor you will be mixing learning methods to suit the needs of each individual pupil, combined with the all-important PRACTICE.

The skill of the teacher is to find a mix that works, or be prepared to change to a different mixture if necessary.

The key to good instruction is the flexibility of the instructor to be able to work out what is best for the pupil, and adapt the teaching to suit.

Attitude

Positively developing a driver's attitude is no different from developing the other transferable skills. You must have the correct attitude towards driving in order to be able to transfer a similar attitude to your learners.

You will need to develop your learners' assessment and decision-making skills so that they become compatible with your own. Remember, you must be able to persuade learners how to do what you want them to do, in the way that you want them to do it. For example, do your learners:

- show courtesy and consideration for other road users at all times?;
- reduce the risk of accidents by planning well ahead?;
- follow the rules in the *Highway Code*, keeping within the law?;
- think defensively instead of aggressively?;
- always consider the consequences of unsafe actions?

Encouraging the correct attitudes can sometimes be quite difficult to achieve, especially when teaching adults. Previous knowledge and learning can get in the way and old attitudes are difficult to modify.

The learner comes into this world with no attitudes about anything. Attitudes are formed early on, mainly by association with friends, relatives or groups with strong views on particular subjects. In the driving task, a learner who, for example, has spent a lot of time as a passenger alongside an aggressive experienced driver may regard this driver's behaviour as the norm and is likely to adopt a similar attitude. When the learner realizes that this attitude is different from yours, they may attempt to put on a show just for your benefit, or for the benefit of a driving test examiner.

Attitudes are formed from three constituents:

1. KNOWLEDGE

2. MOTIVATION

3. EMOTION

The attitudes of learners can be changed, through skilful persuasion, by modifying their views and the decisions they make in any given situation.

To assist in this modification of attitude, you could use accident statistics regarding new drivers, safe driving videos, the high cost of insurance for newly qualified drivers, the New Driver Act and the possibility of losing their licence, or apply coaching techniques to help them modify their own attitude.

> *There is little doubt that attitudes have an enormous influence on the behaviour of the driver and the development of favourable attitudes is probably the most effective long-term method of reducing road accidents.*

By far the most useful aid to attitude development is the continual use of the DEFENSIVE DRIVING theme, pointing out the safety benefits to your pupils.

Defensive driving

You can contribute positively towards reducing the risk of accidents by teaching your pupils defensive driving techniques and attitudes. The development of a defensive attitude is probably more important than skill development. It is good to be able to get out of trouble when a potentially dangerous situation arises, but it is much more effective and sensible to avoid getting into trouble in the first place!

The theory of defensive driving relies on the fact that human behaviour is generally motivated most powerfully by a desire to preserve one's own safety. Defensive driving develops this concept by instilling in drivers an attitude designed to do just that, coupled with the advanced observation of potential accident situations. It may be defined as 'driving in such a way as to prevent accidents, in spite of adverse conditions and the incorrect action of others'. The need for teaching defensive driving skills is emphasized by the DSA's introduction of 'hazard-perception' testing.

An accident has been described as 'an unforeseen and unexpected event', but in many cases potential road accidents *can* be foreseen and in most cases, when they happen, are caused by driver error. Everyone then asks who was to blame. Of far more value to driver education is to consider: 'Was it preventable?'

A preventable accident is one where a driver – not necessarily at fault – could reasonably have taken some action to prevent it happening.

The Driving Instructor's Handbook gives more detail on hazard awareness, reducing risk and the theory of defensive driving. Some of the factors involved in road accidents include:

- visibility;
- weather conditions;
- road conditions;
- time of day;
- the vehicle;
- the driver.

In this section we will be concentrating on the driver and how we can instill into our learners a 'defensive attitude'.

Human actions which may contribute to accident situations are:

- committing a traffic offence;
- abuse of the vehicle;
- impatience;
- sheer discourtesy;
- lack of attention.

The defensive driver will consider all the factors in the first list, making a continuous and conscious effort to recognize each hazard in advance, understand the defensive attitude needed, and apply the skill required to take preventive action in sufficient time.

You should encourage your pupils to drive with full concentration to avoid potential accidents caused by other drivers and road users.

> *A constant awareness is required so that, no matter what they do, other road users will be unlikely to be involved in an accident with drivers you have trained.*

If another driver clearly wants priority, train your drivers to give way – better a mature decision than a lifetime of suffering as the result of an accident. Teach your pupils how to avoid confrontation and to keep a cushion of safe space around their vehicle at all times. This should include advice about drivers who follow too closely.

Get them to continually ask themselves, 'What if...?' – in this way they will improve their anticipation skills and be able to take defensive action before a situation develops into an accident.

Teach them to consider using the horn to let others know they are there; just a gentle tap on the horn can sometimes prevent an accident. It is far better for your pupils to sound the horn to alert another person than not to sound it and have to carry out an emergency stop, especially if there is somebody else close behind.

As well as thinking defensively, favourable attitudes should be developed towards:

- vehicle maintenance and safety;
- traffic law (for example: safe use of speed, traffic signs and road markings, parking restrictions, drink/drive laws, dangerous driving implications);
- the more vulnerable groups of road users;
- reduced-risk driving strategies;
- further education and training for advanced/defensive driving;
- learning and studying.

Developing study skills

You will need to develop your study skills because your self-development programme is dependent on studying. However, driving is mainly practical so you will be studying, literally, while 'on the job'.

You may at some stage in the future wish to gain extra qualifications or take some remedial or specialist training – this will also involve you in studying.

Your learners too will need to study between lessons in order to prepare for the theory test. You will need to assist them in the studying and preparation process.

In developing study techniques one needs to:

- make time available;
- find the right place;
- formulate a study plan.

Making time available

You will have to emphasize the importance of revising between lessons and explain to pupils why they may need to reorganize any social activities so that their studying is effective.

The key is to help them establish a balance between each demand on the time they have available. They should not be forced to devote all of their time and energy to studying at the expense of other interests and activities as this may cause resentment.

You may also have to consider the needs of your pupils' families. One of the best ways of achieving this is to get the family involved with the studying, perhaps by helping to test the student's knowledge, or looking through any written work which has been done.

Time management is crucial. Whenever possible, exploit those times of the day when the student is in the best frame of mind for studying, scheduling any other interests around them.

Initially, the student should try out different times until a routine is established which allows time for studying alongside other demands.

The key ingredients contributing to the success of any studying are self-discipline and determination. Inability to sustain this motivation will make learning much less effective.

To reinforce this determination, the student should continually go through all the benefits that will be acquired after successfully completing the course of study.

Finding the right place

This is almost as important as making the time available. The quality of learning is improved dramatically if the environment is 'conducive to learning'.

Certain types of learning – for example memorizing information – require a quiet environment, free from distractions. For most people a room at home which is quiet and respected by other family members as a study room will be the best setting.

There needs to be space available for books, etc, and a chair and table suitable for writing. Noise distractions should be kept to a minimum as they will reduce concentration and impede the learning process.

When a time and place for studying have been found, they should not be wasted. A structured approach to studying will give the best results.

Formulating a study plan

Studying is a skill which, like all skills, will improve with practice, determination and a planned approach.

Some people are naturally studious – they are content to spend hours at a time studying and reading. For others, studying requires effort. Other interests have to be shelved, distractions removed, and full concentration given to the task. To help in improving the quality of studying, students need a plan. For example the student should:

- set a personal objective and a time by which to achieve it;
- decide how much time each day/week will be needed to achieve the objective by the deadline set – students should be guided by other learners/ instructors/tutors as to how much time might be needed;
- prepare a formal study timetable for the duration of the learning programme, on which target dates for completing the component parts of the subject can be indicated;
- make sure the timetable includes relaxation time between study periods, with at least one whole free day per week and one or two study-free weeks if the programme is protracted;
- keep a continuous check on the progress made so as to adhere to the study timetable and not fall behind;
- not get dispirited if they fall behind but decide whether any leisure activity can be sacrificed to catch up with the study programme;
- not panic if pressures from studying build up, and discuss the pressure with friends, relatives, other students or instructors/tutors;
- consider lowering their targets and, perhaps, revise the timetable to extend the deadline if this is possible;
- never let the study programme get on top of them, but keep on top of it!

OVERCOMING BARRIERS

As well as being aware that your pupils will learn at different rates, and that your training will need to be structured to take this into consideration, you need to know that some of them will experience *barriers to learning*.

These barriers may affect:

- learners' studies for their theory test;
- the rate at which they learn to drive the car;
- a combination of both.

There are many barriers to learning that you will need to help your pupils overcome. As a general rule, the older the student, the greater the barriers tend to be.

Learning is the bringing about of more or less permanent changes in knowledge, understanding, skills and attitudes. Adults in general find that learning new skills and developing fresh attitudes is more difficult than gaining knowledge and understanding. Barriers to their learning may have to be overcome in any or all of these areas.

In adult learning the most frequently encountered barrier is *previous learning*.

Previous learning

Take the young man who has developed a partial sense of speed as a passenger, perhaps being driven by an aggressive young company car driver. He will have subconsciously formed an impression of speed norms gained while sitting next to his friend. This could be detrimental when the novice tries to emulate the experienced driver. Unless dealt with in a sensitive but firm and positive way by his instructor, this could not only seriously hinder the progress of the learner but may also be dangerous.

Consider a situation where a pupil who comes to you from another instructor who is less up-to-date than you are, or has had 'lessons' privately with an older relative who may have been driving for 30 years or more. The pupil may have been misinformed, or may have misunderstood the requirements for driving in today's conditions.

For example, two widely held – but false – conceptions are that it is good driving practice to:

● Always change down progressively through the gears when slowing, rather than using a combination of brakes and selective gear changes.

● Always signal for every manoeuvre including moving off, parking and passing stationary vehicles, whether or not there is someone to signal to or who will benefit from the signal.

Where the novice has been influenced by out dated views it is likely to become a barrier to learning and cause conflict with the new information given by you.

When this type of interference occurs, you must find ways of convincing the pupil that a change in ideas is necessary.

You will need to exercise considerable sensitivity, tolerance and patience during this period of unlearning.

One of the ways of overcoming the problem would be to show the pupil the 'official view' in *The Official DSA Guide to Driving: the essential skills*. This will add weight to your words and help to convince the pupil that change is necessary.

Another way would be for you to prepare a balance sheet, listing the benefits of carrying out the correct procedure (your method) and then asking the pupil to write down all the benefits of carrying it out their way.

Lack of motivation

This is also a barrier to learning. However, where driving instruction is concerned, because of the costs involved, this is not a common problem (as was stated in the section dealing with motivation for learning). You could, however, have some pupils who are not paying for lessons personally, such as those whose employer wishes them to pass the test in order to help with the firm's business activities. These people may have no desire at all to learn to drive.

To overcome this lack of motivation, you would need to outline the personal benefits of learning and also the consequences of not keeping the boss happy!

Other barriers to learning are:

- ILLITERACY;
- DYSLEXIA;
- COLOUR BLINDNESS;
- LANGUAGE DIFFICULTY;
- DEAFNESS;
- PHYSICAL DISABILITY.

Illiteracy

Being unable to read and write can be a barrier to learning how to drive. However, if you are prepared to adapt your teaching to suit the needs of your pupil you will usually find ways of overcoming these problems.

Two-fifths of the world's population are deemed to be illiterate but, in Northern Europe, the incidence of illiteracy is extremely rare. Very often, people who cannot read or write make up for these inabilities by being very practical and dextrous and frequently pick up driving with little or no instruction at all!

You will need to use visual aids, discussion and demonstration to get your message across. It would also be useful to involve the pupil's family in assisting with study and learning. Help will be needed particularly with the *Highway Code* and other essential reading materials.

Dyslexia (word blindness)

The inability to recognize certain words or letters is known as dyslexia. Neither its cause nor its effects are easily explained. Partially genetic, it can be described as a disorganization of the language area of the brain which, in turn, produces problems connecting sounds with visual symbols.

The end result is more readily understood. A person who is dyslexic may experience some learning difficulties with reading, writing and arithmetic. Ignorance of dyslexia in the past has meant that many people who suffered from the condition were regarded as stupid or unintelligent. However, there is no link between dyslexia and intelligence.

Dyslexia is uncommon and, again, should not present a problem if you are prepared to vary your instruction to suit the needs of the pupil. Visual aids should be used and help given in recognizing and acting on traffic signs.

More help may be needed when learning *Highway Code* rules and driving principles. You should also try to encourage the pupil's family to help with the study.

Interactive computer programs are now available to help people with dyslexia overcome some of the problems.

Colour blindness

This is likely to cause problems only when dealing with the different types of traffic light controlled situations such as junctions and pedestrian and level crossings.

Rather than focusing on the colours, you will need to base your explanation on the positioning and sequence of the lights and what each of them means.

Language difficulties

If pupils' understanding of English is very poor, this can be a barrier to learning and, in extreme cases, the learner might need the help of an interpreter.

Providing the pupil has some knowledge of English, the use of visual aids, demonstrations and getting to know what the limitations are, will help you to overcome these difficulties.

It is important, right from the start, for you to encourage pupils to say if there is anything they have not understood.

If there is someone in the family who speaks better English than the pupil, it may be useful to have a debriefing with them present. This should enable you to clarify specific requests to the pupil and also allow the pupil to convey any queries to you.

Teaching people who have hearing difficulties

This section gives guidelines that should help you to adapt the PTS in this book when teaching people with hearing problems.

There are about 50,000 people in the UK who were either born without any hearing or who lost it during early childhood. There are several thousand others who have become profoundly deaf in adult life, well after they have learnt to speak, read and write. By the time they reach the age of 17 and are thinking about learning to drive, those with severe hearing problems may have had most of their education in specialist schools or units. Some will have speech, but this may be difficult to follow – especially for anyone who is not used to dealing with this type of disability. They will probably use sign language and may also be able to lip-read.

With understanding and patience from an effective instructor, people with hearing difficulties should be able to assimilate all that is necessary to learn to drive.

Although not being able to hear will undoubtedly be a barrier to learning, an understanding of the pupil's special problems will quickly enable you to overcome them.

People who cannot hear do not regard themselves as being disabled. Indeed, deafness is not classed as a driver disability so no restrictions are placed on the full licence.

It is particularly important for people with hearing difficulties, and those with no useful hearing at all, to disclose this fact in the 'Disabilities and special circumstances' box in the DSA application form for the driving test (DL26). This will ensure that the examiner will be prepared to modify the method of delivery of instructions to suit the candidate's particular needs.

Test candidates who have neither hearing nor speech will be allowed a special interpreter.

When no interpreter is to be present, you must find time to talk to the examiner well before the date of the test so that you can explain which method has been used to give directions and instructions during training. The examiner can then give directions and instructions that are compatible. This will mean that the pupil on test is much more likely to be relaxed.

Most instructors are only asked infrequently to teach pupils who have hearing problems, and when asked are sometimes reluctant to do it. This is mainly because there is a widespread lack of understanding of the problems of people with hearing difficulties and the ways in which they are able to communicate. For many instructors the task may seem too daunting. As a result, people without hearing often find difficulty in obtaining expert tuition and tend to rely on parents and friends – people who may be good at communicating with deaf people but who are not necessarily able to teach safe driving for life. Driving instructors who are specialists in communication, have good PTS and who understand the effects of not being able to hear are better equipped to teach than friends and relatives.

After adapting your PTS for people with hearing difficulties, you will find the experience both rewarding and enriching. The problem for you will be to learn the best way to transfer your knowledge, skills, understanding and attitude to these pupils.

It is not necessary for you to learn the British sign language used by people with hearing problems, but you must use simple straightforward words which have only one meaning, avoiding those that might be ambiguous.

As lip-reading depends as much on the clarity of the speaker's lip movements as on the ability of the pupil, it is essential that you speak slowly and distinctly, and move your lips to form each word. Face-to-face conversation while stationary becomes more important than with a hearing pupil. Never shout – the pupil cannot hear what you are saying!

With impaired hearing, sight and touch become a great deal sharper and this helps pupils to overcome the disadvantage of not being able to hear. They are likely to be much more aware of what is happening on the road ahead and will quickly master how to assess risk.

People without hearing also develop great sensitivity of feeling over the normal course of living in silence. Consequently, they often acquire clutch control and coordination with the accelerator fairly easily.

People with hearing problems normally have better powers of concentration than learners with normal hearing.

Pupils who cannot hear:

- do not lack intelligence;
- are eager to learn;
- are less likely to forget something they have been taught.

Communication between you and pupils with any hearing difficulty, whether this be through the use of visual aids or signing, should be reinforced with demonstrations.

When teaching those with a hearing problem it is vital that a method of communication acceptable to both of you is established at the beginning of their first lesson.

No matter what problems a pupil may have, the normal skill-training pattern of *Explanation – Demonstration – Practice* must be followed. However, because of the risk of any danger arising through misunderstanding, the *explanation* needs to be more thorough. You must ensure that learners with hearing problems fully understand the safety aspects of any driving skill before being allowed to practise it.

Pre-prepared cards which cover *what, how, when* and, most importantly, *why* can be used. The cards can be used to reinforce the KEY POINTS of any manoeuvre or exercise with drawings of pedestrians, cyclists and cars indicating the involvement of other road users. A magnetic board can be useful to recreate situations quickly and easily.

When giving directions, a simple form of sign language can be used provided you both agree and understand the signs to be used. These signs, because they are being used while the vehicle is moving along the road, will not be the same as those used in the British sign language. This must be explained to, and fully understood by, the pupil. For example, putting a thumb up will mean 'good', whereas putting a thumb down will mean 'incorrect'.

As a large amount of learning will take place through the eyes, it must be understood how the task of teaching people with hearing difficulties becomes easier with the use of visual aids and demonstrations. Visual aids are not only invaluable, they are essential. (See Chapter 3 – Visual Aids.)

Face-to-face conversation, simple language and written notes should cover all of the other needs of most pupils.

Because you will not be able to use an effective question and answer technique while on the move, diagrams will be invaluable when teaching pupils with hearing difficulties. More time will need to be spent parked somewhere safe so that non-verbal instruction can take place.

A complete practical teaching booklet produced by the late Elwyn Reed MBE explains in detail a system for teaching pupils who have profound hearing difficulties. This is recommended to anyone who is considering extending their PTS by undertaking this worthwhile activity. Details of the booklet, which has been approved by The British Deaf Association, are available from:

The Institute of Master Tutors of Driving
12 Queensway
Poynton
Cheshire SK12 1JG

Tel: (01625) 872708

The diagrams and illustrations in this booklet, together with your own visual aids and PTS, will be of great assistance in your work.

It is important to acquaint pupils with all the safety requirements of the 'L' test outlined in the DSA publication *The Official Guide to Learning to Drive*. Ensure that they completely understand what is expected from them when carrying out the set manoeuvres, particularly regarding the observations to be made.

Learning the theory of driving for pupils with hearing difficulties

The DSA CD ROMs and DVDs on the *Highway Code* and *The Official Theory Test* will be useful for pupils to study in between lessons. Questions can be devised in written form to test their understanding of the rules.

Always have a writing pad handy so that any questions and answers can be written down.

If any problems arise, you will benefit from talking to the parents or relatives of pupils and getting in touch with any local associations for deaf people or:

The British Deaf Association
1–3 Worship Street
London EC2A 2AB

Tel: (020) 7588 3520

Physical disability

Physical disability need not be a bar to driving. There are thousands of people with disabilities, some quite severe, who have passed the driving test. Many have proved their skill by also passing an advanced test.

Teaching people with disabilities can be very rewarding as they usually have lots of motivation to learn and often put in more effort than their able-bodied peers.

If you do accept the challenge, the PTS in this book will help you to improve the quality of learning taking place. In particular, you will need to pay special attention to the following:

- *Flexibility* – being able to adapt your usual teaching methods to suit the perceived needs of the pupil.

- *Lesson planning* – being prepared to build in rest breaks and taking care not to spend too long on manoeuvres which may put physical strain on the pupil.

- *Body language* – watching carefully for signs of strain.

- *Feedback* – offering feedback only on things that are controllable. Telling a pupil that they are not reversing properly because they are not turning round in the driving seat sufficiently is not very helpful if they are unable to turn any further owing to the disability. In this situation another solution must be found – for example, fitting extending side mirrors.

Fitting out a vehicle with lots of modifications to suit a wide variety of disabilities can be very cost prohibitive, unless you have a wide catchment area of prospective pupils. Sometimes an automatic vehicle may be all that is needed to overcome the problems of some disabilities.

Three fairly common disabilities which can be overcome relatively simply, enabling effective teaching are:

- having only one leg;
- having only one arm;
- restriction of head, neck or body movement.

Someone with no left leg should be able to drive an ordinary automatic vehicle, while somebody with no right leg will be able to get pedal extensions/adaptions to enable the accelerator and brake of an ordinary automatic vehicle to be operated with the left one.

Someone with only one arm should also be able to drive an automatic vehicle with a steering-wheel spinner fitted. These can be fitted or removed in a matter of minutes.

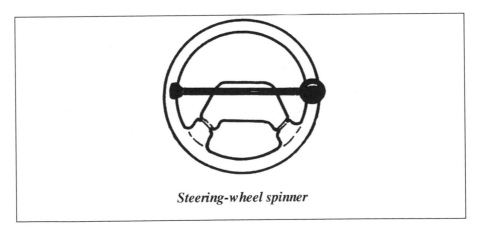

Steering-wheel spinner

There are number of different types of spinner to suit the individual needs of the person. See examples overleaf:

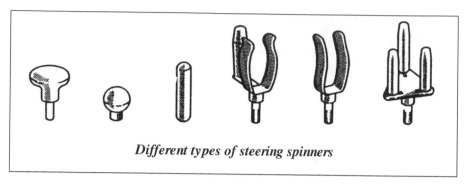

Different types of steering spinners

Using this type of adaptation means that a standard automatic transmission vehicle could be used by disabled people and the steering spinner easily removed for use with able-bodied pupils.

For those with restricted movement of the head, neck or body, special mirrors may be fitted to remove the need to look round before moving off or changing lanes.

Those people who have quite severe disabilities should normally be advised to seek an assessment from specialists at one of the mobility centres around the country. A list of these is included in *The Driving Instructor's Handbook*. If it is considered that they will be able to learn successfully, they will be advised on how a suitable vehicle of their own could be adapted to help overcome their problems. Lessons will, in these cases, be conducted in the pupil's vehicle.

You may need to allow extra time at the beginning and end of lessons for the pupil to get in and out of the vehicle. Frequent breaks may be necessary during lessons if the pupil is prone to tiring easily or becomes uncomfortable after sitting in the same position for a while.

You will need to assess each pupil's personal requirements, and adapt your teaching methods to suit them.

Some people tire very easily as the day progresses. Lessons should be arranged at appropriate times so that pupils will be 'at their best'. This will ensure that as much learning as possible takes place. You will need to find out pupils' weaknesses and strengths and work out the best ways of dealing with them so that problems are minimized.

If you wish to specialize in this kind of work, it is recommended that you attend a course for instructors in teaching people with disabilities. Details of available courses can be found in *The Driving Instructor's Handbook*. Courses are conducted at various centres around the country, including special courses for ADIs at the Queen Elizabeth's Foundation Mobility Centre at

Carshalton. Full details of all available courses and centres can be found in *The Driving Instructor's Handobook*.

Other impairments

Mere discomfort can be a barrier to learning. You need to be able to recognize whether or not your pupils are comfortable. Discomfort can have many causes, ranging from toothache to sitting in an incorrect position, or being told, 'You must keep your heel on the floor when using the clutch' when the pupil's feet are too small or their legs too long to do this comfortably.

Allowances may have to be made for very tall people – they will need the seat as far back as possible with the back rake adjusted to give more leg room. If the tuition vehicle is very small, it may even be necessary for you to advise them to take lessons with another instructor who has a larger car with more headroom.

Pupils of small stature may be assisted by securing cushions underneath and behind them, and pedal extensions may be needed for those with short legs or small feet. Your terminology may also need to be adjusted to allow for pupils not being able to keep their heel down when controlling the clutch.

If a pupil is not driving as well as usual there may be some simple explanation. For example, was the driving seat adjusted properly on entering the vehicle, or was the pupil in too much of a hurry to 'get going'? Make sure these minor procedures are carried out correctly otherwise you may both be at a loss as to the cause of the problems and the lesson may be wasted.

If the pupil is having an uncharacteristically bad lesson, it may be due to something as simple as wearing different shoes, or as complicated as having problems at home.

Ask tactfully if you think a pupil may not be feeling well. The lesson may be completely wasted if a minor illness is causing a distraction. You could even be aiding and abetting an offence if the pupil is taking drugs which affect driving.

Others barriers to learning to drive can be caused by the use of alcohol which, as well as being illegal, can cause a false sense of confidence and impetuous risk-taking. If you think a pupil has been drinking, ask tactfully and abort the lesson if necessary. On no account do you let the pupil take the test if they have been drinking.

Anxiety, emotion and stress can all affect concentration. If a pupil's driving is not up to the usual standard and they have recently had personal problems, it may be advisable to postpone the lesson. Explain that it is not the best time to drive as they will not be able to concentrate on the road and traffic environment.

We are all affected by the ageing process. For those who decide to learn to drive later on in life the going can be difficult. You should explain that it will be more difficult to learn and to remember new procedures. Things may be more easily forgotten and concentration more difficult to sustain. Problems may be even greater for those in this age group who have decided to learn to drive because they have lost a partner or close relative. You will need lots of patience and understanding if you are to help these pupils attain their goal.

Continually assess your own effectiveness by asking yourself:

- Do I stress the benefits of learning to drive in order to motivate my pupils?
- Do I structure my teaching to make it easier for the pupil to memorize, understand and do things?
- Do I pay enough attention to developing or modifying attitudes towards driving and other road users?
- Do I help pupils to develop their studying skills, setting them enough 'between-lesson tasks'?
- Do I help pupils to overcome any barriers to learning which they may have?

2

Communication skills

We learn all the time in everything we do. If we did not, we would not be able to deal with the everyday environment in which we live. We would constantly stub a toe on furniture, burn our fingers when using the cooker, or press the wrong buttons on the TV remote control.

Because the driving task is technically demanding for the novice and is a potentially dangerous situation for the newly qualified driver, the instructor needs to accelerate the learning process. There is a need to ensure that your pupils are taught to understand hazards and how to deal with them as soon as possible. In this chapter we deal with the essential *Practical Teaching Skills* (PTS) of communication that help bring about learning when teaching people to drive. These PTS include verbal, non-verbal and listening skills.

According to Driving Standards Agency criteria to become an efficient instructor – and to pass the ADI exams – you need to be:

- *Articulate.* This doesn't mean that you need to be a fluent public speaker, but it does mean that you should language that is clear to your pupils and that can be easily understood by them.

- *Enthusiastic.* Always endeavour to create a supportive learning environment by showing enthusiasm for the work and for your pupil's efforts.

- *Encouraging.* Give encouragement to the pupil when deserved, but balance this with criticism when required. Any criticism given should be constructive and related to the requirements of the particular task.

- *Friendly.* The way you approach the teaching of your pupils should be in a friendly but professional manner, creating a relaxed atmosphere in which learning can take place.

- *Patient.* As with your own driving, show patience and tolerance, both with other road users and with your own pupils when they make mistakes or are not as efficient as you would like them to be.

- *Confident.* Have confidence in your own ability as a driver and as an instructor, but also develop the skill to help your pupils build confidence in their own driving.

Communication should be a two-way process between you and the pupil. This means listening to them and observing their actions as well as talking. Make sure that any communication from you to the pupil is at a level that is easily understood by them.

As a driver, you communicate with other road users by various means, including indicator signals, brake lights, positioning, flashing headlights and the horn, as well as by eye contact. Similarly, as an instructor you will develop different ways of communicating effectively with your pupils. You will often have to vary and adapt your methods and terminology to suit the needs of individual pupils, so that each of them clearly understands your message or instructions.

To communicate effectively with your pupils you should develop a variety of methods, including:

- Establish an appropriate level of understanding for each pupil.

- Explain any new principles in a clear and straightforward manner.

- Use visual aids where appropriate to give the pupil a clearer picture of what is required.

- Consider whether a demonstration would be effective for a particularly complex procedure or manoeuvre.

- 'Talk through' any new procedures or routines to develop the pupil's confidence.

- Give any directional instructions clearly and in good time, allowing the pupil plenty of time to make decisions and respond accordingly.

- Use positive feedback and praise where appropriate, in order to encourage and motivate the pupil.

- Use questions to ensure that the pupil has a thorough understanding of the task.

- Encourage pupils to ask questions and allow sufficient time for them.

Whatever means of communication you use, make sure that the pupil fully understands what is required and be ready to modify your methods to suit the needs of the individual pupil.

Use each lesson with a pupil as an opportunity to practise your communication skills. At the end of each lesson, you should analyse your own performance with a view to improving your ability and skills.

Ask yourself:

- Have I spent sufficient time looking at, and listening to, my pupil?
- Have I misinterpreted or not seen any silent signals?
- Have I missed the pupil's control faults or observational errors by not watching them carefully enough?
- Has my own body language been positive?
- Have I encouraged or discouraged the pupil by the way in which I reacted to their actions or responses to my questions?
- Could I have communicated more effectively with the pupil during the lesson?

All of these points are dealt with in more detail later in this chapter.

VERBAL COMMUNICATION

As an instructor you must make sure that you use speech effectively and in such a way that your pupils will hear and understand what it is that you need them to hear. For example, even though you may be frustrated or exasperated, you may not want your tone of voice to convey this to your pupil. There are, however, certain times when for safety reasons, you have to get your point across reasonably forcefully. The elements of speech that help you to communicate effectively include:

- tone of voice;
- use of emphasis;
- content of speech;
- use of figurative language;
- use of humour;
- speed of speaking;
- use of pronunciation;
- pitch of your voice;
- use of implied speech.

The tone of your voice

When you speak to your pupils it is important to put them at ease and maintain their interest and attention. If they are not paying attention, it is doubtful whether they will learn anything at all.

Your tone of voice conveys your emotions and feelings, such as annoyance and pleasure, and supports the content of what you are saying. As the tone of voice often conveys the true meaning of your message, it is important that you sound friendly and relaxed even though you may be feeling the opposite!

Consider the following question: 'Why did you slow down?' If you pose this question in a harsh tone of voice, you will sound as though you are telling the pupil off. If you ask the same question with a soft tone of voice, you are showing interest in the pupil's actions.

Practise asking the question in different ways and attempt to convey different meanings to it.

When teaching, you need to consider the tone of your voice, in order to give a clear meaning of the words and to add variety to their delivery. This is essential if you are going to retain the pupil's interest and attention. If you restrict yourself to only one tone, your delivery will become monotonous and it is likely that the pupil will lose interest.

The use of emphasis

By putting greater stress on certain words you can alter the meaning of a sentence. For example:

'*What* are you looking for?'
'What *are* you looking for?'
'What are *you* looking for?'
'What are you *looking* for?'
'What are you looking *for*?'

Practise asking this question out loud and, each time, put the emphasis on the word in italics. In the first question, you are asking about the action of looking itself. In the second you imply disbelief that the pupil is bothering to look at all. The third sentence queries whether it is the pupil who should be looking – perhaps somebody else should be looking! In the fourth example you are questioning the action – perhaps there is no point in looking at this moment in time. In the last question you are probing the pupil's understanding of what needs to be seen as a result of looking.

Now try using each of the questions again, continuing to emphasize the word in italics, but try to vary your voice to express concern, anger, and amazement.

As well as saying the words in a particular way you can sometimes stress a particular consonant or vowel to accentuate your meaning. For example, 'Slooowwwlly let the clutch come up.'

People who are practised and skilled speakers, such as politicians or lawyers, often use emphasis to considerable effect not only to help the listener to understand the message but also to indicate hidden meanings, which otherwise might not have been obvious. Sometimes it is only when a speech is heard rather than read that you understand what message is being conveyed.

The content of speech

As well as the tone and emphasis you use when speaking, the words themselves are vital if you wish to be effective in communicating.

The use of an unambiguous vocabulary is vital when teaching people how to drive. You should always try to match the words you are using to the level of understanding and ability of the pupil. The skilled trainer will be able to put trainees at their ease by talking with them at an appropriate level.

> *There is no point in using long and complicated words when teaching somebody who cannot understand them. The best advice is to keep it simple as this is more likely to bring about learning.*

Getting to know your pupils will help you to use suitable words and phrases that they will readily be able to understand. One common criticism of less able instructors is that they tend to use inappropriate phraseology that is not easily understood. The use of jargon should be avoided where possible. If it *is* necessary, make sure that the expressions have been explained to the pupil.

When dealing with the controls of the car it is best to explain to the pupil not only what the control does and how it is used, but the words that you are going to use when dealing with it. This will avoid your pupil becoming confused with possibly dangerous results. For example, if you are going to call the accelerator the gas pedal don't suddenly confuse the pupil by calling it the 'throttle'.

While communicating with pupils, you should avoid talking about race, religion, sex and politics. Remarks of this nature may be offensive to the person in question and, even if they are not, they will devalue whatever else you may be saying, causing the pupil to 'switch off'.

The use of figurative language

Always try to make the content of your message interesting to listen to. There is nothing worse than boring your pupil. You can avoid doing this in a number of ways by using FIGURATIVE LANGUAGE. By this, we mean using such things as:

● METAPHORS;

● SIMILES;

● HYPERBOLE;

● ANALOGIES;

● PERSONAL EXPERIENCES.

A METAPHOR is used to imply a similarity between things or situations which are not really associated – for example, 'crawling along at a snail's pace'.

A SIMILE is a figurative comparison using terms such as 'like' or 'as'. An example would be to say that a bad driver was 'driving like a lunatic'.

HYPERBOLE is the use of deliberate over-exaggeration – for example, 'That gap is big enough to get a bus through.' (You must be careful when doing this that you avoid using sarcasm.)

An ANALOGY is a comparison made to show a similarity in situations or ideas – for example, 'If you have time to walk across, then you will have time to drive across!'

PERSONAL EXPERIENCES (or ANECDOTES) allow you to compare situations happening now with those that might have happened before. For example, if you had a pupil who tried to emerge unsafely, you might say, 'I had a pupil last week who tried to emerge from a junction without looking. If I hadn't used the dual controls, we would have hit a cyclist!'

By using all of these figures of speech you will make your lessons more interesting and the messages less likely to be forgotten. Care must be taken however that you do not overuse them to the extent that the intended content of your message is diluted or lost.

The use of humour in speech

Instructors who are humorous often maintain their pupils' attention and interest very effectively but it does not work for every pupil or every instructor. If you try to be funny unsuccessfully you could lose your credibility. We all know someone who, when telling a joke, invariably forgets the punchline. You should not tell jokes during the lesson time as this will annoy most pupils, and in no circumstances should you tell racist, sexist, religious or dubious jokes.

Many instructors can be extremely amusing without telling jokes. They can put a message across using wit but, again, not every pupil will respond well to witty remarks and some may take offence, especially if they do not realize that you are trying to be witty. You can often bring a smile to your pupil's face without trying too hard just by being alert and responding to a possibly difficult situation with a humorous remark. For example, you might be waiting at traffic lights which turn to green and your pupil does not move – you could gently ask, 'What colour are we waiting for?'

You should avoid using sarcasm however, as it could cost you a pupil and adds nothing to the learning process.

The speed of speaking

The speed at which you speak can help to maintain the interest of your pupils. You can create anticipation by increasing the speed of speech as you build up to an important point. You can also use silence, or pauses to allow things to sink in before you continue. If you pause while you are talking you can indicate a sense of deliberateness to give emphasis to certain key points. For example: 'MIRRORS (pause), SIGNAL (pause), MANOEUVRE'.

You can also use pauses to give you time to think before delivering your next piece of information, but such pauses should not be excessive otherwise you will lose your pupil's attention completely. Try not to fill in the pauses with 'ums' and 'ahs' as this will irritate your pupil and detract from what you are saying.

Slowing down the speed at which you say a single word can be useful in indicating the speed of action required by matching it with the speed of the delivery of the word. For example, 'Slooowwwllyy let the clutch up, squeeeezze the gas' or 'Geennntttly brake'.

Pronunciation

It is important that as an 'expert' you pronounce the words you use correctly. Your pupil will expect you to be fully conversant with the subject you are talking about and if you mispronunce too often you could damage your credibility, distract your listeners from what you are saying and reduce their attention. If you come across new words when reading books on driving and intend using them but are unsure of their pronunciation, then it is best to refer to a dictionary.

For example, when teaching the emergency stop many instructors mispronounce the word 'cadence' as in cadence braking. Try looking it up in your dictionary and see if you are pronouncing it correctly!

Pitch

Pitch is a combination of the tone that you use and the loudness of the sound that you make. Considerable emphasis can be given to the instruction or direction you are giving by varying the pitch of your voice. Pitch is particularly useful when you wish to convey urgency, caution or importance either to whatever it is that you are saying or the way you wish your pupil to react to the words you are using.

Care must be taken not to over-exaggerate the pitch of your voice because it can be a distraction to your pupil. Your speech should be a comfortable variation of harsh and soft tones and of loudness and softness.

Speaking loudly will not always get the attention you desire. You only have to think of British tourists abroad trying to communicate with somebody with no English. In vain they end up almost shouting – *'DO YOU SPEAK ENGLISH?'*!

Pitch is useful when using keyword prompts, particularly those which require urgent action such as 'WAIT', 'HOLD BACK', or 'STOP'.

Implied speech

Speech can be used to convey your feelings and especially your attitude to a given situation. The dictionary meaning of the words you are using is not as important as what they imply.

It is therefore not only the words being used but also the way in which they are delivered that gets the message across.

Initial speech will sometimes be used to 'break the ice'. For example, if you ask 'How are you today?', it not only puts the pupil at ease but also gives you some feedback, which might be useful when structuring the lesson content. If the pupil is feeling good, then perhaps you will set the objective for the lesson high. If they are not feeling good then perhaps your sights will be lowered to maybe consolidating an existing skill.

When meeting people for the first time, one often talks about the weather or the journey they have had to get to the meeting. The person opening the conversation might genuinely not be interested in these things but is really saying, 'I wish to communicate with you, please respond.'

All of the above elements of speech can be developed. Whether teaching in the car, in the classroom or speaking to larger groups at meetings and conferences, it may be useful either to tape record or, better still (because you can also see what visual impact you are having), video the proceedings with a view to assessing and improving your performance.

There are certain speech distractions which should be eliminated where possible. The most common is the frequent use of speech mannerisms such as, 'OK', 'right', 'you know', 'I mean', 'well then'. This trait gives the impression of a lack of confidence or nervousness, neither of which will help to put the pupil at ease or inspire trust. Also, the use of the word 'right' to mean 'correct' could be misleading and dangerous.

Talking plays a great part in teaching people how to drive and you should take every opportunity to further develop your speaking skills. Remember that, when speaking, you are not only giving a verbal message but also conveying your feelings and attitudes.

> *By varying your speech you can drastically change your listener's interpretation of what you are saying, whether you are talking on a one-to-one basis, or to small or large groups.*

Other common mistakes that speakers make which, particularly when they are talking to groups, can cause their listeners to become bored and lose their concentration are:

- repeating things they have said before;
- getting too technical for the audience.

Telephone conversations form a valuable part of your life given that the initial contact with a potential customer is often made on the telephone. Much of what has been said about speech also applies in this situation.

The problem is that you are unable to read the body language of the person you are speaking to. If you cannot see the gestures and facial expressions of the other party you lose some insight into what they are thinking while they are speaking.

> *Communicating is not just talking, but should be a two-way exchange of ideas and information. You will therefore need to develop your listening skills.*

Developing the communication skills of speaking and listening will help you in presenting a driving lesson. Similar rules will apply to presentations to larger groups but in this section we will concentrate on the one-to-one lesson.

LISTENING SKILLS

We have two ears but only one mouth and we should use them in those proportions. We will learn more about our learners' needs by asking questions and listening to what they say than we will by talking.

You need to pay particular attention to anything that your pupils say voluntarily and try to look at them when they are talking so that you can pick up the silent signals as well. These non-verbal messages will often reinforce the verbal message and help you to understand what people are really feeling. This may often be at variance with what they are saying.

You can then use questions like: 'You don't seem too happy with that. Is there anything that you don't understand?'

When people are listening, they tend to show their interest and attention both verbally and non-verbally. They will nod their heads, lean forward, and say things like, 'Yes, I see', 'That's true', 'I absolutely agree' and 'Hear, hear'.

On the other hand, if they are not listening, they do not look at you, they yawn or they do not respond. Any of these responses will indicate to you that they are bored with the proceedings and that you need to alter your approach to this part of the lesson.

You can develop your listening skills in the following ways:

- 'Listen' with your eyes as well as your ears. By looking at the speaker you will not only hear the words but detect the silent signals which help you to understand the *true* meaning of what the person is saying.

- Ask questions. If anything is unclear, do not be afraid of asking for it to be clarified, and if you disagree with the point being made, then say so, but give your reasons why.

Use open-ended questions to test pupils' understanding of anything you have explained to them and seek their views and opinions on what you are saying. When they respond, hear them out; do not interrupt – wait until they have finished speaking before replying.

BRIEFINGS AND EXPLANATIONS

You will often need to give your pupils BRIEFINGS in which you explain what is to be covered during the lesson to come. These briefings will usually include a statement of the objectives for the lesson, and a short summary of the key points of WHAT is to be covered.

The briefing will usually be followed by a more full explanation of HOW to do whatever is being taught; WHEN to do it; and, particularly, WHY it is important for the content to be taught in a certain way.

Communicating information of this nature plays a vital part in the normal skill-training technique of EXPLANATION, DEMONSTRATION and PRACTICE, which is covered in Chapter 3.

Care must be taken not to 'overload' the pupil. Information should be divided into the following categories:

- MUST KNOW;
- SHOULD KNOW;
- COULD KNOW.

You should be able to identify the 'key points' of the message and then concentrate on making sure that the pupil understands these MUST KNOW elements. Further information from the SHOULD KNOW and COULD KNOW categories may be given in response to questions from the pupil or filled in later, possibly on the move as situations develop which require this further information to be given.

Making sure that pupils know and understand everything that they need to know can be achieved by:

- breaking the information down into its component parts;
- using mnemonics to make routines more memorable – for example, M S M, P S L and L A D (see pages 81–82):
- using word associations like 'Creep and Peep';
- using visual keys like 'Think of the thickness of a coin';
- slowing or quickening the speed of your speech to match that at which you want the action to be carried out;
- using pauses after important points have been made;
- using the Q & A technique after each key point has been made to confirm the pupil's understanding of what has been said;
- using visual aids where appropriate and, if the subject is technical, giving handouts for pupils to refer to after their lesson.

At the end of each lesson that has contained a briefing or full explanation, assess your own performance. Ask yourself, 'Has the pupil understood all the key points that I have explained?'

Problems will arise during driving lessons if the instructions and directions are not given in a clear and unmistakable manner. You need to take account of all the previous points made about verbal communication but you should also take special note of the following:

- Use language that will be readily understood by the pupil to avoid any confusion arising.
- Avoid ambiguous words which might be misinterpreted by the pupil. For example: 'Right', meaning 'OK' or 'correct', could cause the pupil to think you want them to turn right; 'top', meaning top gear, could be misheard as

'stop', especially on a hot day with all the windows down and noise from traffic.

- When on the move give the instruction and directions early enough for the pupil to do whatever is necessary without rushing.

- Match the level of the instruction to the ability of the pupil. A novice will need almost total instruction in what to do, whereas a trained pupil may only need the occasional 'keyword' prompt.

- Use the ALERT–DIRECT–IDENTIFY routine. For example: 'I would like you to…' (ALERT) '… take the next road on the left please.' (DIRECT) 'It's just around the bend.' (IDENTIFY).

Remember to take into account that less-experienced pupils will take longer to react to the instruction or direction. An instruction given too late is likely to result in the pupil:

- missing out important observations;
- losing control with feet or hands;
- assessing situations incorrectly;
- making poor decisions;
- losing confidence.

When teaching a pupil who is at an advanced stage, you should transfer the responsibility of working out where the various junctions and hazards are by not giving too much help. For many pupils the driving test will be the first opportunity that they have to drive on their own without your help.

A very good way of transferring responsibility and finding out whether the pupil is ready to drive unaccompanied would be to say 10 minutes before the end of the lesson: 'Do you think you could find your way back home from here on your own?' If the answer is yes, then let the pupil drive back without any instructions or directions being given.

Once the pupil is nearly at driving test standard you should make sure that you use phraseology similar to that of the examiner as a way of preparing for the test situation. It is extremely important that you 'sit in' on a driving test occasionally so that you can reaffirm your understanding of how an examiner gives directional instructions and the timing of them.

One of the most common criticisms of ADIs is that of over-instruction. This happens because the instructor does not know when to 'drop out'. Are you guilty of 'over-instructing'? If so, what are you going to do about it?

At the end of each lesson you will need to ask yourself:

- Were the instructions and directions given to my pupil in a clear and unmistakable manner?

- Did the timing of the directions given allow the pupil to do all the things necessary to deal with situations?

- Was there any ambiguity in the instructions and directions given?

BODY LANGUAGE

Whenever we communicate with others, we use body language – it is unavoidable and instinctive. Speech and the development of language began about 500,000 years ago but it is probable that body language has been used for at least 1 million years.

Because body language is so deeply ingrained in us, it is difficult to disguise and even when you are not speaking you are sending messages to others, sometimes without even being aware of it. Your physical appearance, posture, gestures, gaze and facial expressions indicate to others your moods and feelings.

It is important for you as an instructor to be able to use positive body language and interpret the body language of your learners.

Because the body language of your learners may give you more information about their mood and receptiveness than what they are saying, being able to interpret accurately these silent signals will assist you in deciding whether to modify your delivery, back off, or even change the activity entirely. For example, should the face of your pupil show frustration when failing to master a reversing exercise, you may decide to switch to something that is less demanding in order to boost the pupil's confidence rather than destroy it.

The ability to interpret body language will also enable you to tell whether there is any difference between what the pupil is saying and what they really think. The driving instructor needs to develop a high degree of perceptual sensitivity to read accurately the silent signals being sent by pupils.

Body language is particularly important in interviewing, negotiating, selling and buying situations. Although the general rules regarding body language will apply at meetings, in the classroom or during social encounters, when you are giving driving lessons your skills will need to be adapted to take account of the fact that, on the move, you can only see the side of your pupil's face. (We do not encourage our pupils to look at us while they are driving!) Of course, while stationary you will often be able to see their eyes as well.

If you want to be able to use your own body language in a positive way and be able to read that of others, you need to recognize the constituents of it. There are seven main constituents, some of which are more relevant to driving instruction than others:

- FACIAL EXPRESSIONS;
- GAZE;
- POSTURE;
- GESTURES;
- PROXIMITY;
- TOUCH;
- PERSONAL APPEARANCE.

When teaching in the car, you will need to spend much time not only reading the road ahead but looking at the face, eyes, hands and feet of the pupil. Although the hands and feet will tell how well the controls are being used, the face and eyes will not only show where pupils are looking but also what they may be thinking or feeling.

Facial expressions

In driving instruction facial expressions are most useful. The face is highly expressive (even in profile) and is capable of conveying one's innermost feelings. Think of the expression on the face of someone who has just failed the driving test and then compare it with that of someone else who has just passed!

The face is a very spontaneous communicator of messages and will generally convey the feelings of its owner in a uniform way. The face is, therefore, a fairly reliable indicator of happiness or despair, pain or pleasure. Consequently, when teaching, you should ensure that your facial expressions do not contradict what you are saying – if they do, it will have a disturbing effect on your pupils.

Gaze

When explaining things to your pupil, or debriefing at the side of the road, or in a classroom situation, you will normally have eye-to-eye contact. The eyes can tell you a great deal about what people may be feeling but, with skill and practice, your eyes can tell others what you want them to think you are feeling. Poker players and salesmen use this technique to good effect, sometimes with high stakes to play for.

A strong gaze usually shows that you are being attentive and concentrating on what the other person is saying. However, in some cultures it is seen to be impolite to stare. When people become embarrassed they will often break eye contact and look away.

Breaking eye contact may show that you have made an error or cannot answer a question, while a reluctance to look at someone at all may show your dislike or distrust of that person.

However, establishing strong eye contact will show that you have a genuine desire to communicate and will be seen by your pupils as an invitation to speak. It is a cultural expectation that people look at each other when communicating. If you are reluctant to look someone in the face when talking to them, or continually shift your eyes around, you will not inspire trust.

Your emotions, attitudes and honesty, as portrayed by your eye contact, make gaze an important constituent of your body language. Aggressive stares and shifty looks should be avoided. You should try to develop a strong gaze, with an occasional blink or look away which will make people feel more comfortable and receptive.

Posture

In the confined space of a motor car, when your feet and hands are occupied, posture is not quite so revealing as in a classroom situation where how you stand or sit and the position of your arms and legs will reflect your feelings and attitudes to others.

A normal seating position, which allows the pupil to reach the foot and hand controls comfortably, will of course determine the 'angles' of their legs and arms.

You can display a warmth and liking for someone by leaning towards them slightly, with your arms relaxed. You can show your disgust at their actions by turning away and looking out of the window. You must be careful not to hover over the dual controls with your feet as this will unnerve pupils and destroy their self-confidence. You should avoid continually looking round to check the blindspots on the move for the same reason. Careful and subtle use of your dual mirrors will achieve the same objective but without worrying the pupil.

In meetings or in the classroom, your posture becomes much more important. An erect posture will indicate a sense of pride, confidence and self-discipline, while stooping shoulders and head down may be interpreted as being slovenly or lacking in confidence. Your impressions of others and their impressions of you will be influenced by posture and gait. When walking across the room, you should therefore adopt a confident purposeful walk, which will indicate self-assurance, confidence and personal dynamism.

When giving presentations, you can use posture and body movements to help to bring your story to life, supporting any verbal message, thus maintaining the interest of those who are watching and listening.

Gestures

Gestures may occasionally be used instead of words in certain circumstances. If you are trying to communicate with someone who has hearing difficulties, or who does not speak English, gestures will help you to communicate. Your hands can be used to demonstrate how the clutch plates come together, for example.

A nod of the head, or a wave of the hand are friendly, passive signals which may be given to other instructors or road users to acknowledge a courtesy, whereas a shaking of the fist conveys aggression. Sometimes your gestures will be involuntary. For example, scratching your head or chin may signal that you are uneasy or concerned about what your pupil is doing. Driving instructors who constantly fidget or wave their arms about will give their pupils the impression that they are nervous or worried. This will do little to build up pupils' confidence! Gesticulations of this nature or pen waving while going along the road will also distract the pupil from concentrating on the road and could be dangerous.

To control them, you need to be aware of your gestures, especially those that may be distracting to others. If you give presentations at meetings or in the classroom, a videotape of your performance will be invaluable in helping you to recognize those gestures that are weak and those that are effective in emphasizing and reinforcing your verbal messages. If you are uncomfortable using deliberately planned gestures, rehearsal and practice will allow you to deliver them in such a way that they appear to be spontaneous and natural rather than forced and awkward.

Proximity (personal space)

You should be aware that each pupil needs a certain amount of personal space (a 'space bubble') with which they feel comfortable. Encroaching on this personal space may make the pupil feel uncomfortable, and could even cause them to change to a different driving instructor.

You need to make sure that this space is not so great that your teaching loses its effectiveness. The following diagram shows the different environments and situations and the amount of space required. You will see that the driving instructor is in the privileged position of being allowed to get closer than almost everybody else, with the exception perhaps of the family doctor!

The amount of personal space required is sometimes dependent on the cultural background of the person. In many Mediterranean countries and in Norway, for example, people feel comfortable almost rubbing shoulders. For most British people this would be quite unacceptable.

You will need to be very sensitive to the needs of each individual pupil in this respect and generally should avoid getting too close wherever possible. This can be difficult in a small car, especially if both you and the pupil are quite large!

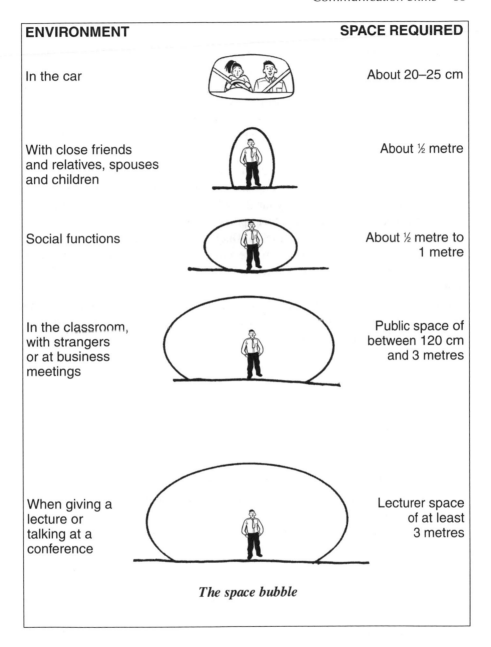

ENVIRONMENT	SPACE REQUIRED
In the car	About 20–25 cm
With close friends and relatives, spouses and children	About ½ metre
Social functions	About ½ metre to 1 metre
In the classroom, with strangers or at business meetings	Public space of between 120 cm and 3 metres
When giving a lecture or talking at a conference	Lecturer space of at least 3 metres

The space bubble

In the classroom, distance can be a barrier to communication, as can speaking from behind a desk, or up on a rostrum. Avoid being seen as authoritarian and try to establish an informal atmosphere. For instance, it can sometimes be more effective to sit on the edge of the desk than behind it.

Touch

Formal touches are important when meeting someone for the first time, like a new pupil. A firm (but not crushing) handshake will indicate self-confidence, which is especially important with new customers. A limp handshake implies weakness and it would be better not to give one at all.

At the end of a lesson a handshake is not really necessary and a wave or pat on the back might be more effective. These can also be nice gestures when the pupil passes the driving test.

You must be extremely careful not to touch pupils in the car unless it is for reasons of safety. Touching pupils may make them feel uncomfortable or threatened and cause them to distrust your motives. Pupils often change instructors because unnecessary physical contact upsets them.

Cultural backgrounds sometimes influence the desire to touch and be touched. For example, people from the Greek island of Rhodes continually touch each other during conversation so, if you have a pupil from this lovely island, watch out!

If a pupil has just received some distressing news you might feel tempted to give them a hug but, generally, a sympathetic ear is just as effective and certainly less likely to be misinterpreted as a social advance.

Personal appearance

When you are a driving instructor, from the moment you leave home to the moment you return back at the end of the day, you are under scrutiny from the public, particularly if you have your name on the car! Your appearance, dress and grooming may create an initial impression that is very difficult to change.

When considering body language, your personal appearance, hair and the clothes that you wear are of great importance because you may well have more control over them than your facial features and posture. There is little we can do to change our shape, features and size, but much can be done to improve our appearance, the suitability of our clothes and the general impression that we convey.

When teaching people to drive, you do of course have to take account of the weather conditions and, while it might not be necessary to wear a three-piece suit, you can still dress casually but smartly. In the summer and winter you will need to dress for comfort, but never forget that your appearance can influence your impact on people and can help to create a favourable or an unfavourable impression.

Propriety of dress is particularly important for the female instructor to help overcome possible problems with male pupils who might see revealing clothes, together with the natural caring attitude of the teacher, as an invitation to develop social relationships.

Pupils' body language

All the constituents of body language that we have discussed in the previous section may combine to present a positive image to those you come into contact with.

It is equally important that you recognize the silent signals your pupils give out. We have chosen common signs that your pupils may give you to indicate the way they feel. Getting to know your pupils better will assist you in accurately interpreting their body language. Generally speaking, the following rules apply.

Pupils who are willing to listen:

- sit with their head on one side;
- look directly at you;
- rest their chin on the palm of their hand;
- nod in agreement;
- say things like 'I see.'

Pupils who are pleased:

- smile;
- use strong eye contact;
- can't stop talking;
- use humour in their speech;
- are polite and courteous.

Pupils who are anxious to ask a question:

- lift a hand or finger;
- shift their sitting position;
- fidget with their ear or chin;
- look intently at you with their head on one side.

Pupils who are annoyed with themselves:

- shake their heads;
- tightly cross their arms;
- hit the steering wheel;
- exhale loudly;
- frown.

Pupils who have had a fright:

- cover their eyes with their hands;
- open their mouth and put their head back;
- bite their bottom lip;
- become red in the face;
- inhale sharply.

Pupils who are disappointed:

- frown or scowl;
- drop their shoulders and let their head drop forwards;
- let their arms fall into their lap;
- droop their mouth.

Pupils who are nervous:

- talk incessantly about nothing;
- tighten their grip on the steering wheel;
- lick their lips;
- bite their nails or chew their fingers.

Looking at your pupils will not only allow you to see and interpret their body language, but also assist you in identifying faults being made which involve their feet, hands and eyes. If you do not see the fault, how can you suggest a remedy for it?

FEEDBACK

Feedback is an important part of the learning process. A simple example might be where the driver hears an ambulance approaching from behind and pulls over to let it pass. Another example would be when the 'feel' from a flat tyre alerts the driver to the fact that something is wrong.

Giving and gaining feedback are useful PTS, especially when teaching on a one-to-one basis or in small groups.

Feedback is usually preceded by an enquiry, a prompt or a physical action. For example, the facial expression of pupils after having carried out a manoeuvre will often give a good indication of how well they feel they have done.

Feedback is obtained and 'fed back' to the initial prompter as a direct result of the initial action. It can be given verbally, physically or sometimes by body language, and can relate both to people and machinery.

In the driving instruction experience, feedback can occur from:

- the car to the pupil/instructor, eg engine labouring;
- the pupil to the instructor;
- the instructor to the pupil;
- the pupil to other road users;
- other road users to the pupil;
- the examiner to the pupil;
- the pupil to the examiner;
- the trainer to the trainee;
- the trainee to the trainer.

Using a question and answer routine is only one way of giving and obtaining feedback.

When teaching learner drivers you should give feedback on what they are doing well and what may need improving. Just as important is finding out from pupils how well *they* think they are doing. They might think they are doing brilliantly when they are really struggling. Alternatively, pupils might think they need extra tuition on a particular topic, whereas you might think this is unnecessary. Every pupil will benefit from extra lessons, so never discourage them from booking more if they feel they need them.

Many driving instructors do not understand feedback and give instead constant criticism, which only destroys what confidence pupils may have and leaves them feeling dejected and wanting to give up.

Many potentially good drivers give up because they do not receive support and encouragement from their instructors. Invariably these pupils will start learning again, as they really need to drive. However, they nearly always go to a different instructor. Never forget that if you are not fulfilling the needs of your pupils, there are plenty more instructors for them to choose from.

Feedback should therefore be offered in a sensitive way, so as not to hurt the feelings of the pupil.

A number of guidelines need to be followed when giving feedback to your pupils.

- Feedback should always focus on what actually happened rather than on what should or might have happened.

- Suggest that pupils comment on their own performance before giving feedback. They will often be more self-critical than you expected.

- Make sure that you balance pupils' strengths and weaknesses.

- Concentrate on areas where you know that the pupil is capable of improvement; don't dwell on points that you know they are not able to alter. This is most important when pupils are aware that they have limitations.

- Be helpful rather than sounding judgemental. For example, rather than saying 'You will fail your test if you do that', you could try 'Your passengers will have a much more comfortable ride if you do this'.

- Try to 'round off' any feedback by stressing the good points.

- Above all, feedback should be seen by pupils as being constructive and positive.

Hopefully the guidelines above will help you to give feedback in a 'human' way, as this will build the confidence of your pupils and their confidence in your ability to teach!

After each lesson, analyse any feedback you have given. Decide whether you could have improved the way in which you presented the feedback to your pupil.

Think carefully about how your pupil reacted to the feedback. Did you tell the pupil what they had done well or did you just criticize their driving?

3

Lesson structure and content

Any presentation is much more likely to be effective and achieve its objective if it is sufficiently prepared for. Remember: 'failing to prepare means preparing to fail'!

Chapter 5 covers the specific requirements for presenting a lesson during the ADI Part 3 test. In that situation, the supervising examiner will actually set the objectives for the lesson and determine the character of the pupil. There is also a limitation on the time available for the lesson.

With a real pupil on a real driving lesson, it is your responsibility to set the objectives and plan the use of time, taking into account the specific needs of the pupil. You usually have the advantage of knowing your pupil.

The best way to plan a lesson is first of all to think of the pupil and their level of ability. Then ask yourself the crucial 'teaching' questions – WHAT?, WHY?, HOW?, WHERE? and WHEN?

- What does the pupil already know?

- What are we going to teach, and Why do we need to teach it?

- How are we going to get the message across?

- Where do we need to go to carry out the main part of the lesson, and When should we get to the main content of the lesson?

- How are we going to manage the time available?

Only when you have answered all of these questions can you get to work in planning the lesson and delivering the presentation.

In any teaching/learning situation the lesson should be structured. This is known as PUPIL-CENTRED LEARNING. For you and your pupil to achieve your separate objectives, you will need to involve the pupil, and the following communication skills will help you to do this.

> *You should start each lesson with a clear idea of* **WHAT** *you are going to teach and* **WHY** *you are going to teach it,* **WHERE** *the lesson is going to take place,* **How** *the timetable is to be utilized and* **How** *the lesson is going to be structured.*

At the start of a Check Test, the examiner will often ask the instructor, 'What is your lesson plan for today?' It is not unusual for the reply to be, 'Well, I just thought we would drive around for a bit and see how things develop'!

Professional driving instruction should not be a matter of driving around for a bit to see what develops. An effective instructor should:

- have a clearly defined plan of what is going to be taught;
- take into account the level of ability of the pupil when setting the objectives for the lesson to be given;
- know in advance what activities are going to take place during the lesson and how the pupil is going to be kept interested and attentive;
- be prepared to modify the lesson plan if the need arises during the lesson.

To obtain the top grading the instructor will need to:

- have specified learning goals for the student;
- vary the teaching methods to suit those goals and the characteristics of the student;
- demonstrate a range of skills when using these teaching methods and any visual or learning aids;
- carefully manage the time, structure and content of the lesson;
- adapt the lesson to suit the perceived needs of the student where necessary;
- identify, analyse and correct faults;
- identify any problem areas, taking remedial action or recommending further training where necessary;
- comply with DSA examination requirements when appropriate;
- take account of the safety of the student, the passenger and any other road users at all times;
- offer feedback to the student during and at the end of the lesson, where appropriate;
- link forward to the next lesson;
- evaluate what learning has taken place.

Your lesson plan may need to be changed if problems are encountered as the lesson progresses. For example, you might plan to teach the pupil how to carry out one of the manoeuvres but, on the way to a suitable place, the pupil fails to see a pedestrian who is just about to step onto a pedestrian crossing. This causes you to have to use the dual controls.

In view of the seriousness of the error, it would make sense to postpone the original manoeuvre planned and spend some time on dealing with how to approach pedestrian crossings, stopping when necessary.

This should not present any problems for the learner as long as you explain why the lesson plan has been changed, and that the original subject will be covered in a future lesson.

The following is an example of a formal lesson plan.

Lesson plan for a partly trained pupil needing instruction on turning on the road

Instruction in turning the car round to face the opposite way using forward and reverse gears.

Objectives

By the end of the lesson the pupil will be able to:

1. choose an appropriate site for the manoeuvre;

2. coordinate the controls with reasonable smoothness;

3. take effective observation before and during the manoeuvre;

4. carry out the manoeuvre with reasonable accuracy.

Taking account of the individual needs of the pupil, the lesson plan will also need to be linked in with:

● matching the level of instruction to the ability of the pupil;

● route selection and planning.

	TIME	MAIN POINTS AND METHOD	TEACHING AIDS
	4–8 minutes approx	Q & A recap and briefing: explanation of manoeuvre	DSA books diagram
	5–10 minutes approx	Demonstration if appropriate, then full talk-through practice	
	5 minutes approx	Debriefing, feedback, encouragement, praise, fault analysis	DSA books diagram if appropriate
	5–10 minutes approx	Remedial practice; prompts if necessary	
	5 minutes	Debriefing, feedback, encouragement, praise, fault analysis, link forward to next lesson	

These timings are only a guide and will need to be varied depending on the individual pupil's receptiveness and ability.

To appreciate the extent of the task that faces you, consider how you would plan a lesson for each of the potential pupils listed below – what type of routes you would choose and how you would vary your level of instruction:

- an absolute beginner;
- a partly trained pupil;
- a pupil at about 'L' test standard;
- somebody who has recently passed the 'L' test but has never driven on motorways;
- somebody who passed the 'L' test a few years ago but has not driven since;
- a full licence holder who wishes to take the IAM or RoSPA advanced test;
- someone who has a full licence for cars with automatic transmission but has not driven a vehicle with manual gears;
- a company driver taking a 'defensive driving' course;
- the holder of a full foreign licence who has never driven in this country or on the left-hand side of the road;

- somebody who is just about to appear in court on a traffic offence and who needs an assessment and report;
- somebody who has to retake the driving test as part of a court order;
- somebody who has to take an *extended* test as part of a court order.

At the end of each driving lesson, you should ask yourself:

- Did the lesson plan help the student to achieve the objectives stated at the beginning of the lesson?
- Did I involve the pupil in the lesson sufficiently?
- Should I have changed the lesson plan to take account of perceived problems?
- Did I give the pupil enough feedback on how well they were doing?
- Did I plan the lesson thoroughly?
- Were the routes chosen correctly?
- Was the level of instruction pitched appropriately for the pupil?
- With hindsight, was there anything I should have done differently?

OBJECTIVES

The theory of teaching by objectives is covered in more detail in *The Driving Instructor's Handbook*. In this section of the book, we will be explaining how to put the theory into practice, using your practical teaching skills. General objectives give the teaching goals. These tend to be broken down into more specific objectives, which allow pupils to determine whether they have attained those goals.

In Chapter 1 we dealt with the learning process, including: learning to memorize something; learning to understand something; learning to do something; and attitude development. When teaching someone how to drive, it is not very helpful to separate these activities. The learner needs to practise all of the above, and then reflect on the experience with guidance from the instructor.

Driving instructors are rather like babysitters. They spend time with their charges for perhaps only one or two hours a week. As soon as the children they are looking after can fend for themselves, the babysitter is no longer required. Once learner drivers have passed the 'L' test, they have no further need for their driving instructors and will possibly never seen them again unless they are persuaded to take some extra training under the Pass Plus scheme or in preparation for one of the advanced driving tests.

Given the limitations of time and money, all we can hope to achieve when teaching our learners is that they know 'where they are going, and how they are going to get there' in terms of their progress through the learning process.

There will probably be large gaps in their knowledge, understanding and practical skills. Almost certainly there will need to be a modification of attitude from time to time. They will undoubtedly take risks along the way, but, hopefully, they will learn from the experience.

So, faced with this problem, how can we make the best use of the short amount of time available for teaching? We need to ask ourselves:

- What are our pupils setting out to achieve?

- What is the best way of helping them to achieve it in the time available?

If we are absolutely honest with ourselves, the answers to these questions will probably be 'pass the "L" test' and 'plan a course of lessons linked to the requirements of the test'.

Because of the public perception about 'passing the test' it is often left to instructors to use their professional skills to persuade their pupils that the main objective of a course of lessons is to teach '*safe driving for life*'.

Whatever the type of course or subject matter, the objectives for each particular pupil will need to be clearly defined and stated.

Teaching by objectives, or using a 'stepping stone' approach, will make the learning process more enjoyable for pupils in that they will be able to recognize and measure how their skills are progressing against the requirements of the 'L' test.

One of the biggest problems for learners when they first start their lessons is that they have a feeling of insecurity. This is due largely to them not being able to compare their progress, or lack of it, with that of their peers, who may also be learning to drive.

Using a stepping-stone approach leading up to the test does help to overcome this problem. When the pupil has achieved one objective, then they move on to the next one, and so on. If they are unable to achieve an objective, then this is where your skill as a coach is put to the test. You will have to find the right method for your pupil – one which ensures that each one will learn something. Knowing when to encourage, praise, question, explain, demonstrate and assess are the skills of the teacher.

It is essential to remember that there is no such thing as a bad learner. The inability of the pupil to learn is much more likely to be the fault of the teacher! Your skill will be to set the objectives for the pupil at an appropriate level, so as to give the pupil a realistic target. When the target is hit, the pupil should feel a sense of achievement, which will stimulate the desire to make more progress.

The most important factor in the selection of objectives is that both the instructor and the pupil agree what they are to be, and that some record is kept of progress made. Using this system gives an immediate progress chart for each pupil and will also act as a memory prompt for you so that you will be able to remember which particular item is the next one to be covered.

By using a log book or progress report, another instructor would be able to pick up where the previous instructor has left off.

As well as giving each pupil feedback on their progress on a record or appointment card, you should also keep a master list in the car so that each pupil's progress can be monitored. Progress sheets can be filed on a clip board in alphabetical order by surname.

Do not lose sight of the fact that as well as giving pupils an individual 'test-related' programme of learning, we are also preparing them for a lifetime of safe driving. The requirements of the test go further than performing the set exercises. Knowledge, understanding and attitude all come into it as well as practical skill. Your course of instruction should cover all of these.

In using objectives based on the DSA syllabus we are giving our learners a firm foundation. Drivers will reflect on their performance long after they have passed the driving test. There will undoubtedly be gaps which are likely to be filled as they gain experience.

The LEARNING CIRCLE of learning, practice and reflection which we saw in Chapter 1 will hold good for the rest of their driving lives!

When teaching by objectives you will need to ask yourself at the end of each lesson:

- Have I set the objectives at a realistic level for the pupil?

- Am I concentrating too much on 'getting them through the test' instead of teaching safe driving for life?

- Am I paying enough attention to knowledge, understanding and attitude, or spending too much time on skill training?

- Have I kept my pupil's progress chart or driver's record up to date?

- Have I kept my own progress chart for this pupil up to date?

LEVELS OF INSTRUCTION

In most driving lessons, the professional instructor will be involved in the following activities:

- teaching new skills;

- consolidating partly learnt skills;
- assessing skills already learnt or partly learnt.

Some lessons may contain a mixture of some or all of these activities. Many instructors make the mistake of trying to cram too much into one lesson to the detriment of the learning process.

As well as planning the content of the lesson to be given, you need to consider carefully the routes and areas chosen and the level of instruction required for each particular pupil.

One of the problems for instructors is knowing when to 'drop out' and transfer to the pupil the responsibility for solving problems and making decisions. The sooner your pupils start to think things out and make decisions for themselves, the sooner they will be ready to drive unaccompanied.

For many learners, the first time they ever drive 'unaccompanied' will be on the 'L' test, when the examiner is there purely as an observer.

The skilful instructor knows when to stop talking. Of course, in most driving lessons, you will need to give directions but, during the lessons immediately before the test, it would be very beneficial to the learner if you say, 'Let's see if you can drive home on your own, without me saying anything at all. You make all the decisions and pretend that I am not here.' You would, of course, need to be sure that the pupil knows the route to be taken.

In this situation, the only time you should intervene is for safety reasons. This exercise will boost the confidence of the pupil coming up to the test, and also give you a measure of the pupil's readiness to drive unaccompanied. At the end of the 'unaccompanied drive' it will be useful to ask the pupil: 'How did you feel about driving on your own then?'

Some feedback would then need to be given to the pupil. A requirement for more lessons might be necessary. Two very common instructional errors arise from instructors not matching the level of instruction to suit the level of ability of their pupil. This can take the form of over- or under-instruction.

Over-instruction

This often occurs when the instructor is teaching a new skill, or who has identified a problem area and is giving the pupil a complete 'talk-through' on a subject. The new skill will probably be mixed in with the skills that are already learnt or partly learnt.

For example, the instructor may be talking the pupil through a difficult junction, with the added problem of roadworks. When the junction has been negotiated, the pupil is asked to pull in and park somewhere convenient, so that they can discuss what happened. The instructor forgets that the pupil knows how to park unaccompanied and says: 'Gently brake to slow; clutch down; gently brake to stop; apply the handbrake; select neutral.'

The pupil may have parked a hundred times unaided, without any problem. What has happened is that the instructor, who has got so involved in the 'talk-through' mode, has forgotten when to keep quiet.

You should therefore try to restrict your prompted practice or talk-through to those aspects of driving which are new to the pupil, or which are as yet unaccomplished. Over-instruction is particularly common when the pupil is approaching test standard. It is as if the instructor is reluctant to 'let go of the reins'. Always remember that at this level your pupils will learn a lot more by doing it themselves, even if they get it wrong, than by listening to you telling them what to do.

Under-instruction

This is particularly common when the pupil is in the novice stage or is only partially trained. When teaching new skills you need to control the practice so that, where possible, the pupil gets it right first time. There is nothing more motivating for the pupil than success, even though that success may be the result of you prompting or talking them through the task. Your function is to talk the pupil through each stage of the operation, skill or exercise until they develop the ability and confidence to do it for themselves.

The need for a full talk-through is greatest in the early stages of learning a particular task so as to lessen the risk of vehicle abuse and inconvenience or danger to other road users.

The talk-through must give the pupil enough time to interpret and execute your instructions comfortably. The speed with which each pupil will be able to do this is likely to vary. You therefore need to match the level of instruction and the timing of your delivery to the particular needs of the pupil.

Knowing when to drop out is important. If you leave the pupil on their own too soon, resulting in a poor execution of the task, it can be very demotivating. However, when you consider the pupil is ready to take personal responsibility, you should encourage them to do so. Some pupils will need plenty of encouragement to act and think for themselves. Others will make rapid progress when left to work on their own initiative.

You might need to change from 'talk-through' mode to 'prompted practice' mode. Prompting is the natural progression from controlled practice and will largely depend on the ability and willingness of pupils to make decisions for themselves.

If conditions become too busy for the pupil's ability or if potential danger is a factor, then the pupil may be reluctant to make any decisions at all. Where these situations arise you must be prepared to step in and prompt when required.

The use of detailed instructions should decrease as the ability of the pupil increases, thereby transferring the responsibility from you to them for making decisions and acting on them.

In the last few lessons leading up to the driving test, it should not be necessary for you to prompt the pupil at all. If this is not the case, then you have a selling job to do. You need to either sell more lessons and the necessity for further practice or postponement of the test.

At the end of each lesson ask yourself:

- Did I match the level of the instruction given to the ability of the pupil?
- Did I over-instruct on things that the pupil should need no instruction on?
- Did I leave the pupil to do things without prompting or should I have given more help?

ROUTE PLANNING

Route selection and planning is itself a *practical teaching skill* and is an essential part of lesson preparation and planning. Part of an instructor's role is to create a situation in which learning can take place, and the selection of routes is an integral element in this process.

The ideal route would be one that takes account of the character and level of ability of the pupil. It should be designed to stretch them but not be daunting.

Using training routes which are not relevant to the needs of the pupil or not appropriate to the requirements of the lesson plan can have an extremely negative effect on the training.

The confidence of some learners is destroyed because they are taken into difficult situations which require good clutch control before they have mastered this skill. Imagine how you would feel if you were sitting at a red traffic light on your first driving lesson and you stalled the engine a couple of times!

If new drivers are unnecessarily exposed to road and traffic conditions with which they are unable to cope, it is quite likely that the amount of learning taking place will be reduced. In the most extreme case, the pupil's confidence will be severely affected, with a detrimental effect on learning or even a reversal of the learning process.

At the other end of the scale, restricting the experienced learner to inappropriate basic routes will not encourage them to develop their skills.

When planning routes, you should consider some of the main requirements:

- the specific objectives for the lesson;
- the standard and ability of the pupil combined with the need to introduce or improve any skill or procedure;

- any particular weaknesses or strengths of the pupil;

- any hazards or features that you may want to include or avoid in the overall lesson plan;

- the length of time available for the lesson;

- whether any danger or inconvenience might be caused by using a particular area at a particular time;

- if any unnecessary or excessive nuisance would be caused to local residents.

Ideally, you should have a thorough knowledge of the training area and any local traffic conditions. However, as this is not always practicable or possible, you will need to take care to avoid any extreme conditions.

If, because of the road layout and the limited time available, complex situations cannot be avoided, consider whether you should drive the pupil to a more appropriate training area. In this event, use the drive to give a demonstration of any relevant points and to include a 'talk-through' of what you are doing.

Training routes and areas tend to fall into three main categories: nursery or basic, intermediate and advanced. There will not be a clear division between the three groups and there will often be a considerable overlap from one group to another. Nevertheless, it is important that you have a clear idea of the appropriate routes within your own working environment.

Nursery Routes – These will normally include fairly long, straight, wide roads without too many parked vehicles and avoiding pedestrian crossings, traffic lights and roundabouts. This type of route will incorporate progressively most or all of the following features:

- roads that are long enough to allow for a reasonable progression through all the gears and for stopping from various speeds;

- several upward and downward gradients suitable for starting and stopping;

- left- and right-hand bends to develop speed adjustment and gear changing skills;

- left turns from main roads to side roads;

- left turns from side roads to main roads;

- right turns into side roads and onto main roads.

Intermediate Routes – These should include busier junctions and general traffic conditions. At this stage, try to avoid dual carriageways, multi-lane roads and any one-way systems. Some or all of the following features might be incorporated in the routes:

- crossroads and junctions with 'stop' and 'give way' signs;
- several uphill, give-way junctions;
- traffic lights and basic roundabouts;
- areas for manoeuvring.

Care should be taken to avoid too many complicated traffic situations – for example, right turns onto exceptionally busy main roads or complex junctions.

Advanced Routes – These will incorporate most of the features of the intermediate routes and should be extended to give a wider variety of traffic and road conditions. They should include, where possible, dual carriageways, multi-lane roads and one-way systems as well as residential, urban and rural roads. A properly planned 'advanced' route will provide the opportunity to conduct mock tests without using actual test routes. You should be able to find routes that include:

- different types of pedestrian crossings;
- roads with varying speed limits;
- level crossings, dual carriageways and one-way streets;
- multi-laned roads for lane selection and lane discipline;
- rural, urban and residential roads.

Starting with nursery routes, try to introduce new elements and situations at a controlled rate bearing in mind the needs of the individual pupil and the level of their ability. Get used to what seems to be 'their own pace' – one at which they feel comfortable.

There may be occasions when a mixture of all types of route may be incorporated into one lesson – for example, when making an initial assessment of a new pupil who has previous driving experience.

Ideally, you should start off with a fairly wide selection of routes. This will give you the opportunity to vary and extend them with experience. Retain a certain amount of flexibility in using the planned routes because you may, for instance, need to spend more time than anticipated on a topic that the pupil is finding more difficult than expected.

If a specific problem is identified, you may need to demonstrate or contrive to bring the pupil back to a particular junction in order to 'recreate' a situation.

Excessive repetition of identical routes will often lead to a lack of interest or response from the pupil. This in turn will lead to slow progress in learning and may also be counterproductive. Some variation of routes is essential to the learning process and will sustain the pupil's interest and motivation. Occasionally, however, you may decide that a certain amount of repetition is necessary to work on a specific task relevant to the objectives for a particular lesson.

Remember that training routes are often a compromise between the ideal and the reality of local conditions in the training area. The nature of traffic conditions can vary enormously from time to time and from lesson to lesson. You may find that a carefully planned route may unexpectedly prove unsuitable and you are faced with a situation that the pupil is not ready for. Careful route planning can, however, keep these incidents to a manageable level. Be ready to extend the length of a lesson for a particular pupil if appropriate training routes are not readily available in the immediate vicinity.

At the end of each lesson, ask yourself:

- Did I choose a route that was suitable for the level of ability of the pupil and for the objectives stated?

- Did I vary the route sufficiently to sustain the interest of the pupil?

- Am I using routes which stretch the ability of the pupil but without destroying their confidence?

FAULT ASSESSMENT

This section deals with fault recognition, assessment and correction.

Driving faults normally fall into two separate categories: in the car (control skills) and outside the car (road procedure errors).

You will often find that 'in-car' errors will lead to errors of road procedure, lack of accuracy or failure to respond correctly to traffic situations

You will need to use your eyes, dividing your attention between what is happening on the road ahead, what is happening behind and what your pupil is doing with their hands, feet and eyes.

Try not to:

- watch the pupil so intently that you miss important changes in the traffic situation ahead to which your pupil should be responding;

- watch the road and traffic so intently that you miss faults that are happening in the car.

An effective way of coping with all the visual checks required is to use the M S M, P S L, L A D routines, but from an instructional point of view. For example, when approaching a hazard you should check that your pupil:

M – checks the rear view mirrors; look in your own mirror to confirm what is happening behind; check that your pupil acts sensibly on what is seen;

S – is signalling properly, when necessary and at the correct time;

M – carries out the manoeuvre correctly;

becomes:

P – positions the vehicle correctly for the situation;

S – slows down to a suitable speed and selects an appropriate gear when necessary;

L – is looking early enough, at the correct time, and that the observations are effective and include use of the mirrors;

becomes:

A – assesses the situation correctly;

D – makes a good decision as to how to deal with the hazard.

Continuous assessment should be sensitive to the pupil's needs and is concerned with improving performance. In the last few lessons leading up to the 'L' test, the continuous assessment should give way to 'objective' or 'mock' testing. The purpose of this is to assess the pupil's readiness to take the test and it should be matched to the requirements of the test itself.

Grading of errors

Try not to think of errors as being black or white. In driving, there are many shades of grey, and the circumstances surrounding the error need to be taken into account. When assessing driver error, you should take into consideration the following:

- an error can involve varying degrees of importance;

- some errors are of a more serious nature and can result in more severe consequences than others.

Driver errors will generally fall into one of four categories:

1. **Not marked** – This is where the fault is so slight that you decide not to mention it.

2. **Minor** – This is where the fault does not involve a serious or dangerous situation. No other road user is involved either potentially or actually.

3. **Serious** – A serious fault is one which involves potential risk to persons or property.

4.   **Dangerous** – This is where the actions of the pupil cause actual danger to persons or property.

There is a need for some standardization between the consistency of assessments made during driving lessons and those used for the driving test. Full details of the Driving Standards Agency fault assessment categories can be found in *The Driving Instructor's Handbook*.

Having said this, there is no necessity for you to grade errors exactly to DSA test criteria. Remember that we are teaching safe driving for life. Consequently, some instructors may aim for a much higher overall standard of ability than that required on the 'L' test.

This can be beneficial to their pupils. It would be true to say that most learners do not perform as well on the driving test as they do while out with their instructor on lessons. Pupils who have been trained to a higher standard should therefore stand a better chance of passing. Even if they do not drive as well on the test as on previous lessons, they are still likely to pass, provided that there are no serious or dangerous errors. In any event, the extra training before taking the test will mean that these pupils are better prepared to drive unaccompanied after passing.

Fault assessment on its own will do little to improve the performance of learners. To benefit learners the following procedure should be adopted:

●   recognize the fault;

●   analyse the fault;

●   correct the fault.

Fault recognition

Having recognized a fault, you should identify it as being minor, serious or dangerous. Minor faults can normally be corrected on the move. However, if a recurring pattern of minor faults is identified, you will need to spend some time on dealing with them before they become more serious.

Minor faults could include errors in coordination and inefficient or uneconomic driving style, slight inaccuracies in positioning (either travelling along the road or during the set manoeuvres) and harsh use of the controls.

Serious or dangerous faults will need to be discussed more fully. This discussion should be carried out while parked somewhere safe. Do not get into discussions at road junctions, or while pupils are trying to negotiate hazards – this will only confuse them which could lead to even more serious faults being made.

Fault analysis

When analysing faults you need to compare what your pupil is doing, or has done, with what you would be doing or would have done in similar circumstances.

Before analysing the fault you should give some general encouragement and feedback on any progress made before the fault occurred. This will make the pupil more receptive to the criticism which you are about to give. Another useful approach would be to ask the pupil: 'How do you think that drive/manoeuvre went?'

It may be that the pupil realizes that a mistake has been made, in which case you could help them to analyse the fault for themselves.

Whichever method you use, you should:

- explain what was wrong (both the cause of the error and its effect and consequences);

- explain what should have happened;

- explain why it is important (paying particular attention to how the error could affect other road users).

Consider using a visual aid if you need to recreate a difficult situation or explain incorrect positioning on the road, or illustrate how other road users were involved. Diagrams, models and magnetic boards are useful aids.

After analysing the fault, use your question and answer technique to make sure that the pupil has fully understood what went wrong, what should have happened, and why it is important. This will then lead to the last, and most important, part of the routine.

Fault correction

Remedial action will need to be offered while the fault and the improvements needed are still fresh in the pupil's mind. It is of little use to say that you will come back to the fault on the next lesson as by that time the pupil will have probably forgotten what to do.

If the fault involved the way in which the pupil dealt with a particular hazard or junction, the most effective way to correct it would be to get the pupil to approach the same situation again. Depending on the fault, you may decide to talk the pupil through the situation, or just prompt on the points which need improving. The main thing is that success is achieved. If time allows, a third approach to the same situation will help to validate your instruction, this time leaving the pupil to deal with it entirely unaided. Praise must be given when improvement has been made.

At the end of each lesson, you should ask yourself:

- Did I identify all the main faults made by my pupil?

- Did I correct all the minor faults on the move and stop to analyse the major faults as soon as convenient?

- Did I analyse the faults made with regard to what went wrong, what should have happened, and why it was important?

- Did I offer appropriate remedial action, bringing about improvement?

HAZARD PERCEPTION

Hazard perception is part of the theory test for learners and the ADI Part 1 exam. It is a subject that instructors need to be expert at – both in theory and practice.

The driving skills involved include:

- scanning the road well ahead;

- anticipating the actions and reactions of other road users;

- being aware of following traffic;

- planning an appropriate course of action;

- maintaining a safe and appropriate distance behind the vehicle in front;

- driving at a speed that is appropriate to the conditions.

However, the main element is CONCENTRATION!

As an instructor, your own perception of hazards is even more important. You should also be able to develop these skills in your learner drivers by utilizing a variety of *practical teaching skills*, but mostly by effective 'Q & A' techniques.

A 'hazard' is usually defined as anything that might cause us to change our direction or to alter the speed of our vehicle. Some of these will be static hazards such as road junctions or bends; others might be moving hazards, such as pedestrians, cyclists, horse-riders, motorcyclists and other vehicles.

Using your 'Q & A' techniques you should be able to help your pupils to improve their skill in recognizing and dealing with all types of hazard.

The ultimate aim of your instruction will be to enable your pupils to:

- scan the road ahead and behind effectively;

- anticipate the main points of danger;

- recognize that what we *can't* see is often more important than what we *can* see;

- think about what *might* happen as well as what *is* happening;

- give themselves time and space to carry out a particular manoeuvre or to avoid a problem;
- maintain absolute control of their vehicle while carrying out correct driving procedures.

Encouraging your pupils to look well ahead, keeping the eyes moving all the time and continually looking for clues as to what might happen, can achieve this.

EXPLANATION, DEMONSTRATION, PRACTICE

When teaching a skill as complex as driving a car, you must have clearly in mind all the component parts of the skill. Before attempting to teach the skill, you will need to ask:

- What knowledge does the learner need in order to carry out the task successfully?
- What attitudes should the learner have towards carrying out the task?
- What manipulative and/or perceptive skills does the task involve?

Each component part of the skill will have a 'prepared' position from which the actual performance commences. This may involve positioning of the hands and/or feet and the use of the eyes in anticipation of carrying out the specific task. Being poised ready for action can be important from the point of view of smoothness, control, accuracy and safety.

For example, moving off requires the car to be in 'a prepared state': ie, gear selected, gas set, clutch to biting point, handbrake prepared. This will be followed by checking ahead, checking mirrors, checking blindspots, assessing whether it is safe to go and whether a signal is necessary, releasing the hand-brake, slowly bringing the clutch up and increasing the gas, and putting the hand back onto the steering wheel.

To help the learner to memorize this sequence, the following mnemonic could be used:

P (Prepare) – O (Observe) – M (Move)

An experienced driver gets into the car, starts up and moves off in a matter of seconds without having to think about it.

For the novice, things are not so simple. As the moving off procedure and the coordination of the clutch and gas is so vital for many other driving tasks, much practice will be needed to get it right.

With all these basic formative skills most pupils will benefit from a demonstration. It is all too easy for the instructor to assume that the pupil knows, understands, and can do what is required.

Prior to practising a new skill the learner should understand:

- WHY is has to be learnt;

- WHEN and WHERE it should be applied;

- WHAT is expected in learning the skill;

- HOW the skill is to be performed.

The most effective sequence of skill training is: 1) EXPLANATION; 2) DEMONSTRATION; and 3) PRACTICE. This teaching routine is a prime example of how many of the PTS in this book can be brought together to form a strategy for learning.

Explanation

Briefings and explanations have been covered more fully in Chapter 2. The explanation should be tailored to take account of the level of ability of the learner. During the early stages of learning to drive, it might sometimes be better to concentrate on the KEY POINTS, so that the pupil is not OVERLOADED with information.

Once these key points are fully established it will be easier for the learner to understand and retain additional information given at a later date.

Most explanations will need to include the following:

CONTROL – Briefings will need to cover control of the vehicle and speed approaching or dealing with hazards. This should include the manipulative aspects of driving; coordination of controls; smoothness; securing the vehicle when stationary.

OBSERVATIONS – This will contain necessary information on the LOOK, ASSESS, DECIDE routine; skills of perception; safety margins; attitudes towards other road users.

ACCURACY – This section will cover aspects of steering; positioning and general accuracy; course and lane discipline where appropriate.

Any visual aids or diagrams that will clarify, reinforce or add authority to an explanation should be used. You will also find it useful to refer to the official DSA publications:

The Highway Code;
The Official Guide to Learning to Drive;
The Official DSA Guide to Driving: the essential skills.

These can be used to 'add weight to your words'.

Demonstration

A demonstration is useful in that the pupil will be able to see a model of correct behaviour which they can then imitate. Complex tasks can be broken down into component parts which can be demonstrated before the learner practises and repeats them until mastery is achieved. The advantages of you giving a demonstration are:

● you can adapt the demonstration to suit the specific needs of the pupil;

● you are there to answer any questions which the pupil may wish to ask.

The demonstration must not be used to impress the learner with your own expertise. The key points in the preceding briefing or explanation should form an integral part of the demonstration by way of an abbreviated commentary.

A learner may often be genuinely unaware of a mistake. A demonstration will help to show them where they are going wrong and what is needed to correct the problem. This is especially so when the pupil's perception of safety margins, the need for 'holding back' procedures, and speed approaching hazards, is poor.

You might mention slowing down approaching a hazard and get no response from the learner if your pupil's understanding of 'slow' is different from your own. Under these circumstances a demonstration can be a valuable aid to you in persuading the pupil to modify what they are doing to fit in with how *you* want the manoeuvre carried out.

It may be helpful to pupils if you SIMULATE what they are doing so that they can appreciate the difference.

This technique would be particularly useful when giving feedback on the pupil's performance in the set manoeuvres.

Points to remember

● Explain beforehand why you are going to demonstrate and what it is all about.
● Pitch the demonstration and the commentary given while carrying it out to the correct level for the ability of the learner.
● Make the demonstration as perfect an example as possible of what you want the pupil to do.
● Restrict the commentary to key points only and those that are necessary for that particular learner.
● Consolidate afterwards with a debriefing and controlled practice.

The demonstration should be concluded with a summary of the key points, which might then lead to a Q & A session to identify any aspects of the task which the learner still does not understand.

Practice

Having demonstrated the skill you should then allow your pupil to practise it as soon as possible. The first time the pupil attempts the skill, it is important that success is achieved.

There is nothing more demotivating for a learner than to watch you carry out a task perfectly and then to fail miserably trying to copy it. You could find that there is a need for prompting if the pupil is encountering difficulties or deviating from what they should be doing. For example, if the pupil is practising the turn in the road and not turning the wheel effectively, you may need to say: 'Use longer movements of the steering wheel and turn more briskly.'

> *Establishing good habits in these early stages while practising the manoeuvre will pay dividends for the learner later on.*

When the pupil is practising new skills, check on the body language for signs of stress, frustration or despair. Be prepared to intervene if necessary. Encouragement and reassurance may be needed. Be prepared to change your lesson plan and go back to consolidating previously learnt skills to boost flagging confidence.

Controlled practice will allow the beginner to remain safe, and not be too unsympathetic to the vehicle. It involves the learner in following simple verbal instructions to carry out the component parts of the skill which, when brought together, form complete mastery.

The speed with which the learner interprets and responds to the instruction needs to be taken into account. This may vary from pupil to pupil. With some pupils it may be necessary to carry out tasks more slowly than normal.

The instructions given should eventually be reduced to prompting. As soon as the learner appears to be able to cope independently, the instruction should gradually be phased out.

The amount of prompting given will depend on the ability and willingness of learners to make decisions on their own. Some learners will require a lot of encouragement to act and think for themselves.

> *The ultimate objective is to get the learner to carry out each skill under all normal traffic conditions with no prompting from you at all.*

Many learners complete their programme of training being able to carry out all the driving tasks required of them, but unable to do any of them particularly well. This is not helpful to the pupils, who may themselves feel that 'all is not well'.

The sequence of development should be:

- CONTROLLED PRACTICE;
- PROMPTED PRACTICE;
- TRANSFERRED RESPONSIBILITY;
- REFLECTION;
- REVISION.

Prompting should not be necessary where the learner is about to be presented for the 'L' test!

After using the 'explain, demonstrate, practise' (EDP) routine, you will need to ask yourself:

- Did I use the EDP routine to good effect?
- Did my briefing or explanations cover all the key points?
- Did my demonstration have the desired effect on the pupil?
- Did I assist my pupil to achieve initial success by prompting when necessary?
- Did I take account of the body language of the pupil when practising new skills?
- Am I flexible enough to change back to the pupil's previously learnt skills in order to boost confidence?
- Did I transfer responsibility as soon as it was appropriate to do so, or did I 'keep instructing' when it was no longer necessary?

PUPIL INVOLVEMENT

To help maintain the interest and attention of your pupil you need to bring the lesson to life, personalizing it and making it enjoyable. At the end of any lesson your pupils should leave the car feeling not only that they have learnt something and achieved the objectives of the lesson, but also that they have enjoyed themselves.

A proportion of your pupils will probably come to you having had lessons with another instructor. Why is this? It is often because they feel they were not making progress with the previous instructor or were not enjoying the lessons.

Don't forget that each pupil is an individual. Use first names during the lesson and make eye contact when discussing things while stationary. Use the different speech elements we discussed in the previous chapter – metaphors, hyperbole and similes – to add interest and perhaps a touch of humour to the presentation.

Use visual aids when explaining things, and make sure that pupils can actually *see* what it is that you are showing them. So many instructors cover up what they are showing with their hands so pupils cannot see or understand the points being made!

Another way to make lessons more interesting for pupils is to INVOLVE them as much as possible by using the 'question and answer' technique. ('Q & A' is dealt with in more detail later in this chapter).

We have already talked about asking yourself questions to help you plan the lesson. Later in this chapter we will show you how to ask similar questions during the presentation to ensure that the pupil is participating.

VISUAL AIDS

A learning aid is any medium you might use to enable you to present your ideas, concepts, knowledge and skills in a manner that is more easily understood by your learner.

> *Learning aids can assist the learning process by helping to hold pupils' attention and generate an interest that stimulates the desire to learn.*

It has been said that, 'The purpose of a learning aid is to liberate the teacher from the limitations of their own speech.' But, while learning aids may help to make a good instructor even better, they will not compensate for bad teaching.

Learning aids range from a simple notepad and pencil to sophisticated driving simulators. Between these two extremes, there is a vast range of aids available to the instructor, many of which are visual. In this section we will concentrate on those aids of a visual nature that can be used in the car.

'A picture paints a thousand words' – provided it is a good picture! It is amazing how many instructors say to their pupils: 'I am not very good at drawing, but I am going to draw you a diagram to explain what I mean.'

The visual aids you use are limited only by your imagination. You can use your hands to explain how the clutch plates come together; you can use your fingers to show 'the thickness of a coin' when explaining the biting point; you can produce pre-prepared diagrams to assist you in explaining various aspects of road procedure, manoeuvres, etc.

Be careful, however, not to overuse visual aids to the extent that they detract from the basic message you wish to put across.

Visual aids offer the following benefits:

- they add structure to your lesson;
- they provide a change of activity for the learner;
- they will assist you by reminding you what needs to be said;
- they will allow the pupil to recall and visualize previously encountered situations;
- they can help to clarify difficult concepts or show specific positions required when manoeuvring or dealing with hazards;
- they stimulate the interest of the learner and help to maintain attention.

> *By being skilful in designing, creating and integrating visual aids in your presentation, you will be able to bring the lesson to life.*

When using visual aids in the car you should:

- avoid just reading from a script;
- talk to the pupil and not to the visual aid;
- turn the aid around so that the pupil can see it – it is for their benefit, not just for yours;
- avoid covering the visual aid with your hand – you may need to hold it with your right and use your left hand, or a pen, to point to the key parts;
- avoid 'pen-waving' because it can be threatening to the pupil;
- once you have used the aid, put it away before it becomes a distraction.

The following ABC of visual aids used should be borne in mind:

ACCURACY – Try to ensure that the visual aid accurately recreates the situation you are trying to depict.

BREVITY – Keep drawings/diagrams simple and avoid having too many words or unnecessary detail.

CLARITY – Ensure that letters or words are big enough to be seen by the pupil.

DELETION – Use them then lose them, otherwise they become a distraction.

EMPHASIS – Make sure that the visual aid stresses the key points.

At the end of each lesson ask yourself:

- Did I take every opportunity to use visual aids in order to assist the learning process?
- Were the visual aids stimulating and effective?
- Did I identify any situations where a visual aid could have been useful? If so, should I think about designing one for future use?

QUESTION AND ANSWER TECHNIQUE

Of all the teaching tools available to you, the question and answer technique (Q & A) is probably the most useful. Using an effective Q & A technique can serve two major purposes:

- teaching understanding;
- testing understanding.

You will need to think carefully which use you have in mind before posing questions. More often than not you will need to use 'testing' questions at the start and at the end of the lessons, and 'teaching' questions during them.

At the start of lessons you should ask a few questions to test whether or not pupils remember what happened during the previous lesson. Pay particular attention to the 'successes' and 'achievements', especially if new skills were used and mastered.

Using questions at the start of lessons in this way will get pupils into the habit of answering them. This will make things easier for you when you get to the more important 'teaching' questions, which we cover in more detail later in this section.

Your purpose in using these 'teaching' questions is to motivate pupils by challenging or intriguing them and helping them to work out solutions and reasons for doing things by themselves.

There is nothing more frustrating than getting 'zero response' to your carefully thought out questions. Your pupils therefore need to be encouraged and conditioned to answering your questions.

At the end of lessons you can use 'testing' questions as a means of reminding pupils what took place during the drive and any improvements or achievements that have been made.

Asking appropriate questions while stationary and on the move will enable you to gain feedback on pupils' knowledge, understanding, experience and attitudes. Further questions can then help you to improve, alter or amend pupils' understanding.

Since the main part of most lessons (the exception being the 'Controls' lesson) will be on the move, it is the 'teaching' questions that will benefit pupils most.

> *The most important thing when using Q & A is that you ask the most suitable question for the situation you find yourself in!*

Choosing appropriate questions

The questions you use must take account of the level of ability of the pupil and what is happening in the driving environment. Each drive will prompt a different set of questions. These may generally be broken down into two categories:

● What is happening or should be happening inside the vehicle.

● What is happening outside the vehicle, and how the pupil should be responding.

For pupils in the early stages of learning you are likely to need to ask 'in-car' questions concerning control, technique, smoothness, the use of mirrors and general observation.

With more advanced pupils, who should be able to control the vehicle in a reasonably safe, smooth manner, most of the questions should find out:

● Whether they are aware of what is happening in front, behind and around the vehicle.

● What action, if any, needs to be taken to deal with the situation, with safety in mind.

You will need to take account of:

● the pupil's ability;

● what is happening in the vehicle;

● what is happening outside the vehicle (ahead, behind and in the blind areas);

● the presence and actions of other road users;

● the weather conditions and visibility;

● road signs and markings.

Your job as an instructor is to read the road far enough ahead, getting the 'big picture', so that you can anticipate what is likely to happen, leaving you enough time to ask the appropriate questions to get pupils involved in the decision-making process.

Some of the most important questions you ask should be designed to test pupils' hazard awareness. Remember that a hazard is anything around that may require you to alter your speed, change direction or stop.

With years of driving and instructional experience behind you, it is so easy to assume that your pupil will see and, more to the point, take the necessary action, to deal with hazards or other road users.

It is particularly important that your pupils are taught to respond to the more vulnerable road users – pedestrians (especially children and older people), cyclists and motorcyclists, people who may be disadvantaged by disability, a parent struggling to cross the road with a pram and toddlers.

In all of these cases, your vehicle may pose a threat to others. Your questions can help to ensure that pupils not only see the situation, but have the correct attitude to take the appropriate action to defuse it.

Some situations may arise where other vehicles pose a threat to yours – large lorries struggling to negotiate roundabouts, or swinging wide when turning into narrow entrances; buses stopping and moving off; refuse-collection vehicles and skip lorries; goods vehicles making deliveries; emergency vehicles fighting to get through traffic; aggressive drivers who are in a hurry to get somewhere and may be setting the worst possible example.

Changes in the environment may also pose a threat – blind bends, narrow roads, poor surfaces, patchy mist or fog, sudden rain or snow, late summer sun low on the horizon, bright lights or oncoming headlights when driving after dark. Most of these hazards will require at the very least a reduction in speed.

As an instructor, you can capitalize on all these potentially dangerous situations by asking questions that will ensure that the pupil:

- has seen the hazard;
- has the correct attitude towards it and understands what action needs to be taken;
- takes the appropriate action.

Of course, with pupils at any level there may occasionally be emergency situations which develop so fast that you have no time to start asking questions! In these circumstances, in the interests of safety, you have no alternative but to intervene.

After situations such as these, you can then put Q & A to good use by asking, 'Why do you think I took control then?'

The most effective questions are OPEN-ENDED QUESTIONS which need to be answered with some information rather than just a 'Yes' or 'No'. For example, if you ask a pupil if they have understood your explanations, the answer can only be 'Yes' or 'No'. This does not indicate whether the pupil has *actually* understood. You would, therefore, need to ask further questions in order to decide whether any learning had taken place.

Open-ended questions usually begin with the words: WHY, WHEN, HOW, WHO, WHERE, WHAT and WHICH.

The weakest of these is WHICH because this could be answered with a guess. You would then need to ask another question to find out if the pupil had simply guessed correctly.

The most powerful teaching word is WHY. For example, if you asked your pupil which signs are the most important, round ones or triangular ones and the pupil answered, 'Round ones' you would then need to ask the question, 'Why are round signs more important than triangular ones?' It would have been better to have asked that question in the first place.

You should always try to ask a question which will give you the answer that you are looking for. The idea is not to baffle pupils but to help them to work things out for themselves.

Open-ended questions can be used on the move to test a pupil's awareness of approaching hazards and what action should be taken. However, they should not require lengthy answers or a discussion. You can sometimes ask two questions at once – for example, 'What does this sign mean and how are you going to deal with it?'

Questions which require a long answer or a discussion should only be used when parked at the roadside somewhere safe and convenient.

Avoid asking questions while a pupil is trying to negotiate a junction or other hazard. This may confuse them and could result in a loss of concentration, leading to further driving errors.

The skill of the instructor is to choose questions wisely to get the pupil thinking and involved in decision making.

You should always confirm your pupils' understanding of what has been explained by careful use of the question and answer technique. Think about how you phrase the question:

● use simple wording that can be easily understood;

● make sure the questions are answerable and reasonable.

Try to avoid using questions that can be answered with any number of replies. Do not use trick questions which will only undermine the confidence of the pupil, make them feel foolish and defeat the objective of the question.

Most driving instructors are very good at telling their pupils what to do and how to do it, but very few ensure that learning and understanding have taken place by skilful use of the question and answer technique. As well as using questions yourself, invite questions from your pupil – 'Is there anything you are not sure about?'

Never ASSUME that your pupil has understood everything you have said!

As in all things, PRACTICE MAKES PERFECT and you will find that the more you use the Q & A technique, the more accomplished you will become. After a while you will build up an armoury of questions designed to suit most pupils and most situations.

Never assume that pupils will see and interpret things in the same way that you do. When a difference of opinion does occur, you may have to ask more searching questions, perhaps while stationary, until you can persuade pupils to see things in the way that you see them.

Remember that the benefits of doing things 'your way' usually include:

- improved safety;

- more smoothness;

- less effort involved and greater efficiency;

- cost savings through more economy or less wear and tear.

Give plenty of praise (positive reinforcement) when questions are answered well, even if they may only be partly answered. In this case you could rephrase the answer, filling in the gaps and thus making it complete.

Do not be disparaging or sarcastic about incorrect answers, otherwise pupils may 'clam up' and be reluctant to answer future questions.

Until it comes naturally to you, try asking yourself questions when you are driving alone. This is very similar to the technique used by police drivers of 'giving a commentary' but more productive for driving instructors in that it will help you to improve your Q & A technique, thus making lessons more effective both for you and for your pupils.

Always give pupils time to answer questions. Never ask another question until the first one has been answered. Be careful not to bombard them with questions or turn lessons into 'interrogations'. If necessary, find somewhere safe to stop so that you can discuss a pupil's response to questions.

During every drive there will be situations on which you can base your questions. These questions will help pupils to see things as you see them, stand them in good stead once they have passed the test and help them to achieve 'safe driving for life'.

Once you have become skilled at using Q & A, don't forget that, as pupils near test standard, you should be reducing the number of questions you are using. By this stage you should have transferred responsibility so that pupils are making their own decisions without help from you. The problem with many instructors is that once they get proficient at asking questions, they don't know when to stop – so don't get bogged down with asking irrelevant ones.

If you still need to ask questions in the last few lessons leading up to the test, you should ask yourself the one final question – 'Should this pupil be taking the test at all?'

At the end of each lesson, when analysing your own performance, ask yourself whether the questions you used during the lesson achieved their objectives.

INTERVENTION

Some learner drivers may fail to recognize potentially dangerous traffic situations in time to employ the necessary procedure or defensive strategy.

Instructors must read the road well ahead. They must also learn to anticipate a learner's incorrect response to situations and be prepared to compensate for it, either by verbal or physical action.

When giving driving lessons you must maintain a safe learning environment for your pupils by:

● planning routes that are suitable to their ability;

● forward planning and concentrating on the overall traffic situation – front, rear and to the sides;

● being alert and anticipating learners' incorrect actions or lack of activity in difficult situations;

● giving clear instructions in good time for them to respond;

● overriding learners' decisions when necessary;

● being prepared to intervene verbally or physically.

Many learners show a reluctance to slow down, give way, stop, or hold back when necessary. This is usually because they have an innate fear of stopping. If they stop, they know they then have to get the car moving again – one of the most difficult things for learners to do in the early stages!

This reluctance to deal with hazards defensively may cause the situation to develop into an emergency. Where the situation is allowed to reach this critical level, there are two possible unwanted reactions:

- the pupil may do nothing and remain frozen at the controls;

- they may over-react at the last moment, resulting in harsh, uncontrolled braking, the effect of which is difficult to predict.

It is in situations like this that expert instructors prove their worth. By intervening, either verbally or physically, a possible accident situation can be avoided.

There are four main reasons why you should intervene:

- To prevent risk of injury or damage to persons or property (including the driving school car).

- To prevent the pupil from breaking the law which could lead to you being prosecuted for 'aiding and abetting'.

- To prevent excessive stress to the learner in certain unplanned circumstances (for example, an emergency situation).

- To prevent mechanical damage to the vehicle (for example, in the event of an injudicious gear change).

Because intervention can undermine confidence and inhibit the progress of the learner, it should be kept to a minimum. Verbal intervention should, if time allows, be used before considering the use of physical intervention or the dual controls.

Verbal intervention

A verbal instruction or command will usually be successful in dealing with most traffic situations or driver errors, providing it is given early enough.

Verbal instructions and memory prompts will be used more frequently in the early stages of learning to drive, and may take the form of more specific instructions such as: 'Use the mirrors *well* before...', 'More brake!', 'Ease off the brake' and 'Clutch down'.

These more positive commands will often be needed to make sure that your pupil slows down early enough on the approach to a potential hazard.

'Hold back!', 'Give way!' and 'Wait!' are other examples of *positive* instructions which require a *positive* response or reaction from the pupil, but which also leave some freedom of judgement.

When using this type of command, the pitch and tone of your voice should be used to convey the degree of urgency to the pupil.

The use of the word 'Stop' should generally be restricted to those occasions when other instructions have not been followed by the pupil or when the pupil has not responded positively. Incorrect use of this command could mean that your pupil over-reacts and stops too suddenly or in an unsuitable position. Unnecessary and too frequent use of the word 'Stop' – for example, when parking – could have the effect that pupils will not respond quickly enough in urgent situations.

Physical intervention

Use of any form of physical intervention, or the dual controls, should be restricted to situations when the verbal instruction has not been followed or there is insufficient time for it to be given or acted on.

In these situations, you may need to consider the main alternatives:

● use of the dual brake and/or clutch;
● assistance with the steering.

Using the dual brake/clutch

The following points need to be considered:

● Avoid sitting with your legs crossed when teaching. When approaching hazards, keep your right foot discreetly near the dual brake but not riding on it.

● Avoid unnecessary or 'fidgety' movements of your feet as this may unnerve your pupil.

● Only use the dual clutch when it is absolutely necessary and *never* to 'make things easy' for the pupil.

● Make effective use of the dual mirror before using the dual brake.

● If your pupil has 'frozen' on the gas pedal, avoid using the dual clutch as this could cause a blown head gasket.

● Give the pupil time to use the brake before intervening. If you both use the brake at the same time, this could cause problems.

- Consider using the dual brake to help you to 'buy time' if you have to help with the steering. This applies particularly where the pupil may be trying to turn a corner too fast.

Assistance with steering

This should only be used to make slight alterations to road position. It would be better for you to tell the pupil to 'Steer to the right' or 'Steer to the left'.
   Bear in mind the following points:

- Minor corrections with steering are usually more practical and safer alternatives to using the dual brake.
- Use only your right hand when assisting with steering.
- Avoid physical contact. If you get hold of the pupil's hand or arm and they let go of the wheel, you have lost control.
- If you wish to steer to the left, hold the wheel near the top so that you can 'pull down'.
- If you wish to steer to the right, hold the wheel near the bottom so that you can 'push up'.
- If the situation is such that more drastic turning of the wheel is required, it would be safer and much less worrying for the pupil if you used the dual brake.
- Never get into a fight with the pupil over the wheel – you might lose!

There may be occasions when assistance with both steering and braking are required. For example, it may be essential to hold the steering wheel while using the dual brake to prevent the pupil from oversteering. In order to gain more time, you may need to reduce and control the speed of the vehicle with the dual brake, particularly when the pupil has 'frozen' on the gas pedal.
   In any potentially dangerous situation, you will need to use your experience to decide which method of intervention is required. You may need to use the dual clutch at the same time as manipulating the gear lever to prevent an inappropriate gear change. This will allow your pupil to concentrate on maintaining the correct speed and position.
   Examples of other types of physical intervention which crop up from time to time include:

- selecting a missed gear at a critical time or place;
- preventing an incorrect gear selection by 'covering the gear lever' until the correct speed is reached;

- covering the dual clutch so as to be ready to prevent the car moving off at an inappropriate time;

- rectifying an error with the handbrake when there is no time to tell the pupil to do so;

- switching off the engine to prevent mechanical damage;

- cancelling an injudicious signal with safety in mind when there is no time to tell the pupil to do so.

The need for any kind of intervention can be kept to an absolute minimum by careful route planning and matching the road and traffic conditions to the ability of the pupil.

You may encounter some resentment against any form of physical interference or the use of the dual controls. This could result in the pupil losing confidence in themselves and in you as a teacher. You should therefore make sure that:

- You do not get into the habit of using physical intervention or the dual controls excessively or unnecessarily.

- Having used any physical intervention, you fully explain to the pupil WHAT you did to control the car, and WHY it was necessary to do it!

CHANGING ATTITUDES BY COACHING

Persuasion

As a good, effective instructor you need to be able to persuade pupils to do want you want, in the way that you expect them to do it.

When 'selling' your ideas informally on a one-to-one basis you should involve the pupil in what is expected by explaining the benefits of following your advice and then by listening carefully to their response.

Whenever you are conveying ideas and concepts you must, of course, be as knowledgeable as possible about the issue under discussion and you will need to make effective use of your communication skills that were described in Chapter 2. In particular you will be using:

- your verbal skills;

- your listening skills;

- your use of positive body language and the interpretation of pupils' body language.

When selling ideas you first of all need to explain:

- WHAT it is that you require pupils to do or understand;
- HOW you want it done or carried out; and finally:
- WHY it is important to carry out the task in a particular way.

The most important element is the WHY as there is no point in pupils knowing WHAT is supposed to be done if they don't know WHY it needs to be done in that particular way.

The skilful use of *coaching* techniques, including effective question and answer routines, will help you to achieve all three objectives.

Good instructors will help pupils arrive at their own conclusions by guiding any discussions with appropriate prompting.

As in any form of *selling*, you need to deal with any objections raised by asking pupils further questions and giving more explanations. It is therefore very important that you listen carefully to everything pupils say. You need to draw them into discussions rather than appearing to be giving a lecture.

Whether you are in the classroom or a car, your body language must be positive and should endorse what you are saying. For example:

- Forceful hand gestures may be used to emphasize important points.
- Strong eye contact should be made to show your sincerity and belief in what you are saying.
- Nods of approval, coupled with smiles, should be given when pupils reach good conclusions – this will encourage them to participate further.

Carefully watching pupils' body language will assist in identifying any resistance to your ideas.

Once you have identified the problem, you should handle it like any other objection by outlining the benefits of doing or seeing things your way. Remember, the benefits should nearly always relate to *SAFETY*, *CONVENIENCE* and *COST SAVINGS*.

For example, you might be trying to convince a pupil that a signal is not required every time they move off, especially if there's no other road user to benefit from one. The de-briefing might go something like this:

'OK, how did you think that part of the drive went?'

'Well, I don't think it was too bad. I know I was a bit jerky with the clutch when I moved off.'

'It was a bit jerky but we can work on that and you'll get better with practice. I liked the way you waited for the red car to pass us from behind before you moved off, but do you really think you needed to signal?'

'Well, my Dad said it's always best to signal just in case.'

'Yes, I agree that in a busy area a signal might be worthwhile, but not if the signal could cause a misunderstanding. For instance, what if you signalled unnecessarily and it made someone pause because they thought you were going to move off?'

'Well, I suppose it might cause some confusion.'

'Yes, so can you see that it's important to think about what's happening around you and then decide whether to signal or not?'

'Yes, I can now!'

'As well as that decision, what about the timing of the signal? I had a pupil on test the other week and the examiner stopped her on a busy road to give his next instruction. Before moving off again, she checked her mirrors, saw a bus coming along and decided to give a signal. The bus driver, perhaps thinking she was on test, decided to stop for her. This resulted in the girl becoming confused, not knowing whether to go or wait. In the meantime, the bus driver became fed up with waiting and started to move. Unfortunately the girl decided to go at the same time, resulting in the examiner having to intervene by stopping the car. If the pupil had assessed the situation correctly, decided to wait and not give a signal, there wouldn't have been a problem would there? If there was a bus coming along you wouldn't move off in front of it would you?'

'No, not really!'

'Good. Well let's try moving off again. This time, I'd like you to assess the situation yourself and then decide if you need to signal. Try to get used to assessing each situation and to base your decisions on safety.'

Coaching through questions

At various points in the book you will see that we have used expressions such as 'pupil-centred learning' and the importance of questions and answers. There has been emphasis on 'nothing is taught until it is learnt' and the need for pupils to feel involved if they are to be properly motivated and able to take responsibility for themselves and, to a certain extent, their own learning. All of these elements should be regarded as part of a system of *coaching* rather than purely *instructing*.

It is perhaps unfortunate that we are called 'instructors', because we should be *coaching* our pupils, not merely 'instructing' them what to do. One aspect of coaching is that the pupil (or trainee or 'coachee') should, in many situations, set their own agenda. In particular they should decide on their goals for achievement in each individual training session or lesson.

In the past this has been done at the start of lessons with recap questions such as:

> *'Any questions left over from the previous lesson?'*
>
> *'Any particular doubts or problem areas?'*
>
> *'Any particular topics to be dealt with today?'*
>
> *'What do you feel you can manage to do?'*

The lesson is then based on the answers and general response from each pupil. If we take this approach a little further we can effectively get pupils to decide on the appropriate lesson plan – except, of course, that they will be guided by your use of questions relating to the subject that you would have chosen in the first place (see 'Persuasion').

All of this can be put in context by using the following dialogues as examples.

At the start of a lesson

An old-style instructor might say:

> *'Today we are going to deal with emerging at T-junctions. Is that OK with you?'*
>
> 'Fine.' (Thinks: 'Oh no! I'm dreading this because I can't even deal with turning corners yet. I don't know how I'll cope with all the other traffic.')

Using a coaching dialogue:

> *'OK, we've got a one-hour lesson today. What do you feel we need to achieve by the end of the session?'*
>
> 'Well, I don't know – that's up to you isn't it.'
>
> *'Is there anything left over from last time that you feel could be improved?'*
>
> 'Well, quite a lot, I suppose.'
>
> *'Anything in particular?'*
>
> 'Not sure.'

'How did you think the last lesson went?'

'Reasonably well.'

'Were you happy with the way you were turning basic corners and dealing with the limited amount of traffic that we met?'

'Yes, I think so.'

'Do you feel that you're ready to take it a little further and deal with slightly more complex junctions and a bit more traffic?'

'Possibly.'

'So, if we spend a little time in consolidating what we did last time and then move on to, say, emerging at junctions you'd feel that's what we should do?'

'Yes, I think I'll be happier with that.'

'Right, so that means that the goal for today is to be able to emerge properly at T-junctions?'

'Yes, that's fine.'

'You're happy with that goal that you've set yourself?'

'Yes.'

'Fine, let's make a start, shall we?'

(Thinks: 'I'm pleased that we're going to do it that way and that I was able to make up my own mind about how the lesson was going to be structured.')

During a lesson (ie, at the end of a particular part of the session)

Example: Turning in the road.
Dictatorial style:

'Well, that wasn't too bad, but you could have controlled the car a bit better and your steering wasn't as effective as it might have been. We'll do it again, OK?'

'Right.' (Thinks: 'I didn't think it was all that bad for a first attempt – I got round in three without hitting anything.')

Coaching method:

'How did you think that went?'

'OK, but perhaps not as good as I would like.'

'In what way?'

'Well, I didn't seem to have the car under complete control and the steering when I was reversing didn't seem quite right somehow.'

'Why do you think that would be?'

'Don't really know.'

'Do you think that it might be anything to do with the speed of the car?'

'Possibly.'

The instructor would possibly wait a few seconds to give the pupil time to think and respond.

'Maybe if I went a bit slower?'

'How much slower?'

'As slow as possible?'

'Do you think that's the only reason?'

'Well, maybe I could turn the wheel a bit quicker.'

'Do you think that going a bit slower will give you more time to steer?'

'Er, yes, probably.'

'Why don't you try it that way and see if it works?'

'OK.' (Thinks: 'I'm glad I worked that out for myself.')

Using reversing as an example:
Old-style instructor:

> *'Your regular instructor has told me that today we are to deal with reversing' or, 'If you remember, last time I saw you I told you that today we would be making a start on reversing.'*

'Yes, OK.'

'Right, this is what we do.'

(Thinks: 'How can I tell him that I know half this stuff he's telling me?')

Coaching style:

> *'Just going back to our previous lesson, do you remember what we said we would be doing today?'*

'Er, I think we said reversing.'

'Oh yes, that's right. What do you know about reversing?'

'I know that it's part of the test.'

'Yes, but we don't need to worry about that yet – have you got any thoughts about what we're going to do?'

'Well, yes. And in fact, at the weekend, I had a chance to do a bit of manoeuvring in my Dad's car in the big yard at the back of the house.'

'Oh good – how did you get on?'

'Well, quite reasonable, I think.'

'You probably know quite a bit about handling the car then, so what we'll do today is build on that.'

'Good.'

'What do you think will be the big difference between what you did at home and what we're doing today?'

'Well – er – other traffic, I suppose – pedestrians, cars and so on.'

'That's right, so those are the things that we'll have to deal with in today's lesson. At the same time though, we'll check your control of the car and the accuracy of the reversing.'

'That's fine.'

'OK, so let's imagine that we've now got to turn the car round and the only way we can do so is to use that side road on the left. Are there any rules about what we do? For example will it be safe to reverse in this area or might we be affecting other traffic?'

(Thinks: 'What a good job I was able to explain what I'd done.')

These are all examples that involve:

- coaching principles;
- pupil involvement;
- use of Q & A;
- persuasion;
- most of the elements described previously in this book.

By using this style and method of teaching, your pupils will be more likely to develop self-awareness and they will be encouraged to take more responsibility for their own learning. Both of these are important elements of an effective coaching environment.

4

Structured driver training

LESSON PLANS

Teaching driving as a life skill in today's congested traffic conditions is a challenging occupation. In order to ensure that your pupils become safe and competent drivers, as well as being able to enjoy their motoring, you need to:

- understand and be able to apply all the teaching, coaching and learning principles covered previously in this book;
- be able to develop confidence and safe attitudes in your pupils;
- structure your training to follow the 'known to the unknown' and 'simple to complex' rules of learning.

You will find detailed information about what to include in your syllabus and which PTS to apply when teaching the subjects listed in this chapter in the various publications that you should already have. They include:

- *The Official Guide to Learning to Drive*;
- *The Official DSA Guide to Driving: the essential skills;*
- the ADI26 forms, as illustrated in *The Driving Instructor's Handbook*; and
- if you are preparing for your ADI exam, ADI14 – *Your Road to Becoming an Approved Driving Instructor.*

In this chapter we have deliberately not repeated all this information but present the syllabus in a way that will be helpful in developing your teaching skills.

You will see that the topics have been dealt with in slightly different styles or formats. With some we have taken a relatively formal approach and include *the introduction*, *objectives* and so on. With others, we give examples of how to set up more of a coaching approach by way of a dialogue with the pupil in order to encourage more self-learning, self-awareness and motivation. With other topics we simply offer a few guidance notes on the important key points.

With experience, you should be able to decide for yourself the method and approach that will best suit your own particular teaching style and the one that will also be most appropriate for any individual pupil or specific circumstances.

Focusing on your job as an ADI, and not the instructional test, this chapter contains a training programme that follows a logical sequence incorporating the above principles. If you learn how to apply these effectively, you should be well prepared to teach drivers at all levels of experience and ability and to adapt to the role-play situation of the instructional ability test.

When you are carrying out your job as an ADI, all of the topics detailed on pages 114 to 182 should be covered within your programme for new drivers.

Beginning with the introduction of the car's controls and how to move off and stop, we progress through all of the different stages of learning to drive in a logical sequence.

The programme is not 'set in stone' and because of various factors, including local geography and different students' rates of learning, you may need to teach some of the subjects in a different sequence. Also, if you are dealing with a pupil from another driving school or are preparing for your instructional ability test, you will need to adapt your lesson to suit the:

- stated level and ability of the pupil; and/or
- the limited amount of time available.

You need to do this by:

- the use of Q & A to establish the base line for the lesson;
- adapting your teaching method to suit progress made during the lesson;
- ensuring some positive learning takes place through practice within the time scale.

Throughout this chapter you will find examples of the types of question you could use to suit the pupil's experience, the topic under instruction and the circumstances. You will need to formulate your own questions, as every time you meet someone new, or go out on the road, everything will be different. Chapter 3 of this book should help with this.

Whatever the subject or level of ability of your pupil, your aim should always be to:

> *Ensure some learning takes place and to encourage pupils' progress and confidence.*

Lesson ingredients

Every lesson, no matter what the subject matter is, should follow a similar pattern. There should always be:

a beginning, a middle, and an end.

The main ingredients should be:

- *Beginning*
    - greeting;
    - recapping on the previous lesson;
    - stating the objectives and aims;
    - establishing prior knowledge and understanding through Q & A;
    - setting the base line according to the above.
- *Middle*
    - working from the known to the unknown;
    - following the pattern of explanation – demonstration – practice;
    - applying the appropriate teaching, instructing and coaching skills;
    - creating opportunities for learning to take place through practice.
- *End*
    - giving the appropriate feedback in a summary, including praise for procedures and routines learnt and carried out correctly;
    - looking forward to the next lesson and giving information for your pupil to research.

The following is an example lesson plan.

Greeting

'Hello Wayne, how are you today?'
'I'm fine thanks.'

Recap

'*You did really well on your last lesson and were getting quite good at moving off, stopping and changing up and down the gears.*'

'Yes, but I remember crunching the gears a couple of times.'

'*Don't worry about that: if you take your time a little more, your gear changing will soon become smooth.*'

Stating the objectives

'*By the end of today's lesson we should have sorted out that little problem and also learnt how to turn left and right at T-junctions. How do you feel about that?*'

'That would be great.'

Establishing prior knowledge

'*So, Wayne, can you tell me what routine you need to apply for moving off and stopping? You know, that little three-letter sequence.*'

'Oh, you mean Mirror Signal Manoeuvre.'

'*Yes, good. And why should we check the mirrors before we stop?*'

'So that we know what's behind.'

'*Good, any other reason for checking them?*'

'I'm not sure.'

'*What about checking to see how close they are and what speed they're travelling at?*'

'If we know they're there, why does all the rest matter?'

'*Because it's going to determine whether we need to signal a little earlier to give them plenty of notice that we intend to stop. By doing this, it will give that following driver more time to respond.*'

'Oh right, I never thought of that.'

'*So you see how important the M S M routine and how we apply it is!*'

Setting the base line

'*What we're going to do today then, is learn how to break down that routine into more sections and apply it to turning left and right at junctions.*'

Working from the known to the unknown

This particular pupil knows a little about the basic M S M routine in straightforward moving off and stopping situations, but now needs to be taught how to apply it to turn left and right at junctions.

Explanation – demonstration – practice

You need to analyse the routine by explaining in detail the M S M – (mirrors-signal-manoeuvre), P S L (position-speed-look) and L A D (look-assess-decide) routines. A visual aid will be useful as you can use it as a memory jogger while your pupil will be able to see exactly what you mean.

A demonstration is sometimes useful when dealing with a more complex topic but when dealing with straightforward tasks such as simple junction work, talk-through teaching will leave much more time for practice.

Apply the appropriate teaching, instructing and coaching skills

The subject in hand, the level of skill of your pupil and the road and traffic circumstances, will all need to be considered when you decide on the most appropriate teaching method to be applied.

Normally talk-through instruction will be needed when dealing with a new subject and, as confidence and skills increase and in order to develop safe attitudes, coaching will become more appropriate.

Create opportunities for learning to take place through practice

Select a route that will allow plenty of opportunities to apply the appropriate routines and skills. The more time that is allocated to the practice element, the more the pupil is likely to achieve success and confidence.

Give feedback and praise

If you are to encourage your pupils to work with you, and to leave at the end of each lesson wanting more, you need to give them some positive feedback. This should include praise for procedures and routines learnt and carried out correctly, use of Q & A to confirm understanding and giving advice on where improvements can be made. See Chapter 2 for guidance on giving feedback.

Look forward to the next lesson

It's important to give your pupils something to think about before their next lesson. Tell them what you will be covering and give them an indication of where to find appropriate information. Give them some incentive to do a little research by confirming that you will be asking a few questions at the beginning of their next lesson.

MAIN CAR CONTROLS

Objectives

The main objectives of this lesson are to:

- get to know a little about the pupil;
- find out what has motivated them to want to learn to drive;
- discover why they chose you as their instructor;
- let them get used to you and your style of instruction;
- teach them about the main controls of the car;
- familiarize them with some of the terminology you will be using;
- gain their confidence;
- and, by the end of the lesson, let the pupil gain some experience in moving off and stopping.

Getting to know the pupil

One of your main aims, when meeting a pupil for the first time, is to sell yourself by promoting a caring and understanding image and ensuring that you inspire confidence. To do this, try to imagine how your pupil may be feeling faced with, what to many will be:

- the daunting task of learning to drive;
- being in the confined space of a car with a complete stranger.

For this lesson, you will need to drive to an area that is reasonably quiet, with as long a stretch of straight road as is available to practise moving off and stopping (see route planning in Chapter 3). Obviously the area you use will depend on the locality of your office or the pupil's pick-up point. You will sometimes have to adapt your instruction to suit less than ideal conditions – this is often the case on the instructional ability test.

During the drive to the training area find out if your pupil:

- has a valid and signed driving licence;

- can read a number plate at the prescribed distance;
- is studying for, or has already passed, the theory test.

Get to know a little more about your pupil by asking questions such as:

'Why do you want to learn to drive?'

'How did you hear of me? Was I recommended by someone?'

'Do you have any experience in driving a car?'

'Do you ride a motorbike?'

'When you've been a passenger, have you been watching what the driver was doing?'

If your pupil is a little shy, you may have to 'back off' a little. However, try to avoid silence – this will only make a nervous pupil even more tense.

> *Remember, part of your job as an instructor is to gain the confidence of your pupils and put them at ease.*

Driving deliberately and a little more slowly than usual, give a simple commentary on what you're doing. Focus mainly on the application of the M S M routine and its application to the various situations you meet.

> *Remember, you are your best salesperson – make sure your driving is impeccable.*

Select a training area that is safe, legal and will cause as little disruption to other drivers as is possible – in other words, convenient. Park where:

- you can safely carry out your explanation of the main controls;
- the pupil can get some stationary practice in their use;
- there is plenty of opportunity to learn how to move off and stop.

Vehicle familiarization

To make the most effective use of your time, and to avoid repetition, it is sensible to get the pupil into the driving seat so that you can explain where the controls are and they can practise using them. This will also mean you have plenty of time for the pupil to get practical experience at moving off and stopping before the end of the lesson, which in turn should help to meet some of their expectations.

The first thing you need to get your pupil to think about is getting out of the passenger seat, around the car and into the driving seat safely. This should include:

- Checking around before opening the passenger door. You could ask something like: 'Is anyone near the car on the pavement?'
- Making sure it's safe to walk into the road, around the car and to open the door, ask: 'Is there any traffic coming up that might make it unsafe to step out or that you will affect by opening the door?'

Entering the car and getting into a correct seating position is commonly called 'The cockpit drill' and includes:

- *Doors* – ensuring they are properly closed.
- *Seat* – correct adjustment of seat, back rake, head restraint and other ancillaries as are available and necessary such as steering column and seat height.
- *Steering* – hands can be comfortably moved from top to bottom of the wheel.
- *Seatbelts* – correctly put on and removed (no twists); driver's responsibilities.
- *Mirrors* – all mirrors are correctly adjusted.
- *Ancillary controls* – to avoid overloading your pupil with too much unnecessary information, only cover those that are needed for the conditions, for example wipers and lights.

Main controls

These fall into three categories:

1. hand controls;
2. foot controls;
3. ancillary controls.

It is not essential to cover these in the sequence listed. However, from experience, it does help pupils if you deal lastly with those controls that will be used to make the car go and stop – that means the foot controls. Apart from the indicators, the ancillary controls you will need to cover should depend on the weather and light conditions.

Hand controls

Explain that, although there are lots of dials, switches and gadgets in the car, there are three main hand controls:

1. steering wheel;

2. handbrake;

3. gear lever.

1. The steering wheel

You can use coaching skills to find out which hand position is most comfortable for your pupil. First of all get them to place their hands on the wheel at around 'ten to two' and watch the pupil, encouraging them to hold it gently with the thumbs along the rim rather than around the wheel. Ask how it feels when they slide their hands to the top and bottom. If it's not comfortable, get them to drop the hands a little and try again. Try this procedure until the pupil can move the hands comfortably around the wheel – as long as they aren't at rest too near the top or bottom.

Explain that, since the wheel shouldn't be turned while stationary, as this can damage the steering mechanism and tyres, they should refer to *The Official DSA Guide to Driving: the essential skills*, for a full explanation of the official 'pull-push' method of steering.

Turning the wheel using this method does not come naturally to many drivers and everyone's body and range of movement are different. Exercise tolerance and some flexibility with those who find it easier to turn the wheel by going over the 12 o'clock point (rotational steering) – as long as the car is in the correct position on the road, they don't completely cross their arms, and they can return the wheel to its normal position in safety. You should be aware that rotational steering generally results in a quicker response in some emergency situations.

Describe how it's natural for the hands to follow the eyes. Ask your pupil if they've ever experienced a situation when they've been walking along and something to the side has caught their attention and when they've looked forward again, they've gone off course. Confirm that this can happen while driving and that's why it's so important to look well ahead up the road at where they want to go.

INDICATORS. Remember – new drivers will have been pedestrians and passengers and will be aware of the use of indicators. To avoid being patron-izing try to get them to discover for themselves where they are and in which direction they will need to be operated. Use questions such as:

'What are the orange flashing lights for on the front, rear and sometimes the sides, of cars?'

'When do you think they should be used?'

'Which of the controls on the steering column do you think is the indicator switch?' If the pupil has a problem, follow this up with: 'OK, find the switch with the arrows on.'

'If you're intending to turn right which way you will turn the wheel? Now tell me which way you think the indicator switch will need to be operated.'

Allow the pupil to practise switching the indicators on and off (preferably using the fingertips while keeping the hand on the wheel), confirming that they should normally self-cancel after going around corners. Explain the audible and visible warnings that will tell the driver when the indicators are operating.

HORN. The *Highway Code* could be mentioned again to confirm that this is a warning device and should only be used in cases of the threat of danger or damage. Watch your pupil to ensure they don't try to activate the horn and confirm one of the main rules is not to use it when stationary unless under threat from another moving vehicle. You could then ask them to check up on the other rules because you'll be asking some questions on their next lesson.

ANCILLARY CONTROLS. As your pupil has to take on board lots of infor-mation on this lesson, it's very important to consider how much of it is likely to be remembered. Overloading them at this stage with information they are unlikely to remember in any case, is going to inhibit their progress and confi-dence.

Only cover those ancillary controls that are necessary according, mainly, to the weather and light conditions. If it's not raining and light conditions are good, you'll not need to cover the lights, washers, wipers or demisters. Confirm that you will show the pupil where these are and how they work on another lesson.

2. The handbrake

By telling your pupil this is often referred to as the 'parking brake' they should be able to give you at least one answer if you ask: 'When do you think you might use it?' Confirm that it secures the car once stopped by locking up the rear wheels. As well as for parking, it should be used for stops of longer than a few seconds, on hills to prevent rolling forwards or backwards and for safety when stopped for pedestrians on crossings. (When driving automatics, the handbrake should be used more often to compensate for their tendency to creep.)

You will need to ensure the car is secure. You can either apply the dual footbrake or, because you also need to encourage an understanding of the relationship between the two braking systems, you could say something like: 'Press the middle pedal down with your right foot. This is the footbrake and I'll be explaining about it in a few moments.'

Explain that the handbrake has three positions: on, off and, when the button is pressed, ready to release. Demonstrate how to properly release and apply the brake and then allow the pupil to practise this a couple of times.

If the pupil doesn't follow your example and release the ratchet, explain that this can eventually cause wear, resulting in the brake not holding properly. Ask what they'll do if they leave their car parked on a hill and when they return it's no longer there!

3. The gear lever

Find out what the pupil knows about the use of gears. Usually if they have experience in riding a cycle they will have a little understanding. However, in order to develop your PTS, we will deal with the subject as it should be taught to someone with no knowledge.

First of all, explain about the power to speed ratio and, while serving as a memory jogger for you, a visual aid may assist your pupil in understanding this principle (see 'Visual Aids', Chapter 3).

Confirm that, because of the weight of the car and its occupants, you will need more engine power to get moving. The lower gears, first and second, are the most powerful and normally first is used for moving off. Second is useful for moving off down hills where gravity will help in getting the car rolling more quickly. We will need to accelerate to build up speed and then change up into the higher gears. These allow us to drive at a wider range of speeds while using less power.

To assist in the pupil's understanding, you might ask:

'When you're walking uphill what happens to you?'

'Do you start to slow down and then have to put in more effort?'

'If you were cycling up a hill, what would you have to do?'

You will then be able to confirm that this is exactly what happens to the car by saying something like: 'Because of the hill slowing the car down, in order to keep going at the same speed, we will need to give it more power by changing into a lower gear.'

You should also explain that, because all cars differ in size and power, the speed at which the gears will need to be changed varies. However, after a few lessons they should become familiar with the sound the engine makes as it 'tells' them when a change is required. Confirm that you will help them to recognize these sounds and to build up their vehicle sympathy so that they will eventually feel the car is part of them.

As one of the main objectives of this lesson is vehicle familiarization, plenty of stationary practice should be allowed so that they will be able to 'find' all the gear positions while looking through the windscreen. This can be done without switching on the engine, but it might be useful to get the pupil to push down the clutch (confirming that you will explain this pedal later) to establish the relationship.

Allow your pupil to take an initial look at the lever and identify the different gear positions. It might help, in the early stages, to relate the position of the first four gears in the form of the letter H to the position of the road wheels so when a change is necessary, and without looking down, they should be able to move the lever in the appropriate direction.

The gear lever in most modern cars is usually 'spring-loaded'. As well as demonstrating (with your right hand) how to select all of the gears using the 'palming' method, you will also need to emphasize this bias as you talk the pupil through the various changes so that they experience success and confidence is built up.

Allow the pupil to practise all of the gear change combinations. That is, as well as showing them how to change in sequence up and down, explain about selective changing and talk them through these changes with a couple of examples of where they might be used.

This practice is very important because, the more confident the pupil becomes with gear changing while stationary, the easier they will find it when they are on the move.

Foot controls

Unless you are teaching in a car with automatic gears, confirm that there are three foot controls:

1. accelerator;
2. footbrake;
3. clutch.

Ask your pupil if they know which foot operates which pedal and what each does, for example:

'Do you know what the pedal on the right does?'

'What's the pedal in the centre for and which foot will you use to operate it?'

'Do you know what following drivers should see when the footbrake is used?'

'What's the pedal on the left for?'

If you are teaching in a car with automatic transmission, then you will need to explain that the right foot is used for the two pedals. You will also need to explain about the gear selector.

1. Accelerator

Because you will sometimes need your pupil to respond quickly to a request, for example to start slowing down, it's easier to say: 'Off the gas' than it is to say: 'Off the accelerator'.

If you ask, 'What does the gas pedal do?' most pupils will say that it makes the car go faster. Very few will realize that it is also the first means of starting to slow down the car. However, this point should become clear if you use a simple comparison such as how a tap works, explaining that when the pedal is pressed down more fuel will flow into the engine to make it go faster; and when the pressure is eased the flow will slow down.

The pedal is sensitive and should be used gently.

2. Footbrake

Operating on all four wheels to slow down and eventually bring the car to a stop, explain that:

- a mirror check should be made prior to braking;
- this is also a sensitive pedal and should be used gently and progressively;
- the stop lights will be activated as soon as pressure is applied to it.

3. Clutch

To maintain the co-working relationship ask questions such as:

'Do you know what the clutch does?'

'Do you know when you'd use it?'

Depending on the pupil's responses, using a visual aid, either confirm or explain in simple terms the clutch's main purpose. This is to disconnect the engine from the gearbox in order to make smooth changes from one gear to another and to ensure that the engine keeps running when the car has been stopped.

Stationary practice

To familiarize the pupil with the terminology you will be using and, in order to build up your pupil's confidence in using the main controls, you will now need to explain how to safely start the engine.

Demonstrate how to check that the handbrake is firmly applied and that the gear lever is in neutral. Ask your pupil to make these checks and then allow plenty of stationary practice in:

- setting the gas;
- covering the brake pedal;
- finding the 'biting' point.

Dealing with 'main controls' on the Part 3 exam

You will be advised of the subject you are to be tested on at the test centre. This will give you the opportunity to drive the pupil to a suitable training area, just as you would drive a new client away from the meeting point. The examiner will assume that you are not familiar with the area and will direct you to a suitable location.

You will be given a brief description of the pupil's background and previous experience. Your examiner will then go into role as the pupil and will play either the role of a pupil with no experience or of someone with a little knowledge, for example a young garage mechanic. You must respond and immediately take on the role as the instructor giving the pupil their first driving lesson.

As you will only have about 25 minutes for this part of the test, don't feel you have to squeeze in as much as you would with a real pupil on an hour's lesson.

Because you may not have enough time to cover moving off, this may be the only test that gives you the opportunity of demonstrating your knowledge and teaching skills without being affected by a changing set of circumstances.

Even though you will be conducting most of the lesson in a stationary situation, your examiner will still introduce errors to test your fault identification, analysis and ability to correct errors sympathetically. These could include:

- trying to use the controls as soon as you mention them;
- fiddling with ignition keys;

- fidgeting with hand or foot controls;
- using the controls unsympathetically.

Your instruction may be under even closer scrutiny because it will be mainly verbal and with the car stationary. You must therefore ensure that:

- you use Q & A to confirm any prior knowledge;
- the information you give is accurate;
- you listen carefully and respond to what the pupil says;
- your instruction is clear and simple;
- your instruction allows for routines to be practised in the correct sequence;
- you watch the pupil closely;
- you respond to what the pupil does;
- you give any remedial advice in a sympathetic manner.

You must do all of these things in order to demonstrate that your instruction will:

> *Encourage pupils' progress and confidence.*

MOVING OFF AND STOPPING

You would normally teach your pupils how to move off and stop during their first lesson when you have explained about the main controls. You would simply carry on to talk about the M S M routine and the practical skills needed to move off and stop safely. This is how we will deal with the subject here and at the end of the section we will cover the differences you need to consider if you are preparing for your Part 3.

Confirm that your pupil understands about the main controls by asking a couple of questions such as:

'Do you feel happy with what we've covered so far?'

'Is there anything you're not sure about?'

'Would you like to practise anything again?'

Setting the objectives

You are now ready to continue the lesson by setting the next objective. This is to learn how to move off and stop the car safely. If your pupil has already told you they are preparing for their theory test, ask if they know anything about the M S M routine and give praise if they have even only a little knowledge. In any case, you will need to give a breakdown of the routine to ensure that all the important points are covered.

Explanation

Mirrors

- Explain the difference between the flat glass of the interior mirror and the convex glass of the exterior ones. Confirm why any decisions must be based on the true image seen in the interior mirror.

- Confirm that not all areas to the rear and sides are covered by the mirrors and demonstrate what a 'blind area' is by selecting a point, such as a driveway, to the pupil's right. Confirm why it's important to look over the shoulder prior to moving away to make sure no one, for example a cyclist emerging from that drive, is at the side of the car.

Signal

- Introduce the *Highway Code* and confirm that drivers should use signals to warn or inform other road users of their intentions.

- Confirm that if, after checking the mirrors and all around, there is no one about to benefit from a signal, then it's pointless to give one. Explain that you will help with these decisions to begin with.

Manoeuvre

- This means any change in speed or direction. Moving off involves getting the car moving, building up speed and getting into the normal driving position; and stopping involves slowing down, moving back towards the kerb and stopping.

Although normal teaching practice involves explanation, demonstration and practice, with simpler tasks the demonstration can be omitted so that more time can be allotted to the practice element.

Practice

Moving off and stopping

You will need to give full talk-through instruction in:

- making the safety checks prior to starting the engine;
- preparing the car to move;
- taking full all-round observations;
- moving the car when it's safe;
- stopping where it's safe, legal and convenient;
- moving off on the level and on uphill and downhill gradients (where suitable opportunities arise);
- moving off, building up speed and changing through the gears;
- slowing down and stopping.

Be patient and give as much help as necessary, particularly with the less able. As skill increases, start dropping off your instruction. However, always be ready to come back with more help when needed.

Fault identification, analysis and rectification

Be positive when you make corrections and give your reasons. Common errors during these early stages of learning are:

- *Moving away before or without checking blind areas.* Ask: 'Is there anyone in the blind area? You wouldn't like to move out when there's a cyclist at the side of you, would you?
- *Lack of coordination between gas and clutch.* By being totally in tune with your car, and giving positive instruction, you can do much to ensure your pupil's confidence is built up. By encouraging your pupil to listen to the sound of the engine and feel for the biting point, you can do much to prevent a stalled engine and, at the same time start to develop vehicle sympathy.
- *Looking at the controls.* Confirm that the hands will follow the eyes and that's why we need to look well ahead up the road when we're driving.

Feedback

Throughout the lesson, give lots of praise for routines carried out correctly. End the lesson by confirming where progress has been made, and look forward to the next lesson when more practice will take place prior to learning how to apply the M S M routine to turning left and right.

Dealing with 'moving off and stopping' on the Part 3 exam

If you are dealing with a pupil who has had lessons with another instructor, or you are preparing for your instructional ability test, you will need to recap on the pupil's previous experience, for example entry and pre-start checks and moving off and stopping. You will then need to adapt your lesson to suit the:

- stated level and ability of the pupil; and/or
- the limited amount of time available.

Use Q & A to establish the base line for the lesson, for example:

'On your last lesson did you switch on the engine and learn how to find the biting point?'

'Did you move off and stop?'

'Can you tell me what the M S M routine is?'

'Where are the blind areas?'

'Where would it not be safe, legal or convenient to stop?'

It's extremely important to listen to all the responses otherwise you may be pitching the level of your instruction either too low or too high (see Chapter 3).

Create as many opportunities as possible to allow for practising all of the procedures for moving off and stopping under different circumstances, building up speed and progressing through the gears. Then follow the general lesson ingredients given at the beginning of this chapter to ensure you demonstrate to your examiner that you understand and are able to apply all of the necessary instructional techniques and practical teaching skills.

USE OF MIRRORS

Objectives

The main objectives of this lesson are to ensure your pupil fully understands the importance of correct mirror adjustment and use.

The following is an example of a statement of objectives:

'There are four main objectives in today's lesson and by the end of it you should:

- *be able to adjust all of the mirrors so that you have the maximum possible view around the car with the minimum of head movement;*
- *be aware of the areas not covered by the mirrors;*
- *understand the importance of responding properly to what you see;*
- *be able to apply the M S M routine'.*

Set the base line

Confirm what your pupil has remembered from previous lessons by asking questions such as:

'When you get in the car, how should you adjust the mirrors?'

'Tell me which is the offside and which is the nearside mirror.'

'Do the mirrors cover all areas around the car?'

'Why is it important to check over your shoulders before moving off?'

'Why do you need to check the mirrors before putting on a signal?'

'What routine would you apply for moving off, passing parked cars and stopping?'

Explanation

Give praise for correct answers and give more information where knowledge or understanding is weak.

Confirm that, when a change in direction is involved the mirrors should be used in pairs. For example, before moving out to pass a parked car a check of the interior mirror should be made, followed by a check in the offside door mirror. Before moving back in to the left, the interior mirror should be checked again and this should be followed by a check in the nearside door mirror. Similarly, prior to turning left, as well as checking the interior mirror a check should be made to the nearside for any cyclists.

Explain why it's important to check the mirrors well before deciding when to signal. For example, before signalling to turn right, it's important to know what's behind, how fast it's travelling and whether anyone is going to overtake you. In this case, applying a signal too early may cause confusion all around so it would be better to delay it until the vehicle's gone by. On the other hand if you intend to turn left and there's someone following closely, giving an early signal will be of benefit as it will give the other driver plenty of warning of your intention and time to react to you slowing down.

This is another subject where practice rather than demonstration will help develop your pupil's awareness and skill in mirror use.

Practice

Unless the pupil has had several lessons, has been to another driving school or you are on your Part 3 test, full talk-through instruction may initially be required to establish the need for regular checking of all the mirrors. Encourage general mirror checks every few seconds so that eventually, when there's a hazard that requires a change in speed or direction, checking will become automatic.

As your pupil's mirror work develops, drop off your instruction but when any lapses occur, give a reminder. You can do this by either physically watching them or by using an extra mirror trained on their eyes. The latter can be beneficial in that you can avoid giving hints to your pupil to check the mirrors by not having to look directly at them at the appropriate time.

Fault identification, analysis and rectification

One of the basic ingredients of safe driving is being aware of what's happening all around and responding safely. In order to establish safe routines, it's extremely important that you identify any weaknesses in pupils' mirror use during their early stages of learning. You will need to watch for pupils:

- not adjusting mirrors correctly;
- exaggerating head movements when checking the mirrors;
- making late mirror checks;
- checking mirrors at the same time as signalling;
- not checking mirrors before speeding up, slowing down, changing direction or stopping;
- playing about with the anti-dazzle setting;
- not checking blind areas;
- not using door mirrors;
- not responding correctly to what is happening.

Each error must be identified, analysed and corrected (see Chapter 3). Always try to give reasons for using the mirrors effectively by explaining the consequences on other road users of incorrect responses.

You then need to create opportunities where you can emphasize the need for using the mirrors correctly and responding safely. This may sometimes mean reverting to talk-through instruction until you can see that the pupil's understanding is improving.

Feedback/recap

Give praise where improvement has taken place and confirm by looking back over a few of the situations that arose, where any weaknesses have to be worked on.

Remember that feedback is a two-way process. At the end of the session confirm, through Q & A, that the pupil understands the importance of correct mirror use and ask if there are any points they are not sure about. Explain where any misunderstandings may be occurring.

Look forward

Link the use of mirrors to the application of the M S M routine and confirm that, on the next lesson, you will be covering the correct use of signals. Refer them to the *Highway Code* and *The Official DSA Guide to Driving: the essential skills* for more information.

Dealing with 'mirrors' on the Part 3 exam

If this topic is included on your test, it will be combined with the emergency (controlled) stop. You will need to direct your 'pupil' to a suitable area, where this can be carried out in safety. It is therefore sensible to make full use of the time to deal with mirror adjustment and use at the beginning of the lesson and during this drive.

You will need to incorporate the points listed in the previous lesson plans and watch for similar errors, giving the appropriate feedback and corrective advice.

USE OF SIGNALS

Up to now in this chapter, lesson plans have been dealt with in detail for each subject and, by now, you should be getting familiar with their basic structure.

Most of the remaining topics within the syllabus are dealt with slightly differently. Rather than repeat each element of lesson format, we concentrate on the key points and give guidelines on how to teach them, including example questions.

Signalling

The use of signals, and response to those given by others, is not a subject that you can teach in isolation. It should be taught from lesson one and as part of the general routine for driving.

Make sure that your pupils are aware of the many different ways in which drivers communicate with each other, including:

- indicators;
- arm signals;
- brake lights;
- horn;
- headlights;
- road positioning;
- eye contact;
- signals given by police officers and school wardens.

The following are some sample questions you could use to test pupils' knowledge and understanding:

'How can we tell other road users of our intentions?'

'How does a following driver know when you're slowing down?'

'When could you use the horn?'

'What does the *Highway Code* say about using hazard-warning lights?'

'When would you signal to move away or stop?'

'Do you always need to signal to pass parked cars?'

'When might you use an arm signal for slowing down?'

'Apart from the indicators, how can you tell following drivers that you're going to pass parked vehicles?'

'If you wanted to allow another driver out of a side road when it's busy, how could you do this without waving them out?'

'Why do you think it might be dangerous to beckon pedestrians onto crossings?'

'If someone flashed their headlights at you to turn in front of them into a side, would you automatically assume that your way was clear?'

During pupils' early lessons, you should ensure that they get plenty of practice in applying the M S M routine in all situations. As the basic car control skills improve and the pupil becomes more confident, encourage them to judge when to use signals. They should learn to:

- Look all around and check the mirrors before moving, working out whether anyone will benefit from a signal.
- Make regular checks of all mirrors and decide on the best way to tell others of their intentions to pass parked vehicles, for example moving out earlier.
- Use the brake lights as an early indication of slowing down for lower speed limits.
- Respond correctly to other road users' signals for moving off, stopping and turning.
- Check for themselves that it's safe to proceed when others beckon them on.
- Use eye contact.
- Work out when a short beep on the horn might be used to warn others, for example when they see someone reversing out from a driveway or where there is a blind summit.

As this subject will apply to every lesson, you should give the appropriate praise when the correct routines are applied and good discrimination is demonstrated, and positive advice on where more practice is required.

Dealing with 'signals' on the Part 3 exam

You will probably have seen from the 'pre-set test forms' that this subject is coupled with pedestrian crossings. You should use Q & A to establish the pupil's knowledge and understanding. Listen carefully and give advice if there are shortcomings. All the time the pupil is driving, you should watch for:

- incorrectly used, mistimed or misleading signals;
- unnecessarily signals for moving off, passing parked vehicles and stopping;
- unsafe beckoning of drivers and/or pedestrians;
- improper use of the horn and/or flashing headlights;
- failure to cancel signals after stopping or leaving roundabouts;
- lack of response to the signals of other road users.

Again, using Q & A and incorporating your summary on signals with pedestrian crossings, give the appropriate feedback and advice.

Be tactful if you ask when you should signal and get a response such as: 'Well my Dad says you should always signal, just in case!' Don't insult Dad.

Just confirm what the *Highway Code* advises and explain the logical reasoning behind the rules.

TURNING AND EMERGING AT JUNCTIONS

As with all topics, first of all establish the base line for the lesson so that you are able to pitch the instruction at the correct level. Remember, in this chapter we are dealing with how to teach the subject to one of your regular pupils who has no experience of the subject. You can set the base line, therefore, by asking a few questions relevant to what was covered on the previous lesson. Here are a few examples:

> 'Do you remember our discussion on the last lesson about the routine for moving off, stopping and passing parked cars?'
>
> 'Why do you think that it's important to use the mirrors before signalling?'
>
> 'What if there is some traffic behind, for example, a motorcyclist who is about to overtake? How would that influence your signalling?'
>
> 'What do you think you should you look for when you're turning into a side road?'
>
> 'What does the *Highway Code* say you should do if there are pedestrians who are about to cross the side road?'

Early in the pupil's training you should ensure that your instruction will result in the correct routines being applied. To do this, you will need to start giving your instructions early enough to allow the pupil plenty of time to carry out each individual element comfortably.

As they are the most simple, begin with left turns into and out of T-junctions. Do a few circuits of these and then, as skill improves and confidence increases, introduce turning right following a similar pattern of circuits.

Where there are any weaknesses or misunderstandings you must create opportunities for more practice on appropriate junctions so that positive learning and improvement can take place. To achieve this, you may find that you have to change places with the pupil and drive from one area to another to avoid the pupil having to deal with situations that are too complex for their ability. It might be helpful to use these opportunities to give a demonstration with commentary, keeping this to a level that will suit the pupil's capabilities.

For all types of junction make sure that:

- The Mirror-Signal-Manoeuvre routine is applied correctly.

- Signals are properly timed, taking into account any following traffic and the location of the junction.

- Full control of the car is maintained by effective use of the brakes.

- Any downward gear change is done only after slowing down with the brakes – this should be emphasized from the start, otherwise the pupil mistakenly gets the impression that gears are needed for slowing down.

- Road position is appropriate for the direction being taken, the width of the road, and the presence of other road users.

- The car is secured with the handbrake when waiting to emerge for more than a few seconds.

- Full all-round observations are made. Keep checking that your pupil is looking effectively, as well as making sure that it will be safe for them to complete the turn or to emerge.

During the initial stages of training you might include questions such as:

'How far down the road can you see?'

'Have you checked your mirrors?'

'What are you going to do about the motorcyclist behind us?'

'At what point do we need to change down?'

'Have you released the clutch?'

'Have you seen the cyclist coming up on the nearside?'

'Have you taken account of those pedestrians waiting to cross?'

'What will you do if they step out?'

'Do you think you've time to turn right before that oncoming car reaches us?'

'Have you looked to the right to see what's happening in the new road?'

'How far can you see in both directions?'

'Tell me what's happening on the main road to our left.'

'What's happening at the bus stop?'

As skill increases, transfer the responsibility for decision making and introduce more difficult and busier junctions.

Only allow your pupil to turn or emerge when it's safe.

Always bear in mind that, no matter what their level of ability, you are responsible for the safety of all your pupils, other road users and, of course, yourself. Don't let an unsafe situation arise and put someone else at risk when it could easily be avoided by giving a simple instruction such as 'Wait' or, if really necessary, 'Stop'. (More detail on 'fault analysis' can be found in Chapter 3.)

At the end of each lesson you should offer a summary, including a few questions such as:

'Why do you think that we should look into a junction before turning in?'

'How would you deal with a slightly more complex situation such as...?'

'Why was it necessary for us to...?'

As well as you using Q & A to recap on the lesson, allow time for the pupil to ask questions. Make sure your pupils go away with an understanding of the principles covered during each lesson. (Feedback is dealt with in Chapter 2.)

Finally, 'look forward' by briefing the pupil on the next training topic. This would probably cover 'crossroads' as an extension of junction work or, if progress is slow, maybe a lesson consolidating on 'junctions'.

Dealing with 'junctions' on the Part 3 exam

This subject is included in both phases of the test, and even if you get it on the Phase 1, your 'pupil' may have some previous experience at dealing with junctions. You therefore need to listen very carefully to the description of the pupil and the stage reached in their training.

Make sure that the following key points are covered, either in your briefing, during the practical part of the 'lesson' and/or your fault analysis:

- the M S M routine;
- turning in and emerging from junctions;
- observations – including the extra ones needed at crossroads;
- crossing other traffic;
- pedestrians.

Faults that the examiner could introduce include:

- inadequate use of mirrors and incorrect response;
- late signalling;
- incorrect positioning for direction being taken or width of road;

- coasting (either clutch down too early while using intermediate gears, or when driving around corners);

- speed on approach (too fast or too slow);

- swinging out on left turns;

- crossing the path of other traffic;

- cutting right corners;

- lack of awareness of pedestrians and/or failure to respond to them.

CROSSROADS

The introduction to this subject should include a brief recap on turning left and right into and out of minor roads.

At this stage in a pupil's training, it would be much more appropriate to use 'coaching' techniques as the basic elements of the subject are not completely new as they have been learnt and applied to T-junctions. Because of this, and because the pupil should be studying for the theory test, you should be able to encourage some transfer of learning.

A few questions to recap will be appropriate, particularly if there has been a gap between lessons and if the pupil is normally getting private practice. Here are a few examples:

'Have you been able to get some practice in?'

'How did you get on?'

'Why do you think that it's more appropriate for us to slow down by using the brakes, rather than using the gears as your brother/father/grandfather says?'

'If we can see that we're going to have to stop – for instance at a red light – do we need to change gear?'

'Did you check on that *Highway Code* rule regarding pedestrians – what did it say?'

To introduce the subject of crossroads you might use the following types of question:

'Have you dealt with crossroads at all while you were practising?'

'Compared with a T-junction, what extra observations do you think you'll have to make?'

'Who has priority at a crossroads if we are going ahead and the oncoming traffic is turning right?'

'Can you explain the sequence of traffic lights?'

'What do you think "amber" means?'

'Which is potentially more of a problem – a light that's green as we approach, or one that's been red for some time?'

'Why do we need to look to the right when we are about to turn left?'

Before introducing more complex situations such as traffic light controlled junctions, allow for practice at various types of less busy crossroads and include turning:

- left from main roads into side roads;
- left onto main roads;
- right onto main roads;
- right from main roads into side roads.

When the pupil is applying all of the principles, particularly the extra observations required at crossroads, select routes where there are different types of traffic light controlled junctions.

Remember that your job is to produce skilled and safe drivers. This means that you not only have to work on their practical ability but you also need to develop in them sensible attitudes towards other road users in situations that aren't always straightforward. An example is at traffic light controlled crossroads where there are no markings and decisions need to be made as to whether to turn right using the offside to offside, or nearside to nearside method.

Make sure that your pupils understand the principles involved and that they are able to make sound decisions based on the size of the junction, its layout and the position of any oncoming, right-turning drivers.

For all types of crossroads, make sure that:

- The M S M routine is correctly applied, particularly when turning right for the first few attempts.
- Signals are timed correctly.
- The pupil responds safely to road signs and markings.
- Observations are made all around no matter what direction is being taken.
- Pupils are fully aware of pedestrians who are about to cross side roads.
- There is a correct response to other drivers, cyclists and motorcyclists.

At the end of the lesson, recap with Q & A to ensure that your pupil is fully aware of any weak areas of skill or understanding, but balance this against any good points and confirm where improvement has taken place. As with all lessons, allow time for the pupil to ask questions.

Look forward to the next few lessons, confirming that you will be introducing more complex junctions, busier crossroads, dual carriageways and roundabouts.

Dealing with 'crossroads' on the Part 3 exam

You will need to ensure that the key points previously mentioned are all included and watch for errors including:

- Failure to make all-round observations at all types of crossroad.
- Incorrect positioning on the approach and at T-junctions.
- Lack of or incorrect response at traffic lights.
- Cutting corners.
- Incorrect response to other turning traffic.
- Crossing the path of others.

MEETING AND DEALING WITH OTHER TRAFFIC

The objectives are to encourage pupils to respond safely to other drivers when:

- travelling on narrow roads;
- there are obstructions on either or both sides of the road;
- passing parked vehicles;
- turning right across the path of others.

Because of the design of roads in built-up and rural areas, the volume of parked vehicles, and the need to keep traffic flowing, pupils have to be taught how to deal safely with these subjects from quite early on in their learning.

Explanation

Meeting other traffic

The most common 'meet' situation is where there are vehicles parked at the side of the road. If these are on the nearside, using a visual aid, you could ask your pupil:

'Where are you going to have to drive to pass the parked car?'

'Who should have the priority then?'

If the obstruction is on the other side of the road, similarly you could ask:

'Who will have priority then, when the obstruction is on the other side of the road?'

'What if the other driver doesn't wait, though?'

'Do you think it might be sensible to be ready to give way, just in case they keep coming?'

'So, it really doesn't matter whose priority it is, does it? You should consider that you never really know what the other driver is going to do, be prepared to give way, and look after number one!'

'Sometimes it's even more courteous to give way to the other person. For example, if they're driving a large vehicle uphill it's going to be much more difficult for them to move off again if you make them wait for you.'

Clearances

To encourage the development of sensible and safe attitudes your pupils will need plenty of practice. In the early stages this should be in fairly quiet areas with the occasional parked vehicle, progressing to busier areas where there are vehicles parked on both sides and oncoming traffic to deal with.

Initially, when dealing with one or two cars parked on the nearside, you need to explain about the need to give sufficient clearance to allow for:

- car doors opening and drivers stepping out;
- pedestrians, particularly children, or animals wandering into the road from between the parked vehicles;
- drivers moving off without signalling.

You need to include in your explanation:

- Planning ahead and applying the M S M routine for approaching the hazards.
- Deciding on whose priority it is and whether to give way.
- The ideal clearance – give a demonstration of this by getting your pupil to check the road and then open their door to see exactly how far into the road it goes.

- At busier times of the day the need to keep the traffic flowing by creeping slowly through some of these gaps – the reduction in speed compensating for the lack of clearance and creating more time to respond should a door open.

- Being prepared to move into passing places on the left to allow oncoming drivers through.

Crossing the path of others

Teach your drivers to be courteous in all situations and not to make any other road user have to take avoiding action. The key points to cover are when:

- Turning right – encourage pupils to work out whether they have enough time to turn, that they have checked on what's happening in the new road and that they won't make any oncoming road user slow down.

- Driving in lanes – ensure they check what's happening all around them before deciding to change lanes.

Practice

Normally, talk-through instruction should suffice in the early stages, developing pupils' awareness and skills until you can transfer the responsibility for decisions to them.

Use routes that have varying amounts of parked and moving traffic and encourage them, through early planning and 'holding back' allowing time for hazards to clear and to try to keep the car moving.

Demonstration

If you have a pupil who has difficulty in understanding the principles and cannot grasp what you mean by 'adequate' clearance, then you may need to demonstrate exactly what you mean by driving at the appropriate speeds, allowing the relevant safety margins.

Fault identification, analysis and rectification

Some of the more common faults include:

- Lack of planning and response to oncoming vehicles.
- Not giving way to oncoming vehicles.
- Arriving at hazards at too high a speed and having to stop at the last moment.

- Steering in towards the kerb instead of keeping out towards the centre of the road.

- Steering out too far for passing.

- Driving too close to vehicles parked on the left.

- Driving too far out and getting too close to those parked on the right.

- Failing to anticipate doors opening.

- Lack of response to pedestrians waiting in between parked vehicles.

Feedback

Feedback should always be used to encourage positive improvement. Confirm where the pupil has learnt and shown improvement and explain where there are weaknesses.

Recap

Apply your coaching skills to help pupils analyse their own actions, emphasizing the reasons why they need to change their approach. The following are two examples:

Example 1

'*When we were driving down that steep hill why did you not give way to the bus driver?*'

'Because the parked car was on his side!'

'*Yes I know, but don't you think it might be difficult to get a large vehicle like that moving up a steep hill?*'

'I hadn't thought about that, I just thought it was my right of way!'

'*Well, actually, no one has right of way anywhere and even if it is your priority it doesn't mean it's always the best way. Try to remember what problems you used to have moving off uphill and then think about trying to move a bus.*'

'I think I see what you mean. So you think it would have been better for me to let the bus driver through then?'

'*Well, that's what I would have done. So will you think about that the next time we have a similar situation?*'

Example 2

'On whose side of the road was the parked car when you squeezed through that gap and made the driver of the black BMW slow down?'

'I think it was on our side.'

'You're right, it was on our side. Whose priority should it have been then?'

'Well, I thought as I'd got there first he'd wait for me.'

'But he was driving quite fast and, anyway, it was his priority as you had to drive onto his side of the road. How do you think you'd feel if he'd done the same thing to you?'

'I suppose I'd have been a bit annoyed.'

'So, in future will you plan a bit further ahead and consider giving way, no matter which side of the road the parked vehicle is on?'

You can create this type of discussion around any weaknesses to encourage pupils to arrive at their own conclusions and, by underlining the reasons, you will help create much better attitudes towards other road users.

Look forward

Confirm that during all future lessons you will be encouraging your pupil to develop their planning and decision-making skills. The next lesson will deal specifically with how to anticipate and make allowances for the actions of other road users, including drivers, cyclists, motorcyclists and pedestrians.

Overtaking

As an instructor accompanying learner drivers, you will find that very few opportunities will present themselves for teaching them how to overtake. However, it will be your responsibility to ensure that they know about the dangers involved and how to carry it out safely. When driving along dual carriageways opportunities will occur when there are vehicles driving at speeds much lower than the legal limits, but overtaking on this type of road is much safer as there won't (hopefully) be any oncoming traffic. First of all you need to stress the important questions of:

Is it safe? Is it legal? Is it NECESSARY?

Points you then need to cover include:

- Keeping back from the vehicle to be overtaken.

- Looking ahead and working out the speed and distance of any oncoming vehicles.

- Checking to see that it's safe by looking for bends, junctions, dead ground, etc.

- Checking the mirrors to see what's happening to the rear and sides.

- Moving to get a view along the nearside of the vehicle ahead.

- Checking the mirrors again and moving out to get a view ahead and to decide on whether anyone (including the driver to be overtaken) will benefit from a signal.

- Adjusting the speed, including selecting a lower gear to give sustained power.

- Moving out to pass, giving plenty of clearance.

- Checking the mirrors and in some circumstances deciding on whether or not a signal will be beneficial (for example on dual carriageways when a driver is approaching from behind at high speed).

- Moving back to the left without cutting in.

- Accelerating away and changing gear as normal.

If opportunities don't present themselves during a pupil's course of driving prior to their driving test, you should certainly include it as part of their training under the Pass Plus scheme.

Dealing with these subjects on the Part 3 exam

Following the same format as on previous lesson plans, you need to use Q & A to find out the level of knowledge and ability of your 'pupil' so that you can set the base line at the correct level.

Use all opportunities that arise to assess whether or not your pupil understands about dealing with other traffic and watch out for errors similar to those listed in the foregoing lists. Make sure that, when you identify the errors, you finish with a sound reason for dealing with them your way – that is the way in which they are described in all of the official textbooks.

MANOEUVRES

The manoeuvres included in the official syllabus for learning to drive include:

- reversing round left-hand corners;

- turning the car round in the road;
- reversing on right-hand corners;
- reverse parking at the side of the road;
- reversing into bays (left and right).

These notes are designed to help the new instructor who has little or no experience with learners, and who is dealing with a pupil who has no previous experience in manoeuvring the car.

Before starting to teach any manoeuvres, it is worth making sure that the pupil is completely skilled and confident with uphill and downhill starts and stops. Experience is also needed in angled starts on up and down gradients, so that the pupil has complete control of the car in all of these circumstances.

For example, moving away straight ahead downhill is relatively easy because you don't need too much coordination between the foot controls and the steering – as soon as the handbrake is released the car is on its way! With an angled start, though, there is a need to introduce the use of the footbrake and coordination between that and the clutch to avoid the car running away too quickly and to allow sufficient time for steering round the obstruction (or to turn into the main road). This exercise is often neglected by some instructors. The result of this is that their pupils are not properly prepared for similar situations on the turn in the road and reversing exercises when careful control is needed for stopping and starting on uphill and downhill cambers.

The manoeuvres do not necessarily need to be taught in the order listed above, but there is a certain amount of logic in dealing with reversing before introducing some of the other complicating features of the turn in the road and reverse parking exercises. A lot of the time it will depend on the availability of suitable roads and corners in your own locality.

Introducing the subject

Make sure that you emphasize the need to be able to manoeuvre the car as part of a driver's everyday requirements, rather than just 'because it's part of the test'. If the pupil persists with raising the question of the driving test, make it clear that we are dealing with driving safely and manoeuvring for convenience and that test procedures will be outlined on future lessons.

To achieve this, ask a few questions:

'How do you think we would turn the car round if there was no opportunity to go round the block or to turn at a roundabout?'

'Would we use a side road on the right or the left?'

'What if we're in a car park or a dead end where we can't use any side roads or entrances to turn round?'

'Should we back into a parking space in a car park or is it better to drive in forwards?'

'Why do we need to reverse into a parking space at the side of the road – why not drive in forwards?'

'Why should we reverse into a side road and not out?'

There are many other variations to these questions that you should be able to work out for yourself.

Setting the base line

With all of the manoeuvres it's important to recap on what the pupil has covered on previous lessons by asking a few appropriate questions, for example:

'As this is the first manoeuvre you'll be carrying out and good clutch control is required, tell me how you would creep forwards at a junction to get a better view.'

'What would you do if your car started to creep forwards before you wanted to move?'

'Why is it important to keep the speed very low when you're moving out from behind a parked car?'

'What did you need to check up and down the road for when you were turning the car round in the road last week?'

'What happens to the front end of the car as you're reversing round a left corner?'

'What should you do if you see another driver approaching as your car is about to swing out?'

Explanations

With any manoeuvre always get the pupil to consider – is it safe? Is it legal? Is it convenient?

Confirm that, because they are part of normal everyday driving requirements, the manoeuvres are included in the training programme so that new drivers will have the ability to control and manoeuvre the car in various confined areas such as car parks, no-through roads and in driveways.

Demonstrations

A demonstration can be useful for any of the manoeuvres, but particularly with the turning in the road because pupils often find it difficult to visualize the overall requirement or the individual parts of the exercise. Please note that any demonstration should be free from faults.

Talk yourself through each element, carrying out the manoeuvre a little more slowly than normal. This will allow the pupil time to take note. Be able, if necessary, to carry out certain parts in slow motion. You may sometimes need to replicate the way in which a pupil has carried out a manoeuvre so that they can compare the two.

Practice

Don't expect perfection first time!

For pupils' first attempts use an appropriate amount of 'talk-through' so that a reasonable degree of success is achieved and they are not put off or demoralized by getting it completely wrong.

Watch for, and correct right from the start, any basic errors of control or observations. However, you should make allowances for the fact that the pupil has not done this particular manoeuvre previously and there are several elements being combined. These are: car control skills, observations and accuracy.

On subsequent attempts, transfer some of the responsibility by gradually reducing the amount of 'talk-through'. When a reasonable amount of consistency is achieved, introduce slightly more complex situations.

At the end of the lesson

Use Q & A to obtain some verbal feedback from the pupil to find out how they feel about the lesson.

Give them feedback, balancing any discussion on areas of weakness with comments on the good points.

Summarize the overall content of the current lesson and emphasize the reasons for each particular manoeuvre and confirm how to make sure they are legally carried out.

Look forward to the next lesson by discussing what will be covered, confirming any preparation work that you require the pupil to do.

Manoeuvres on driving tests

Only during the latter stages of pupils' training will you need to point out that, although they will be tested on some of the manoeuvre exercises, they are only included as a means of assessing their ability to handle the car in confined spaces. This means that, to a certain extent, they are slightly contrived 'test exercises'.

For example, we wouldn't normally make a decision to turn the car round in a road where it's relatively busy and when it would be far safer and more convenient to use a different means of turning. Neither would we reverse into a parking space at the side of a busy road unless the existing parked vehicles were close together – we would simply drive forwards into the gap. Even when using a car park, rather than reversing in, we might prefer to drive forwards into the space to allow us to load lots of shopping into the boot on our return.

In all these respects, the manoeuvres are included in the driving test to assess, in a controlled environment, the candidate's ability, observations and responses.

Dealing with the 'manoeuvring exercises' on the Part 3 exam

As with any lesson, you will need to set the base line at the correct level. The examiner may opt to play the role of a partly trained pupil who has never carried out the manoeuvre, or someone who is near test standard and requires remedial practice. Use Q & A to determine prior knowledge and understanding.

If the pupil has had previous experience, confirm any correct answers given and fill in with any supplementary information. Create as many opportunities to practise as the time allows. Try not to use the same site for more than three attempts as it can cause offence to local residents.

If the exercise has never been carried out before, you will need to give an explanation, using a visual aid if it will help. Try not to make this too long-winded though – keep it simple. Because of the time constraints, you will probably not have the opportunity to give a demonstration. However, you can still offer one if you think that it's appropriate for the circumstances or with a particular type of 'pupil' – that is, one who appears not to understand you too well. You could say something like: 'Would you like me to show you how it's done?'

More information on preparing for the Part 3 is given in *The Driving Instructor's Handbook*.

In each of the following sections on manoeuvring we have included a few sample questions that might be useful in your teaching. You will need to modify these to suit your own particular circumstances and training routes. You will also find places where you can add your own notes about routes, locations, questions, key learning points and exam references.

As with all of the lesson plans in this chapter each one should consist of the same set of ingredients. These are listed here as a reminder:

Introduction

Stating the objectives

Confirming prior knowledge

Setting the baseline

Questions such as

– Can you…?

– Have you…?

– What if…?

– Why…?

Explanation

– Is it safe, legal, convenient?

– Control, Position, Observations

Demonstration if appropriate

Level of instruction

Full talk-through

Practice

Fault identification, analysis, rectification

Giving and receiving feedback

Recap, summary, look forward.

REVERSING AROUND CORNERS TO THE LEFT

Introduce the subject by confirming that reversing is a part of normal driving and is required, for example, when parking, entering property or for turning round.

As always, at the start of the lesson establish the pupil's previous knowledge:

- Have they done any reversing while they've been practising?
- Do they understand about low speed control, for example when creeping forwards at junctions?
- Do they appreciate that it's important to make lots of all-round observations?
- Do they know why the normal rules about steering do not necessarily apply?

If the pupil has done a little reversing previously, for example for the turn in the road manoeuvre, find out exactly what. The following is a scenario where a pupil has had lessons with another instructor:

'Your driver's record and lesson notes show that you haven't done this particular manoeuvre before – is that right?'

'Well, on my last lesson with Bill we did do a bit of reversing in a straight line, but not much.'

'OK, so what do you remember about turning to look through the back window? You might need to release the seatbelt and turn round more in the seat.'

'How do you feel about the steering?'

'Did it feel uncomfortable to maintain the position of your hands on the wheel while looking back?'

'Do you think it might be better to put your hands in a different position?'

'Why don't you try with the right hand at the top of the wheel?'

'When we start turning a corner, how do you think the wheel should go?'

Explanation

As with any manoeuvre, drivers should ask themselves – is it safe, legal, convenient? Ask if the pupil has read the *Highway Code* or *The Official DSA Guide to Driving; the essential skills.* Confirm that when reversing around a corner to the left this would include:

- only reversing from main roads into side roads and not into main roads;
- using only T-junctions, avoiding reversing at crossroads;
- keeping well away from school entrances or where other people would be inconvenienced, for example near driveways,
- not reversing into one-way streets.

If the pupil has no previous experience, you could give an explanation using a visual aid.

Demonstration

A demonstration combined with an explanation could be helpful in allowing the pupil to see what's required. The demonstration may be appropriate if, for instance, the pupil is particularly nervous about the manoeuvre, or they obviously do not understand the requirements from your explanations.

Keep any demonstration simple and carry it out at a slower than normal speed.

Key teaching/learning points

- Look *through* the back window, not at it. (It is not a particularly good idea to put markers in the window as pupils will focus on these and not where they're going.)

- The speed of the car should be kept as slow as possible by effective clutch control.

- One-handed steering (at the top of the wheel) is ok when going backwards.

- Pull/push is not always the most effective or comfortable steering method when reversing round a corner at slow speed.

- Explain that there is a delayed action with the steering, because the rear wheels are now being used to steer with.

- The starting point for starting to turn can be judged by lining up the rear of the car with an appropriate mark on the pavement (a tree, fence, street name).

- Look across the rear corner of the car – not at the side – to judge the amount of steering.

- Once in the new road, get the big picture by looking down the side road. This also gives a view of what's happening on the road and whether there are others approaching.

- Line the car up in the new road by looking through the back window – avoid the temptation to look down at the side of the car.

- Avoid 'over-steering' – think about how you only have to make small adjustments to the steering when going forwards. Remember, though, the delayed action on the steering.

Observations

A constant check should be made throughout the manoeuvre, looking all around for traffic. The pupil should be encouraged to watch carefully for pedestrians – particularly anyone crossing the road they're reversing into. Remember that there's a blind area to the right when they're looking over the left shoulder.

If other traffic is approaching the junction from the side road, the pupil should be prepared to give way – either by waiting or, if necessary, by moving forward to the start position.

Feedback

After completing the manoeuvre, ask a few questions such as:

> 'Did that seem OK to you or could it be improved in any way?'
>
> 'Do you think that by looking around a bit more and getting the wider picture you would be able to steer more effectively?'
>
> 'What do you need to see and be aware of?'
>
> 'How would you feel if you'd been walking across a road and a driver continued to reverse in front of you?'

Depending on the pupil's responses, follow up with:

> 'What you're saying is that you feel that by going a bit slower, you would have more time to steer?' 'OK then, let's try it.'
>
> Or: 'You're telling me that you think that you need to feel more aware of the traffic around you. I'd agree with that, so what if we did the manoeuvre extra slowly so that you can check that out for yourself?'
>
> Or: 'How do think it would work if we did...?'
>
> 'Why not try this approach...?'

Dealing with 'left reverse' on the Part 3 exam

Refer back to the main heading 'Manoeuvres' for a general explanation.

Fault identification, analysis and rectification

Faults to watch for are:

- seating position not adjusted to afford the best view;
- poor coordination skills;
- under- or over-steering;
- lack of observations;
- ineffective observations resulting in lack of response to others.

TURNING IN THE ROAD

Introduction

The lesson should begin with an introduction of the subject and by defining the objective:

'To turn the car round in the road by using forward and reverse gears.'

Use Q & A to establish the reasons for being able to carry out this manoeuvre and also to establish the 'base line' for the lesson. By this stage in the pupil's training, they should be able to respond to this approach much more readily than by giving them a lecture on the subject. For example:

'Why do we need to do be able to do this manoeuvre?'

'Because it's part of the test!'

'Well, we need to be able to turn the car round in confined spaces such as car parks, dead-end streets and other places where there's no opportunity to use side roads or roundabouts to enable us to turn round.'

'But it is part of the test?'

'It's only a set part of the test because it gives an examiner the opportunity to assess your ability to control the car in a confined space and to see how you deal with other traffic at the same time. In normal driving you would only need to do this manoeuvre in a relatively quiet location – you wouldn't do it in a busy main road for example, would you? But on test the examiner has to find a suitable road where there is at least some traffic about. Anyway, today we're not concerned with the test – that's a long way off, and we'll have more discussions about that another time.'

By using this type of discussion you can lead in to the topic, rather than simply stating an objective.

Whatever the circumstances, as with all the other manoeuvres that have previously been covered, we always need to consider:

'Is it safe; is it legal; is it convenient?'

More Q & A can be used to check on the pupil's prior knowledge and understanding and to make sure they're studying for their theory test. Try to encourage the pupil to work with you and give you some answers, again avoiding a one-way lecture. For example:

'How do you think safe, legal and convenience apply to the turning in the road? Give me some examples of where you think you shouldn't do it.'

'Let me think a minute. Near junctions, school entrances, pedestrian crossings, driveways, obstructions, bus stops. Where there's a solid white line across the road?'

'Good.'

Setting the base line

At this point, as with all the other subjects, make sure that you establish exactly what the pupil already knows and what level of understanding they have. Asking a few relevant questions can achieve this. For example, if the pupil is one of your regular customers you could start with:

> *'Do you remember that on our last lesson we dealt with reversing round a corner and previously to that we covered hill starts and stops?'*

> *'How do you think that those skills relate to what we're going to be doing in today's lesson?'*

If it's the pupil's first lesson with you:

> *'I see from your driver's record and your previous instructor's notes that the programme for today is going to be "turning in the road" and that you have already dealt with reversing and uphill and downhill starts. Is that right?'*

> *'How do you feel about those manoeuvres? Is there anything you're not sure about?' 'OK, in view of what you're saying we'll spend a few minutes on a reverse then the hill starts before moving on to the turning in the road.'*

> *'Why do you think that we normally deal with hill starts and reversing before tackling the turn in the road?'*

> *'How do you think the skills on those manoeuvres are connected to what we're going to be doing today?'*

With any of these discussions you'll be starting a dialogue with the pupil to get them involved in the learning process and encouraging them to take some responsibility for their own learning.

The variations of questions will depend on whether the pupil has previously been trained by you and also on their responses to your questions. Always be ready with a follow-up question to keep the dialogue moving in the direction you want it to go so that you achieve your objectives. Either way, you should be able to get a clear indication within a few minutes of how to plan the rest of the lesson.

Explanation

'To turn the car round by using forward and reverse gears.'
Emphasis needs to be placed on:

- *Control of the car:*
  - slow speed;
  - fast turn of the steering wheel, using the whole of it to give maximum leverage;
  - low speed control both uphill and down;

    – opposite lock on the steering to help with the following movement;

    – positioning of hands on the wheel – right hand high in preparation for going forward, low for starting to reverse.

● *Observations:*

    – keep looking all round for other traffic;

    – make eye contact with others and either wait for them or carry on as appropriate and depending on the other driver's anticipated actions;

    – on the reverse movement, look through the back window, then over right shoulder – judge the back of the car in relation to the kerb or any obstructions;

    – discourage beckoning others unless the road is absolutely clear in the opposite direction.

Practice

Don't expect perfection first time!

Find a road that is fairly wide, flat and quiet before introducing more difficult situations on narrower roads, where there's more traffic and on steeper cambers.

On the pupil's first attempt, give 'talk-through' instruction to prompt the pupil where necessary to avoid any unnecessary errors. This will promote reasonable success and should motivate and encourage the pupil. On subsequent attempts, or with more experienced pupils, reduce the amount of prompting.

Watch for, and try to correct from the start:

● *Poor coordination of the foot controls* – this can be caused by the pupil not having had sufficient practice at uphill and downhill starts and stops, or simply because the driving seat has not been adjusted sufficiently for them to be able to turn and look while retaining full control of the clutch.

● *Steering* – emphasize the need to keep the speed very slow so as to give time for full steering (that is – 'fast hands, slow speed'). Encourage 'opposite lock' towards the end of each part of the manoeuvre so that the wheels are then pointing roughly in the new direction.

● *All-round observations* – encourage the pupil to look along the road in each direction for approaching traffic. This should be done before moving off and in the first part of each section of the manoeuvre. Observations should be made through the rear window to check for obstructions such as trees, lampposts and pedestrians immediately behind the car. Halfway through the reverse movement, observation should be made over the right shoulder to check for position in relation to the kerb.

- *Response to approaching traffic* – encourage the pupil to judge the speed and position of any oncoming vehicle and to make eye contact with the driver if possible. Don't be tempted to direct the traffic. Wait to allow the other driver to make a decision to proceed, but be ready to move away or carry on if it's obvious that they are waiting. In some circumstances it may be more convenient for everyone for you to get the pupil to complete the turn.

Feedback

After the first attempt you should be able to obtain some feedback from the pupil by asking a few questions. These might include:

'How did you feel that went?'

'Well, OK, but you were helping me a lot.'

'That's true, but for a first attempt it was pretty good.'

'Would I pass the test?'

'We're not going to deal with what happens on the test yet – you'll be having a lot more practice on different roads and with more traffic and with less prompting from me. What do you think we need to do to improve...?' etc.

or:

'Well, I don't think it was very good.'

'In what way?'

'I didn't seem to be in complete control.'

'Do you mean with the accuracy?'

'Yes.'

'Well, for a first attempt it was very good, but how do you think it could be improved?' etc.

After the second attempt, the discussion might be along similar lines:

'Did you feel that was better?' 'What was different?'

'You're saying that by going a bit slower you might be able to achieve more?' 'Did you feel that you got in the way of the other traffic?'

'How would you feel if you were walking along the pavement and you saw a car reversing across the road towards you?'

'How do you think we could avoid that situation?'

'When do you think it might be better to keep moving rather than wait for the other traffic?' 'What about when you're just about to start one of the movements?'

'What would you do if it was a much larger vehicle?'

'OK, let's try it the way you've just described.'

Using this type of discussion encourages the pupil to think that they have made decisions about how to carry out the manoeuvre.

Recap and summary

As with all lessons, end by using Q & A and give a brief recap on the main points, that is: the reasons for carrying out the manoeuvre and how to make sure it's legal. Give a summary of the good points and some of the weaker areas, trying to balance the two.

Look forward

Discuss the next lesson with the pupil and give an indication of the subjects to be practised or learnt.

Personal lesson plan notes

Key learning points to include:

- Coordination of all the controls to give maximum time for steering and observations.
- Using the whole wheel to ensure maximum turning is achieved.
- Looking in the direction the car is travelling.
- Making all-round observations throughout the manoeuvre.
- Responding safely to other road users, including pedestrians.

Routes and location:

- Early practice should be given on roads that are wide enough to achieve turning in three movements, and level so as to avoid rolling onto kerbs.
- As skill develops introduce roads that are narrower and have cambers to encourage the development of good coordination.

Dealing with 'turning in the road' on the Part 3 exam

As with any lesson, you will need to set the base line at the correct level. The examiner may opt to play the role of a partly trained pupil who has never carried out the manoeuvre, or someone who is more experienced and requires remedial practice. Use Q & A to determine prior knowledge and understanding.

If the pupil has had previous experience, confirm any correct answers given and fill in with any supplementary information. Create as many opportunities to practise as the time allows. Try not to use the same site for more than three attempts as it can cause offence and inconvenience to local residents.

If the exercise has never been carried out before, you will need to give an explanation, using a visual aid if it will help. Try not to make this too long-winded though – keep it simple. Because of the time constraints, you will probably not have the opportunity to give a demonstration. However, you can still offer one if you think that it's appropriate for the circumstances or with a particular type of 'pupil' – that is, one who appears not to understand you too well. You could say something like: 'Would you like me to show you how it's done?'

More information on preparing for the Part 3 is given in *The Driving Instructor's Handbook*.

REVERSING AROUND CORNERS TO THE RIGHT

This exercise should be introduced when your pupil has become fairly proficient with reversing to the left. Your lesson plan, incorporating all the usual ingredients, therefore, should be to build on these skills.

Your pattern of teaching/coaching should follow the usual routines of using Q & A to establish whether the pupil understands the reasons for the manoeuvre and to fix an appropriate base line for the lesson.

Questions at the start of the session might include:

'Why do we need to do this manoeuvre?'

'Because it's part of the test?'

'That's not the best reason. Can you imagine a situation where you need to turn the car round, but there are no other junctions available?'

'Well, I could turn into the junction and reverse out to the left.'

'Do you think that would be safe? What if there was someone travelling fast along that road?' 'What if you were driving a vehicle with a restricted view, say a van or a full-loaded car with not much view through the back window?' 'Do you think it might be better to reverse to the right in those circumstances?'

Always refer to *'Is it safe? Is it legal? Is it convenient?'*

The objective is to turn the car round safely by reversing around a corner on the right.

Explanation

Using a visual aid, explain the manoeuvre, highlighting the differences between the right and left reverse and emphasizing the importance of effective observations as the car is being driven along the wrong side of the road.

Demonstration

By this stage, and because the pupil will have had lots of practice at turning in the road and reversing to the left, most pupils won't need a demonstration. However, for those who have more difficulty in acquiring new concepts and skills, it might help.

Key points

- Initial positioning for the manoeuvre, that is, to drive the car across to the right side of the road.
- Before starting to reverse, full observation for oncoming traffic, pedestrians and traffic in the side road.
- Slow speed control and observation along the offside of the car for accurate positioning.
- Forward, side and rear observations for other road users – particularly pedestrians and cyclists.
- Taking the car far enough back into the side road to clear the junction.

Feedback

At the end of the first attempt use Q & A and coaching techniques:

> *'Your control of the car was very good – and your positioning, for a first attempt, was quite reasonable. How did you feel about dealing with that other traffic?'*

> 'Well, I'm on the wrong side of the road, I suppose, but shouldn't they wait for me because I'm a learner?'

> *'Were you aware of the driver waiting in the side road for you to complet. What might you have been able to do to help?'*

'Signal?'

'Would that have solved the problem? How do you think using a signal would have helped?'

'Perhaps I should have moved forwards out of the way then?'

'What, when you were part way round the corner and it would have meant driving round on the wrong side of the road?'

'On reflection then, I suppose it might have been better for me to keep going and get out of his way.'

'How far down the road do you think we should go before stopping?'

'About three car lengths, like on the left reverse.'

'And what if someone were to drive around the corner fast?'

'Should I go further back then?'

'Yes, at least twice as far as for the left reverse. So, why don't we do it again, bearing in mind those points that we've just spoken about.'

After a second attempt you could develop another discussion along the lines:

'How did you feel about doing it that way? Were you happier with your control/ positioning/observations?'

'Did you feel that you were able to deal with the other traffic/pedestrians that time?'

'Did you feel there was anything different from the first time?'

Recap

At the end of the lesson use Q & A to recap on the main points:

- moving across to the right-hand side of the road;
- looking over the right shoulder for position, but all around to watch for traffic and pedestrians;
- looking well back down the road for position;
- go far enough back to be able to move over to the left side of the road.

Feedback

ummarize and give praise on the good points and identify the weaknesses that
ed to be worked on.

Look forward to next lesson

'We'll be dealing with a mixture of left and right reverses, and using slightly busier junctions. I'd like you to refer to the Highway Code *and* The Official Guide to Driving *to refresh yourself on the rules and procedures.'*

Dealing with 'right reverse' on the Part 3 exam

The format for your lesson will be similar to that described for the other manoeuvres.

Fault identification, analysis and rectification

The following is a list of problems to watch for:

- incorrect application of the M S M routine for driving across the road;
- ineffective observations;
- lack of response to others;
- under- or over-steering around the corner and during straightening up;
- failing to look well down the new road;
- finishing too near to the corner.

REVERSE PARKING

Following the usual lesson format, the following are some suggestions for introducing this subject:

'You'll remember that on previous lessons we've stopped at the side of the road where there were other parked cars.' 'Do you remember how much space it took to drive in and get parked properly?'

'About three car lengths?'

'Yes, why do think we needed that much space?'

'I'm not sure.'

'Well, it's to do with the fact that the front wheels do the steering and the back wheels are always straight.'

'Oh yes, I remember that from reversing round a corner. So that means it'll take a while for the front of the car to drag the back in does it?'

'That's right, so how can we deal with that when the space available is much shorter?' 'Do you think that by reversing we can put the back of the car in, and then the front will follow?'

'I'll take your word on that one as I'm still not quite sure.'

'So to demonstrate what I mean, we'll practise first of all where there's only one car, with nothing behind it. Then when you feel confident, we'll move to where there's a proper parking space in between two cars.'

Setting the base line

As the pupil will, by this stage, have had lots of practice at the other manoeuvres, use Q & A to determine their understanding and to establish where to set the base line for the lesson. Here are a few example questions:

'We've dealt with reversing to the left on previous lessons so tell me a couple of the important things you need to do.'

'Can I just make sure that you've dealt with reversing with your previous instructor?'

'How did you get on?'

'Is there anything that you're not sure about?'

'Before we get on to the reverse park we'll just recap on slow speed car control in forward and reverse by moving slowly forwards and back along here.'

'That's fine.'

Objective

Confirm with a simple statement what you're going to doing: 'Today, we're going to learn how to park the car at the side of the road where there are other parked vehicles.'

Ask a couple of questions to confirm that the manoeuvre will be safe, legal and convenient at the site selected, for example not too close to junctions or on a busy road and where other drivers are likely to be affected.

Explanation

Explain that, under normal driving conditions, this manoeuvre would be carried out where there were two vehicles close together. However, for the purposes of training we'll initially be doing it where there's only one car parked. This sets up a slightly artificial situation as we'll be able to park at the side of the road before starting the manoeuvre – a luxury that is not available in a real situation when there will usually be following traffic and only a confined space to park in.

Using a visual aid, talk the pupil through each part of the exercise, including the key elements:

- M S M to get into position to begin the exercise;
- initial positioning at the side of the leading vehicle;
- getting into a seating position that will allow good all-round vision and control;
- coordination of all of the controls to maintain a low speed;
- all-round observations throughout the manoeuvre;
- responding safely to other road users;
- accurate steering;
- checking clearance given to the leading vehicle;
- straightening up to finish reasonably close to the kerb.

Use Q & A to confirm the pupil has understood the main elements. For example:

> *'Where do you think we should be looking for other traffic?'*
>
> *'How does that vary from when we did the left reverse round a corner?'*
>
> *'What would you do if there was a large vehicle behind you as you approached the parking space?'*
>
> *'What if you were to move half into the space to allow the following traffic through?'*
>
> *'What signals would you give?'*

Demonstration

As this is one of the more complex manoeuvres you may find that a demonstration is needed more often. If your pupil appears to be a little worried and unsure, give another explanation as you are demonstrating how to park. Remember, keep the speed a little slower than normal and make sure your parking is accurate.

Practice

You will normally need to give full talk-through to ensure that a reasonable degree of success is achieved.

During the manoeuvre check on:

- Whether the pupil has the driving seat adjusted so that they can turn to look through the rear window while retaining steering control.

- Coordination of the foot controls – compare this to the speed of the car when reversing round a corner, or creeping forward at a junction.

- Observations for other road users – including pedestrians crossing the road.

- Appropriate responses to approaching traffic – whether it would be safer to wait or to continue with the manoeuvre.

- Correct observations to the rear for positioning in the parking space.

After a couple of attempts, make sure that you get feedback from the pupil by asking a few more questions, such as:

'Other than indicators, what signals do we have that would warn other people about what we're doing?'

'Would it be a good idea to let other people know what we're doing by using an arm signal?'

Only when you are sure the pupil can cope, should you start transferring the responsibility to them. It would be wise to drive to another site and give them a change of activity before reversing around another car.

Feedback

As with all lessons, it's important to give and receive some feedback. Use Q & A to find out whether the pupil feels confident about parking. Give praise for those elements that have been improved on and reminders about where more practice is needed.

Look forward

Confirm that more practice will be given on the next lesson and you will also be introducing reversing into a parking bay to the left – such as in a car park. To establish some of the point you have previously raised, ask a couple of questions such as:

'Would it be better to reverse into or out of the space?'

'Why might it be better to reverse in and drive out?'

Dealing with 'reverse parking' on the Part 3 exam

This exercise is only included as a Phase 2 subject when the examiner will ortray an experienced pupil.

The briefing might be that the 'pupil' has recently failed a test on the reverse park; or one who has been to another instructor who didn't cover this manoeuvre. In the latter case you would cover the exercise as described above.

Your discussion with the 'pupil' who has failed a test could be something like:

'I understand that this item was marked on your test. Is that right?'

'Have you got the failure sheet with you?'

'What do you think might have gone wrong?'

'Are you saying that you might have got in the way of other traffic?'

'Why do you think that was?'

'Would it have helped if you had been going a bit slower?'

'Would it have been safer and more convenient if you had completed the manoeuvre, rather than hesitating?'

There are many more variations you could use to stimulate response and gather information, but the main theme is to encourage the 'pupil' to think about what might have gone wrong and how they could improve. The discussion will, of course, be guided by you so as to extract the information you need to establish your base line.

Fault identification, analysis and rectification

As well as the items listed above under things to check on during the manoeuvre, watch for:

- incorrect application of the M S M for stopping;
- failure to turn enough in the seat to get a proper view;
- starting from the wrong position;
- lack of proper coordination;
- reversing too quickly and passing the point at which to start steering;
- steering too early;
- steering too quickly – particularly prevalent in cars with power steering;
- lack of all-round observations throughout the manoeuvre;
- incorrect response to others;
- not checking the front end clearing the leading car;
- steering back too early or too late;
- finishing at an angle to the kerb.

EMERGENCY STOP

Objective

To stop the car promptly, safely and under complete control.

Introducing the subject

Using Q & A, confirm with your pupil that they stopped in various types of situation on their previous lesson, for example at junctions, at the side of the road, and in specific places such as: 'by the second lamppost'.

Emphasize that an 'emergency stop' is only an extension of what they have done before. The main difference is that the brakes will need to be applied more firmly.

Ask questions to confirm previous knowledge and understanding, for example:

> *'Why is it necessary to apply progressive braking?'*
>
> *'Do we need a gear change when stopping?'*
>
> *'Why is it important to keep both hands on the wheel when we are braking firmly?'*
>
> *'Do we need a signal?'*
>
> *'What about the handbrake?'*

Discuss possible situations where an emergency stop might be needed, for example if a child ran out from a gateway into the road. Relate this to their previous hazard perception understanding when they will have been responding mainly to things they could see.

Explanation

You should include information on:

- the fact that there may not be enough time to check on what's happening behind, because of the need to stop quickly;
- prompt reaction in moving from gas pedal to footbrake;
- use of the footbrake – progressive, firmly;
- maintaining steering control because the weight of the car is thrown onto the front wheels;
- avoiding locking wheels;

● having the clutch down just before stopping;

● securing the car after stopping;

● all-round observations before moving away.

Emphasize the need for both hands remaining on the wheel to keep the car going on a straight course, and of controlled braking. Confirm this by giving an example such as, 'There's no point in avoiding the child who's run out if we then slide across the road and hit other pedestrians.'

Confirm the pupil's understanding of braking distances. For example:

'What is the thinking distance if you're travelling at 30 mph?'

'At 70 mph how far would we travel before starting to brake?'

'How does that relate to a number of cars' length?'

'How far do you think it takes to stop from 20 mph? (Or any other speed.)

'Tell me how far that is in terms of the distance from here?'

In preparation for their theory test pupils should be doing some homework on reaction times, and thinking and braking distances. Make sure they realize that there is a straightforward means of calculating the distances and that they are not random figures. For example:

The thinking distance is based on an average reaction time of 2/3 second. This equates to about 60 feet (or 18 metres) when travelling at 60 mph (88 ft per second).

The braking distance at 20 mph is 20 feet (6 metres) and it increases with the square of the speed. That means that if you travel at twice the speed, the braking distance is multiplied by four times.

Confirm that on future lessons thinking, braking and stopping distances will be discussed and related to practical situations.

Practice

Find an area where it's going to be safe to practise and make sure your pupil understands that you will check there's no following traffic before giving the signal to stop. Explain how you will give the instruction and signal for stopping.

On the first few attempts at an emergency stop check on the pupil's:

● slow reactions to respond;

● prompt movement from accelerator to brake;

- harsh or too gentle use of the footbrake;
- left hand off the steering wheel before stopping;
- clutch being pushed down too early or too late;
- lack of adequate precautions after a stall;
- failure to secure the car when stopped;
- lack of all-round observations before moving off.

Look forward to future lessons by indicating that this exercise will be repeated at different speeds and in varying situations, unless, of course, real emergencies crop up.

Dealing with 'emergency stops' on the Part 3 exam

The emergency (or controlled) stop exercise is combined with mirror adjustment and use. Errors introduced are generally similar to those listed above. However, some are likely to be exaggerated, for example:

- stamping down on the brake;
- trying to change gear while braking;
- pulling on the handbrake before coming to a complete stop;
- moving off unsafely.

PEDESTRIAN CROSSINGS

The point at which you introduce pupils to pedestrian crossings will depend, to a large extent, on the area in which they live and where the nearest crossings are situated. However, they should have reached a stage at which they can consistently apply the M S M routine to hazards and be able to cope with more traffic and pedestrian activity.

Objectives

As pedestrians, your pupils will have used most types of crossing. Try to avoid patronizing them by treating the subject as if they know nothing about it.

Indeed, the lesson objective will be to build on this existing knowledge by introducing the differences between how, as pedestrians, they will have used crossings and how drivers should deal with them. (See 'Transfer of Learning' in Chapter 1.)

Set the base line

First of all you need to recap on the pupil's previous progress, using Q & A to confirm that the M S M routine is properly understood. Find out what they understand about the different types of crossing and then set your base line according to their responses. The following are a few sample questions:

'When should you apply the M S M routine?'

'Can you name three different types of pedestrian crossing?'

'How would you recognize a zebra crossing?'

'How would you claim priority at a zebra crossing?'

As always, listen carefully to your pupil's responses and set the base line according to their level of knowledge and understanding. In any case you need to ensure that all of the basic principles in dealing with the different types of crossing are covered.

Explanation

Information on the following should be included:

- the different types of crossing, ie: zebra, pelican, toucan, puffin and equestrian;
- why these differences are in place;
- signs and markings and what they mean, including the rules relating to waiting, overtaking, parking;
- the sequence of the different traffic lights;
- how to look and plan well ahead, applying the M S M routine in good time to stop safely when necessary and securing the car;
- the use of arm signals when appropriate.

As this subject is very wide-ranging, and so that the lesson doesn't become a one-way lecture, keep your pupil involved by asking the occasional question. For example:

'What do the zigzag lines on approach to crossings mean?'

'What's the sequence of lights at a pelican crossing?'

'What does the flashing amber light mean?'

'What's the difference between a pelican and a toucan crossing?'

'What would you do if you saw someone waiting at a zebra crossing?'

Level of instruction

To avoid over-instruction, you will need to ensure that the pupil is allowed to demonstrate their skill in subjects learnt previously. For example, by this stage their car control skills should be reasonably well developed and they should be able to deal virtually unaided with simple junctions.

When you approach the new situations, and to ensure the pupil is able to deal safely with the crossings, give talk-through instruction until the correct routines and procedures are grasped.

Practice

Depending on your area, try to incorporate as many types of crossing as you can so that your pupil will see what the main differences are. Ensure that all of the basic routines are carried out, particularly in relation to planning ahead and approaching them at safe speeds.

Fault identification, analysis and rectification

Initially, as you should be giving full instruction, there should be few faults. However, as the pupil's skill improves, and you start transferring to them the responsibility for making decisions, errors are bound to occur. (Some examples are listed under the heading 'Dealing with pedestrian crossings on the Part 3 exam'.

Watch carefully for these mistakes and give positive correction. Analyse what happened and explain what should have been done to deal with the situations safely.

Feedback/recap/summary

At the end of the lesson make sure you give positive feedback and praise where the pupil improved on skills previously covered and has learnt how to deal with the new topics.

Recap on the most important points that arose and give an overall summary on applying the M S M routine to dealing with crossings.

Look forward

Advise your pupil on which reference materials to study, confirming that you will be asking a few questions on crossings and getting in some more practice on approaching them during the next lesson.

Dealing with 'pedestrian crossings' on the Part 3 exam

Dealing with this subject when you have a pupil who's been to another driving school, or with the examiner playing the role of a pupil, you will need to follow the guidelines given previously.

Use Q & A to determine previous experience, listening very carefully to the answers and then decide where you may need to set the base line. According to the pupil this could be at one of many levels. Be extremely careful in avoiding under- or over-instruction.

Faults introduced could include:

- ignoring signs and markings;
- not responding to pedestrian activity around the crossings;
- incorrect application of the M S M routine;
- approaching crossings at too high a speed;
- not stopping when necessary;
- stopping late, giving little notice to any following driver;
- failing to secure the car when appropriate;
- waving pedestrians across;
- blocking crossings in queues of traffic;
- moving off too soon at pelican crossings.

Ensure that any corrections made include an explanation of what might happen when incorrect actions are taken and why it's important to follow safe procedures.

ROUNDABOUTS AND DUAL CARRIAGEWAYS

Whichever topic you are dealing with, your lessons should all follow the pattern described previously in this chapter. This is listed here as a reminder:

- recap, including Q & A to establish prior knowledge and understanding;
- statement of objectives;
- setting the base line;
- working from the known to the unknown;
- explanation, demonstration (if applicable) and practice;

- feedback;
- look forward to next session.

It is normal to deal with two-way roads, T-junctions and crossroads in order to build up pupils' confidence in applying the basic driving routines before introducing more complex road systems. However, depending on the area you are working in, or where each pupil lives, you may need to be flexible with the introduction of these two subjects and in any case, in some quieter areas where most basic training should be carried out, there may be mini roundabouts to be dealt with.

In most areas, you will need to deal with roundabouts in combination with driving on dual carriageways.

Mini roundabouts

These are usually sited in reasonably busy areas where the minor roads used to have 'Give Way' or 'Stop' signs. They allow better traffic flow by allowing drivers in the minor roads to merge more easily. The following are a few sample questions you could use to establish pupils' understanding:

'Which routine do you need to apply when you're approaching junctions?'

'What does the "give way" sign mean at a T-junction?'

'Who will you have to give way to at a roundabout?'

Following on from these questions you will need to transfer pupils' prior knowledge and develop it to include the different rules to be followed. For example:

- looking and planning ahead for signs and markings;
- applying the M S M routine;
- selecting the appropriate position (lane) in the road;
- making full all-round observations;
- giving way to traffic from the right;
- maintaining the correct position through the roundabout;
- checking the mirrors;
- signalling for leaving if appropriate and where it won't affect the steering.

Create plenty of opportunities for practice at as many different mini roundabouts as the training area will allow. Begin with straightforward left turns and then approach from different directions, explaining about the need to adapt road positioning to suit each individual roundabout.

For pupils' first few attempts, you will need to give talk-through instruction on the unfamiliar aspects. Extra help will often be needed to merge when traffic is arriving at the junction from all directions at the same time.

Depending on how quickly they pick up the new routines, gradually transfer the responsibility of decision making when you feel they can cope.

Fault identification, analysis and remedy

Some of the common faults to watch for at mini roundabouts are:

- lack of application of the M S M routine;
- failure to respond to signs and markings;
- incorrect lane selection;
- emerging in front of other drivers;
- missing opportunities to proceed;
- not signalling when required;
- signalling when not required or when it interferes with steering;
- not maintaining lane discipline.

Roundabouts

If the training area you are working in dictates that you have to deal with mini roundabouts first, then you will be able to transfer this knowledge and introduce the differences that apply to the larger ones.

To deal with larger roundabouts first, you will need to give a full explanation of all the items listed under mini roundabouts, but more information will be required on signs, markings, lane selection and discipline.

Using a visual aid, explain how to deal with a straightforward four-exit roundabout, beginning with turning left. Use Q & A to confirm pupils' prior knowledge of applying the M S M routine as you talk your way through your diagram. For example:

> *'Who has priority at a roundabout?'*
>
> *'Will you need a signal for turning left at a roundabout?'*
>
> *'Do you always need to stop at a roundabout?'*
>
> *'What does the broken white line mean?'*
>
> *'Where should you be looking?'*

Remember that Q & A should be used to get some feedback and not as an interrogation tool. Pupils often become anxious when faced with new and complex situations, so respond to body language, be prepared to back off and give more help if necessary.

Explain the procedures the pupil will not yet be familiar with and then continue by describing the procedures for going ahead and turning right. No matter which direction is to be taken, emphasis needs to be placed on:

- looking ahead for signs and markings;
- application of the M S M routine and maintaining full control of the car;
- looking early for gaps in the traffic from the right;
- watching for traffic coming around the roundabout from other roads – these often create gaps by preventing the traffic directly to our right from emerging;
- continual observations in all directions so that we know what's happening to the right and in front, and to help maintain our position;
- maintaining position and lane discipline throughout the roundabout;
- signalling for leaving so as not to hold up those waiting to merge into the roundabout.

Practice

Each pupil will have their own individual rate of learning, ability and aptitude. This means that the amount of training each one needs will also vary.

Roundabouts also come in many varieties. As the pupil's competence and confidence improve, plan your routes to cover as many different types as possible, including roundabouts with more than four exits.

Your questions might include:

'How do think you should signal if you were taking the second exit?'

'Where should you position on approach for taking the third exit that is just beyond the 12 o'clock position?'

As pupils' ability improves in applying the basic routines, you will need to focus on their skills at looking and planning ahead, making good progress and taking safe opportunities to proceed.

Fault identification, analysis and remedy

Errors will generally be similar to those listed under the heading mini round-abouts. However, the larger roundabouts are generally busier and carry traffic that's often travelling much quicker. In particular you will need to watch for pupils:

- failing to read and respond to signs and markings;
- approaching too fast to allow themselves sufficient time to start looking;
- making unnecessary gear changes;
- looking only at the traffic in the roundabout and not at the gaps;
- not preparing the car in time to move into suitable gaps;
- failing to take opportunities to move;
- concentrating on making observations to the right – this often results in them not keeping to the left as they move into the roundabout and not being aware of what the driver ahead is doing;
- straddling lanes;
- not checking mirrors before signalling or changing lanes;
- leaving in the incorrect lane.

Recap

Some of the questions you could use to further develop pupils' understanding include:

'Why is it important to be planning ahead and looking for signs and markings?'

'Who has priority at roundabouts?'

'If you were going to travel straight ahead at a roundabout would you need to signal on the approach?'

'Which signal should you use for leaving a roundabout and when should you put it on?'

'Where should you check before moving across into the left lane?'

'Why do you think it's important to keep looking both ways at a roundabout?'

'What might happen if you wander across into another lane on a roundabout?'

'What might happen if you fail to move into safe gaps in the traffic?'

The list is endless and you need to develop your own question bank and adapt each one to suit the circumstances.

As with all lessons, you need to give positive feedback on areas of improvement and advice on where more practice is needed. Use Q & A and encourage your pupils to ask questions if there are particular aspects they don't quite understand.

Look forward

Confirm that, to become consistently skilful in dealing with these busier junctions, lots of practice will be needed; and that during the rest of their training with you, you will help them become confident and able to cope in as wide a variety of circumstances that the area allows.

Dual carriageways

Recap

Before introducing dual carriageways, a recap on driving on two-way roads could include the following questions:

'Where do you normally drive on a two-way road?'

'What is the most dangerous manoeuvre on a two-way road?'

'What's the speed limit in built up areas and on other roads?'

'What routine should you always apply when dealing with hazards?'

Objectives

The objective is to teach your pupils how to join, drive along and leave dual carriageways safely and efficiently. Because there are numerous types of dual carriageway you will not be able to achieve this in one lesson – it will be a gradual process over a series of lessons up to and beyond the driving test (Pass Plus scheme).

Depending on the location of dual carriageways in your area, you will need to incorporate as many types as you can to build up your pupils' skills and confidence so that they can not only cope with the different types of road, but also keep up with the traffic flow. Your statement of objectives should be something like:

'Over the next few lessons we will be learning about dual carriageways and how to join, drive along and exit them safely.'

Explanation

You will need to confirm that dual carriageways come in lots of different designs and layouts. Some of the variations are the:

● number of lanes;

● speed limit;

● methods of joining – ie roundabouts, T-junctions, slip roads;

● volume of traffic;

● parked vehicles.

The following are some questions you could use to confirm what the pupil knows about dual carriageways:

> *'What's the speed limit on dual carriageways where the national limit applies?'*
>
> *'What's the speed limit in built-up areas?'*
>
> *'Tell me what a "repeater" sign means?'*
>
> *'Where should you normally drive on a dual carriageway?'*
>
> *'What's the right lane for?'*
>
> *'Why do you think it might be important to plan further ahead and use all of the mirrors more frequently?'*

It might be useful to use visual aids to help the pupil 'see' what you mean, particularly when you're describing how to turn right onto dual carriageways from side roads. You will need to explain the differences that apply where the width of the central reserve varies. The most important key elements you should include in your explanation are:

● joining from roundabouts;

● turning left onto dual carriageways from T-junctions;

● turning right onto dual carriageways through narrow and wider central reserves;

● driving in the left lane unless passing parked vehicles, overtaking or turning right;

● planning further ahead – for parked vehicles or slower moving traffic;

● using the mirrors more frequently;

● positioning in the centre of the lane;

● planning for junctions and applying the M S M routine early;

● changing lanes safely;

● keeping up with the traffic flow.

The following are some of the questions you might use to coach the pupil:

> *'Why do you think you might have to look and plan further ahead on dual carriageways?'*
>
> *'How often should you use the mirrors?'*
>
> *'Why do you think you have to start the M S M routine earlier than on normal roads?'*
>
> *'How would you turn right if the central reserve is narrow?'*
>
> *'What would you do if the central reserve is very wide?'*

As with any other complex subject, the list of questions is endless and you will have to devise questions that suit each particular set of circumstances.

Demonstrations

Unless your pupil has difficulty in understanding, 'hands on' experience is the most effective way of learning to apply the different rules. You may, in some particularly difficult situations, decide that a demonstration would be the safest way to initially explain how to deal with them.

Practice

For the first few outings on dual carriageways, practice will need to be guided. Although your pupil should by now have good car control skills and can apply the M S M rules on normal two-way roads and at junctions, you will need to revert to 'talk-through' instruction in these new situations.

Make sure, at this stage, that your talk-through is restricted to the unfamiliar procedures. If you're not careful, it's very easy to revert to giving basic instructions in those skills the pupil has already mastered.

Depending on the road systems in your area, practice should be given on all of the procedures listed under the explanation section.

Fault identification, analysis and rectification

Some of the problems that arise during the early development of skills in driving on dual carriageways are very similar to those listed under roundabouts. Other faults include:

- Failing to look ahead and respond in time to parked vehicles – this can often result in either the pupil becoming boxed in or signalling and pulling out in front of another driver.

- Not keeping up with the traffic flow and causing problems for others.

- Keeping up when the other traffic is breaking the speed limit.

- Not planning early enough for junctions.

- Blocking a carriageway by failing to work out the width of the central reserve before pulling across.

- Moving onto a dual carriageway and failing to build up the speed effectively.

Feedback, recap and look forward

Following the normal lesson format, give positive feedback and advice on aspects that need more attention, recapping on the strengths and areas of weakness.

Formulate questions similar to those listed under other subjects in order to coach your pupil and develop better understanding and attitude.

Confirm that, as with roundabouts, driving on dual carriageways requires lots of practice and experience in order to build confidence.

MAKING PROGRESS AND ROAD POSITIONING

When you have covered most of the elements within the 'syllabus for learning to drive', and so that your pupils will be able to drive consistently and effectively in today's congested road conditions, you need to teach them:

- to maintain the correct position on the road;

- how to respond positively;

- to take safe opportunities to merge into traffic at all types of junction;

- to drive at appropriate speeds to keep the traffic moving.

Your statement of objectives could be something like:

'During your next few lessons we will be driving in more congested areas to build up your confidence and improve your personal driving skills. We will be focusing on:

- *road positioning and lane discipline;*

- *how to judge safe gaps in the traffic to emerge into;*

● *driving on higher speed and multi-lane roads so that you learn how to keep up with the flow of the traffic.'*

Setting the base line

By this stage pupils should be able to apply the basic driving routines to most situations. The following are a few examples of questions to confirm understanding:

'What's the speed limit in a built up area?'

'Give me a few examples of when and where it wouldn't be safe to drive up to the speed limit.'

'At what speed would you drive past a school around lunchtime?'

'What's the normal driving position on a two-way road?'

'When do you think it might be safer to drive a little further out in the road?'

'What's the national speed limit on a two-way road?'

'Why do you think it's sensible to drive up to the national limits when it's safe?'

'What might a following driver be tempted to do if you're driving too slowly for the conditions?'

'Why should you be ready to move away promptly at junctions?'

'When you're waiting at a roundabout, why is it important to look to the left as well as to the right?'

'What do you think might happen if you miss a suitable gap in the traffic at a roundabout?'

'Where should you position the car when you're driving on multi-lane roads?'

Using Q & A at this stage should help you establish in your pupils an awareness of the need to remain alert to the all-round traffic situation and to always be:

travelling in a safe position on the road, at the correct speed for the circumstances.

Explanation

Through discussion on these points, you should be able to explain to your pupils what is required in order to become a good and confident driver. Listen carefully to their responses and guide them towards the correct answers, giving added information as necessary.

Level of instruction

At this stage, pupils' driving skills should be fairly well developed. Give them the responsibility for making decisions in the types of situation they have previously experienced.

You may need to give talk-through assistance at the busier junctions in order to encourage them to take suitable opportunities to emerge and make good progress along the road.

Practice

By selecting appropriate routes, create as many opportunities as you can to cover as wide a variety of road and junction type as is possible within each session.

As you see confidence growing, back off and transfer the responsibility to the pupil. Obviously how long this will take will vary from pupil to pupil and you may sometimes have to adapt your teaching to suit their progress.

Fault identification and analysis

As with all other subjects, use your pupils' mistakes as opportunities to coach them into being better drivers. You need to ensure they are able to:

- move off promptly when safe;
- build up speed and change through the gears positively;
- apply the M S M routine effectively at all types of junction;
- take opportunities to emerge safely into traffic;
- travel at speeds appropriate for the road type and traffic conditions and drive in the correct position;
- Look and plan well ahead to minimize unnecessary stops at hazards.

Feedback/recap/summary

This is another area where the use of Q & A and guided discussion on what occurred during each session can help improve pupils' understanding of the principles involved in becoming effective drivers.

Remember to give praise where pupils demonstrate good decision-making skills and use any incidents that arise to confirm the reasoning behind the need to apply the principles in *The Official DSA Guide to Driving: the essential skills*.

Look forward

At the end of each lesson, confirm that on the next you will be introducing even more complex situations in order to build up their experience and ensure they will be confident to drive unaccompanied when they have passed their test.

Refer them to any extra reading material that may help in their development.

Dealing with these subjects on the Part 3 exam

This should not really be much different from the basic lesson plan. The main difference will be that, as *it is a test*, the examiner will introduce more challenging faults than most learners would. Some of the more common ones include:

- driving too close to the kerb or too far out in the road;
- straddling lane markings;
- not responding to signs and markings;
- making last minute lane changes;
- being unaware of traffic to the sides and in blind areas – through ineffective use of the mirrors and/or application of the M S M routine;
- positioning incorrectly for the type of junction;
- missing safe opportunities to emerge at junctions and roundabouts;
- moving off cautiously and not changing efficiently through the gears;
- not driving up to speed limits when it's safe to do so.

Ensure that you analyse the errors, giving reasons that are designed to encourage understanding and the development of positive and safe attitudes.

ANTICIPATING THE ACTIONS OF OTHER ROAD USERS

Today's roads are really congested, with everyone trying to get from A to B as quickly as possible, often with little thought given to those around them. All of your pupils will have been passengers and will probably have observed some of the unsafe actions that have from time to time put them at risk.

Objectives

Teaching anticipation cannot be done in one lesson, it is an ongoing process. You will need to use all opportunities that present themselves from a pupil's first lesson right up to the day they take their test, to encourage them to drive defensively by anticipating what others may do and to work out the safest way to avoid conflict.

Through the use of coaching you can use pupils' previous experiences to develop their awareness and anticipation and hopefully, by encouraging them to come to their own conclusions, you will influence safer attitudes.

Using all of the teaching, instructional and coaching skills described earlier in this book and in the lesson plans contained in this chapter, make sure that your pupils are able to deal safely with:

- Other car drivers. They may pull out from side roads or turn across their path, push their way through spaces between parked vehicles, overtake unsafely or follow too closely.

- Riders of cycles and motorcycles. Beware of: them creeping up at the sides of the car, or in between lanes in queues of traffic; being less easy to see at junctions; or of cyclists riding off the pavement onto the road, etc.

- Drivers of larger vehicles, for example anticipating that they may straddle lanes in roundabouts and will require more room when turning into and out of junctions.

- Emergency vehicles. Listen for sirens and watch for flashing lights: encourage pupils to be prepared to make room for them to pass.

- Pedestrians. Expect children to step into the road, to mess around with their friends around school time, to misuse crossings, etc. Expect older people to misjudge speed and distance, to be hesitant and to take longer to cross the road.

- Animals. In urban and rural areas they are unpredictable. Allow plenty of time and clearance.
- Differing road, light and weather conditions. These influence the driver's needs. For example, being dazzled by the headlights of oncoming or following drivers.

Before applying for a driving test your pupils should be able to drive consistently safely in all types of road and traffic conditions and to anticipate and deal safely with other road users.

When they pass their test, pupils are only at the beginning of their career and they should be encouraged to enrol on your 'Pass Plus' course to broaden their experience.

If you follow this systematic method of teaching driving, not only will it make the learning situation enjoyable, but, by the end of their course, your pupils should also be able to safely share the road with us.

5

The ADI exams

PART 1 – THEORY AND HAZARD PERCEPTION

The purpose of this book is to improve your *practical teaching skills*. It is therefore not our intention to cover in detail information that you will find in the other reading materials recommended by the DSA for this test.

This short section on the ADI Part 1 is included to ensure that you are aware of the wide range of knowledge and understanding you will need for the Part 1; and to emphasize that this will also give you a good grounding for the practical elements of the ADI exam – and, of course, for your future as a driving instructor.

The Part 1 syllabus

The subjects covered are:

- the principles of road safety;
- the techniques of driving a car correctly;
- the theory and practice of learning, teaching and assessment;
- the tuition required to teach pupils how to drive a car;
- *The Highway Code;*
- the DSA publications;
- interpretation of the reasons for test failure;
- knowledge for the needs of driving instruction.

All of the questions taken from the syllabus have been grouped into 10 subject areas and these are grouped into four main categories as follows:

- road procedure;

- traffic signs and signals, car control, pedestrians, mechanical knowledge;

- driving test, disabilities, law;

- publications, instructional techniques.

To prepare yourself properly for all three parts of the ADI exam you need to have a thorough knowledge and understanding of:

- *The Official DSA Guide to Driving: the essential skills*, ISBN 0-11-552641-2;

- *The Highway Code*, ISBN 0-11-552449-5;

- *Know Your Traffic Signs*, ISBN 0-11-551612-3;

- *The Official Guide to Learning to Drive*, ISBN 0-11-552608-0;

- *The Driving Instructor's Handbook* (14th edition), ISBN 0-7494-4746-X;

- *The Official DSA Theory Test for Car Drivers*, ISBN 0-11-552682-2;

- *Helping Learners to Practise – the official guide*, ISBN 0-11-552611-0

- *The Motor Vehicles (Driving Licences) Regulations 2004*, ISBN 0-11-050334-1;

- *Driving Test Report Form* (DL25A/B) – details in *The Driving Instructor's Handbook*;

- *Pre-set Test marking sheets* (AD126PT) – these forms are reproduced in *The Driving Instructor's Handbook*;

- *What you need to know about driving licences* (D100);

- *Registering and licensing your motor vehicle* (V100);

- *Application for a driving licence* (D1);

- *Practical Teaching Skills for Driving Instructors*.

D100, V100 and D1 are all available from the DVLA at www.dvla.gov.uk or from main post offices.

As you can see, this list is quite extensive and covers a wide range of subject knowledge.

> *Do not fall into the trap of believing that you will be able to memorize the question bank by rote learning.*

For one thing, there are over 900 questions in the official bank and, because they are computer-generated, the papers vary. Secondly, some of the questions are designed to test your understanding – not just your memory.

Remember, you are not only preparing for the theory test. You will also need an understanding of the principles involved in safe and effective driving for the Part 2 test; and also those involved in good teaching practices to prepare you for the test of instructional ability.

Hazard perception

Hazard perception testing is included in the ADI Part 1 exam and follows on from the multiple-choice questions. This section of the exam tests your ability to identify hazards. You can develop these skills in a practical way in our everyday driving and also by using 'The Official Guide to Hazard Perception DVD' from the DSA.

More detail about Hazard Perception is given in *The Driving Instructor's Handbook*.

Developing study skills

In preparation for the ADI Part 1 test, you will need to develop your study skills so that your learning is effective. This will be even more important if it is a long time since you have studied for any sort of theory test. Developing your own study skills should also stand you in good stead later, should you wish to take further qualifications for continuing professional development.

Some of your learners, too, will need advice when organizing their studies for the theory part of the 'L' test.

In developing these study skills, you will need to:

- make time available;
- find the right place to study;
- formulate a study plan.

Various types of courses are available, ranging from distance learning to intensive residential courses. Whichever type you choose, there is a lot of subject matter to study and you will need to spend a considerable amount of time working on these materials at home.

Organize your study time so that you maximize your learning. This means fitting it in around your other commitments and in a quiet place where you will be able to concentrate properly.

Making time available

Depending on how quickly you want to progress through your course, you may need to consider putting on hold for a while some of your social activities.

You will need to consider the impact of this study period on your close relatives. Try not to let yourself become so involved that they become resentful. This will only cause personal stress for everyone, and this, in turn, will affect your learning rate. You could try to get them involved by asking them to test you. This may even benefit them by updating their knowledge of the *Highway Code* rules and other information.

Time management is crucial. Whenever possible try to arrange your studies to fit in with the times when you know you will be in the best frame of mind to concentrate. You may have to experiment by studying at different times of the day.

> *The key ingredients to successful studying are:*
>
> - *Motivation;*
> - *Self-discipline;*
> - *Determination.*

Finding the right place to study

Being in the right place is just as important as studying at the best time. The quality of your learning will be enhanced dramatically if the environment you choose is 'conducive to learning'.

Some types of learning, for example 'learning by rote', require a quiet environment that is free from distractions. Rote learning is where you are learning things by memory, for example, a set of facts or figures.

Whatever the type of learning, you still need a relatively quiet environment. Provided that those sharing your home understand and respect your needs, you will probably be able to 'shut yourself away' without creating too much disturbance.

As this course involves such a large amount of reference material, you will need lots of space in which to spread your books around. You should try to get yourself properly organized with these and some writing materials before you start each session.

Some people like a little background music, but noise should be kept to a minimum as it can be a distraction and cause you to lose concentration.

Having established the time and place for your studies, you now have to ensure that you have a properly organized study plan.

Formulating a study plan

Studying is another skill that, like other skills, will improve with practice, determination and a planned approach.

Everyone is different. Some people are naturally studious and content to spend hours at a time studying and reading. Others find it not so easy – especially if they have not been in a learning environment since leaving school.

Remember, you may have to accept that some of your other activities are going to have to be shelved so that you can concentrate fully. To help maximize the quality of your studies, you need to formulate a plan. Try the following:

- Set personal objectives that you should be able to achieve within the time you set for them.

- Decide how much time you will need to set aside each day or week in order to achieve any deadlines that you set for yourself. You may need to take advice from your tutor or course organizer on the timetable for preparing for the exams.

- Formulate a timetable on which you can set targets for completing each specific module of the syllabus.

- Try to organize the material so that you are reading about similar subjects in one study session.

- Make sure that your timetable is not too restrictive by including some relaxation time between study periods. Leave yourself at least one whole day a week; and one or two study-free weeks if you are finding the course a bit 'heavy going'.

- Monitor your progress to ensure that you are not falling behind.

- Try not to become despondent if you feel you are falling behind and ask yourself if you are able to devote a little more time to the work.

- Don't panic, as this would only lead to stress and would do nothing for your learning process. Discuss your problems with your course provider, other trainees, close relatives or friends.

- If the pressures are too great, then it is better to consider revising your timetable. It would be better to delay taking the test than to take it before you have a thorough understanding of the course materials.

- Never let a study programme get on top of you but *KEEP ON TOP OF IT*!

After you have qualified as an ADI, this list of 10 key points will help you in advising your pupils on how to study effectively for their theory test.

As the ADI test covers such a wide range of subject knowledge, you need to properly organize your studies so that in any one session you are reading about related topics. This will prevent your suffering from an overload of mixed information that can often end up with nothing being remembered.

Various structured training programmes are available from several of the main training suppliers. These programmes encourage you to train in a logical sequence and that you are properly guided through the different topics and related bands of subjects.

A properly structured programme will usually ensure that you are not missing out on any important information. For details of materials and suppliers, see *The Driving Instructor's Handbook*.

The ADI theory test is taken at most 'L' driver theory centres and therefore appointments are quite readily available. Before applying for your test, you should feel confident that you have carefully studied all of the recommended materials and that you have a thorough understanding of all of the rules, regulations and teaching principles involved in driving and driving instruction.

On the test day

Allow plenty of time to get to the test centre with a few minutes to spare. Remember, these days you cannot predict how long a journey will take. If you are late, you will become stressed. Hardly the right frame of mind for concentration!

Take with you the appointment confirmation and your driving licence. If you do not have a photocard licence, you will also need some sort of photographic identification, such as your passport.

The test is computer-based with one question at a time being shown on the screen. It doesn't matter if you are not familiar with computers as you will be given a few minutes to practise and there will be someone on hand to assist.

The test paper has 100 questions, each with a choice of four answers, only one of which is correct. Some of the questions will have two or more correct answers from a selection of five. Where this is the case, an indication is given alongside the question. Read each question very carefully at least twice. It may sometimes be easy to eliminate an obviously incorrect answer, but the choices remaining may be very similar. Some questions will even expect you to remember exact wording from the reading materials. This is why your study and understanding of the textbooks is so important.

If you're unsure about any questions, the computer system allows you to go backwards and forwards through them and to change your answers. If you're really not sure about one, it's better to tick the answer you think is the most appropriate. After all, you won't lose any more marks with a wrong answer than you would have by not having answered it.

You are allowed an hour and a half to complete the test. Make good use of any time left to re-check your answers. Don't be distracted when you see others leaving after only a short while. As well as other ADI candidates, there will also be learners taking their theory test and they have far fewer questions to answer. Anyway, the trainee instructors may have given up because they didn't study properly!

The result will be given to you before you leave the test centre. When you pass, you will also receive an application for the driving ability test. If you fail, you will be given an application for a further attempt.

PART 2 – DRIVING ABILITY

Although this section deals in detail with the ADI test of driving ability, you should be teaching your pupils to drive to a similar style as that required of you.

It is accepted that although new drivers preparing for the 'L' test can't be expected to drive at the same standard as you, they should be taught the same syllabus – that is, a syllabus that will result in 'safe driving for life'.

As you read through this section, therefore, you should consider how you will structure your courses to ensure that, as far as possible, you apply a similar set of criteria when teaching drivers at all levels of ability.

The major difference will be in how you will be assessed and how your learner drivers are assessed.

For this part of the exam your personal driving skills must be of a very high standard. You should not be trying to drive merely as a very good learner – the test is much more stringent than that.

The DSA expects you to show that you have a thorough understanding of safe and effective driving techniques; and that you are able to demonstrate these skills efficiently. In particular, you must be able to put into practice all of the following subjects:

- expert handling of the controls;

- application of correct road procedures;

- anticipating the actions of other road users and taking appropriate action;

- sound judgement of distance, speed and timing;

- consideration for the convenience and safety of other road users;

- moving away straight ahead and at an angle;

- overtaking, meeting or crossing the path of other vehicles, and taking an appropriate course without undue hesitancy;

- turning left- and right-hand corners correctly and without undue hesitancy;
- stopping the vehicle as in an emergency safely and under full control;
- reversing into limited openings to the left and right;
- reverse parking into a space behind another car;
- reverse parking into a parking bay;
- turning the vehicle to face the opposite direction using forward and reverse gears;
- the application of environmentally friendly driving techiques.

During the test you should endeavour to drive as normally as possible. In other words, don't try to 'put on an act' for the benefit of your examiner. The examiner would undoubtedly see through this and, anyway, you would probably not be able to keep the 'act' going for the duration of the test. It could also distract you, taking away your concentration from what's happening around you.

As with the practical 'L' test, the examiner will explain a few of the 'ground rules' before you start the test. These will normally include:

- *'Follow the road ahead unless I give you an instruction to turn off.'*
- *'I will tell you in good time if we are going to turn to the left or the right at a junction.'*
- *'If you are unclear about any of my instructions, don't be afraid to ask – they will then be repeated or clarified.'*
- *'Drive as you normally would – but remember that a high standard of competence is required.'*

As well as driving over a varied route incorporating different types of road and traffic conditions, the test will include, if practicable, any of the following manoeuvres:

- up- and downhill starts;
- emergency stop;
- left and right reverse;
- reverse parking;
- turning in the road.

During the test your driving will be assessed on all of the following:

(Note that the numbers in brackets in the section headings that follow refer to the corresponding headings on the DSA form DL25.)

Vehicle checks (7)

You will be asked to describe how to carry out three vehicle safety checks, and to then demonstrate checks on two others.

The subjects covered include:

- tyres and wheels;
- lights, reflectors and direction indicators;
- braking systems;
- steering;
- audible warning devices;
- any liquids used in the engine, braking and steering systems.

Precautions (11)

Make sure that you:

- are in the correct seating position;
- are able to reach and use all of the controls safely;
- check that the vehicle is secure before starting the engine.

Control (12)

Use the *foot controls* progressively and smoothly.

- Push gently on the *footbrake* to begin with, gradually increasing the pressure and, to achieve a smooth stop, ease the pressure just before the car comes to a complete stop.
- Use the *clutch* smoothly for moving off, stopping, changing up and down through the gears and for low speed manoeuvres. Avoid 'coasting' after changing gear and when stopping.
- The *accelerator* should also be used smoothly and gently. Use '*accelerator sense*' to begin the slowing down process on the approach to hazards. This should avoid the need for last minute harsh braking.
- The *footbrake* should be used gently and progressively. Plan well ahead for hazards and brake gently and in good time so that you can either proceed if the hazard clears, or you can come to a smooth stop in the correct place.

- Use *gears* to match the speed and power requirements dictated by the road and traffic conditions. Selective gear changing up and down the box will demonstrate that you are planning properly for hazards and driving economically.

- The *handbrake* should be used to avoid the car rolling either backwards or forwards, for stops that are likely to last for more than a few seconds, or when parking.

- Use the steering smoothly. Using the whole wheel and looking where you want to go should help avoid under- or over-steering when cornering.

Move off (13)

- Check all the *mirrors* and *blind areas* before moving off. You need to cover all of those areas to the sides and rear of your car that are not seen in the mirrors. You are checking, for example, for traffic emerging from side roads and driveways, or cyclists or pedestrians who may be crossing the road diagonally behind you.

- *Signal* only if it will be of benefit to another road user, including pedestrians. This will show that you are looking and thinking effectively.

- Move off *smoothly and under control* in all circumstances by coordinating the hand and foot controls, handbrake and steering. For moving off downhill use the footbrake and clutch effectively to avoid coasting.

Position for normal stops (25)

As an experienced driver, you should know where it's legal, safe and convenient to park without causing problems for others.

- Look and plan ahead and choose a suitable place for stopping, taking into consideration any signs, road markings, openings/driveways, junctions.

- Stop close to the edge of the road.

Controlled stop (2)

You will be expected to demonstrate a high level of skill at bringing your car to a controlled stop.

- React promptly to the signal.
- Keep both hands firmly on the wheel to maintain a straight line.
- Brake firmly and progressively as dictated by the road and weather conditions.

As a good driver you should be able to avoid skidding. If you feel the wheels start to lock up, release the brake momentarily and then re-apply the pressure. Do this in an 'on-off' manner (called *cadence* braking) until you regain control. Even if your vehicle has an ABS system, try to avoid braking so hard that it activates.

You will be stopped in a driving position so remember to check nearside and offside before moving off again.

Reversing left, right and into a parking space on the road or a parking bay and turning in the road (3, 4, 5 and 6)

All of your manoeuvres should be carried out efficiently – remember, *you are an experienced driver.*

- Assess the gradient;
- while maintaining full control of your car, keep checking in all directions for other road users, giving them priority where appropriate.

Use of the mirrors and rear observations (14)

Use all of the mirrors effectively.

- This means constantly taking into account what is happening all around you and acting safely so that you don't inconvenience any other road user.
- Apply the M S M routine and check your mirrors *well before* reaching any hazard and before slowing down, signalling and changing direction. By doing this you will be better placed to decide whether or not a signal will be helpful and when to time it.

Signals (15)

- Use the signals shown in the *Highway Code* when they will be helpful to inform any other road user (including pedestrians) of your intentions.
- Use signals in good time so that others have time to respond; and ensure they are cancelled after use.
- Avoid giving a signal when it might cause confusion. For example, using a right signal for passing a line of parked vehicles where there is also a right turn.

Positioning (23)

- Keep well to the left in normal driving – about a metre from the kerb.

- If there are lots of parked vehicles, maintain a position to pass them all unless there are junctions on the right where vehicles may emerge.

- Look and plan well ahead for signs and lane markings.

- Position early for any changes in direction.

- When driving in lanes, keep well to the centre so that you don't straddle the markings.

Clearance to obstructions (16)

- When there are obstructions in the road, be prepared to slow down or stop and give way to oncoming vehicles.

- As you pass parked vehicles, give plenty of clearance, allowing for children running out from between them, doors opening or drivers pulling out without warning.

Responding to signs and signals (17)

- You should constantly scan the road well ahead, looking for all signs, road markings and traffic lights.

- Plan ahead and work out what might happen at traffic lights. Try to anticipate any changes and have your car under full control so that you can either stop comfortably or proceed safely. Remember that a green light means '*go if it's safe*'. Check in all directions as you proceed through any junctions.

- Obey signals given by police officers, traffic wardens and school patrols.

- React promptly to signals given by other road users, including those in charge of animals. Remember some drivers use unofficial signals – check all around for yourself before proceeding.

Use of speed (18)

- Taking into account the road, weather and traffic conditions, and any road signs and speed limits, make safe and reasonable progress.

- Remember that a speed limit is the *maximum* allowed for the road you are travelling along. There are many times when you may need to be travelling much more slowly, for example when driving past schools where there may be children about.

Following distance (19)

- Keep a safe distance between you and the vehicle ahead.

- In wet conditions maintain a bigger gap to allow for the longer stopping distances.

- By applying the '*two-second*' rule where there is a speed limit of 40 mph or more, you should be able to stop comfortably.

- If you are being followed too closely, increase your distance from the vehicle ahead to allow yourself more time to brake gently. This will give the following driver more time to respond.

- Keep even further back when following large vehicles, as it will give you a better view of the road ahead, particularly if you are considering over-taking.

Maintaining progress (20)

- You are an experienced driver – drive at realistic speeds to suit the conditions so as not to impede other drivers.

- Plan well ahead and take opportunities to proceed at all types of junction as soon as you can see that it's safe to go.

Junctions (21)

- Apply the M S M routine early.

- Check for signs and road markings.

- Take up an appropriate position for your intended direction.

- Your approach speed should be such that you can either proceed if it's safe, or stop comfortably when necessary.

- Maintain a safe position throughout by avoiding cutting right corners or swinging out on left turns.

- At roundabouts demonstrate good lane discipline and watch for other vehicles cutting into your lane.

- Prior to turning, check for cyclists or motorcyclists on your left, and for pedestrians crossing the road.

- At some junctions, where the view is restricted, you may need to 'creep and peep' before you can take *effective observations*. Check for other clues by taking advantage of reflections in shop windows, telephone boxes, or by looking through other vehicles' windows. Do not proceed until you are absolutely sure that you can see far enough to make a safe decision to go.

Judgement (22)

- Before overtaking you need to ask yourself: *'Is it safe, legal, and is it necessary?'* You must also decide if you have time to complete the manoeuvre without causing problems for any oncoming drivers or the one you are passing.
- When overtaking cyclists and motorcyclists allow plenty of room in case they wobble or swerve.
- After overtaking make sure you allow plenty of room before pulling in again.
- Where there are obstructions on your side and the width of the road is restricted, be ready to give way to oncoming drivers. Remember – not all other drivers are courteous. You may also need to give way to an oncoming vehicle even when it should be your priority! It's also easier for you to give way if you're travelling downhill, particularly to larger vehicles.
- When turning right and it's not busy, look and plan well ahead. Try to time your arrival so that you can keep moving. However, make sure you do have plenty of time! If there are oncoming vehicles, you should not make them slow down, swerve or stop so that you can make your turn.

Pedestrian crossings (24)

You should be aware of the different types of crossing and show consideration to all groups of pedestrians.

Your speed on the approach should be appropriate to:

- the type of crossing;
- traffic and road conditions;
- pedestrian activity.

Whatever the type of crossing you are approaching, if there are any pedestrians using it you must stop:

- At *zebra* crossings plan ahead and be ready to stop if anyone is waiting to cross. (You may consider using an arm signal to inform any oncoming driver.)
- Give way to pedestrians on *pelican* crossings when either the red or flashing amber lights are showing.
- At *toucan* crossings, you should also give way to cyclists.
- At *puffin* crossings be aware of the light sequences and act appropriately.

- Where a police officer, traffic warden or school patrol is controlling the traffic, you must obey their signals.
- Before moving off, check all around for pedestrians and cyclists.

Awareness and planning (26)

You can only anticipate events if you are constantly scanning ahead and all around and making effective use of the information you are gathering. You should:

- consider what is happening on the road;
- take account of the traffic and weather conditions;
- anticipate what might happen;
- take early action to maintain full control of your vehicle.

You should also:

- judge what other road users are going to do;
- predict how their actions are going to affect you;
- take early action to avoid problems and conflict.

In particular you should consider the more vulnerable groups of road user, such as:

- young, old or infirm pedestrians;
- cyclists and motorcyclists;
- people with animals.

Ancillary controls (27)

You should understand the function of all of your car's controls and switches. You should always maintain full visibility and operate your vehicle in safety. The main controls for this are:

- indicators;
- lights;
- windscreen wipers/washers;
- demisters;
- heaters;
- air conditioning.

When needed, you should be able to locate and operate ancillary controls without looking at them.

Preparation for the ADI Part 2 exam

The standard of driving required to pass this test is extremely high. Although you may have had many years of accident-free driving you will almost certainly have picked up a few habits that detract from the overall efficiency of your performance.

> *You must remember that there is no substitute for effective coaching from an experienced tutor.*

There is a limit of three attempts for this test. Rather than wait until you have failed, it makes sense to have an assessment with an expert (check the ORDIT Register on the DSA's website).

An assessment taken early on in your training will give you more time to make any necessary adjustments to the style of your driving and any changes made will also become more natural to you.

Whether or not you are taking a test, you should always try to drive:

- smoothly;
- sympathetically;
- briskly;
- efficiently;
- economically;
- courteously;
- with your vehicle under full control at all time.

Good forward planning and anticipation are the foundations of effective and safe driving in today's difficult traffic conditions. As an instructor, you need to be looking and planning even further ahead and working out all of the possibilities in time to get your pupils to react safely.

Take the advice of your tutor and:

> *Only take the test when you feel that your vehicle handling techniques and road procedures feel completely natural in all situations.*

This book is aimed at improving your practical skills. A full breakdown of the DSA's marking system for this test can be found in *The Driving Instructor's Handbook*.

PART 3 – INSTRUCTIONAL ABILITY

This part of the ADI exam is designed to test your *practical teaching skills* and is structured in a way that will assess your ability to teach drivers at different levels of driving skill.

This is done by breaking down the test into two phases. The first phase tests your ability to teach a novice or intermediate learner. The second assesses how you would deal with a more experienced learner or someone who has a full licence.

The test is also designed to assess:

- the knowledge you gained while studying for the theory test;
- whether you can put that knowledge into practice by teaching 'safe driving for life'.

The practical teaching skills described in this book will not only give you a good foundation on which to build your instructional ability and prepare you for this test, but should also provide you with an insight into what is involved in the ADI's everyday work.

Your trainer should teach you how to put your knowledge into practice in the car through:

- explanation;
- demonstration;
- role play;
- practice.

Driver training syllabus

Your initial instructor training should include a properly structured syllabus which covers the complete range of subjects, rather than just those that are tested in the Part 3 ADI exam.

You will need the ability to teach your pupils these additional subjects if they are to be prepared for 'safe driving for life'. In addition, if you are trained effectively in all subjects, you will be much better prepared for the exams.

The full list of topics includes:

- the function and operation of the main controls;
- moving off and stopping safely;
- effective use of the steering;
- changing up and down through the gears smoothly;
- braking exercises, including the emergency stop;
- safe application of the M S M routine, including effective decision making from what is seen in the mirrors and using signals correctly when appropriate.
- Turning left and right at road junctions.
- Emerging left and right from side roads.
- Driving through, turning and emerging at all types of crossroads including those controlled by traffic lights.
- Approaching and negotiating roundabouts.
- Driving on dual carriageways and other roads with national speed limits.
- Dealing with other traffic safely when meeting, overtaking and crossing their path.
- Allowing safe clearance to parked vehicles, giving way when appropriate – whether the obstruction is on the near- or offside of the road.
- Manoeuvring the vehicle, including turning in the road, reversing right and left and reversing into parking places behind other vehicles and into bays.
- Dealing safely with the different types of pedestrian crossings.
- Driving at speeds suitable to the road, traffic and weather conditions.
- Encouraging effective and positive progress when conditions allow.
- Positioning the vehicle safely for driving on single and multi-lane roads.
- Developing vehicle sympathy, forward planning, anticipation and hazard awareness skills in order to encourage economical driving and to avoid conflict with other road users.

This part of the exam is designed to test, through your practical teaching skills, your knowledge of the rules, regulations and procedures for safe driving. You will therefore need to keep up to date with the knowledge you gained when preparing for the theory test.

The test is conducted in two phases. The *first phase* is structured to test your teaching skills and you will be asked to deal with a learner with no, or very little knowledge of the subject. The *second phase* is to test how well you can assess the driving of a more able learner and give corrective advice and training that results in improvement. The examiner may, on this phase, portray a full licence holder.

Some of the teaching topics are tested in both test phases. The reason for this is to assess whether or not you can properly adapt your teaching to suit drivers with differing levels of skill and aptitude.

Lesson notes

Part of your job as an instructor is to instill confidence in your pupils. To do this, you will need to display confidence in yourself, and you will hardly do so if you have to open a textbook to give an explanation. However, the use of training aids is quite acceptable and will add weight to your explanations.

During the initial stages of your training you should have prepared some lesson notes listing the key elements of each subject in the syllabus. If you have sufficient training and practice before you take the Part 3, you may find that by this stage you no longer need them.

For in-car use, you may find *visual aids* more helpful. While your pupil can *see what you mean*, you can use them as a memory jogger. Using a picture, you can talk yourself through the elements of the subject as if you were carrying out the procedures as a driver.

Many candidates think visual aids should not be used on this test. However, you are supposed to be demonstrating what you would do as an instructor. If you think your 'pupil' is experiencing some difficulty in understanding a complicated procedure and would benefit from seeing a picture, use one!

Route selection

Route planning is dealt with in detail in Chapter 3. However, don't worry about having to work out a route for your test in what may be an unfamiliar area to you.

For the purpose of the test, your examiner will select the training route. This is because:

● you may not be completely familiar with the training area;
● the examiner will know the most appropriate areas for teaching and practising each specific subject;
● the examination can be structured more efficiently and effectively.

At the beginning of the test your examiner will establish a method of communicating to you where you are required to take the 'pupil'.

Again, time constraints may mean that the route may not be one hundred per cent suitable. Don't let this be a distraction. Your examiner is also under the same constraints and has to adapt to the time available. You have to be prepared to adapt your instruction to suit the road and traffic conditions.

For example, if you were teaching a real novice how to move off and then stop, you would drive them to a quiet area with a long straight stretch of road away from other traffic and hazards. However, most test centres are situated in towns and you will not have the luxury of 10–15 minutes to drive away and find somewhere more appropriate. You will therefore need to adapt your tuition and time your instructions to get the 'pupil' moving away safely into gaps in the traffic. As long as you give the correct instructions, the 'pupil' should respond by carrying them out properly.

Adapting the lesson to the time available

Lesson planning is dealt with in Chapter 4. This covers planning for normal lessons, rather than for the ADI exam. Due to the time restraints on the Part 3 exam, you will need to adapt your lesson plans to fit the time available, while still ensuring that it suits your pupil's level of ability. For example, if you were giving a normal on-road lesson of an hour's duration to a complete novice, you should have sufficient time to get them on the move by the end of it. However, since you now have less than half this time, you may not be able to achieve these same objectives.

You should bear in mind, however, that this is a practical test. Do not spend too much time stationary – but cover the necessary teaching points and get on the move so that your 'pupil' can *learn through practice*.

Each lesson should be planned as follows:

- Introductions. At this point you might find it helpful to jot down the 'pupil's' name and also the subject to be dealt with.
- Set the baseline by establishing prior knowledge.
- Explain any new elements for the 'beginner/novice'; or confirm prior knowledge of the more experienced 'pupil' through Q & A.
- Create opportunities for learning to take place through practice.
- Make corrections on the move as appropriate.
- Park up to discuss more serious problems.
- Create opportunities for correct procedures to be practised.
- Give positive feedback of progress, confirming areas that need more practice.

Setting the baseline for the lesson

No matter what subject is being taught and which phase you are dealing with, you will need to *set the baseline* for each lesson. To do this you need to establish what the 'pupil' already knows and can do by:

- Listening carefully to the 'pupil's' description, making a mental note of previous experience.
- Asking one or two questions to confirm knowledge of the subject.
- Listening carefully to the responses for any hint of misunderstanding.
- Correcting or confirming any response.

This procedure should take no longer than a couple of minutes – do not put the 'pupil' under any undue pressure by 'giving them a grilling'. Watch for, and respond to, body language and 'back off' if necessary.

Setting the objectives for the lesson

Any training session, no matter what the skill or subject being taught, should begin with a *statement of objectives*. All this needs to be is a simple statement such as: *'By the end of today's lesson you should understand and be able to deal with basic roundabouts.'*

Giving a briefing or explanation

We have already spoken about the time constraints of this test. Again, your explanation of the subject will have to be adapted to suit the time available – and of course it should also be adapted to suit any previous knowledge or experience your 'pupil' may have.

A few carefully worded questions at the beginning of each phase to establish the pupil's prior knowledge and understanding of the subject matter can prevent problems during the practical element of the test.

The questions will need to be:

- relevant to the pupil's perceived experience;
- to the subject matter.

As with setting the baseline for the lesson, *listen carefully* to the responses. It is your job to work out what the 'pupil' already knows, and your explanation should be designed to give any new information on the key elements of the subject, or to *top up* existing knowledge.

Remember that this is supposed to be a test of **instructional** *ability. You are not expected to try to include in your briefings every single element you can think of relating to the subject matter.*
YOU DO NOT HAVE THE TIME FOR THIS!

A full breakdown of the syllabus for the instructional ability test can be found in:

- *The Driving Instructor's Handbook;*
- *The ADI 14 – your road to becoming an Approved Driving Instructor.*

You will also find in Chapter 4 of this book detailed lesson plans for a syllabus in driver training. These should help with your everyday work and in preparation for the Part 3.

For any driving lesson to be effective you need to ensure that your pupil is not overloaded. This means you have to prioritize between what the pupil:

- *must know;*
- *should know;*
- *could know.*

When you have your own pupils you will normally have some prior knowledge of their aptitudes and the stage of driving they have reached. Notwithstanding this, your lessons should always begin with a Q & A recap session.

You do not have the advantage of knowing the 'pupil' on the Part 3. Therefore, listening carefully to the scene set by the examiner is extremely important and following this up with relevant questions will help you develop an idea of where to pitch your instruction.

ROLE PLAY

Role play is often used in the training environment to create situations where either learning or assessment of specific skills can take place in safety.

In the case of the ADI exam, if a real learner were used, it would be extremely difficult to set up situations that would test these areas of your skills.

While preparing for the Part 3, you should have become accustomed to your trainer role-playing different learners in a variety of situations. This should stand you in good stead for the test.

One of the most difficult drawbacks, however, is that you will know in your own mind that the person sitting beside you 'putting on an act as a learner' is really someone with a great deal of knowledge about driving.

You must try to overcome this barrier by being prepared to 'take part in the game'. Have the courage of your convictions that you have a good deal of knowledge – gained through studying for the test of theory – and that your driving skills have been proved by your passing the Part 2. All you have to do now is pass on that knowledge and ensure that the person beside you is advised on how these principles should be applied on the road.

To 'take part in the game' you must:

- concentrate;
- listen very carefully to the description of the 'pupil' being portrayed;
- either make a mental note, or write down anything you think is not understood;
- ask questions relevant to the subject;
- listen carefully to the responses;
- be prepared to give extra information or corrective advice.

By the time you have done this, you should have started to relax a little and be settling into your role as the instructor. The following are a few sample questions.

General introduction questions

- *'How long have you been learning?'*
- *'Are you able to practise between your lessons?'*

The answers given by your 'pupil' may generate other questions. If the 'pupil' is someone with very little experience and you have been asked to teach a manoeuvre, you could ask:

- *'Have you done any reversing yet?'*
- *'Can you move off on hills and from behind parked cars?'*

Following this you should be able to make a definite link to the lesson and ask the 'pupil' to:

- *'Tell me how you would control the car so as to creep forwards slowly to get a better view at a blind junction.'*

With a Phase 2 'pupil', you could ask:

- *'Have you taken a test yet?'*
- *'Can you remember what the examiner discussed with you at the end of it?'*

The roles used in the test

Examiners conducting the ADI exams have all been trained in playing different roles. The role selected will depend on the:

- subject being taught;
- level of ability of the 'pupil';
- aspect of your teaching skill that is being assessed.

Linked to these, the examiner will either play a *proactive* or a *reactive* part and this will be done through one of the following roles:

- negative;
- simple;
- average;
- testing;
- knowledgeable.

Normally the examiner will begin each phase in the *proactive* role in order to introduce realistic faults. This will then enable an assessment of whether or not you are responding by giving correct instruction to which the examiner will react positively.

Proactive

Should you give no positive advice, the examiner will remain in this role and continue making similar mistakes. Questions may then be asked in order to give you a prompt and to test your flexibility. If this happens, the examiner is asking you for more help and information. Don't ignore this hint – remember to teach safe driving, the 'learner' needs to have good reasons for doing things.

Roles played under this heading are:

- *Negative* – the Supervising Examiner (SE) will wait for you to use Q & A to establish knowledge and understanding and when you ask 'Did you understand that?' replies simply 'Yes'.

- *Simple* – does not respond to technical instruction, waiting for you to adjust the level of your terminology to suit the 'pupil'.

- *Average* – asks questions in a normal way and relevant to the subject.

- *Testing* – the 'pupil's' questions go beyond what is being taught. For example 'What if …?' The examiner will then wait for you to deal positively with this.

- *Knowledgeable* – this is the 'know it all pupil' who will challenge everything you say and will pick up on any doubtful instruction by asking: 'Why must I do that then?'

Reactive

Unless possible danger is involved, whether your instruction is correct, incorrect or late, the examiner will do exactly as told.

Roles played under this heading are:

- *Negative* – the SE will respond normally to your questions and may ask further questions to clarify a point.

- *Simple* – when you adjust the level of your instruction to suit the 'pupil', the SE queries you on more technical matters.

- *Average* – your instructions, whether correct or incorrect, will be followed to the letter, unless they are unsafe.

- *Testing* – when you react and take control, the SE will keep to the subject but will be ready for the 'What if…?'

- *Knowledgeable* – when you take control, the SE will offer less challenges but will pick up on any incorrect instruction by saying, for example, 'But my last instructor said…'

The SE will use a role felt to be appropriate for the 'pupil' and level of ability being portrayed. Examiners do not normally play the same type of personality for both phases of the test and rarely choose to play the *average* learner.

Whatever two roles your examiner plays, you must try to become positively involved and deal with each in a way that is:

- sensitive to their needs;
- tactful – you do not want to insult your 'pupil';

- adjusted to suit any lack of response;
- likely to result in positive learning taking place.

During the first part of your test, the examiner will be testing your teaching skills. You must listen and respond very carefully to what is said and done and then adapt your teaching to suit. You must give as much help as is necessary to ensure some positive learning takes place.

The second part of the test is designed to give you an opportunity to demonstrate your assessment and corrective skills. Make sure you treat the 'pupil' as a more experienced driver by allowing them to show what they can do. Follow this up with any positive advice and create opportunities for the correct procedures to be practised.

During each phase, and no matter what level of skills the 'pupil' has, you must ensure that:

- the 'pupil' learns about the relevant procedures and how to carry them out;
- some understanding is achieved;
- improvement takes place;
- a change in attitude is achieved;
- your instruction is positive;
- no potentially dangerous situations are allowed to develop;
- you deal tactfully with each character being portrayed;
- your instruction is pitched at the correct level to suit each 'pupil's' ability;
- you identify and analyse most of the faults;
- you give positive feedback and remedial advice;
- opportunities are created for each 'pupil' to practise the correct routines and procedures.

Your instruction will be assessed under the following categories:

1. Core competencies:
   - identification of faults;
   - fault analysis;
   - remedial action.
2. Instructional techniques:
   - level of instruction;
   - planning;

    – control of the lesson;

    – communication;

    – Q & A techniques;

    – feedback/encouragement.

3.   Instructor characteristics:

    – attitude and approach to pupil.

For more information on how the test is marked refer to Chapter 5 of *The Driving Instructor's Handbook*.

Before taking your test, you need to feel confident that you can deal positively with pupils at all levels of skill and aptitude. You should be able to cope well with the test situation if you have:

- taken sufficient, high-quality training;

- a thorough understanding of good practical teaching skills;

- prepared your lesson plans and visual aids properly;

- listened to the advice given by your tutor.

When you attend for the test, remember to take with you all the relevant documents, your lesson plans and visual aids.

Plan your journey so that you will arrive at the test centre in plenty of time, allowing for any unforeseen traffic hold-ups. If you have to rush to make it on time, you will not be feeling very relaxed nor in the right frame of mind for a test!

As well as ensuring that your car is roadworthy and clean (see the ADI 14), it might be useful to take along some of these *extras*:

- a window leather;

- sunglasses;

- some mints to combat 'that dry mouth feeling';

- a soft drink;

- a round tray in case you need to allow the 'pupil' to practise steering method.

Some of the main reasons for the high failure rate of this test include:

- Insufficient training.

- Poor preparation.

- Candidates' inability to adapt to the role-play situation, resulting in a failure to treat the examiner as a 'learner'.

- Failure to listen properly to the description of each 'pupil' and their current level of ability.

- Ineffective use of Q & A.

- Failure to listen and react to the 'pupils' ' responses.

- An inadequate introduction and briefing to the topic to be covered.

- Lack of in-depth knowledge of the subject resulting in a poor explanation and ineffective practical session.

- Spending too much time on briefings, leaving insufficient time for practical application of the correct procedures.

- Under-instruction, resulting from an inability to give sufficient help according to the 'pupil's' stated or demonstrated level of skill.

- Over-instruction, resulting from a lack of response to the pupil's stated and demonstrated level of skill.

- Lack of control resulting from failure to respond to the *Phase 1* 'pupil's' unsympathetic use of the car.

- Failure to take opportunities to stop to discuss major incidents with the *Phase 2* 'pupil'. This often results in a takeover by the 'pupil' and more and more uncorrected errors being committed.

- Minor errors not being corrected on the move, resulting in too many stops and lack of time for sufficient practice.

- Poor fault assessment.

- Inadequate analysis of faults leading to a failure to give remedial advice and allow for positive practice to take place.

- Failure to use effective Q & A for positive feedback purposes.

- Failing to respond to feedback from the 'pupil'.

- Lack of praise and encouragement resulting in a failure to build up the 'pupil's' confidence.

You should have no problems passing this test if:

- you apply all of the PTS covered in this book;

- your instruction is positive;

- you stay cool, calm and collected;

- you are firm, fair and friendly and – most importantly:

- each of your pupils learns something.

TRAINING FOR THE ADI EXAMS

This section is designed to help you decide on the training plan that will best suit your particular needs. It may help if you refer to ADI 14, *Your Road to Becoming an Approved Driving Instructor* to remind yourself of the full syllabus and the stringent requirements of this exam.

The importance of effective training

> *Today's driving instructor has to be an effective teacher – not just someone who rides around telling people where to go and what to do.*
>
> *This means that you will need to be able to coach new drivers to understand the main principles involved in safe driving.*

It is vital to remember that, although you are initially training for an examination, you are also preparing yourself for a job that involves potential danger. You will therefore need to commit yourself to having sufficient training in order to achieve both of these objectives.

The pass rate for the theory test is less than 50 per cent. This should emphasize the need to study the recommended reading materials thoroughly in order to gain a proper understanding of the principles involved in safe driving and effective teaching.

For the ADI driving test, the pass rate is under 45 per cent. Again this figure would point to candidates not being thoroughly prepared. Too many candidates are not fully aware of the high standard of driving skills required.

The first-time pass rate for the Part 3 exam is even lower, at well under 25 per cent. This would seem to emphasize even further the fact that far too many candidates are ill-prepared. There are two main reasons for this high failure rate:

1. Many trainees look for cheap options and use trainers with little expertise. Your local instructor may be extremely good at 'L' driver training and have an excellent pass rate. However, training to teach requires totally different skills from teaching driving.

2. Too many candidates have insufficient training and are not properly prepared for the exam nor for the job of an efficient instructor.

A good course should not only include those subjects on which you might be assessed during your Part 3 test, but also provide you with training in other important topics included in the *official syllabus for learners*. These include:

- dual carriageways;
- roundabouts;
- rural roads and other driving situations not included in the Part 3 syllabus.

Through your studies for the theory test and preparation for the ADI driving test, you may know the subject well and are able to apply the correct driving rules and procedures effectively in all situations. However, putting over that knowledge to new drivers in a way that will encourage learning to take place is a totally different matter.

> *To learn how to become an effective driving instructor you will need plenty of expert guidance.*

A good trainer will be able to teach you how to:

- find out what your pupil already knows;
- establish a baseline for each lesson;
- pitch the instruction at a level to suit the pupil's ability and personality;
- analyse any problem areas;
- give positive and constructive advice;
- allow for practising the correct routines;
- teach *safe driving for life*.

You will also need to be taught to cope with the complexities of teaching a wide range of subjects, in a moving classroom and to pupils with different abilities, personalities and weaknesses.

Think of your training fees as being an investment towards a new career. Don't opt for what might appear to be the cheapest and shortest course. *THERE ARE NO SHORT CUTS!*

Selecting a course that suits you

The course you select will obviously depend on your particular circumstances. However, before making your final decision, you should bear in mind that the structure of the exam, together with the waiting time for practical appointments, means that it is not a process that you can rush through within a couple of months.

To be realistic, if everything goes well and you pass each element at the first attempt, it will take you *at least* six months from beginning your studies to the registration stage. If you opt for the *Trainee Licence* scheme, then the process could take much longer if you are to gain the full benefit of the six-month licence period.

Training options

The three main options are:

1. part-time studies and training organized around current work commitments;
2. an intensive course that involves classroom studies and in-car work for all three elements of the exam;
3. studying for and passing the theory test, training for the driving and instructional tests, and taking out a six-month *trainee licence*.

Part-time studying and practical training

This option best suits those who are in full- or part-time employment and wish to fit in their training around these commitments.

As explained earlier in this book, the syllabus for the theory test is very comprehensive and you need to be prepared to devote quite a lot of your spare time to your studies. The more thoroughly you understand the principles covered in this syllabus, the better prepared you will be for your practical training.

As previously indicated, make sure that your training is properly structured by using a system that covers the entire syllabus in a logical sequence. Training programmes are available from various suppliers.

It is most effective to overlap your preparation for the three elements of the exam. While learning the rules and regulations for driving and teaching in readiness for the theory test, your trainer will ensure that you are putting them into practice when you drive. You will also see at first hand how your trainer applies the teaching principles in preparing you for the two practical tests.

Establishments offering this type of part-time individual course normally charge you for each training element. This means, therefore, that you will be able to spread the cost over the duration of your training period.

Everyone has a different rate of learning and training needs vary from one individual to another. Unlike many of the intensive courses, which usually stipulate within the fee a specific amount of training per exam element, the part-time course means that the amount of training will be structured to meet your personal needs.

However, you may prefer to share a course so that you can experience interaction with other trainees.

Intensive courses

There are many different types of intensive course available. These vary in structure and duration. The syllabus should be compatible with the DSA's requirements for the ADI exam and also with their *recommended syllabus for learners*.

Much of the work is carried out in the classroom. This normally includes studies for the theory test and tuition on the principles involved in good driving and how to structure driving lessons.

Practical training is usually carried out on a ratio of one tutor to two trainees. The DSA recommends this to be a maximum and some people might benefit from watching as well as being actively involved. If there are three trainees to one trainer, learning will become less effective and, obviously, less time will be available to deal with your specific training requirements.

No matter what your personal needs may be, the course fee may be restrictive in terms of how much training you are allowed for each element of the exam. You may be required to pay for any supplementary training you need.

Planning for any additional training to be outside the 'intensive course' timetable may also sometimes be difficult, as the establishment will normally have to schedule this at a time that suits you and another trainee.

If you opt for this method of training, you may be required to pay part or all of the fees in advance. Remember, there are absolutely no guarantees that you will pass all three tests. You should be made fully aware of the costing structure and whether or not you will be entitled to any refund of fees should you not be able, for any reason, to complete the course.

Practice

With both part-time and intensive courses, you can get practice instructing friends or relatives. You must remember, however, that you are not allowed to take any form of payment. You cannot even take money for fuel or any other costs incurred. If you are attending a course with other trainees, you may wish to practise with each other.

If you select either of these methods of training together with:

- listening to the advice given;
- having as much tuition as is recommended;
- the tuition being of sufficiently high quality;
- your trainer being experienced in ADI training and expert at role play;

you should be able to qualify independently of the *Trainee Licence* system.

The trainee licence

This system allows you to get practice with paying learners while preparing for the Part 3.

You have to pass both the theory and driving tests before being considered for a *trainee licence*. (You can do this through either of the above two methods.) You then have to be sponsored by a qualified instructor, whose driving school address will be shown on the licence. This instructor should take responsibility for your training and supervision.

The *trainee licence* option will normally entail you in taking up a full- or part-time position with a driving school. There are various schemes available, many of which include taking up a franchise with one of the larger schools.

If you already have a job, you need to consider this option very carefully. You will probably have to give it up in order to work in line with the conditions set out by the sponsoring driving school. (Remember, there are no absolute guarantees that you will pass the Part 3.)

Before you can apply for a *trainee licence* you must receive 40 hours training from a qualified ADI. You must receive training in all the following subjects:

1. explaining the controls of the vehicle, including the use of the dual controls;
2. moving off;
3. making normal stops;
4. reversing, and while doing so entering limited openings to the right or to the left;
5. turning to face the opposite direction, using forward and reverse gears;
6. parking close to the kerb using forward and reverse gears;
7. using mirrors and explaining how to make an emergency stop;

8.   approaching and turning corners;

9.   judging speed, and making normal progress;

10. road positioning;

11. dealing with road junctions;

12. dealing with crossroads;

13. dealing with pedestrian crossings;

14. overtaking, meeting and crossing the path of other road users, allowing adequate clearance;

15. giving correct signals;

16. comprehension of traffic signs, including road markings and traffic control signals;

17. method, clarity, adequacy and correctness of instruction;

18. general manner;

19. manner, patience and tact in dealing with pupils;

20. ability to inspire confidence in pupils.

You should bear in mind that **you are responsible for making sure that you get this training**. A record of it must be kept on the form ADI 21T. This has to be signed by yourself and your trainer and sent in with your application for the licence.

Under the *Trainee Licence* scheme, you are not allowed to advertise yourself as a fully qualified instructor and you must keep to one or other of the following conditions:

(a) Twenty per cent of all of the lessons you give must be supervised by your sponsoring ADI. A record must be kept on the form ADI 21S of all of the lessons you give and the supervision received. This form must be signed by yourself and your sponsor and returned to the DSA as soon as the licence expires.

or

(b) You must receive a minimum additional 20 hours training covering all the listed topics. This training must take place within three months of issue of the licence, or before you take your first attempt at the Part 3, whichever is the sooner. A record of this training must be kept on the form ADI 21AT and must be sent to the DSA before the end of the three-month period, or presented to the examiner conducting your Part 3 test if this is the sooner. At least 25 per cent of this must be in-car training, with a maximum instructor : trainee ratio of no more than two trainees to one ADI.

If option (b) is selected and you fail at your first attempt, an additional five hours' training must be taken before you will be allowed to take a further test. This also applies if you fail at the second attempt. A declaration that you have had this extra training must be signed by you and your sponsoring ADI and handed to your examiner on the day of the test. If you do not do this, then the test will be cancelled and you will lose the fee.

For full information about the legal requirements of this system, refer to the *ADI 14 – Your Road to Becoming an Approved Driving Instructor* (Car).

Selecting your trainer

Selecting a good trainer is your first step to achieving your goal of becoming an effective driving instructor. Good trainers are able to help you:

- understand the importance of the instructor's role and of teaching safe driving skills;
- develop your attitude and skills so that you will become a proficient and responsible instructor;
- communicate effectively;
- prepare thoroughly for all three parts of the ADI examination;
- learn to teach effectively in the car, and in the classroom where applicable;
- construct an effective and flexible training programme to suit the needs of individual pupils;
- seek further training for personal development;
- with advice on ADI and road safety organizations;
- prepare for running your driving school business.

Role play

Many candidates for the Part 3 experience difficulty in dealing with the role-play situation. It is unnatural to try to treat someone as a learner when you know they are an extremely proficient driver. One of the most important assets of the good trainer, therefore, is having the ability to role play effectively while still maintaining safety. A good trainer should be able to:

- simulate drivers at all levels of experience and ability;
- play the role of people with different characteristics, for example: shy and retiring; forthright; argumentative; indifferent;

- introduce a wide variety of driver errors relating to the different topics under instruction;

- do only what they are told to do – in spite of an instruction being incorrect, a good trainer must go against instinct and do only as instructed, for example when given an instruction to select a gear before being told to push down the clutch;

- create opportunities for you to make positive correction through not responding properly to the road and traffic situation.

Experiencing the role-play situation in a wide variety of situations should give you a good grounding for dealing with your examiner.

There are currently no mandatory qualifications for the trainers of driving instructors. It is accepted, however, that qualifications other than that of ADI can be helpful. These include:

- AEB/DIA Diploma in Driving Instruction. (Preparing for this qualification gives the prospective ADI trainer a good foundation of knowledge.)

- Cardington Special Driving Test. (In seeking personal development through taking this test, the trainer is able to maximize efficiency and performance by training Part 2 candidates to a similar style and standard.)

- City & Guilds 7307 Further & Adult Education Teaching Certificate. (A qualification particularly useful for those engaged in classroom teaching.)

- City & Guilds 7254 Certificate in Training Competence. (Most appropriate for those preparing candidates for the practical elements of the ADI exam.)

- NVQ in driving instruction. (The role-play aspect of this qualification is extremely useful for ADI trainers.)

- NVQ Assessor's Award. (Useful for those mentoring ADIs for the NVQ in driving instruction.)

- ADI National Joint Council Tutor's Certificate. (A good foundation for those involved in the training of new instructors and the updating of ADIs preparing for the Check Test.)

- MSA GB Tutor's Certificate. (Similar advantages to the above qualification.)

Training establishments

There is currently no mandatory register for instructor training and there are many training establishments throughout the United Kingdom offering a variety of different types of course. Many of these are independent and offer excellent training.

There is, however, a voluntary scheme that many establishments have opted to join. This is ORDIT – the Official Register of Instructor Training.

ORDIT is a voluntary registration scheme administered by the DSA, using criteria that were set originally by representatives of the driver training industry. In Northern Ireland the DVTA (NI) operates the register.

The Register consists of a list of training establishments that have satisfied the DSA criteria of minimum standards of training.

Members of ORDIT offer professional training to a minimum and consistent standard. They are subject to bi-annual inspections to ensure that the standards are maintained. ORDIT members' facilities and courses are designed to:

- develop the skills of trainee and potential instructors;
- further develop the skills of existing qualified instructors.

All training courses are structured to ensure that clients are fully prepared to teach driving as a life skill.

All types of courses relating to driver training are acceptable, bearing in mind that quality, and not quantity, is important in any training programme.

Individual trainers are registered for inclusion in the ORDIT Register when they have demonstrated to the DSA inspector that they can deliver a satisfactory standard of training in any one or all three parts of the ADI qualifying exam. For example, a trainer may be registered to give only Part 1 (theory) or Part 2 (driving) training. A trainer who is assessed as giving satisfactory ADI Part 3 training will also be registered for Part 2 training.

The DSA is taking a positive role and is working with the industry to develop and improve the quality of training. The ORDIT Register requirements are regularly reviewed and the DSA is committed to keeping the industry fully informed about developments that might affect training establishments and trainers.

Full details of ORDIT terms and condiitons of membership are in *The Driving Instructor's Handbook* and in the ADI 14 starter pack.

6

The ADI Check Test

After you have qualified as an ADI, there is a legal requirement for you to take a test of 'continued ability and fitness to give instruction' whenever required by the Registrar. This test is more commonly known as the 'Check Test' and is an opportunity for the DSA to assess whether your instruction is still up to the standard required for inclusion on the register of ADIs.

The testing and checking of driving instructors is the responsibility of a relatively small team of the DSA's Supervising Examiners who have undertaken extensive specialist training. You and your pupil should be aware that the Check Test is not related to the 'L' driver testing system. The examiner is there to assess the quality of the instruction being given and not your pupil's driving.

When you first qualify, you will be seen within a few months for an 'educational' visit by your local SE. At this stage you would normally be assessed and allocated an appropriate grading.

Changes to the ADI regime over the past few years mean that the Check Test is assessed to the same criteria as the Part 3 Test of Instructional Ability. This is to ensure that, irrespective of how long an ADI has been registered, the standard of instruction given to all their customers is of a reasonable and consistent standard.

Because of the higher standards now required to achieve the minimum acceptable grade of 4, many instructors are worried about their Check Test, particularly in view of the fact that more ADIs are being removed from the Register for substandard tuition than ever before. Sometimes, especially if it is an instructor's first Check Test after qualifying, it is 'fear of the unknown' that causes the problem.

This unfounded fear often results in instructors presenting lessons differently from their normal pattern, simply because they are being 'watched'.

We should all welcome the Check Test as an opportunity to demonstrate our teaching ability and to benefit from the advice of the Supervising Examiner.

There is a saying that:

POOR PREPARATION = POOR PRESENTATION

This chapter offers advice to all instructors, no matter what their experience, on how to properly prepare for the Check Test.

Good application of the practical teaching skills in this book, and an understanding of how your performance will be assessed against the set criteria, should give you greater confidence when you have your Check Test. It will also help ensure that you achieve the best possible grading for your ability.

Do not try to 'stage' what you think to be an easy lesson by presenting a very good learner dealing with an obviously well-rehearsed subject. Also try to avoid putting on a special show that is different to the way you normally teach. If your pupil sees you behaving differently, they may become confused, which could lead to them making more mistakes than usual.

A pupil who is struggling with a subject may well present a better opportunity for you to display your true skills. It will also make it easier for you and the pupil to concentrate on the job in hand rather than worrying about the SE sitting in the back of the car.

Any test is of little value if the information and feedback gained is not then fed back into the learning process. This means if you do not give a true picture of your teaching skills, how can the SE judge them properly, how can an objective assessment be made and how can corrective advice be given?

The 'L' test, the ADI practical entrance exam and the Check Test are all based on the following principle:

Failure to meet the criteria indicates that the performance is incomplete and needs modifying in some way.

It would be unreasonable to say to one of your pupils who failed the 'L' test, 'Well, you had your chance and you blew it!' Surely, what you would do is arrange further lessons for that pupil to bring about any improvement necessary, before retaking the test.

Irrespective of the grading you receive, you should be prepared to modify your instruction to take into account any weaknesses identified. On your next Check Test, the SE will be looking to see that any previous recommendations have been implemented.

Some driving instructors find it very difficult to stand back and look at what they are doing in the way that the examiner is able to.

They can't see the wood for the trees!

They are often so involved in the teaching that they cannot see whether any learning is taking place.

The Check Test is useful to instructors in that it provides accessible information that can be used to improve the amount of learning taking place during driving lessons.

> *You should see the Check Test as being an independent assessment of your teaching ability, the cost of which is included in your registration fee.*

The test is designed so that the examiner can:

● ASSESS your teaching ability;

● ADVISE you of the outcome and the grading given;

● ASSIST you to make improvements by giving you feedback.

It is natural to be nervous on the test. This, too, is part of your learning process as it will allow you to know first hand what your pupils feel like when they are taking the 'L' test. However, once your natural enthusiasm and the desire to get the best out of your pupil come into play, you should be able to forget the examiner and concentrate instead on giving a normal lesson.

In any examination or test, careful preparation will greatly improve the chances of success. The Check Test is no different.

You need to know:

● what the Check Test is, why it is in place and who conducts it;

● where Check Tests are carried out;

● how the test is conducted;

● how to prepare for your Check Test;

- how to present the lesson;
- how to get the best possible grading;
- the result.

FORMAT

If you have only recently qualified as an ADI, the SE for your area will soon contact you at your home address to invite you to attend for a Check Test. You will be given a date and time, and the test will start from either the SE's office or from your local driving test centre. If the SE's office is in an area which you are not familiar with, you can elect to take it instead from your local 'L' test centre. You should acknowledge the invitation as soon as possible, letting the SE know immediately if you are unable to attend or if you wish to change the venue.

The first Check Test is 'educational' in that it is designed to let your local SE, who may not be the one who tested you on the Part 3 exam, see your work and let you know if there is anything that needs improving.

Provided that your instruction is satisfactory, you will be given a grading, otherwise you will be invited to attend another Check Test within a few months.

If you have been qualified for some time, you will periodically be invited to attend for a Check Test. The grading you received on your last Check Test will determine how soon you will be required to undertake a further test.

Again, you should acknowledge the invitation as soon as possible, letting the SE know if you cannot keep the appointment or wish to change the venue. In this case another date and time, or venue, will be offered.

Check Tests are normally conducted during the SE's normal working hours – ie, Mondays to Thursdays between 8.30 am and 5.00 pm. If you do not have a pupil available, you may give instruction to a full licence holder, as long as this person is not an ADI. If you cannot arrange for a learner or full licence holder to accompany you for your Check Test, then rather than postpone the appointment, you may request a 'role-play' test.

The SE will accompany you while you are giving a driving lesson to a pupil. You are assessed in much the same way as in the ADI examinations but, because the driving lesson is longer than each phase of the Part 3, it allows more time for the pupil to practise driving. The SE will be looking for:

- the method, clarity, adequacy and correctness of your instruction;
- your observation and correction of the pupil's errors;
- your manner, patience and tact in dealing with the pupil, and your ability to inspire confidence.

Remember that the SE is assessing your ability to instruct and not your pupil's ability to drive. You can give a lesson to a driver at any level of ability – a total novice, an 'experienced' learner or a full licence holder – but the lesson must be tailored to suit the needs of the pupil.

If you are not able to produce a pupil the SE will conduct the Check Test in a similar manner to the ADI Part 3 exam by role playing a pupil in a particular situation. If this is the case, the examiner will describe the pupil to be portrayed.

PREPARATION

The vehicle in which you conduct your lesson should be safe, legal and reliable, and must carry 'L' plates if you are teaching a pupil who has a provisional licence. If the lesson is conducted in your own or a school car, this should not be a problem. If the lesson is in the pupil's car, it would be sensible to check beforehand on the state of the vehicle and, of course, the insurance. Your ADI certificate must be displayed if you are charging a fee for the lesson.

How you prepare for the lesson should really be no different from what you do for any other lesson. However, you should also be ready to explain to the SE some background information about the pupil and the lesson you intend to give.

In particular you should let the SE know:

- whether the person is a regular pupil of yours;
- what you know about the pupil's progress;
- what professional instruction the pupil has received;
- whether they are having any private practice;
- any strengths or weaknesses of which you are aware;
- your lesson plan.

Have to hand any teaching aids that you normally use. They should be ready and available for use as and when required during the lesson. Notes and any other written material should only be used for reference and should not be read word for word.

PRESENTATION

The SE wants to see a 'normal' lesson. Do not try to put on a special show. Presenting a lesson is covered in full detail in Chapter 3, but before the lesson begins you need to take account of the special requirements of the Check Test.

You will need to:

- Structure the lesson to last about an hour but allow extra time for discussion with the SE.

- Introduce the pupil to the SE and explain the purpose of the visit to the pupil.

- Emphasize to the pupil that it is your instruction that is being checked, not their driving.

- Encourage the pupil to behave normally and to ask questions if there is anything that has not been understood.

- Remind the pupil that because of the extra weight in the back, the car may handle slightly differently.

At the beginning of the lesson, you may need to confirm with a short recap what was covered in the previous lesson. Asking a couple of questions should tell you whether the pupil has remembered the key points.

Explain to the pupil what is going to be covered in the lesson. This will also let the SE know what the objectives are.

Using your own style, adapt your method of instruction to suit the pupil's ability, personality and progress.

The SE will be assessing your fault identification, analysis and correction. Any remedial advice you give will be assessed for its effectiveness.

If the pupil is not someone you teach regularly, make sure that you find out about any previous experience by asking appropriate questions and by inviting the pupil to ask questions.

Although you will have set objectives for the lesson, be prepared to vary your original plan if necessary. For example, if serious problems arise in other areas, concentrate on correcting these. Give the pupil your reasons for changing the lesson plan and explain that the original topic will be covered in a future lesson.

Your explanations should be methodical and systematic, with a clear definition of the key points of any new subject. Avoid excessive verbalization or repetition and make sure that the information you give is correct. Encourage the pupil to ask questions if you think that any misunderstanding may have occurred. Your answers should be correct and in sufficient detail for the needs of the pupil.

Avoid giving any complicated instructions on the move as this will only distract the pupil and may divert attention away from the driving task. If the pupil asks questions while driving along, answer only briefly, saying 'I want to talk about that when we stop.'

Route directions should be given clearly and in good time. Encourage your pupil to read the road signs and markings. How much guidance you give will depend on the pupil's ability and experience.

Two very common instructional errors arise from not matching the level of instruction to the ability of the pupil. These are: UNDER-INSTRUCTION and OVER-INSTRUCTION.

Under-instruction

This often happens when an instructor tries to conduct a mock test letting the pupil drive around and saying nothing until the end. This gives the SE very little information about the instructor's normal methods of instruction. Even if the pupil is driving reasonably well, a few mistakes are bound to occur and the instructor should work on the positive correction of them.

Many experienced instructors feel that giving positive correction to a pupil at test standard will be classed as 'prompting' or 'over-instruction'. However, positive learning is more likely to take place if the pupil's attention is drawn to a problem before it becomes too serious. Allowing a dangerous situation to develop and then discussing it later is negative or retrospective correction and is not good teaching practice.

For example, there may be an obstruction on the left and you don't feel that it would be safe to allow your pupil to drive through because of approaching traffic. The pupil, however, is making no attempt to slow down and is obviously heading for the gap. To encourage the pupil to make a positive decision about giving way, you could ask, 'Have you assessed whether it is safe to go for that gap?'

This 'prompting' would be far safer than allowing the pupil to scrape through the gap with unsafe margins for error, then saying, 'You shouldn't have gone through that gap – it was dangerous.'

Over-instruction

Unless the pupil is in the very early stages of instruction, or practising a new skill for the first time, try to avoid 'talking them round'. Over-instruction will deter the pupil from thinking and making decisions, and this will inhibit progress.

Over-instruction often occurs when a pupil is practising new skills while consolidating existing ones. For example, you may be teaching the turn in the road and giving a complete talk-through, but forget that the pupil already knows how to move off and stop. Try to restrict your talk-through to the aspects of the manoeuvre that are new to the pupil.

Use of the question and answer (Q & A) technique is covered in detail in Chapter 3. This method of teaching can help to encourage pupils to look and plan ahead. Poor Q & A is a common reason for failing the Check Test. It is vital, therefore, that you fully understand how to apply it effectively. Using good Q & A will:

- tell you what the pupil is thinking;
- test the pupil's knowledge and understanding;
- encourage the pupil to think more about solving problems and making decisions;
- ensure the pupil is participating in the lesson and in the learning process.

For example, if your pupil continually drives too close to parked vehicles, you could ask: 'What should you be looking for around these parked cars?' Or if bends are approached at too high a speed: 'What will you do if there is an obstruction around the bend?'

Because no two situations are the same, each drive should prompt different questions. Your skill in choosing the most appropriate one, while avoiding over-instruction, will depend on:

- the pupil's ability;
- what is happening in your vehicle;
- what is happening outside the vehicle;
- the presence and actions of other road users;
- the weather, road conditions and visibility;
- road signs and markings;
- the urgency of any required action.

Generally speaking, less experienced pupils are likely to need more questions. These questions should be relatively straightforward and uncomplicated. You will probably need to use fewer questions with more experienced pupils, but they should be more searching.

> *As an instructor, knowing when to stop talking and to listen is as important as knowing when to speak!*

The question and answer technique may be useful to encourage your pupil to look and plan ahead. It will also tell you what the pupil is thinking. It not only tests the pupil's knowledge and understanding, but also encourages them to think more about solving problems and making decisions. Using this technique should also result in a greater degree of participation by the pupil in the learning task and a better understanding of safe driving principles.

For example, if you are following a bus, its brake lights come on and you see passengers getting up, ask the question: 'What do you think the bus is going to do?', or, if you see waste bins on the pavements, ask: 'What activity could you be expecting to see in this area today?'

Observation and proper correction of errors

Stay alert and try to show an interest in your pupil. Continually look for ways in which to improve their performance. You should recognize all faults and differentiate between those which require immediate attention and those that are only one-off minor errors.

Constant 'nit-picking' may undermine the confidence of the pupil. Where minor errors occur in isolation that do not affect safety or control, it may be better not to mention them. This applies particularly in the early stages when the pupil may be under pressure while learning new skills. It can, however, also apply in the later stages of learning. For example, while waiting at a red traffic light with the handbrake on and neutral selected, your pupil takes one hand off the wheel to rub an eye. As the car is secured and the discomfort could cause a distraction, is it really necessary for you to tell your pupil to keep both hands on the wheel?

The causes and consequences of errors should be identified, together with the actions required to prevent recurrence. It is important that corrections are made in a positive manner. For example, 'Drive in the centre of your lane' is much better than 'Don't drive on the white line'. The latter comment only confirms and reinforces what should *not* be done without indicating the correct position on the road.

There is little benefit in simply telling the pupil what they did wrong without an explanation and the reasons WHY it is important to do it in a different way.

A good instructor will ask a pupil: 'Why do you think we should keep in the middle of our lane?'

You should identify and correct the *causes* of any errors and not just the effect of them. For example, if your pupil emerges from a junction without taking effective observation, it should tell you that the potential danger from oncoming traffic has not been understood. Rather than merely confirming the error by saying, 'You emerged before you could see properly', it is better to explain the importance of the creep and peep routine – to check for smaller vehicles such as motorcycles.

Whether or not the pupil has understood about limited zones of vision will subsequently be shown by their response in a similar situation. If they demonstrate an ability to use the creep and peep routine, your explanation has obviously been effective. If the pupil still emerges without taking effective observations, then the potential for danger has still not been understood and may be caused by another problem, such as an inability to judge speed. A more detailed explanation may be necessary, followed by further practice.

Because of the need for you to be constantly checking all around, it is not always possible to monitor every single mirror check. To avoid any arguments which might arise from undue criticism, rather than stating 'You didn't check your mirrors!', it may be better to ask 'Did you check the mirrors before signalling?'

The response is not really important. What does matter is that the pupil will know whether or not the mirrors were checked. Your question will therefore have had the desired effect of making the pupil think about using them. You can then expand on this by asking 'Why is it important to check the mirrors before signalling?'

Instructor characteristics

MANNER
- Try to create a professional but relaxed atmosphere in the car, without becoming overly familiar with your pupil.

- Address your pupil in an informal manner, but bear in mind the individual's personality. Using first name terms can often lead to a more relaxed atmosphere, but in some situations you may need to be slightly more formal.

- Physical contact should be avoided whenever possible as it can be misunderstood. Sit in a position where the pupil cannot accidentally touch you.

PATIENCE
- Even if you have told the pupil something several times, do not assume that it will be remembered by them. Be patient! You need to be sympathetic and ready to rephrase your explanations so that they can be more readily understood.

- There are different degrees of 'impatience' which must be avoided. These range from sarcastic comments, an irritated tone of voice and impatient body language, to total loss of control and open hostility towards the pupil.

- Avoid getting upset or annoyed in a situation where the pupil already knows that they have made an error. Patience will help to keep the pupil calm and therefore assist the learning process. This will also lead to a greater degree of cooperation and effort on their part.

TACT

- Always be careful of what you say and do, in order to prevent giving offence to the pupil.
- Try to develop an intuitive understanding of the needs and feelings of the individual pupil.

CONFIDENCE

- Your own enthusiasm will be reflected in the efforts made by your pupils.
- Pupils will not normally make the same amount of effort if they have the impression that you are bored or disinterested.
- Encouragement should be given where appropriate and praise given where credit is due. This is just as important as criticism and the correction of errors, as it will develop the pupil's confidence and inspire further effort.

Lesson summary

At the end of the lesson you should recap by giving the pupil some feedback on:

- how the lesson went;
- what has been learnt;
- what improvements have taken place;
- those topics in need of further instruction.

The lesson should end with:

- a look forward to the next lesson;
- an outline of the topics that will be covered;
- information on the reference materials to be checked beforehand.

Mark down for the pupil a record of strengths and weaknesses. This will demonstrate to the examiner that you are monitoring progress and keeping pupils informed of how they are doing.

GRADING

Proper preparation is essential if you wish to attain the best grading possible.

If it's a long time since your last Check Test, or if you are in any doubt over any particular instructional techniques, you should consider having an assessment with an ORDIT registered tutor. You might find this worthwhile anyway rather than leave it too late only to be told by the examiner that your instruction is 'substandard'.

When selecting a pupil, don't be tempted to take one who is ready for test and won't need you to demonstrate the effectiveness of your PTS. Using one who has plenty of room for improvement will allow you to bring about some progress during the lesson. This should be one of your prime objectives on the Check Test.

Make sure that your pupil is properly briefed about the Check Test – what it is, who will be conducting it and what the procedure will be. Draw up an appropriate lesson plan and make sure that both the pupil and the SE are aware of the objectives for the lesson. Don't try to cram too many things into the one lesson. It is better to bring about some improvement in one aspect of driving than try to improve the overall ability of the pupil in all aspects.

Your instruction should be based on the lesson plan and the pupil's ability but be prepared to modify the objectives if necessary. Flexibility is the key to good instruction.

Brief your pupils at the start of the lesson, give feedback during the lesson if appropriate and make time to give a thorough debriefing and some feedback at the end. Involve your pupils as much as possible by using Q & A techniques and inviting questions from them.

Try to avoid retrospective instruction. Be positive and identify any faults made, analysing their causes. Think about and discuss solutions, getting your pupil to work with you in improving any weak points.

Self-assessment before the Check Test

In assessing your overall instructional ability, the SE will in particular be considering your:

- individual characteristics as an instructor;
- instruction/teaching ability;
- fault identification, analysis, and correction.

Before you take the Check Test analyse your own performance in these three areas.

Instructor characteristics

Clarity – Are your verbal instructions clear and articulate?

Enthusiasm – Do you sound enthusiastic about the subject and the progress the pupil is making?

Encouragement – Do you encourage the pupil as often as you should?

Manner – Are you friendly and able to put your pupil at ease?

Patience and tact – Do you sound impatient or show your impatience or lack of tact when the pupil gets something wrong?

Instructional techniques

Recap at the start of the lesson – Do you use Q & A and coaching techniques to remind the pupil what was achieved in the previous lesson?

Objectives – Do you clearly define and state the objectives for the lesson you are giving?

Level of instruction – Are your directional instructions and explanations unambiguous and easy to understand? Do you match the level of instruction to suit the needs and ability of each pupil?

Instructions given – Are they easy for the pupil to understand or are they sometimes ambiguous?

Language – Do you use language that is easy and straightforward? Do you avoid using jargon and technical words that may not be understood?

Q & A technique – Do you use questions effectively? Do you invite questions from the pupil and allow time for them? Do you follow up any responses from the pupil by asking more questions?

Feedback – Do you give it yourself and gain it from your pupil and, if so, do you act properly on it?

Recap at the end of the lesson – Does your pupil get out of the car knowing what has been achieved and feeling good?

Use of dual controls – Do you use the dual controls only when necessary or do you use them excessively?

Fault assessment

Fault identification – Do you always accurately identify faults made by your pupils?

Fault analysis – Do you analyse the faults made in such a way that your pupils understand what has gone wrong and how to put it right?

Remedial action – Do you make sure that your pupils have the opportunity to remedy any faults made?

Timing of fault – Do you assess faults made while they are still fresh in the pupil's mind, or do you leave it so late that your pupil cannot recall the situation?

If you are in any doubt about any of these check points, you should refer to earlier chapters in this book which cover them in more detail.

Some dos and don'ts

DO:

- prepare in advance – your car, the pupil, the lesson plan;
- take account of any recommendations the SE made in any previous Check Test;
- brief both the pupil and the SE;
- pitch the instruction at an appropriate level;
- use a two-way question and answer technique;
- ensure that some learning takes place during the lesson;
- identify, analyse and correct any faults;
- use encouragement when needed and praise when deserved;
- sum up at the end of the lesson and look forward to the next one.

DON'T:

- choose a pupil for their good driving ability;
- use retrospective corrective instruction;
- involve the SE in the lesson;
- try to carry out a mock test.

You owe it to yourself to obtain the best possible grading. If you are at all worried about the standard of your instruction, then consider taking some specialist training to prepare you for the Check Test. This should be done well before the date so that you have time to improve your PTS.

THE RESULT

At the end of the Check Test the SE will have assessed your instruction. You will be advised of the result and your overall performance will be discussed in order to assist you in bringing about any necessary improvement.

If you have passed, you will be given a grade – 4, 5, or 6. If you are given a grade 4 this means that your instruction was only adequate. A grade 5 means that your instruction was good; a grade 6 indicates that the instruction observed was very good indeed.

At this stage you will be given the opportunity to discuss with the SE anything that you do not understand about the grading given or any recommendations that are made. These recommendations are designed to help you to build on your strengths and correct any weak points.

If you have difficulty in understanding or implementing any of the recommendations, you should contact your SE to make an appointment so that you can be given a more detailed explanation.

The grade awarded will determine how soon you will be asked to take the next Check Test. As a rough guide, you could normally expect to be seen again within two years if you achieve a grade 4, three years if you achieve a grade 5, or four years if you achieve a grade 6.

Grade 6: To obtain the highest grade, your overall performance must be to a very high standard, with no significant instructional weaknesses. In particular, during the lesson you should:

- give a concise and accurate recap on the previous lesson;
- set realistic and attainable objectives for the lesson;
- demonstrate the ability to select (and vary where required) the most appropriate instructional techniques to suit the particular needs, aptitude and ability of the individual pupil;
- recognise and address all relevant driving faults and provide a sound analysis of them;
- apply prompt and appropriate remedial action;
- choose an appropriate route for the pupil's ability and experience;
- take each and every opportunity to develop the pupil's driving skills and awareness;
- create an appropriate learning environment to encourage the development of the pupil's skills and driving practices;
- show a professional attitude and approach to the pupil throughout the lesson.

At the end of the lesson you should:

- provide a concise recap, with an accurate review of the lesson;
- identify the strengths and weaknesses of the pupil and discuss them constructively;
- set realistic and attainable objectives for the next lesson.

Grade 5: For a grade 5 rating you will have shown only a few minor weaknesses in your instructional techniques. These weaknesses might relate to:

- the recap on the previous lesson;
- recognising and addressing important driving faults;
- creating an appropriate learning environment by structuring the lesson appropriately;
- accurately identifying and discussing the strengths and weaknesses of the pupil;
- setting realistic and appropriate objectives for the next lesson;
- providing an accurate overview of the lesson;

Grade 4: If you are given a grade 4 (the minimum acceptable grade), you will have demonstrated only a 'competent' overall performance. There will have been weaknesses on several of the instructional techniques and on the subjects listed above.

Grade 3 or below: A grading of 3 or less indicates that the instruction given was unacceptable. In these circumstances, the instructor is given two or three more attempts to improve their standards. The exception to this is grade 1, which is regarded as potentially dangerous.

At the end of the test, the examiner will give an indication of when you will be required to take another check test.

Any grade below 4 will require a further Check Test fairly soon. If you get a grade 3 you will normally be seen within three months; with a grade 2 you will be seen within two months. In each case, the SE will expect to see a significant improvement on the next Check Test. You should seriously consider taking retraining to bring your instruction up to the required standard.

Should you be given a grade 1 on your Check Test, this would indicate that your instruction is considered to be dangerous. In this case, a second test will be arranged very quickly. If your instruction is still considered dangerous, you would not normally be allowed a third attempt.

If you fail a further Check Test with an SE, you will be required to take another test with a more senior examiner. At this stage, if your instruction has not improved, the Registrar will consider removing your name from the Register of ADIs.

In all cases of failure, the SE will confirm in writing what aspects of instruction were considered inadequate or wrong.

Irrespective of any recommendations that your SE makes, you should always ask yourself:

- Was there anything I could have done to make my teaching more effective so as to bring about more learning for my pupil?

- How can I go about implementing the suggestions made by the SE?

- Would I benefit from investing in some retraining?

Finally, GOOD LUCK when you next take your Check Test!

7

Continuing professional development

When you qualify as a driving instructor, the only skills that the DSA check on are related to driving and the teaching/learning situation in very restricted circumstances. Even then, the driving element is not to a particularly high standard and the instructional exam does not deal with modern methods of instructing through coaching.

After qualifying as an ADI, the only continuing check on your ability is the Check Test conducted by the DSA. This only assesses your ability to deliver a particular lesson to a specific pupil on the specified date. In other words, it's only a 'snapshot' of your overall ability.

The DSA does not currently check your skills with customer care, nor your ability to run a business legally. (In fact, when members of the public occasionally complain about the conduct of instructors, their response is that they are only concerned with the level of instruction given. They do not get involved with any other aspects of their work.) This leads to a situation where most instructors think that the ADI Check Test is the only thing they must concern themselves with.

To be an effective all-round instructor, especially if you are working on your own account (or within certain of the franchises), you need to keep up-to-date and also develop many other skills. You should be continually:

- improving your skills in instructional ability to deal with pupils and trainees at all levels;

- using your driving skills to full advantage by keeping an open mind and not being dogmatic about up-to-date trends in terms of lane discipline (for progress), signalling, steering, fuel economy, environmental issues; and, equally important in this age of consumer rights:

- improving your customer care skills; and

- your business skills – including legal issues, cash flow, insurance responsibilities and public liability.

In this chapter we concentrate on driving skills and instructional matters, with an overview of the other skills (business and customer care) that are dealt with in more detail in *The Driving Instructor's Handbook*.

Continuing professional development (CPD) has been described formally as:

> The systematic maintenance, improvement and broadening of knowledge and skills in the execution of professional duties throughout a practitioner's working life.

It has also been defined (5S Consulting document to ADIs) as:

> Specific and planned activities that serve to enhance our performance in our work role; that is how we:

- carry out our job;
- manage our related administrative and business responsibilities;
- deal with others to whom our job relates, including particularly our employees and customers.

To achieve these aims, CPD can take the form of a variety of different types of activity, including:

- Formal, structured courses provided by specialist external trainers. These might consist of practical or knowledge-based programmes with or without a formal assessment or qualification.

- Seminars or other types of presentation, with the information being presented in a formally structured programme or in an informal discussion setting.

- Self-study or distance learning. This could involve the use of books, CD ROMs or DVDs with the trainees working at their own pace.

- Coaching or mentoring, where the learning and development of the trainee (or 'coachee') is guided by an experienced colleague or 'coach'.

All, or any, of these methods would be appropriate and useful in any programme of continuing professional and personal development. You should aim to be continually enhancing your abilities in the following areas:

- business skills;
- customer service skills;
- assertive skills;
- affective skills;

- problem-solving skills;
- decision-making skills;
- feedback and reports;
- vehicle safety checks;
- own driving skills;
- driving instructor training;
- role play.

BUSINESS SKILLS

These include:

- financial management and planning;
- business administration;
- book-keeping/accounts;
- insurance – vehicle, premises, personal and public liabilities;
- professional indemnity;
- legal responsibilities;
- tax and VAT affairs;
- pension planning;
- financing assets;
- National Insurance;
- banking;
- health and safety matters;
- marketing;
- advertising;
- equal opportunities;
- racial and sex equality.

CUSTOMER CARE SKILLS

These include:

- dealing with enquiries;

- follow-up procedures;
- promotions;
- selling services;
- customer feedback;
- promotional literature;
- customer records;
- communication;
- handling complaints.

Most of these subjects are dealt with in *The Driving Instructor's Handbook*. There are also many other useful books on running a small business, including:

Start Up and Run Your Own Business, published by Kogan Page Ltd – ISBN 978-0-7494-4828 8.

Working for Yourself, published by Kogan Page Ltd – ISBN 978-0-7494-4757 1.

Many instructors are perfectly happy to devote their career to teaching learner drivers, while others feel that they need to broaden their work to give themselves a wider range of customers. Either way, there is a need for all of us to continually look for ways of developing and improving our teaching skills and level of professionalism. After all, *'nothing stays the same for ever – it either gets better or it gets worse.'* It means that you can't afford to stand still – if you think you are standing still, you will, in fact, be going backwards!

If you are looking for more variety in your work you could think in terms of developing your *practical teaching skills* in order to not only improve your levels of driving and instruction, but also to expand your potential market. This applies even if your work is entirely related to teaching learners.

Because the driving school market has traditionally focused on the training of learners in preparation for the driving test, many ADIs allow themselves to be limited by this – even to the extent of them feeling that anything outside the 'L' driver market, by definition, is not for them.

Those falling into this category are often reluctant to work within a group or to cooperate with other instructors, preferring to 'do their own thing', remaining completely independent in their own working environment. Many do not even join any of the professional associations. It is probable that one of the reasons this type of person chose to be an instructor in the first place was that they preferred to work alone, at their own pace and in their own way.

This approach may have been acceptable in the past, but nowadays it is not realistic. To be an effective instructor, there is a need to develop *all* of the required skills, but in particular those relating to instructional ability – *and not forgetting the importance of basic driving skills.*

There is much work and research now being undertaken to review the needs of instructors in the area of not only minimum educational requirements to qualify, but also the area of CPD. This work includes various projects commissioned by the Driving Standards Agency and the Department of Trade and Industry.

The results of these projects should become known and implemented during the next few years, but there are already a few indicators that have emerged. One of the main points is that there is currently no real incentive for ADIs to develop their skills and, in fact, only a very small percentage undertakes any form of extra qualification or training other than that required for the basic DSA qualification.

The general trend in most other professions is for CPD to be much more widely undertaken and, indeed, is an expectation for most people. For example, in the road transport industry there is a European Directive that will soon require all lorry drivers to take a minimum amount of refresher training every few years.

There is clearly a need for more development for instructors, but, as always, it is uncertain how any CPD courses or initiatives will be funded because it is extremely unlikely that the majority of instructors will take training or extra qualifications unless they are obliged to, or are motivated in some way. Nevertheless, it can be shown that CPD is now even more important in a world that is very competitive.

Any properly prepared programme of CPD for driving instructors should include an element of:

- assertive skills;
- affective skills;
- reflective skills;
- problem-solving skills;
- decision-making skills.

The development of these particular skills will greatly enhance your teaching and coaching skills and this is particularly important in the driving instruction environment where we are dealing mainly with pupils on a one-to-one basis.

As previously implied, it is unfortunate that we are called 'driving instructors', because this title indicates that we would be directing and 'instructing' the pupil in exactly what to do and when to do it. This, of course, was the method used in the past by use of rote learning and by repetition work until the pupil had memorized everything that needed to be done.

Nowadays, there should be much more emphasis on developing pupils' skills and behaviour by instructors' use of appropriate questions and skills in motivating pupils to learn. The skill of *coaching* involves the coach and pupil in a structured dialogue with more emphasis on the *learning* than on the *teaching*.

In a previous chapter, we emphasized the importance of persuading pupils to do whatever it is that you would want them to do in the way you want them to do it. Persuasion is necessary not only when dealing with pupils' control of the car and their road procedure, but also when handling other problems that might arise from time to time.

PERSONAL SKILLS

Assertive skills

This is the art of using clear and direct communication in order to persuade others to do what you want them to do, without being dictatorial. When dealing with pupils you will need to be assertive, but in a friendly and sensitive way, sometimes with safety in mind.

Being assertive enables you to:

- be direct and to ask for exactly what you want from your pupil;
- say 'No', clearly and firmly without causing offence or embarrassment;
- take control and responsibility when required, sometimes against the wishes of the pupil.

Some instructors are naturally assertive, while others are a little more reticent and find it difficult to say 'No', or to refuse unreasonable requests. If you are naturally non-assertive, you should persuade yourself that 'being assertive' does not involve aggression, but simply being firm and persuasive and for the good of everyone around.

There are many situations in which you need to be assertive in your instruction, but particularly when dealing with pupils about non-driving topics, for example coping with the pupil who wants to take a test when you feel they are not yet ready for it. You will need to be very persuasive in your arguments, and the most effective way to be assertive without causing offence is to be factual, positive, persuasive and persistent.

Being assertive in a sensitive way is probably easier if you develop your *affective skills*.

Affective skills

'Affective' in this context refers to your feelings and emotions, your attitudes and values and how these 'affect' your interpersonal relationships. How successful you are in dealing with people and problems can often be affected by how you feel at the time, as well as your attitude towards the person or problem that you are dealing with.

Always try to:

- Treat other people with respect. Even if you are feeling low, don't release your own frustrations onto others. Try to control any 'mood swings' that you are aware of.

- Be sensitive to other people's feelings and problems. Try not to unintentionally offend others. Listen carefully to the other person's side of the story. Respect their point of view, but also make them aware of your own view.

- Be polite. Treat others as you would want to be treated yourself.

- Be sympathetic. Show concern for other people's well-being. Learn to pick up both verbal and non-verbal signals that might indicate their concerns. Allow time to find out the cause of their concern.

- Provide support where appropriate.

If and when any confrontations occur, always analyse the way you dealt with the situation. Ask yourself whether you did everything possible to work out any possible alternatives to the problem and how the pupil reacted to your handling of the situation.

Problem-solving skills

Because of the continually changing situation, problem solving in the context of driving instruction often needs to be carried out without the usual amount of time that might be available when solving problems in other situations and environments. When problems arise, decisions often have to be made immediately and usually with safety in mind.

The effective instructor will, if time allows, work with a pupil to solve the problem. The function of the instructor is to 'guide' the pupil towards making the correct decision, presenting alternatives for consideration and asking thought-provoking questions that should help the pupil to consider the possible cause and cure.

If, with your help, your pupils can solve their own problems they will be better able to understand why they arose in the first place and to decide on how similar situations could be avoided in the future. A systematic approach, following a series of stepping-stones, should help pupils to identify the different options available and eventually lead to the most effective solution to particular problems.

You also need to be able to solve other types of problems relating to yourself. For example, if you get a series of test failures where the candidates are failing for similar faults, you need to identify the causes, analyse the weaknesses and decide if you need to adapt your teaching of those particular topics.

Problem solving invariably involves *decision-making* skills.

Decision-making skills

The purpose of *problem solving* is to discover what caused a particular situation so that you are able to use that knowledge to decide exactly how to deal with it.

A key element in decision making involves assessing and balancing risk. For example, a partly trained pupil is approaching traffic lights that have been green for some time. Following your instructions, the pupil slows the car to a speed at which it can be stopped if necessary. Under normal circumstances, you would expect to stop if the lights changed to amber on the approach. You realize that the pupil can, and should, stop at the line, but at the same time you realize that there is a large, heavy vehicle travelling very close behind you.

It's *decision time!* In this situation you need to balance the risk and, because there's not time to consult with the pupil, you probably need to say something positive such as: 'Keep moving!' Had you said nothing then your pupil would probably have stopped quite suddenly – possibly with disastrous consequences.

In this sort of situation, where you have to make a decision for a pupil, you will need to stop at the earliest safe opportunity to discuss what happened. You then need to explain to the pupil why you made the decision for them.

The usual steps in the decision-making process are:

- specifying your aims;
- reviewing the different factors;
- determining the possible courses of action;
- making the decision;
- implementing the decision.

This is fine under normal circumstances when you are making decisions with pupils when the car is stationary. However, when you are travelling along the road and situations are developing rapidly, you need to simplify the process to:

$$LOOK \rightarrow ASSESS \rightarrow DECIDE \rightarrow ACT$$

Part of your job as an instructor is to transfer the responsibility for making decisions to your pupils as soon as possible in the learning process. At the same time you must be prepared to override those decisions, or, in the interests of safety, to pre-empt them.

The earlier your pupils start making their own decisions, the sooner they will be ready to drive unaccompanied. For most pupils, the first time they will drive 'unaccompanied' is on the driving test, when the examiner won't be giving any verbal assistance.

An effective way to introduce them to decision making is, towards the end of a lesson, to allow them to drive home or back to work giving no instructions or directions unless, of course, unplanned or exceptional situations arise and safety is in question.

From time to time everyone makes a mistake. When incorrect decisions have been made, either by you or a pupil, they should be discussed and analysed. You will both learn more from your mistakes than you will through making correct decisions!

FEEDBACK AND REPORTS

Although most driving instruction and assessment is conducted on a verbal basis, you need to be able, when required, to provide written feedback on trainees' progress. This will become even more relevant when the 'Driver's Record' is introduced on a compulsory basis.

It will also be necessary if you embark on the training and assessment of more experienced drivers and full licence holders. Any third party will undoubtedly require some form of written report if they are paying for your services.

Feedback may take the form of:

- recording pupils' progress in a logbook at the end of each lesson;
- providing more detailed written reports to an employer.

To maintain your professional image, you should consider the following when compiling reports:

- The style and format of writing should be appropriate to the individual or company for whom you are preparing them.
- Your grammar and spelling should be correct.
- Reports should be neatly presented, whether they are hand-written, typed or produced on a computer.
- Read through and check reports at least a couple of times before submitting them.

VEHICLE SAFETY CHECKS

It's extremely important that new drivers are able to carry out some basic checks to ensure that the car they're going to drive is safe. For this reason, driving test candidates are asked by their examiner to demonstrate that they can do so.

Teaching them how to carry out the necessary routine checks and identify faults should help the new driver avoid unnecessary delays and breakdowns as well as ensuring that the vehicle is legally roadworthy. Indeed, having a basic knowledge of how a car works should also help your pupils develop vehicle sympathy.

The Driving Instructor's Handbook contains a chapter on 'The car'. This can be used, in conjunction with your own vehicle's handbook, as a reference source when you are preparing your lesson plans.

Items you should cover include:

- re-fuelling the car;

- checking oil, water and fluid levels;

- checking the condition of wheels and tyres;

- checking tyre pressures;

- checking and replacing light bulbs;

- wheel changing;

- routine preventative maintenance.

If you have more than a basic knowledge and level of skill in car maintenance, you might consider slightly more advanced training for your pupils and teach the more enthusiastic of them about car care. The way you go about this will depend on how many of your pupils wish to take up the option and whether you will be teaching them individually or in groups.

On a one-to-one basis you could combine an educational re-fuelling stop with demonstrations of how to carry out the basic checks and bulb replacement. Then use your coaching skills to develop the pupil's knowledge and understanding by the use of appropriate questions and with practice at carrying out the tasks.

For more in-depth teaching, you might need to locate suitable premises where there will be sufficient space in which to work. This could be your own garage, or for more comprehensive sessions you might consider hiring classroom or workshop facilities where you could use models of various parts of the car to show how they work. Whichever option you take, you should use your coaching skills rather than lecturing pupils on the main points to be considered.

DRIVING STANDARDS

Each year about 3,500 people are killed on our roads. Over the past 15 years the figure has been reduced from more than 5,000 and the Government has indicated its intention to reduce it by a further 40 per cent by 2010.

As part of the Government strategy, there is a commitment to a programme of improvements in the areas of driver training and testing. These measures include:

- Instilling in young people the correct attitudes to safe driving by providing presentations in schools and to youth associations.

- Encouraging learner drivers to take a more structured approach to learning and by emphasizing the need for it as a lifetime skill, not just a means of passing the test. The main focus of this is on the introduction of the 'Driver's Record'.

- Raising the standard of driver training offered by instructors through improvements to the ADI exams and the periodic Check Test. Indeed, under current discussion throughout Europe is a project called MERIT – Minimum Educational Requirements for Driving Instructor Training.

- Focusing on the immediate post-test period for newly qualified drivers. This has been partly addressed by encouraging a greater awareness of the 'Pass Plus' scheme. Over the past four or five years, the take up for these courses has increased from 7 per cent to around 14 per cent.

- An enhancement of the various advanced motoring qualifications. The DSA has recently agreed national minimum standards with the organizations that offer advanced tests. These tests are now regularly monitored by the DSA to ensure that the standards are maintained.

> *All driving instructors should, by furthering their own ongoing training and qualifications, be ready to deal with these different aspects of training opportunities.*

It is now even more important that you keep your own driving skills up to date by taking one of the tests offered by:

- The Institute of Advanced Motorists (IAM);
- The Royal Society for the Prevention of Accidents (RoSPA);
- The Driving Instructors' Association (DIA);
- The DSA special 'Cardington' driving test.

During advanced driving courses, and in preparation for a test, you should develop a better understanding of some of the issues relating to driving, such as:

- The importance of fatigue – we all tend to use the roads for much longer periods.

- Fuel economy driving – to lessen the impact of our increasing use of world resources.

- The different types of fuel that are available.

- The growing importance of 'dual-fuel' vehicles.

In our approach to our personal skills, and when teaching our pupils to drive, we need to be much more flexible in today's road and traffic conditions, especially in terms of:

- lane selection;

- selective signalling;

- roundabout procedures;

- right turn positioning;

- use of steering;

- appropriate use of gears;

- the many other procedures that might have been regarded as correct when we took our own driving test, but which we now have to reconsider in relation to the current conditions on the roads.

Taking one of the advanced tests will not necessarily provide all the answers, but your preparation for it will provoke and stimulate you into possibly re-evaluating your style of driving. For example:

- Why do we automatically assume that pull/push is always the best method of steering, especially when it doesn't come naturally to some new drivers who often find it difficult to carry out? Is there a case for using, say, a cross-hand method (rotational steering) in some situations?

- Are we correct, at roundabouts, in dogmatically insisting on turning right and exiting into the left-hand lane?

- Is it always sensible to religiously follow the *Highway Code* advice about lane selection at roundabouts?

- Do we really need to signal our intention to do something when our actions are obvious and when no one will benefit?

All of these, and other important discussion points, would be dealt with on an advanced course.

DRIVING INSTRUCTOR TRAINING

After you have gained some experience as an ADI, have regularly achieved a good Check Test grading and have a constantly high test pass rate, you might consider becoming a tutor or trainer of instructors. This could be as part of your ongoing CPD or supplementary to your ADI work.

To prepare for this change, you will need to:

- Have a thorough knowledge of the syllabus for the ADI theory and hazard perception test and be able to provide your students with the relevant study materials and necessary support.
- Drive to a consistently high standard at all times.
- Have a thorough knowledge and understanding of the official syllabus for learning to drive and of the ADI Part 3 syllabus.
- Have the ability to deliver appropriate practical training.
- Adapt your *practical teaching skills* to suit drivers who will have much more experience than learners.
- Be competent in the skills required to train people to teach, including coaching skills.
- Acquire and develop your role-play skills.
- Undertake training with a specialist organization.

While preparing for your own ADI exams, you should have become fully aware of the in-depth knowledge required for the theory test and the high standard of personal driving skills required for the Part 2 test. However, training to instruct is very different from teaching people to drive. You will need to develop more of your *practical teaching skills* to progress into the field of instructor training.

Some of the skills discussed in previous chapters will certainly be beneficial, but one of the most important parts of the tutor's job is having the ability to stimulate and motivate trainees with varying aptitudes, attitudes and personalities.

Role play takes up a large percentage of the time spent in training new instructors and you will need to develop this skill so that your simulation of the learner driver becomes credible.

Before making the decision to take a course in the tutoring of ADIs, you should already be able to confidently and effectively apply all the essential *practical teaching skills* in your everyday work with learners. Prior to committing yourself and embarking on this more challenging aspect of the driving instruction world, you should seek advice and assessment from a recognized tutor. You will find a list of specialized training establishments (ORDIT – the Official Register of Driving Instructor Training) on the DSA's website: www.dsa.gov.uk and in the ADI 14 starter pack.

ROLE-PLAY EXERCISES

In practice, role play mostly takes the form of short, unscripted 'playlets'. These normally involve two or more participants taking the part of different people in order to satisfy the specific training requirements. For example, in the case of driving instructor training, the trainer plays the part of a learner at a specific level of ability and with a particular aptitude; while the trainee instructor will be learning and practising their role of instructor. Although the role play will be largely unscripted, the dialogue will be structured and controlled by the trainer.

This is another example of where coaching will be used to instigate the correct technique from the dialogue rather than the trainer giving a straightforward instructional session.

The trainer (or coach) should organize each short session of training so that it simulates circumstances similar to those that the trainee will meet in everyday life as an instructor, or in the later stages in the particular circumstances of the Part 3 test.

In order to prepare the trainee to deal with normal everyday situations with learner drivers, different elements should be introduced so that the trainer is able to assess and improve on all aspects of the trainee's teaching skills.

Role play is a valuable training technique; it provides:

- participation;
- involvement;
- opportunities for 'action learning';
- a safe environment in which to learn how to deal with situations that could be dangerous for an inexperienced instructor with a real learner.

In order to prepare trainees to deal with different types of pupil, the trainer should be able to simulate a variety of different personalities. For example:

- the difficult customer who 'knows it all';

- the slow learner who needs constant encouragement, reinforcement and progressive learning steps;
- the indifferent pupil who doesn't put much effort into the learning;
- the over-confident person who thinks their driving is better than it really is.

During any training exercise, the trainee's communication skills, their attitude, behaviour and feelings should form the basis for self-appraisal, with feedback from the trainer. From this feedback, the trainee should learn which type of approach to each pupil would be most appropriate for the circumstances.

Role play can provide a mirror in which the participants should be able to see themselves as others see them. This can give them an insight into their own behaviour and sensitivity towards other people's opinions, attitudes and needs. The benefits of any changes in these aspects can be readily demonstrated during the role play and can therefore bring about the desired modifications.

The benefits of role play as a training tool depend on three elements:

1. the design of the exercise;
2. the quality of the feedback;
3. control of the training session by the trainer.

1. The design

The design of each individual exercise should be governed by the requirements of the overall training objectives. Three factors need to be considered:

a. *Credibility* – the degree to which the trainee can identify the situation as one that is likely to be encountered in real life.
b. *Reliability* – the role-play 'playlet' must allow the trainer to cover all of the desired learning points.
c. *Complexity* – the level of complexity of the exercise must not overwhelm the trainee, but should take into account the trainee's current knowledge, understanding and ability.

2. The quality of the feedback

This must be constructive, otherwise it will become counterproductive by either destroying confidence or erecting barriers to learning. Positive feedback can reinforce effective behaviour, instil confidence and highlight particular areas for improvement in a way that should be acceptable to the trainee.

3. Control of the training session

To get the best out of any role-play exercise, the trainer must maintain overall control in a situation where it is often difficult to predict what will happen. If situations start to arise that are not going to be helpful to the trainee, the trainer must be ready to intervene and to move the dialogue or the action in a different direction. This is particularly important if there is potential for any danger or damage to be caused.

For effective results from role-play exercises, the trainer needs to be:

- *Proactive* – with questions that will test the trainee's knowledge, ability, attitude and understanding. As each session develops opportunities should be taken to prompt the trainee's responses and to test their flexibility.

- *Reactive* – by doing exactly as the trainee instructs them, acting on their level of ability and by responding appropriately to instructions. Directions and instructions given by the trainee should be followed unless it is unsafe or illegal to do so.

When planning exercises it is useful to understand how the SE uses role play for testing purposes on the Part 3 exam. (For details refer to Chapter 5.)

The importance of staying in role

For any role-play exercise to be effective, both parties must stay in their respective role. Because of this, any discussions held during the exercise should be 'in role'.

However, particularly during the early stages of training, situations can arise where the trainee is becoming more and more confused or there is the possibility of danger. In these situations, the trainer must take control – by coming out of role if necessary. If this happens, the departure from role play must be made quite clear to the trainee.

Once 'out of role', the trainer will need to use effective Q & A skills to find out whether the trainee understands why the exercise was interrupted. Depending on the circumstances, and the trainee's responses to the questions, the situation may need to be recreated to give another opportunity for more positive learning to take place.

If the trainee is really struggling, a demonstration may be useful with the roles being reversed. This would entail the trainer taking on the role of instructor with the trainee playing a relatively passive learner. Whatever the circumstances, there must be no doubt in the mind of either party about whether they are 'in' or 'out' of role.

SUMMARY

No matter what branch of driving instruction you intend to focus on, if you are to keep up to date and be able to compete, you should seek to continually improve all of your personal and professional skills. We hope you find this book helpful in enhancing your *practical teaching skills*.

Index

NB: page numbers in *italic* indicate diagrams

INDEX OF ADVERTISERS